WRECK OF THE VICE-ADMIRAL

CAPTAIN WM. PHIPS

Log Cabin Noble

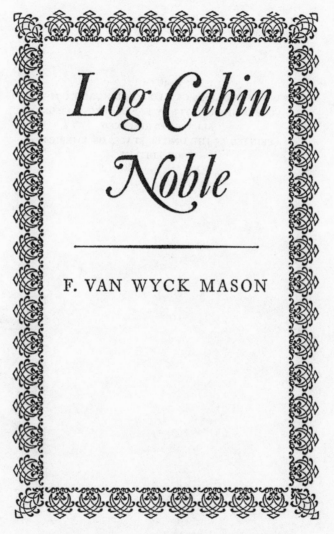

Log Cabin Noble

F. VAN WYCK MASON

DOUBLEDAY & COMPANY, INC.
GARDEN CITY, NEW YORK
1973

ISBN: 0-385-01279-9
LIBRARY OF CONGRESS CATALOG CARD NUMBER 72–95716
COPYRIGHT © 1973 BY F. VAN WYCK MASON
ALL RIGHTS RESERVED
PRINTED IN THE UNITED STATES OF AMERICA
FIRST EDITION

For
those dear and true friends
Irving and Patricia Phelps
1973

Part I

TREASURE FLEET

Chapter I

THE FLOTA SAILS

AROUND MIDDAY OF SEPTEMBER 28, 1641, big guns
in El Morro Castle roared repeatedly, sent huge woolly gray-
black clouds whirling out over the entrance to the port of Havana. Sullenly these commenced to climb a sultry, brazen-
blue sky. Reports rumbled and reverberated over red-roofed
houses, church towers, and caromed among low, gray-green
palm-dotted hills behind the town over which many buzzards
planed and circled in seemingly effortless flight.

Today, to a blaring of trumpets and a clash of Moorish cym-
bals, the *Flota de la Tierra Firma* of 1641, for a second time,
was departing for Cádiz in the realm of His Most Catholic Majesty, Philip IV, King of Spain, King of the Indies, of the Tierra
Firma and of the Ocean Sea.

At the head of the departing convoy sailed *Nuestra Señora
del Rosario*, the Captain-General and Fleet Commander Don
Juan de Campos's high-sided, yellow-red-and-blue-painted gal-

leon. In her wake some thirty flag-bedecked men-of-war and merchant vessels of widely varying rigs, speed and tonnage, straggled past the castle's yellow-gray and smoke-wreathed battlements guarded by a double column of lightly armed frigates, brigantines, and patches.

These last, swift and maneuverable, being lateen-rigged, were intended to maintain communication between the flagship and the rest of the *flota*. This convoy's chief protection—well paid for by practically unarmed merchantmen—consisted of eight majestic galleons each mounting an average of sixty broadside cannons. These highly ornamented men-of-war were characterized by towering many-decked "castles" placed fore and aft.

English, Dutch, and French naval architects long since had lowered or modified such edifices—especially the forecastle—for the good and sufficient reason that such extensive wind-resisting surfaces rendered a high-sided vessel prone to capsize and clumsy to manage in any but a broad-on or a following wind.

On a lofty battlement of El Morro Castle, the Archbishop of Havana raised generously bejeweled hands in solemn benediction as the Captain-General's flagship lumbered by, firing salutes and showing the pious initials *AVMGP—Ave María Gratia Plena*—painted in large black letters across her considerably overlarge main course. Big, blood-red Latin crosses showed on all men-of-war's topsails, royals and gallants.

The glittering group on the battlement included His Excellency the Governor of the Captain-Generalcy of Cuba, the Alcalde of Havana, the Commandant of El Morro Castle, and other richly dressed and jewel-bedecked dignitaries both clerical and secular. This group, without much success, was attempting not to appear bored since the present occasion was something of an anticlimax; only ten days earlier amid much more elaborate ceremonies this same *flota* had departed only to reappear a few days later because dangerous leaks had sprung in the hull of *Nuestra Señora de la Concepción*, the galleon bearing not only Vice-Admiral Don Luis Villavincencio but also the bulk of treasure shipped annually from the New World.

Flocks of harbor gulls and lines of ungainly brown pelicans, having overcome their terror of booming guns, commenced to flap back into the harbor in search of scraps and refuse left by the departing fleet.

From their excellent vantage point on the *todilla*, or uppermost of the three decks composing *Nuestra Señora de la Concepción*'s sterncastle, a pair of off-duty apprentice pilots stood awaiting orders.

Commented Ottavio Gallucio, the taller of the two, a long-faced and fair-complexioned young Genoese: "Yonder's a sight not quickly to be forgotten, eh?"

"Maybe so," drawled Henrico Moreno, a short, scrawny and bandy-legged native of Amalfi, "but 'tisn't up to our first send-off by a long shot. Wonder what they're thinking over there?" His gaze sought a glittering knot of armored and bejeweled officers clustered around their lean, spike-bearded, and hawk-nosed Vice-Admiral, Don Luis Villavincencio, tall and definitely imposing in a gleaming gold-mounted breastplate and scarlet-plumed morion.

Ottavio, whose classic profile might have graced the obverse of an ancient and fine Grecian coin, grunted: "Probably, like you and I, they're wondering how many of us will live to see Havana again."

Nearby, the *Concepción*'s white-haired Chief Pilot, a swarthy and almost toothless Venetian, briefly scanned the cloudless, hot, sapphire-blue sky before commenting to his mate: "Weather seems fair. But that doesn't mean a thing. Man alive, we're departing the Indies *three* weeks after the end of *huracán*-free season so, as you know very well, *ciclones* can without warning strike at any time."

The Chief Pilot nodded then bellowed orders down to the deck to brace about the galleon's huge mainsail suspended from a yard so long and ponderous it might have served as mainmast for a sizable merchantman. Chanting a hymn in order to pull in unison, mariners obeyed in unhurried fashion.

Ottavio and his fellow apprentice being Italians understood all that passed between the Chief Pilot and his mates; even though the rest of a Royal man-of-war's officers were Spaniards to the last man, for some inexplicable reason tradition dictated that in His Most Catholic Majesty's ships all navigators, pilots, and sailing masters must be of either Portuguese or Italian origin.

Alongside cruised a motley collection of canoes and small craft from which white, Negro, Indian, and mestizo hucksters, watermen, and fishermen yelled, waved, and made obscene gestures while singly or by twos and threes the heterogeneous convoy straggled out of the harbor's mouth, flying a garish miscellany of gonfalons, flags and pendants.

From the maintop of the gigantic *Nuestra Señora del Rosario*, flagship of His Excellency, Captain-General Don Juan de Campos, fluttered an admiral's enormous white ensign bearing the Royal Arms of Spain embroidered in full color, surmounted by a golden crown and encircled by the chain of the Order of the Golden Fleece.

A similar flag worn by the last ship in the *flota* to pass El Morro Castle indicated that the convoy's Vice-Admiral Don Luis Villavincencio was on board.

Almost everyone was aware not only that *Nuestra Señora de la Concepción* had been constructed in the New World but also that she was the personal property of no less a personage than Don Diego de Pacheco, Duke of Escalona and Philip IV's recently appointed Viceroy of the Audiencia of Mexico.

Most onlookers stared hard at this particular great green-yellow-and-blue man-of-war whose lofty sides bristled with the red-painted mouths of sixty-odd cannon. Was it not well known that in the *Concepción*'s strong room and lower holds was stowed not only the King's fifth share of the gold, silver, and gems extorted annually from the Americas but also his Viceroy's very considerable personal treasure—not to mention wealth accumulated by Don Diego de Pacheco's principal lieutenants and moneys being sent back to Spain by a number of enormously powerful colonial merchants?

The Royal ships, and not a few of the larger merchantmen, were flying the Spanish National Ensign, red-white-and-yellow horizontal stripes of equal width, but some vessels, in addition, had hoisted colors to indicate their port of origin.

To his companion Henrico, Ottavio identified most banners: for instance, those from Castile showed white fields surcharged in red and yellow with the famous Lion and Castle quarterings; merchantmen hailing from Barcelona flaunted a bright blue flag distinguished by a figure of a black-clad priest; ships out of Galicia flew white ensigns showing in their center a golden chalice surrounded by six red Latin crosslets.

To the relief of sundry anxious pilots, pungent-smelling clouds enveloping the departing ships thinned as the guns in El Morro Castle and those of the departing convoy stopped saluting after *Concepción*, bringing up the rear, had cleared the harbor's mouth and had pointed her intricately carved and gilded beak towards the Straits of Florida and the Gulf Stream's clear and dark-blue expanse.

From the lofty *todilla* Ottavio Gallucio gloomily surveyed the indescribably crowded main deck and noticed that nowhere did there appear to exist an unencumbered square yard. Everywhere mitted weather-beaten mariners, soldiers still wearing corselets and short-tempered because of humid heat, gaunt priests wearing the somber habits of several Orders, homeward-bound minor officials, merchants and a good many obviously very sick passengers, mercilessly jostled and cursed while disputing some spot in which to deposit their belongings.

Long inured to such a scene, the Genoese apprentice watched a corpse being unceremoniously dropped over the side once a black-habited Franciscan had recited the briefest of prayers. All too accurately young Gallucio foresaw that many more bodies soon would follow this one to encourage ever-increasing schools of gray-white sharks already patrolling the convoy.

The dead seldom were mourned; their disappearance afforded additional space, increased rations and more fresh water.

[7]

A Treasury official, on leave from *La Casa de Moneda de Potosí*, the great Royal Mint long ago established in Bolivia, turned saturnine, pock-marked features to the Officer of the Deck. "*Madre de Dios!* Why did those bastard officials in Porto Bello and Vera Cruz so overload these ships? Isn't a one but hasn't become loggy and unhandy through their rapacity."

Creating an obbligato to the conversation from below sounded the endless clacking of crude pumps.

Remarked the Treasury official fingering a gold and amethyst necklace: "I'm no seaman but I've noticed the pumps seem to be working harder every day. Am I right?"

"*Sí*, you're not mistaken."

"But wasn't this the ship that forced our *flota* to return to Cuba that she might be overhauled?"

The Officer of the Deck jerked a nod. "*Sí, señor;* alas, her repairs were only partially completed, for with the *huracán* season so far advanced the Captain-General was most anxious to get the *flota* under way once more." Frowning, he added: "May the Blessed Virgin send us clear of the Bahama Banks without encountering a tempest."

He waved a thin brown hand. "See for yourself, Henrico, some big-bellied merchantmen already begin to straggle out of station."

Standing under the galleon's huge and freshly gilded wrought-iron stern lanthorn, Vice-Admiral Don Luis de Villa-vincencio absently stroked a short and neatly pointed light-brown beard, then took a few short strides which set to glowing a sizable star ruby set in the pommel of a poignard slung at his belt.

He was confident that his bearing was conveying to his staff none of those misgivings which had bedeviled him ever since that day at the Royal Dockyard in Havana when he'd conducted a thorough survey while the *Concepción* lay careened for recaulking.

Even to an unprofessional eye such as his it had been easy to determine that repairs to his ship's hull were being too hurriedly made; at the same time he'd ascertained that the Viceroy's new galleon had been constructed of unsuitable timber much of which had been quite unseasoned. Small wonder the Viceroy's pride had leaked freely from the day she'd been launched. Further, veteran shipbuilders had pointed out to Don Luis that *Concepción*'s rudder was much too small; indeed, quite inadequate of steering this vessel of over 600 tuns burthen.

Long since Don Luis had come to accept a general conclusion: only because she was the Viceroy's own property had she been selected to transport the greater part of that treasure taken aboard in steaming, pestilential Vera Cruz, in addition to riches already fetched there by galleons rendezvousing from Hispaniola and Cartagena bearing wealth collected among the Antilles and along the northern coast of South America. Also conveyed to Vera Cruz had been even more valuable consignments from the Vice Royalty of Chile, and Bogotá in the Captain-Generalcy of New Granada.

It lent the Vice-Admiral small comfort to be aware that in the galleon's strong room and three small holds located directly beneath his great cabin reposed by far the richest part of the *flota*'s enormous treasure.

By degrees the convoy assumed a roughly egg-shaped formation, well over two miles in length, by half of that in diameter at its thickest part with galleons forming the van. An exception, of course, was *Concepción* which, carrying the Vice-Admiral, protected the rear from an increasing number of freebooters sighted cruising on a parallel course but always maintaining a respectful distance.

Along the *flota*'s outer edges sailed a skirmish line composed of perhaps a dozen small, speedy but lightly armed, men-of-war such as brigantines, barks and a few *frigatas*—a fairly new type of vessel.

After drawing their evening ration of stone-hard ship's biscuits and a bowl of greasy goat-and-onion stew, Ottavio Gallucio and his fellow apprentice, Henrico Moreno, picked a devious course across the incredibly encumbered main deck towards the windward bulwarks, for in this weather, as torrid as it was humid, the galleon commenced to reek like a public jakes; with no heads or privies provided, the ship's company were forced to relieve themselves in the scuppers or in any semisecluded area.

Presently the young Italians found seats on the carriage trails of a couple of broadside guns defending the starboard side.

"How many souls d'you reckon we've got aboard?" queried Henrico.

"Quartermaster's mate told me he thinks it's well over five hundred," Ottavio mumbled, mouth overfull. "Be that true, we'll soon be on short water rations if plenty more bodies aren't heaved over the rail."

"*María!* How I pity the poor sick below with rats swarming all over them; I'm told such vermin are eating weak sufferers alive. Somehow, I fear—"

He broke off when a file of unshaven and jaundiced-eyed soldiers in polished breastplates, plumed morions and scarlet-and-yellow uniforms, roughly elbowed their way aft and halted to salute a gilded and beautifully carved crucifix secured to the *toda* or second deck of the sterncastle's base. They then formed up under it in a double rank to be casually inspected by an officer who, though very subordinate, nevertheless was wearing a handsome, gold-chased helmet. Presently the detail tramped down a wide companionway ladder opening at the sterncastle's base.

To Henrico's unvoiced query Ottavio explained: "A new guard on their way to relieve troops on duty before the strong room."

The youth from Amalfi grimaced while gulping the last of his ration, then wiped his mouth on a sleeve. "*Deo!* If only I could be a soldier free for a space to help myself down there." He belched and kicked aside a ragged old fellow who made an attempt to share his seat. "You got any conception of the riches we're practically sitting on?" His voice lowered. "Man! What I saw with my own eyes when they were loading into my ship treasure brought to Panama City by the *flota* of the South Sea! 'Twould stagger the unbelief of Satan!"

"But Panama City lies on the Pacific. How then did the loot get to Porto Bello on the Atlantic?"

"Conveyed across the Isthmus of Panama on muleback. Ah, my friend, you'd have gone mad to behold even a small part of the wealth we stowed in the *Santa Margarita*, my ship before I got tranferred to the Vice-Admiral's."

"Is the South Sea treasure still in the *Santa Margarita?*" Ottavio asked breathlessly.

"No! *Per Baccho*, as I've said, most of it lies beneath our feet at this very moment."

"But why were the Pacific riches transferred?"

"Because—or so everyone suspects—the Viceroy preferred to see the bulk of this *flota's* treasure cross the Atlantic in his private vessel."

Ottavio queried, his color rising: "You actually *saw* some of these riches?"

"Aye. Because I can read and write, I was sent, for a few days, to help the Royal actuaries and assayers in *La Casa de Moneda* of Porto Bello where they were overwhelmed by the responsibility of weighing, appraising, and recording tribute of Bolivia, Peru and Chile."

"What was it like?"

"On counters in the Royal warehouse I saw great heaps of pearls, emeralds, rubies, sapphires, amethysts, and many bright yellow stones I don't know the name for." Henrico's slender shoulders shrugged. "I know you think I lie or am raving."

Ottavio stared out over the darkening sea. "Some might; but me, I'll credit everything you say for in Vera Cruz I witnessed the great hoard from Mexico City being lowered into our holds. Please continue—"

"Don't call me a liar if I tell you there was so much silver brought into Porto Bello there simply wasn't room for it in the King's warehouse. Mother of God! I, myself, saw silver ingots stacked on the dock alongside the *Santa Margarita* like so much

[*11*]

cordwood." Henrico's tone lowered even further; passengers crouched nearby had begun turning and peering in his direction.

"For the love of God, go on," pleaded Ottavio, his lively deep-set eyes aglow in the light of *Concepcíon*'s newly lit great stern lanthorn.

"I saw a big cell heaped ceiling-high with all manner of silver plate, candlesticks, chalices, cups, crucifixes, massive salvers, beakers, censors and altar service—many articles were of massive gold and set with precious stones.

"Then there were Indian ornaments, breast plaques, headdresses, and heathen idols, all wondrously worked out of pure gold. Believe me or no, some images were *that* tall!" Young Moreno's hands became parted by a generous foot.

"I also beheld mounds of jewel-studded daggers, swords, dress helmets, and gorgets. Then there were piles of necklaces, tiaras, brooches, rings and bracelets and—oh-h the sight was maddening, breath-snatching."

Young Moreno broke off chuckling: "Forgive me, my friend, for running on like this; surely you must have seen the like in Vera Cruz?"

Ottavio shook a head close-cropped since he passionately detested body vermin of any description. "Alas, no. In our case the treasures to be carried in this ship already had been packed and stored in the castle of San Juan de Ulloa till we made port so no silver bars were left lying around in the open. However, I watched Royal accountants tally an incredible number of bags, chests and barrels filled with gold and silver reales, pistoles, pesos and doubloons—which last some call 'pieces-of-eight.'"

Henrico's gaze wandered up to the Royal Standard stirring lazily at the maintop. "And so, Ottavio, my fine Genoese friend, a mighty emperor's ransom lies not sixty feet beneath our bottoms. Makes one think, doesn't it?"

"To what purpose?" grunted Ottavio dislodging a shred of meat between his teeth. "Short of a miracle what can humble folk like us do about it?" With a sly grin he added: "Still, miracles have been known to happen, or so say the Holy Fathers."

II

For three torrid days the convoy crept at a snail's pace up the Straits of Florida, propelled more by the Gulf Stream's current than by canvas since, to the Admiral's mounting anxiety, winds remained distressingly light and variable.

Gradually routine and order had become established on the galleons. Officers forcibly divided the motley swarms of passengers into four roughly equal groups which, however, constantly were altering in size and composition.

Pitilessly, hard-bitten soldiers and mariners with blows, curses, and the occasional use of whips drove more or less able-bodied passengers into performing exhausting but essential duties, such as manning the pumps in relays and pulling and hauling on the running gear.

To lower or hoist on *Concepción*'s ponderous yards and upper masts required the combined efforts of many hands so, to co-ordinate such efforts, priests led religious chants which created an effective cadence of scant soul-saving value.

Conditions aboard *Concepción* proved somewhat better than those prevailing on other galleons for, as a fairly new vessel, the Viceroy's vessel's bilges had not yet really begun to fester and exude gagging stenches so characteristic of older ships.

Once the day's burning heat abated passengers, soldiers, and mariners, having won living space on deck, brought out guitars, zithers and concertinas, struck up and sang while the sun, bathed in fiery splendor the sea and the faint black line marking Florida's low-lying coast. Cock fights soon were arranged and frenzied betting began, especially among time-expired veterans whose wallets fairly bulged with severance pay. In addition, hilariously amusing pig races hurriedly were improvised before such animals should be dragged, shrieking, towards the mess galleys.

During the day the Chief Pilot and his assistants would collect on the sterncastle and there conduct a haphazard instruction of apprentices. Ottavio Gallucio soon proved to be among the most attentive and on occasion provoked instructors by putting an overabundance of queries the answers to which the young Genoese recorded in a memory remarkably capacious for one of his age and simple education.

Especially, Ottavio familiarized himself with the use of a mariner's forestaff, learned to box a simple lodestone compass and to operate a cumbersome brass astrolabe, but most of all he enjoyed instruction in the ancient art of navigating by stars.

One duty he abhorred above all others was the necessity of going below decks every few hours to stand his trick in the steering flat where *Concepción*'s massive tiller handle was manipulated through the use of blocks and tackles in response to orders relayed down from the pilot on duty up in the blessed fresh air of the *todilla*.

Three or even four voices in sequence might call down over the creaking and groaning of the galleon's fabric, "Four points port" or "five points starboard!" whereupon the quartermaster's shaggy steering crew would tail onto tackle ropes and heave until the required adjustment laboriously was made in accordance with marks painted on the deck.

As a rule air in the steerage was so foul that four hours in this noxious atmosphere was all any tiller man could endure and remain anywhere near efficient.

Five days out of Havana, Ottavio overheard the Master Pilot comment to his Sailing Master: "Should this wind hold we'll be entering Santarem Channel tomorrow—a prospect I don't in the least enjoy. At best that passage is too damn' crooked and narrow, and in hard weather a pilot's lucky not to get himself piled up on one of those God-cursed cays and reefs along the Great Bahamas Bank, off Anguilla Island or along the coast of Cuba."

He mopped a deeply tanned forehead. "*Per Deo!* I mean to

[*14*]

burn a dozen candles in honor of Peter, Patron Saint of Sea-farers, once this raggle-taggle armada has weathered Salt Cay in safety."

Despite angry threats by Vice-Admiral de Villavincencio and predictions they'd fall easy prey to buccaneers, corsairs, or English privateers, several of the slowest merchantmen now lagged so far astern that *Concepción* found herself no longer able to protect them if she were to remain in position to guard the *flota*'s rear; nothing remained but for *Concepción* to keep on after the bulk of the convoy and abandon sluggish sailers to their fate.

In steadily mounting apprehension experienced mariners, pilots, and passengers alike, watched more reefs and shoals begin to spout and gleam to either side of Santarem Channel. On occasion, pale-blue mountaintops in Cuba could be seen away off to port, shimmering beyond a seemingly endless succession of surf-ringed cays.

On the afternoon of the ninth day at sea certain of the *flota*'s veteran navigators commenced ever more frequently to study the heavens.

"*Sí*, the sky, she begins to 'whiten,'" announced *Nuestra Señora del Rosario*'s wizened Portuguese Chief Pilot.

"To be sure it is," growled his Second. "Next—count on it—the breeze will die out for a space then, with luck, we'll learn out of what quarter a *ciclone* may strike in time to take precaution."

An army captain admitted, uneasily fingering a gold chain about his neck: "I can't explain it, Señor Piloto, but all day I've had a feeling in my bones we're seeing the last of fair weather."

As if to bear out the officer's hunch, sunset that night, al-though cloudless, turned a sickly, greenish-yellow color and ominous gray-black hues commenced to tinge the northeastern horizon.

Passengers lining the lee rail became aware that although triangular shark fins continued to cut the water alongside, por-poises, dolphins, and flying fishes had disappeared. No longer did terns, frigate birds, albatross and shearwaters circle and scream about the convoy's mastheads.

Vice-Admiral Don Luis Villavincencio, having twice sailed this course, experienced misgivings so sharp he instructed his Sailing Master to order all hands on deck to secure movable gear. All gun carriages were to be double-lashed as well as both the galleon's small boats—her *batel* slung along the starboard quarter and the slightly smaller *chalupa* swaying to the port.

Even more, the tall, lean Vice-Admiral was concerned over ever-increasing leaks. For a second time these were becoming a problem of critical importance; despite continual pumping water inexorably had risen in the lowest holds until it had begun to lick at the lower tier of treasure boxes and chests. Should these leaks continue to increase, before long the water might gain the strong room's level and imperil the King's share of minted silver and gold coins, and those ironbound coffers containing the most precious jewels, gems and plate transported in the *flota* of 1641.

Although the ocean was calm and no breath of breeze blew, for some inexplicable reason there was little dancing or singing on the main deck except for interminable lugubrious intoning by priests; nor did cock fights, casting of knucklebones or card games take place. Perhaps the subdued atmosphere was attributable to the fact that during the day an unusual number of the sick had given up the ghost and had been tumbled over the rail.

Towards midnight, despite a complete lack of wind, a curious sea arose composed of long and smooth high rollers. *Concepción* soon commenced to roll, sluggishly at first, then violently, thanks to her lofty topworks and the weight of massive yards and masts.

Raising a shriek and a howl a hurricane out of the southwest, hurling before it tons of almost solid walls of warm rain, bounced upon the now hopelessly disordered *flota*. That this tempest should have struck shortly after daybreak proved a mixed blessing; men on *Concepción*'s upperworks, clinging half-drowned and terror-stricken to shrouds and stays, were able to sight spouting rocks and sand bars in time to avoid them

[*16*]

but, at the same time, were forced to watch three merchantmen become overwhelmed and vanish under the lead-hued surface as suddenly as though by the trick of a magician.

The screaming blast so filled the atmosphere with rain, salt spume and spindrift it proved hard to breathe.

The last vessel of the *flota* to be sighted was a galleon lying on her beams' ends with towering waves relentlessly battering her spars, masts, and rigging.

Any attempt to move about *Concepción*'s deck was to attempt almost certain death; furious green-and-gray combers had begun to sluice through gaps being torn through the galleon's weather bulwarks.

Trapped in the darkness of the steering flat, Ottavio Gallucio prayed to all the saints in the calendar he could remember and clung to a stancheon once the rudder had been smashed and carried away—a disaster which afforded a very minor recompense in that now a few rays of light sifted through splintered planking to reveal complete chaos. The steerage crew was being tossed about like toys; some already had been battered to death, others were rolling helplessly about with shattered limbs.

So deafening had the tumult of the wind become that only on occasion could Ottavio hear howls and shrieks of mortal terror rising from the ship's depths.

On the spray-smothered *todilla* Don Luis Villavincencio, the Chief Pilot and another navigator remained on station thanks only to stout lifelines double-lashed about their waists. All were hatless and drenched but retained presence of mind through awareness of their overwhelming responsibilities.

Speech had become an impossibility. The moment a man parted his lips to speak the wind instantly and grotesquely puffed his cheeks and drove words back down his throat.

Helplessly, those on the *todilla* watched cannon after cannon snap fastenings to rumble crazily about until they smashed through bulwarks and disappeared.

Don Luis felt his arm seized in a spasmodic grip. The Chief Pilot, mouthing unheard words, frantically was pointing towards a half-seen rank of high-vaulting breakers foaming not fifty yards off the starboard beam. Heeled over by forty degrees, the Viceroy's galleon was plunging and reeling like a harpooned sperm whale commencing its death flurry. Don Luis sensed that if this galleon's list increased, no power on earth could prevent her from capsizing.

For only one reason *Concepción* failed to turn turtle. Her mainmast suddenly snapped off at the crosstrees carrying with it the massive mainyard topsails and the upper yards they carried. These surged alongside as a menacing tangle of ropes and lines; for a moment the mainsail remained visible above the raging seas, displayed briefly the inscription *AVMGP* before it vanished.

Dodging cascades of green water, seamen carrying axes appeared under the Sailing Master's orders—that worthy having gone below before the hurricane achieved its present intensity. At the cost of many men washed overboard, *Concepción* at length became able to right herself sufficiently to drift sluggishly before the screaming, rain-filled blast.

Ensued an interminable interval, during which nothing at all could be seen through eye-stinging sheets of spume and rain save rocks and sand bars frothing almost alongside. Only the hand of God could have guided the ship through such a deadly tangle of reefs.

Then followed what seemed an endless period of terrifying confusion during which it remained impossible to tell time beyond realizing that increasing darkness meant that night, bringing new perils, must be falling.

The hurricane blew itself out at the end of what Ottavio believed to be a day and a half, but an endless succession of mountainous waves continued to batter the helpless treasure ship without sign of diminishing. Dismasted, rudderless and therefore unable to navigate, the half-waterlogged hulk blundered blindly on and on. The crew, although sleepless, starving and having all but abandoned hope of survival, toiled endlessly at the pumps against a relentlessly rising tide which filled the lower holds, then forced the strong room guards to abandon their posts once foul-smelling water began sluicing about their waists.

Scarcely had the hurricane ceased than a full gale arose from a different quadrant and created murderous cross seas further to torment the wallowing treasure ship. Now and then persons clinging to *Concepción*'s *todilla* through the storm wrack caught glimpses of sizable but unidentifiable cays and islands and countless coral rocks and reefs.

It proved unfortunate that the Chief Pilot should have been lost overboard when the Viceroy's galleon was hit by a huge freak wave which swept the sterncastle's upperdeck; only he had had even a vague notion of the ship's possible position. Shortly before vanishing, the old Portuguese had hazarded an opinion that the *Concepción* might be floundering somewhere in the vicinity of Puerto Rico.

Other navigators claimed their vessel's position more likely lay near San Salvador or Hispaniola or in the vicinity of Turks Island.

The Sailing Master, sunken-eyed and growing very weak, argued, not unreasonably, that the Virgin Herself *must* be guiding the half-sunk wreck along one of several channels dividing that intricate maze of islands called the Bahama Banks, otherwise, why had she remained afloat? If this were the case, along *which* channel was she being driven? Caicos Passage, Mouchoir Passage, or even Crooked Island Passage? No telling.

Inevitably the great gale blew itself out but only at the end of several days. The sun came out and the sea flattened sufficiently to allow scarecrow survivors, now numbering under a hundred, to rig a jury mast and mount a clumsy rudder of sorts under the direction of the Sailing Master and Don Luis Villavincencio, who displayed that cool, indomitable courage which had conquered and now ruled vast empires in the New World.

Discipline of a sort became re-established. By the time the ship once more could respond, albeit erratically, to her helm it came as a vast encouragement to discover that two of her four anchors somehow remained catted in position. Water and food were broken out, the hurt were bandaged and spirits revived until the officers even spoke of making for a large island barely visible on the skyline.

But then the sky "whitened" and a second hurricane arose with almost incredible suddenness to drive the Viceroy of Mexico's galleon floundering, half awash, towards a semicircle of coral reefs above one of which showed a chimney-shaped projection. Ottavio Gallucio distinctly saw it while, with a handful of half-drowned companions, he swung an ax to cut free the huge port watch anchor. In addition to the anchors, a drag of cannons, lashed together, was contrived to impede the treasure ship's progress towards that half-circle of white-fanged reefs. All at once drag and anchors must have slipped into some profound crevice in the sea's bottom for *Nuestra Señora de la Concepción,* no longer restrained, lurched straight towards the center of that tight semicircle of reefs.

Making horrible grinding noises, the Viceroy's galleon struck so hard she broke in two. Bow and forecastle almost immediately disappeared under surging, frothing seas, but what fate awaited the lofty sterncastle and the vessel's afterend no one could predict.

Part II

FRONTIER ROUGHNECK

Chapter 2

FIRES ALONG THE SHEEPSCOT

HAPPILY YET UNAWARE that this, the eleventh day of August, 1676, was to prove a date that would linger forever in his memory, William Phips strode out to untwist a block and falls dangling from a heavy oaken derrick set at the far end of a fitting-out dock lying parallel to the building stocks of his thriving new shipyard.

The newly risen sun tinted copper-red the young man's bold, squarish features and revealed in full clarity his boxlike jaw and the rather full lips of a wide mouth which ran ruler-straight from one corner to the other.

Will Phips's large steel-gray eyes, widely spaced beneath heavy dark brown brows, traveled across Monsweag Inlet to Jeremesquam Point which lay across that narrow, deep-water bay upon which, after thorough investigation, he'd decided upon as an ideal site for his venture.

He could see under a stand of towering firs the weather-beaten gambrel roof of that log cabin in which, some twenty-four years ago, he'd first beheld the light of day as the twenty-first son born to James and Mary Phips.

Formerly of Bristol, Gloucestershire, in the Old Country, Pa and Ma had emigrated in the early 1640s at the earnest solicitation of the Puritan government of the Massachusetts Bay Colony. Those practical, if dour, officials had noticed that their ever-expanding colony was growing dangerously short of skilled artisans. Therefore, carpenters, bricklayers, shipwrights and especially weavers, tanners, blacksmiths, armorers, and gun-smiths had been offered passage at reduced prices and promised generous grants of land in the new Massachusetts Bay Colony— especially if they respected or adhered to Puritan tenets.

Accordingly, James Phips, master blacksmith and gunsmith of no mean ability, had sold his business in Wales and with wife Mary and the children had embarked for the New World.

Strangely enough, mused the young shipwright, neither Pa nor Ma could recollect just how many of their numerous off-spring had accompanied them on that most uncomfortable and seemingly interminable voyage across the Atlantic.

A pair of otters swam up, bright-eyed, to consider big young William Phips as he stood looking across Monsweag Inlet, glassy-smooth at this early hour.

The shipwright then noticed something unusual. A birch-bark canoe paddled by two Indians had put out from above Spring Cove across the river, and was starting upstream at a hurried clip. Why upstream? Ordinarily, these savages would have headed down the Sheepscot to fish pools in which huge salmon loved to linger.

Well, 'twas no concern of Will's where they fished as long as they fetched him a catch of reasonable size.

Yonder on Jeremesquam Point was where he and a brood of equally tough and boisterous brothers had grown up, toiling from dawn till dark the year round so that the family could not only survive the rigors of this harsh New England climate but even prosper in a modest way amid these dark, perilous, and seemingly endless expanses of incredibly rich timberland.

Now the sun began lifting above serrated ranks of pointed spruce tops beyond Clarke & Lake's shipyard in Spring Cove, lying almost directly across the fast-flowing Sheepscot River. The night's freshness he knew would linger but a short while before windless and humid midsummer heat would saturate the river valley.

Will didn't mind heat since here in the backwoods he could, without criticism, peel down to shirt and breeches and go bare-foot and hatless if he chose. Only thanks to liberal applications of rancid bear's grease such as the Tawnies used could he ward off clouds of "no-see-ums" and black flies by day and, come sundown, mosquitoes which could punish a body like a verita-ble plague out of Egypt. Aye, but anything was preferable to those endless dark months of bone-piercing cold.

He still found pleasure in watching a beaver, an alder branch between huge yellow teeth, go swimming by through water so placid the animal's wake remained visible for quite a distance.

Slowly rubbing huge and thickly callused hands, young Phips continued to view Pa's cabin. Of course, the original, small low-lying structure Pa and his partner, John White, had built 'way back in '45 right after they'd moved from Pemaquid, necessarily had been added onto several times to accommodate a family to which Mary Phips every year added a new member regular as clockwork.

The structure stood on nearly five hundred acres of rich, well-timbered land acquired from one Edward Bateman and had been sited on a low, fir-covered and rocky peninsula jutting into Monsweag Bay to create a short but very deep inlet on which William Phips, last year, had determined to invest hard-won earnings to establish a shipyard where to prove to himself and a group of niggling shareholders that, up here in the wil-derness, it was entirely practicable to construct, very cheaply, stout and uncommonly swift vessels of varying tonnage. Did not all manner of choice building materials grow in abundance right at hand?

[25]

Slowly the young backwoodsman's wide-set and slightly protuberant eyes traversed the inlet until they came to rest on the most ambitious project of his career. A few dozen yards offshore rode the nearly completed brig, the *High Hopes*, 52 feet overall and of 120 tuns burthen. Her yet unpainted hull glowed yellow-brown out of which a pair of sturdy half-rigged masts stuck up stark as hop poles.

No matter. Once he'd sailed her down to Boston and had sold a heavy deckload of choice, twice-seasoned ship timbers he'd be able to add refinements and return before winter set in, in time to lay down a much larger vessel, the plans for which already were taking shape in his imaginative mind.

Absently he watched an osprey dive, then flap off upstream bearing its silvery prey. Even though work on the brig hadn't progressed as rapidly as he'd hoped, it came as some encouragement that the scattering of seafarers living around Monsweag Bay mostly opined that this new vessel seemed extra-well put together and showed lines which promised uncommon speed, which was more than they could say about the sturdy but unimaginative craft turned out in Clarke & Lake's shipyard over yonder.

Still, Will ruminated, he'd learned plenty at Clarke & Lake's during his four-year term of apprenticeship during which he'd more or less taught himself to read, write, and even to make simple mathematical calculations. But for the life of him he could never explain how he'd acquired such an uncanny ability to forecast, pretty accurately as a rule, weather conditions, and to understand seasonal variations in the action of currents and tides.

How well he recalled that glorious autumn day with the maples all aflame when, after four long years of apprenticeship, his employers had presented him with his discharge—plus the customary gift of clothing; one suit to be sure had been of loose-woven homespun but the other had been of really decent serge intended for use on Sundays.

That very same day he'd set out for Boston sailing the *Star of Boston*, a cutter built with his own hands during off hours, deep laden under her cargo of salted codfish.

Phips returned to the present and, more critically than ever, surveyed his brig's lines. Would the original manner in which he'd raked her masts really increase her speed and lend added maneuverability? Pray God, the *High Hopes*'s design *would* prove a long stride towards making good repeated boasts that ere long he'd rank among New England's foremost ship-builders.

Naturally, this, like other pretentions, too often and too loudly voiced, had been sneered at, had evoked plenty of sober folks to deem him a brash, outrageously conceited braggart. But, by the Lord Harry, he'd prove 'em wrong! The public never would comprehend or share his abiding faith in the power of a certain guiding star, nor that the number "seven" would play a decisive part in determining his fate. Did it mean nothing that he'd been his parents' *twenty-first* son?

Once, when warmed by too much Jamaica rum punch, he'd predicted that someday he'd be commissioned to command a King's ship. Jeers had sounded—mostly out of earshot because his shoulders were wide and he stood near five feet eleven inches in Abenaki moccasins which he preferred whenever possible to noisy, heavy and uncomfortable European footgear.

At the end of the fitting-out dock Will Phips noticed that the canoe had disappeared upstream and that smoke was commencing to rise above the handful of dwellings along the river. It remained so still, so peaceful he lingered where he was, head cocked to one side, and reflecting not without satisfaction on certain events.

How come that he, a coarse and almost unlettered back-woodsman, had been able to persuade certain shrewd, well-established merchants and a pair of wealthy young graduates of Harvard College to buy shares not only in the *High Hopes* but also to invest in the yard which was constructing her.

Unfortunately, certain rumors had circulated that credit had been extended largely because of his recent marriage to Mary

[*27*]

Spencer Hull, newly widowed and supposedly pretty well fixed. Although Captain Spencer's petite daughter had not exactly been born into one of the town's foremost families, she and her late husband, John Hull, a successful wool merchant, nevertheless were respected and modestly influential in the community.

His brows merged on recalling how so many people deemed it a minor miracle that Captain Hull's relict should have bestowed her hand on this personable but uncouth and woefully uneducated lout from the Colony's remote and scantily populated Maine District, when so many elegant and well-to-do bachelors were available.

Yes, it was a rare Bostonian who wasn't more or less convinced he'd courted Mary Hull—admittedly four years his senior—only to enhance his financial and social position. The gossips, however, had been mistaken on two important counts.

First off, he'd really fallen deeply in love with that clear-sighted and capable little woman—and she with him. Secondly, Mary had not been left nearly as well off as her God-fearing neighbors imagined—a fact of which he was fully aware before the banns had been published and he and Mary had gone to exchange marriage vows before a stern-faced magistrate.

Phips abandoned reflections when on the placid surface of Monsweag Bay a scattering of small craft appeared heading for his shipyard.

Pretty soon the *High Hopes* would be towed in alongside the fitting-out dock for the amazing rise and fall of tides in these latitudes made it inadvisable to leave an uncompleted vessel tied up.

Soon Phips's foreman, Luke Brodbelt, and Tim Pomeroy, his principal rigger, were boarding the unpainted brig in company with a trio of more or less dependable ship's carpenters he'd brought back from Boston.

Next to appear gliding over the inlet's morning-gilded water came an ungainly birch canoe paddled by a pair of dark-faced Penobscots he'd grown up with. It had been Tookaw—Fast Otter—who'd taught Will Phips how to swim, dive, and maneuver under water better than any of his white or tawny-skinned playmates.

The second paddler was No-me-tha—Red Fish—another mighty swimmer. The younger Indian was quite as skillful with carpenter's tools as he was with a fish spear or diving for lobsters; time and again he'd proved able to remain submerged for three whole minutes, even in icy water.

The tall young shipbuilder strode back to a tool shanty on the dock's landward end and, in passing, cast a cursory glance at those chip-littered stocks in which the keel, for yet another coasting sloop, had been laid the day before; only 40 feet overall, she shouldn't require more than a couple of months to complete so, well before ice formed on the river, the little vessel should be ready to start freighting lumber and firewood down to Boston.

Will was about to enter the supply shed when he noticed a skiff being rowed in great hurry around a rocky point jutting into the Sheepscot about half-a-mile below Fort Arrowsic where John Dale, his local partner and boyhood friend, had built a cabin for Jenny, his plain, red-cheeked bride of a year. Yellow head bent, Dale's big body was swinging so hard his oars were bending and spray was spurting from beneath the skiff's blunt bow. What might have prompted this burst of speed? Almost at once young Phips decided that at long last Jenny's baby must have arrived.

A burst of high-pitched laughter ringing across the spruce-lined inlet returned his attention to the cabin Pa had built on Jeremesquam Point. Those young children romping so noisily along the inlet bore the name of White so were only half brothers and sisters. Most of his full brothers long since had disappeared on their separate ways; only two, both younger than himself, had lingered to earn their bread in the new ship-yard.

Without interest he watched his mother's lanky, deceptively frail-looking figure walk out on the rickety little dock to dip up a mess of lobsters from a pound moored alongside.

Over the whining rasp of a saw, John White, his stepfather,

[29]

hailed from the *High Hopes*'s poop, "Hi, Will! Ain't you got the hardware ready?"

"Keep yer pants on, John, just bring the vessel alongside and I'll have the forge going."

At that moment the two Indians' birchbark canoe grated onto coarse gray shingle on a sharply shelving beach alongside the fitting-out dock.

Fast Otter came running up to the toolshed, narrow black eyes aglitter. "Ill news, oh, Augpac, my brother!" he panted in Abenaki which Phips understood quite as readily as English.

Noting that Dale, though pulling hard, remained still a quarter-mile upstream Phips snapped: "What kind of bad news, oh my brother?"

"Just now—Pennacook trapper ran from Pejepscot—say Squando and Blue Foot right now lead big Abenaki war parties —destroy all whites and settlements south of Pemaquid!"

Muscles on Phips's broad jaw suddenly stood out. "Any places hit so far?"

Fast Otter shook his head, close-shaven save for a low, roached crest of coarse blue-black hair. "Me not know, Augpac, my brother."

Red Fish put in: "Saco, Sheepscot, Damariscotta in big danger—maybe Pemaquid, too."

Keeping an eye on Dale's onrushing skiff, Old Man White grunted, "Them bugtits inland always are throwin' connip-tion fits over nothin'—just like last year."

Drawled Tim Pomeroy, the master rigger: "Maybe them settlers wouldn't act so scary iffen they'd built them a few stronghouses to hole up in, like they do to the south'ard."

"Fat lot o' good such t'would do if King Philip's runners really have 'roused the tribes 'round here," said Phips.

"Who's King Philip?" asked a young carpenter.

"King Philip's a Wampanoag, same one hit the Plymouth settlements so hard last year."

Luke Brodbelt, the yard foreman, shook a big balding head whose scalp was speckled with big, coffee-colored freckles. "Think yer Injun friends are mistook, Will. Philip's been layin' mighty low since his warriors got licked so bad by the Plymouth people and their Prayin' Injuns last winter."

Phips turned, spoke sharply: "Aye, 'tis likely another false alarm. Well, we ain't butterin' any parsnips jawin' and standin' 'round like this. Tim, take some hands and work the brig alongside."

While workers manned a couple of skiffs and started pulling out towards the *High Hopes* Will found time to consider whether those piles of twice-seasoned spars and ship timbers rising at the beach's far end would prove sufficient to satisfy those shareholders down in Boston.

Red Fish suddenly grabbed Phips's arm, grunting: "My brother, look upstream!"

Something like a trickle of icy water suddenly coursed the length of Phips's spine. In the direction of Arrowsic Fort a lazy spiral of blue-white smoke had begun to climb into the windless, blue summer sky above ranks of pointed, dark-green treetops.

"By damn!" swore Old Man White. "Some lunkhead of a new settler must ha' set the woods afire."

Vigorously, Phips shook his head; it wasn't the birth of Jenny Dale's baby which had brought his friend in such a tearing hurry down to Monsweag Inlet. Startled shouts arose when, almost in line with Arrowsic Fort, a second smoke pillar materialized.

The two Penobscots exchanged swift glances; no need to tell Augpac that King Philip's local allies, the cruel, man-eating Abenakis were swarming along the Sheepscot River Valley.

Chapter 3

BLUE FOOT'S BAND

MEMBERS OF THE SIX FAMILIES occupying crude log cabins injudiciously spaced along the Sheepscot's northern shore near Captain Richard Hammond's Fort—which wasn't, in fact, a real fort, only a stronghouse—an extra large cabin equipped with loopholes and a second-story overhang—somehow had failed to notice that not a single watch dog had barked or raised an alarm during the early hours of August 11, 1676. They hadn't because the Abenakis had employed the old trick of loosing in the air odors of a bitch in heat which kept them quiet and lured them to silent destruction.

The inhabitants of Hammond's Fort, including older children, still were yawning and chewing the last of a frugal morning meal before setting about innumerable chores such as felling timber, tending fish traps, mending nets or constructing lobster pots. Women and girls prepared to weed tiny, rock-studded vegetable patches laboriously cleared from the dense and seemingly limitless forest. Presently axes thumped in trimming already felled trees soon to be floated down to Phips's shipyard on Jeremesquam Inlet.

Smaller girls and boys lugged out wooden buckets to milk the settlement's cows of which there weren't many, since along this stretch of the frontier wolves abounded and savages fancied nothing better than a taste of beef as a change from their eternal diet of venison. Moreover, sufficient grazing land hadn't yet been cleared to sustain more than a few head.

Only because beetle-browed and bandy-legged Captain Dick Hammond had paused to repair his wife's butter churn, cleverly fashioned out of a hollow beech log, was he delayed in departing to answer his matutinal call of Nature.

While nearing the family's lean-to "backhouse," he suffered two terrible surprises. First, he discovered Nig, his big, rough-coated black watch dog, lying sprawled in a clump of blueberry bushes with a yellow-feathered war arrow transfixing his throat. Second, from behind the privy, leaped a pair of naked Indians painted in the deadly red-and-black colors of war.

Instantly, the foremost hurled a tomahawk so accurately its blade split Hammond's forehead and sent the black-bearded captain lurching crazily about till he tripped over a root and fell, limbs jerking convulsively even after his scalp had been wrenched off.

Blue Foot's war party had surrounded and closed in on the settlement so silently that auburn-haired Pegeen Hammond, just turned eighteen and soon to marry lanky Tom Booker, observed nothing untoward while deftly milking Bluebell, the family's limpid-eyed black-and-brown milch cow.

The girl had stooped to pick up the half-filled bucket when her fingers closed spasmodically upon its rope handle for, from the direction of Pa's stronghouse and surrounding cabins, a gale of ear-piercing war whoops effectively shattered the morning's warm stillness.

Pegeen's large, heavily lashed and dark-blue eyes formed white-ringed circles while she remained frozen into stark immobility listening to the eerie, shrill screeching of savages

[33]

mingle briefly with deeper-pitched yells raised by white men. These last quickly died out, were replaced by shrieks and screams of pain and mortal terror.

Out of the woods where he'd been busy, bounded Tom Booker, ax in hand. "Injuns!" he rasped and rushed up so fast he startled Bluebell into dashing away into a heavy alder thicket on the river's bank. "Bide here whilst I fetch gun. Be right back!"

"Tom! Tom! Don't go—too late. Savages already—among houses." Gobbling war whoops were attaining a crescendo around Captain Hammond's two-story "fort."

Tom shook off the girl's hand then, yelling his head off and brandishing his ax in a pathetic effort to sound like re-inforcements coming up, bounded out of sight.

Trembling violently, Pegeen debated her immediate course of action. To continue cowering like a frightened rabbit would accomplish nothing. Commonsense, of which she possessed more than her share considering her years, warned she'd better not heed her intended's instructions to remain where she was. So, cautiously, she crept through the underbrush till she could obtain a partial view of that clearing in which stood her father's stronghouse and four nearby cabins.

Pegeen then calmed sufficiently to notice that thus far only a half-dozen muskets had been fired—which argued that Pa and the neighbors must have ignored a fundamental law of survival in the wilderness—no matter what a man was about a firearm must always be kept handy by.

In paralyzed and dry-mouthed horror, the girl watched a swarm of hideously painted, yammering Indians close in on one log cabin after another. The first to be attacked was Asaph Wiggins's place, the sturdy oaken door of which stood invit-ingly ajar because of the heat no doubt.

Squalling like a pig dragged to slaughter angular Mrs. Wig-gins dashed out of her doorway hauling her youngest child by the hand. Skirts flapping wildly, she hadn't completed more than a few awkward strides before a screeching buck leaped onto her shoulders much like a cougar pinning a deer to the ground.

The warrior stooped, made a quick circular movement with his skinning knife, then planted a moccasined foot on Mrs. Wiggins's neck, wrenched free her scalp. Streaming blood, the woman somehow struggled onto her knees all the while shrieking for her child whose meager little body already lay scalped and squirming feebly amid a widening scarlet puddle.

Rooted by terror, Pegeen's attention was diverted to a white man of about Tom's build swinging a clubbed musket in frenzied arcs till he went down under a converging ring of flashing blades and painted tawny bodies.

In rigid horror she watched Pa's nearest neighbor and best friend, Michael Phelps, overtaken and tomahawked at the water's edge while attempting to shove off a canoe. At first glance she'd feared the fugitive was Tom, but it wasn't. Neither then nor later did she catch even a glimpse of her intended.

It was just as well Pegeen couldn't see what was taking place in Pa's stronghouse because of a stand of sugar maples, which Ma had insisted on saving, obscured her view. Long since, Pa, as experienced as he was, had vowed that all trees within bowshot of the settlement must be felled and cleared away, but somehow he'd put off this precaution in favor of more pressing tasks of which there always were plenty. When the hellish clamor commenced to subside to isolated shrieks and screams Pegeen guessed all too well the fate which must have overtaken Pa, Ma, and the neighbors. Possibly a few souls just might have been taken prisoner to be held for ransom? Sometimes the savages did that. But where was Tom?

The auburn-haired girl crouched low among the alders, loins aquiver, and watched a tall, yellow-and-black-painted warrior dash out of the Wiggins cabin flourishing a flaming brand above his roached and shaven head and run, whooping, over to the Booker cabin. Another Abenaki headed for Ben Smiley's place.

In swift succession Blue Foot's warriors set fire to Pa's stronghouse and the other cabins. Because a hard rain hadn't fallen in weeks flames took hold with an appalling eagerness and shingle roofs burned like dry birchbark. Incredibly soon the crackling roar of flames drowned out even triumphant scalp screeches and created billows of pale gray-blue fumes which hung so low in the windless atmosphere as to set a body's eyes to smarting.

A plaintive moo from Bluebell brought home to Pegeen Hammond that absolutely nothing was to be gained through lingering here; she'd soon be as dead as her neighbors if she didn't decamp. So bent almost double, she forced a way through the alder thicket towards a cart track leading to Jeremesquam Point, lying nearly three miles downstream.

The wild-eyed girl's innate commonsense again asserted itself. She figured that once their onslaught on Hammond's Fort was complete the Abenakis next would set about exterminating lonely homes scattered around Monsweag Bay. In that case the savages quickly must reach this same cart track along which they could run her down without effort.

Pegeen, therefore, turned left and worked her way through white birch clumps till she came on a seldom-used foot path running parallel to the Sheepscot. She paused, panting wildly and sweating, long enough to twist her dark-red hair into a knot which grasping branches couldn't get hold of. Then, pulling her heavy homespun skirt and coarse linen petticoat waist-high, she started off, long and muscular white legs flashing while hurdling fallen logs, leaping over mossy rocks and entangling roots. Although stones continually bruised her broad bare feet and wild blackberry briars raked her unprotected legs and branches lashed her face and arms like red-hot wires Pegeen plunged on towards Jeremesquam Point.

Inevitably, she fell several times. Once as she struggled, gasping, back onto her feet, she glanced across the river in time to see a thin, blue-gray column of smoke rising in the direction of Fort Arrowsic—reputedly as ill-defended as Pa's place had been. God's love! The Abenakis must also be rampaging along the Sheepscot's north bank!

To draw even a shallow breath now caused agony but even so she reckoned she just might reach Jeremesquam if a crippling "stitch" didn't develop in her side. She lumbered onwards almost blindly, full young breasts jolting uncomfortably beneath a thin blouse of calico.

The moment she rounded the last point above Jeremesquam she could tell by the way people there were scurrying about they must already have taken alarm. She couldn't know that no less than six pillars of smoke now were twisting upwards to the north and to the west.

At last she lurched across a little potato patch in a clearing back of the Phips cabin to gasp the terrible news from Hammond's Fort to old Ma Phips and a gaggle of frowsy, sunburned, and scared-looking youngsters.

Not long before Pegeen Hammond reached Jeremesquam Point, John Dale, frozen-faced and purple with exertion had rowed into shouting distance.

Phips cupped ears but his partner was so out of breath he couldn't make out what John was trying to tell him.

A few skiffs and canoes now appeared from points scattered about Monsweag Bay; all were making for Jeremesquam Point.

John Dale drove his battered skiff onto the gravel beach and faltered ashore with his slightly straddled, intense dark-brown eyes staring and out of focus, like those of someone who recently has suffered a violent blow on the head.

The yellow-haired young fellow's mouth and nostrils worked spasmodically like the gills of a stranded fish.

Phips ran towards his lifelong friend.

"Tawnies struck maybe—hour ago."

Muscles began to stand out in ridges along the shipbuilder's jaw. "How many?"

Dale used the heel of a hand to shove aside sweat-soaked strands of hair. "No tellin'," he wheezed. "P-painted devils were ever'where—surprised us—complete—no chance—find weapons—put up any kind of—fight."

Phips broke in harshly: "Anyone else get away?"

"Doubt it. I only 'scaped 'cause when they struck I was down by river whittlin' thole pins."

[37]

"Any small craft left whole at Arrowsic? Think hard. 'Tis important!"

Shuddering violently, Dale collapsed rather than settled onto the nearest tide-smoothed rock. "Dunno."

Phips snapped: "Any Injuns attack from canoes?"

"None I noticed, but, like I said, I was workin' below the Fort's reg'lar landin'."

"You don't remember any canoes on the river?"

"No."

William Phips's gaze flitted over the gathering of shaggy-haired settlers and regular shipyard workers. "That's good, if true. Mebbe we'll be granted time to get set."

Dully, Dale queried: "Will, how many men 'round here got firearms know how to handle 'em?"

"Maybe a dozen—a few more if more survivors come in."

Snapped Luke Brodbelt, the foreman: "Must be ten-twenty times as many hostiles closin' in. Look over yonder—" Down-river more small but ominous smoke clouds had begun to lift lazily.

Someone called out: "Hey, Jack, where's yer wife? She get away?"

"No. A passel o' howlin' devils chased Jenny right down to water's edge and—and—" Quivering callused hands covered Dale's eyes. "They rode her down, scalped her then"— he gagged—"ripped off Jenny's clothes, slashed open her belly, snatched the baby out of her body and carried it off, screechin' like trapped lynxes. Oh, God! Oh, my God!"

Phips's powerful neck swelled and he swallowed hard; like some others he knew what this meant. Many Abenakis were cannibals who, like the Mohawks and certain other tribes, deemed an unborn child, gently simmered, to be the most succulent of tidbits.

Phips's hand closed hard on his partner's shoulders. "Steady, Jack. Git a hold of yerself. You certain—sure no one else is likely to show up from Fort Arrowsic?"

"No, except mebbe some of our redskin slaves might ha' cleared out in time; but such wouldn't run in this direction."

[*38*]

Since only a few more hard-eyed and terrified neighbors in ragged homespun or work-shiny buckskins succeeded in reaching the fitting-out dock, the extent of this disaster became apparent. None of these later arrivals actually had suffered attack since all had seen the smokes and had recalled last year's bloody raids down in Massachusetts when King Philip's warlike Wampanoags had launched a succession of cunningly conceived and usually successful attacks. He also had inflamed the Narragansetts, Nipmucks, Potumtucks, and other northeastern tribes to join in a campaign calculated to wipe out or to drive all Europeans into the Atlantic. Warned the Wampanoag sachem, the whites relentlessly were moving inland to trap and farm and all along the coast pale faces were acquiring vast stands of virgin timber from sagamores who, dazzled by gifts of worthless baubles plus plenty of brain-numbing rum, were daubing their tribe's totem mark on one-sided treaties which deeded away tracts to which many signers possessed no real title.

Long before midmorning, William Phips, sweating and hard-eyed, had perceived that the only chances of survival for his neighbors and himself lay in rendering the new brig able to navigate. Accordingly, he ordered the *High Hopes* hurriedly tied up to the fitting-out dock and set all hands feverishly to work. Once Blue Foot's raiders came howling out of the woods there'd be precious little to prevent them from swarming on board and putting a bloody period to the soaring ambitions of James and Mary Phips's twenty-first son.

As, single or by twos and threes, wild-eyed fugitives commenced to appear Phips became increasingly aware of the situation. This raid, it came out by degrees, had been plotted and directed by Squando, a crafty and war-wise Abenaki sachem whose tribesmen had been reinforced by an indeterminate number of Pennacooks, Nashuas, Winnipesaukees, and lesser nations inhabiting the wilderness south and west of the Kennebec River.

Apparently the war party at present ravaging the Sheepscot Valley was being led by Blue Foot, a famous warrior so named because tattooings climbing to midcalf on one of his legs.

If Blue Foot, indeed, commanded the raiders it wasn't welcome news; for over a generation his name had been dreaded along the Maine District's coast from Pemaquid all the way down to Falmouth in New Hampshire.

For all he needed every man to help render the brig navigable, Phips despatched Fast Otter paddling to warn settlers below Monsweag Bay, mostly fishermen and timber cutters, to come arunning or to board the *High Hopes* when, if ever, she appeared downstream. Red Fish, he sent upriver to reconnoiter and attempt to estimate the numbers and probable intentions of Blue Foot's band.

He couldn't know that already King Philip's northern allies effectively had surprised Saghagadoc, Damariscotta, and Saco, which settlements largely had been reduced to mounds of smoldering ruins populated only by mangled corpses. No telling how many lonely lumbering, fishing, and trapping camps might have been obliterated.

By noon Phips, lips ruler-straight and nearly colorless, had concluded that at least two powerful war parties right now were ravaging both banks of the Sheepscot. Probably their intention was to converge upon Monsweag Bay to destroy both shipyards and the concentration of settlers in their vicinity.

It wasn't encouraging, either, when a pair of lean Pennacooks paddled up from the ocean to report in guttural Algonquin that death and destruction had visited several villages in the vicinity of Cape Porpoise. Escape inland, warned the Pennacooks, would be impossible, nor could small, unarmed craft hope to escape to the coast; the hostiles were reported to have collected an indeterminate number of small sloops, shallops, cutters, and canoes.

Over the din of frenzied hammering and sawing, Phips peered intently into the deeply lined features of the older Pennacook and said, "Tollems, old friend and brother, will tribes living inland also turn on us?"

"Some, oh Augpac. Squando and Blue Foot promised them plenty easy scalps, plenty loot."

"What if inland tribes refuse to join in the uprising?"

Tollems spat. "Squando promises to leave them unharmed, but if they believe him they are great fools."

Phips turned to John White, his silver-haired but still sturdy stepfather. "John, 'pears like the Tawnies ain't far from here this minute so get you over to the cabin and tell Ma and the rest to pack eatables fast as they can—warn 'em to bring along just one bundle of clothing apiece."

His gaze flickered to the hot, smoke-streaked sky where, there not being a breath of wind, several strata of bluish-white smoke had formed clouds which hung almost motionless. Since the summer-dried forest now had begun to blaze fiercely in various directions such clouds grew denser.

During the late afternoon Phips became plagued by haggard men who wanted to quit work just long enough to run or paddle back home to retrieve some precious valuable.

"No! Goddam it, no! Ye'd only lose yer hair," snarled the hulking young shipbuilder. "Just 'bide here and help ready this vessel."

"Aye, *your* vessel."

"Know of another can *maybe* carry you to safety?"

"Damn it, Will," snarled George Tolliver, "Mercy's silver spoon's back there. I'm *goin'!*"

"Like hell you are. You shove off, then everybody else will want to leave, too."

"But, Will, that there piece o' silver's the only thing of value we own."

"Shut yer mouth!" Phips dashed sweat from his forehead and stepped forward.

"To hell with you! Me, I'm goin'—"

With a single roundhouse swing Phips knocked Tolliver flat, then towered over him, huge fists balled. "Get up, you bloody fool, and get back to work else I'll kill you!"

Everyone present reckoned Will Phips meant what he said.

First stars were making timid appearances when a final group

[*41*]

of survivors, numbed with horror and leading a few small, whimpering children, reached the fitting-out dock and collapsed onto the *High Hopes*'s chip- and sawdust-covered deck.

Now that dusk was deepening fires flared brighter; some dangerously nearby. Out of the smoky woods appeared a few deer and an elk; these hesitated only a moment before plunging in to swim the inlet at its upper end.

Over by the Pomeroy place a cow overdue for milking commenced a lowing complaint and an abandoned dog suddenly raised such a furious clamor there could be no doubt that the Abenakis were moving out on Jeremesquam Point; immediately Phips ordered the brig's cables cast loose. Only with agonizing deliberation did she commence to drift away from shore towards the dubious safety of open water. In the widest part of the placid bay he ordered the anchor lowered.

Over on that point, known to Indians as "Cher-e-me-squam-me," arose an eerie, heart-stilling chorus of war whoops, while, like giant fireflies, clusters of torches could be seen converging on the Phips cabin. Almost at once flames burst out of its windows and presently soared in vivid sheets from its shingled gambrel roof. Even then old Mary Phips didn't cry aloud, only buried her graying head in the crook of an arm and wept drearily to think on the joys and sorrows she'd experienced yonder where she'd conceived and birthed eleven, or was it twelve or thirteen children.

Her latest young ones clutched her skirts and, in wide-eyed stupor, watched the only home they'd ever known dissolve amid whirlwinds of fire and spark-laden smoke.

Gregory Phips, a stringy, heavily freckled ten-year-old, shook a skinny fist across the cove piping. "Afore I'm done, ye tarnal devils, I'll lift a hundred Tawny scalps on account o' this!"

Huddled amidship, Pegeen watched Will Phips's broad black-haired chest heave spasmodically a few times—but the shipbuilder said nothing. Suddenly he realized he'd not seen his next-younger brother since he'd come in from a timber camp around noon.

"Hey! Anybody seen Brother Jack?"

"He ain't finished staving in small craft along the shore," yelled Brodbelt above the conflagration's awesome roaring.

"He'll show up any minute," predicted Seth Larkin. "You aimin' to spend the night here?"

"If we can. Tide's runnin' too strong 'gainst us; we've too little canvas bent on and there's no wind anyway. No point going aground in the dark."

Mumbled John Dale: "Mayhap, now they've done their damnedest the savages will lose interest and pull foot come daylight? An' if they do, Will, mebbe we can load at least some of our ship timber?"

Phips indicated clumps of shadowy outlines crowding the brig's deck.

"No. Ain't enough space left for a payin' cargo—besides, if I know Blue Foot, his Abenakis won't clear out so long's there's a chance of their takin' this vessel, which they can do easy enough an they discover sufficient whole small boats and canoes."

Hard, red-brown features half-veiled by long brown hair, Phips scowled at the dim outlines of the lumber piles, precious timber he and Dale had selected and weathered for over a year.

What would those penny-pinching shareholders down in Boston say when and if the *High Hopes* made port bearing a cargo of no more value than a parcel of destitute refugees?

Chapter 4

IN THE NARROWS

LONG BEFORE MIDNIGHT William Phips arrived at the conclusion that he'd been correct in assuming that Jeremesquam Point and his boatyard on Monsweag Bay were this particular war party's main objectives.

Disconsolate refugees, having sorted themselves out after a fashion, now were huddled about the incredibly cluttered deck as much out of the way as they could manage. Most were silent but some groups shared scraps of food and in undertones speculated about who else might have got away or been taken captive. The name of a person certainly known to be dead was seldom mentioned.

To William Phips, ranging endlessly along the deck, it was alarming that not one lookout had detected the soft swish-and-drip caused by a paddle drawing near.

He caught up a musket and, from the poop, bellowed, "Who comes yonder?"

"Don't shoot, Will, it's me, Jack!"

"Come in along the port quarter." Although infinitely relieved Phips then took time to berate the watch with a selection of blistering curses for which he was well known.

"Whyn't any of you crotch-blistered bastards notice Jack coming? Be you all deaf and blind to boot? Want the lot of us to lose our hair?" That careful enunciation and elegant turn of speech so painfully acquired in Boston had vanished. His voice sounded harsh as a blade pressed against a grindstone.

His next-younger brother had brought with him a pair of shaggy-headed and jay-naked small boys whose teeth were chattering with cold and fright. "Found 'em clingin' to a driftin' snag; claim they're the only ones left of Tim Clarke's family."

Immediately Jack and the lads had been hauled aboard, Will ordered a ballast stone dropped through the birchbark canoe's bottom. Filling slowly, it drifted out of sight upstream—of no immediate use to Blue Foot's warriors.

"Take the Clarke lads in charge," he instructed Pegeen. "Find 'em food and coverin' of some sort."

"Sure, Will," said she in attempted cheerful tones. "Come along, boys."

"Well, Jack, what'd you find acrost the river?"

The younger Phips grabbed a chunk of bread, tore at it mumbling: "Appears to me like most o' the Abenakis on the north bank ain't headin' straight downstream but seem to be circlin' north and east a bit, perhaps to meet up with reinforcements afore attackin' Fort Pemaquid—"

"Or gettin' ready to cut us off at the Narrows. Yep. *That* must be the reason they ain't yet struck Clarke's shipyard."

In the conflagration's fading light Jack nodded. "Effen the Tawnies come acrost enough small craft they'll likely wait and hit us downstream."

"What else have you heard?"

"Not much."

"While ago I sent Red Fish part way down towards the Narrows but he reported no fires that way."

"You send out Fast Otter, too?"

"Yep. But he ventured only upstream far enough to make sure Blue Foot's hellions have wiped out every settler above Monsweag. Reckon their biggest band must be over yonder or thereabouts." Phips indicated low mounds of embers glowing on Jeremesquam Point.

John Dale, who'd labored all day like a frozen-faced automaton, now showed signs of emerging from shock. When Phips, ceaselessly ranging about the vessel, told him to count heads his partner did so quickly, reported, "Got fifty-three souls on board, all told."

"How many men can prove useful if it comes to a fight?"

"Ten or twelve, and three lads big enough to be of some help an things really go bad."

"And the rest?" From all the smoke he'd inhaled Phips sounded hoarse and harsh.

"Seventeen females and 'round twenty-two sprats of all ages," Dale said. "Some o' the real young 'uns got ary kin aboard so I've ordered such stowed amidships where yer ma, the Hammond girl, and other women can 'tend 'em best they can."

Phips nodded, then ordered all men and the older boys to assemble in the waist; they appeared, many barefoot or only half-dressed. All were too tired and shocked to talk much or even act scared.

Looming fantastically tall in the smoky gloom, Phips spoke briefly, successfully counterfeiting a confident tone.

To Dale he said: "From now on you'll be Chief Mate; Brodbelt, you'll serve as Second Officer."

He next appointed John White, Pa's old partner, to serve as Boatswain. Next, he divided the men and boys into watches. One would be headed by Tim Pomeroy, his boss rigger, the other by Seth Larkin, the barrel-chested ship's blacksmith who aside from the Phipses had been one of the few to fetch aboard his entire family. The big shipbuilder yearned to grant his brother a responsible post but didn't dare; Jack Phips, although big, smart and willing, lacked experience, and too often had proved himself headstrong, even disobedient.

He croaked: "Larkin, your watch will take the first trick and see to it you keep a sharper lookout than we've enjoyed thus far."

Fighting down almost overwhelming fatigue he turned to Red Fish and Fast Otter, who stood silently among the shadows. "My brothers, just before daylight comes, swarm up to the crosstrees. Once we get under way keep yer eyes skinned.

"Minute I pass the word, all women, children, and incapables get below in a big hurry." He kicked the coaming of the main hatch gaping black. "I know it's hotter than Satan's breath down there but I'll be glad if some of you would go below right now." He managed a taut laugh. "'Tis clean-smellin' down there and the 'no-see-ums' and skeeters won't pester you near so bad."

Over in Cold Spring Harbor a clump of pines suddenly flared like gigantic torches in the vicinity of Clarke & Lake's shipyard. Then huge sheets and dazzling banderoles of flame shot up from the frame of a schooner lying half-finished on the stocks, bathing the Sheepscot from bank to bank with an infernal, throbbing radiance.

Phips turned away when a second set of fires burst into brilliance, for this time they were flaring among those piles of precious ship's timber.

It depressed the Master of the *High Hopes* immeasurably that Spotted Skunk, a Pennacook he'd grown up with, was able to swim out to the brig and, quite unobserved, climb the anchor hawser and drop onto the deck, bronze-hued body dripping.

Spotted Skunk, eyes flickering restlessly about, stated that Blue Foot's warriors had discovered quite a number of undamaged small craft.

Phips fingered his big unshaven jaw. "That's bad. When d'you figger the hostiles aim to attack?"

"Just before daybreak, Augpac, my brother."

Phips glancing downriver noted a faint pearling of the eastern

[47]

horizon which he knew well enough was only the breaking of false dawn. Nevertheless, he decided to get the *High Hopes* under weigh, especially since the tide now stood near flood. It seemed wise to set off downstream amid semidarkness and banks of acrid, eye-stinging smoke rather than delay for true dawn and hope for that downstream breeze which usually commenced to spring up about that time.

Once the infirm, the women, and young children had been sent below out of the way, he ordered the few real seamen among the refugees to make sail while half-grown boys and landlubbers manned the barrel capstan's bars and heaved anchor.

He smothered a curse when, after clumsily unclewed sails had been set any which-way, they only dangled slack and useless. Despite the gloom the glimmer of loosed canvas at once was noticed. On Jeremesquam Point and from the Spring Cove side of the river savages started to whoop and yowl once the brig, responding to the onset of the ebb, started almost imperceptibly to drift downriver.

Shaken by a multitude of anxieties, William Phips steadied the tiller's handle. God's blood! Would this untried vessel prove sluggish or overtender in answering her helm?

The false dawn ended and once more smoky gloom shrouded the river. Mercifully, the ruddy glow of those lumber piles smoldering on Jeremesquam Point quickly became lost to sight.

For all William Phips had followed this channel since boyhood it proved disconcerting to be unable to identify even a few familiar landmarks. Gripping the tiller's handle, Phips braced himself against the dull, grinding *crunch* caused by a hull striking one of countless rocks studding this reach of the Sheepscot.

To the shipbuilder's relief there appeared to be no indication of immediate pursuit from Monsweag Bay. If only the *High Hopes* could make better progress; her hastily rigged sails continued to slat limp and useless so she only moved under the current's propulsion.

Eternities seemed to elapse before the eastern horizon brightened sufficiently to disclose that thus far the brig had drifted less than a mile below Jeremesquam Point! Just then John Dale croaked: "Will, methought to feel a breath of air."

"God send you ain't mistook."

Dale hadn't been wrong—a light wind did arise sufficiently strong to stir the canvas and start water gurgling alongside.

The brig barely had acquired a modicum of steerageway than her progress was checked and ominous scraping noises rumbled from her hold, empty save for survivors huddled in apprehensive misery.

To Phips's indescribable relief the *High Hopes* broached-to, then swung sluggishly to starboard before rasping free.

Chapter 5

THE NARROWS

INCREASING DAYLIGHT brought apprehension to William Phips; no real breeze after all had sprung up on *this* of all mornings. Lacking steerageway the *High Hopes* therefore only drifted helplessly, broadside on, towards the open reaches of Sheepscot Bay still a long three miles downstream; worse, the truly safe waters of the broad Atlantic lay a full mile beyond them.

Wearing a battered Monmouth hat the wide brim of which was pinned up on one side, tar-splashed canvas breeches, and a coarse blue dowlas shirt which sagged open down to his navel, Phips reviewed the odds in his favor and found they didn't amount to much.

Firearms fit for use, should the Abenakis come paddling out from some ambush along the Narrows, numbered only eight sound muskets and about half as many boarding pistols. In addition there was a curious assortment of hatchets, axes, pikes, and peaveys—clawed, wood, and iron lumbering levers—which might come in handy as a last resort.

He said nothing but foresaw that everything depended on whether Blue Foot's raiders had come across sufficient canoes, skiffs and similar small craft to launch a waterborne assault in strength.

Due to smoke clouds raised by forest fires blazing at intervals along the river the morning brightened but slowly. Nor was it encouraging to catch occasional glimpses of files of painted Tawnies trotting along the shore towards the Narrows.

He took courage, however, when at long last the brig's hitherto motionless canvas stirred under a faint puff of wind—possibly a precursor of that offshore breeze which at this time of year should have sprung up with dawn. Of greater significance was the fact that lookouts aloft and astride the bowsprit now could recognize landmarks in time to avoid shoals, rocks and reefs.

Once the entrance to the Narrows became visible as a gap about one hundred yards wide opening between tall palisades of evergreens on either bank Phips ordered women and tall youngsters on deck there to don mens' hats and move along the bulwarks in hopes of deluding the Abenakis into believing the brig heavily manned.

The Narrows remained a half-mile distant when Red Fish called down from the foretop that a skiff lay dead ahead but riding so low she must be nearly water-filled.

Soon it appeared that this craft's only occupant was a gray-haired figure who was feebly waving a white rag.

Once the skiff came closer it was seen that aside from the rag waver a slender body lay limp on the rowboat's bottom, half-awash in bloodied water. A lanthorn-jawed trapper suddenly yelled, "Take care, Cappen! That there's Granny Eldritch, the witch!" At the same time the frontiersman forked the first two fingers of his right hand, leveled them at the waterlogged skiff.

Making the same sign others implored, "Steer clear! Yon's a curséd witch!"

Although few people aboard ever actually had seen the Eldritch woman almost every inhabitant of the lower Sheepscot
had heard tell of this woman's Satanic practices when, in lowered voices, talk turned to the practice of witchcraft, as it did
all too often.

The trapper dashed aft to find Phips at the tiller altering the
brig's course to intercept. "Jesus, Cappen! Surely you don't
aim to take aboard one o' Satan's servants!"

"'Twill mean the end of us all an ye succor a witch at a time
like this!" wailed a wild-haired and badly sunburned young
woman whose infant in arms started squalling like a pig suspended for sticking.

Luke Brodbelt cast an anxious glance at his Captain. "With
all the trouble waitin' in the Narrows, ye'd better not risk
takin' yon old harpy aboard."

William Phips made no reply, kept on his course.

"For God's sake, leave her alone!" shrieked a wrinkled crone
with silver-streaked hair and haunted, sunken eyes. "Last spring
plenty of sober folks saw her under a full moon wearin' the
guise of a black billygoat and cruisin' about the bay 'thout the
use of sail or oars."

Phips rasped: "Has yonder female ever been accused, tried
and convicted accordin' to law?"

"Not yet," admitted a brawny young fisherman. "All the
same, everybody *knows* Granny got sore at Job Jones and cast
so evil a spell on his orchard that its fruit all withered and fell
off and his hens quit layin'."

"That's yet to be proved. Anyway, I ain't about to abandon
any white to the savages, any more than I've abandoned the lot
of you. Now quit pesterin' me!"

To John Dale he snapped: "Once I come into the wind stand
by to help the poor creature on board. If that feller on the
bottom ain't real dead bring him, too." He put over the helm
permitting his brig to bear down on the skiff, broadside-on.

"But Granny's oft been heard singing in the Devil's language
which no true Christian can understand."

"Witch or not, she's comin' aboard despite all this—" He

[52]

had started to say "nonsense," but not being knowledgeable concerning witchcraft, checked himself.

Tim Pomeroy, the boss rigger, pleaded: "For God sake leave her be. She's safe enough! Don't you know witches *can't* drown 'cause they can walk on water?"

Phips grabbed up a peavey and started for the vessel's waist. "Anybody forgettin' who's Master aboard this craft had better step forward."

To Phips's astonishment Mrs. White, his own mother, shrilled: "Nobody's forgettin'. All the same, Will, you'll rue this, you headstrong lout."

When fresh cries of protest arose Phips thrust out his box of a jaw. "Be still ye snivelin', heartless swine! Remember, I left behind a rich deck load o' lumber just to keep you from losin' yer hair!"

When the waterlogged skiff, its passenger swaying half erect and the slim, limp figure on its bottom, lay alongside Phips grabbed uplifted hands and pulled the white-haired fugitive over the rail. As he did so he noticed that the survivor's hands weren't bony or clawlike at all, but fairly soft and full-fleshed. Moreover, the Eldritch woman's oval, pinkish-brown features appeared almost unlined and her wildly streaming snow-white hair was plentiful and silky-fine. Beyond a doubt this female hadn't yet reached middle age. For what reason had she gone gray so prematurely?

Once on deck the rescued woman babbled: "May the gude Laird bless and presairve ye, sir-r." She peered up from small eyes so dark that only much later on would William Phips come to notice that the iris of one eye was a very deep blue hue while its companion definitely was black-brown.

Onlookers gasped out in horror when from the front of the rescued woman's faded calico blouse peeked the head of a small and green-eyed black kitten.

"God save us! She's brought along her familiar!"

"Bosh!" roared Phips in rage tempered by unfamiliar apprehensions.

While the young-old woman wrung water from a shapeless

skirt of coarse gray kersey, Phips glanced downwards, saw the body of a half-grown boy lying in pinkish water on the skiff's bottom. Undoubtedly he was dead, must have been shot from behind if a gaping wound in his chest meant anything.

He couldn't have reached fifteen and lay with large and bright blue eyes peering steadily into the smoke-veiled morning sky. Since no weapon was in the skiff and the Narrows entrance now was showing up in greater detail the small boat was left to drift loggily downstream.

Cried Granny Eldritch: "I canna reward ye fair, sir-r, but I predict that sure as Christ's our Saviour, ye'll go far and some-day become a great power i' the land."

Startled, Phipps grunted: "What might be yer true name?"

Ignoring hostile red-brown faces ringing her in, the woman numbly used fingers to push aside lank strands of wet silvery hair. "I was born Betrag Cameron, I'm from Glenelg in Scot-land and widowed these three years."

"Widowed?"

"Aye. I was wedded fair and true to Andrew Eldritch. Andy, our lad, and I crossed the sea five years gone to take up a freehold on this river. We prospered and were unco happy till puir Andrew got killed by a bolt of lightning by mischance on the Haloween. 'Twas then spiteful neighbors started gossip 'twas all my doing! After that my life's become a misery saving for Jamie whose corpse ye saw i' the skiff. The savages slew him just as he was pushing us off. I've been adrift all night. And noo, sir-r, I'll clear oot o' yer way."

Suddenly she stuck out her tongue at the refugees many of whom were pointing forked fingers in her direction to ward off the Evil Eye. "Avaunt, ye un-Christian wretches. I fear ye not!"

Phips's gaze circled the ragged, sun-burned onlookers. "Any-body got sufficient heart to take Mrs. Eldritch below and give her a bait of food? She must be famished."

No one made a move till Pegeen Hammond stepped forward and gingerly took the white-haired woman's hand. "Come along. Neither my Pa nor Tom ever set much store on tales of witchcraft."

With the rock-studded entrance to the Narrows now foaming only a hundred yards off, Phips's manner changed. "Once we enter the Narrows you hatted women will line the rail but keep well down lest the enemy catches on. When the Tawnies start for us go below saving females sufficient strong and bold to swing a broadax like you was splittin' firewood."

Gradually the wind increased until the disheveled little brig really started to answer her helm so readily William Phips felt a surge of pride. Lucifer's tail! If, ill-rigged as she now was, the *High Hopes* could be maneuvered so readily she'd likely prove the hardiest vessel he'd designed thus far. He briefly scanned both pine-studded banks then centered attention on the eddying channel ahead. Hell's roaring bells! Smoke clouds suddenly had begun to rise farther down the Sheepscot.

Fast Otter's thin voice called from the maintop: "Augpac! Small boats and canoes lie behind next point—starboard!"

"How many?" Phips bawled through cupped hands.

"No can tell. Mebbe twice ten, mebbe more. Each carry three-four warriors."

Phips yelled up: "Notice any craft along north bank?"

"Only four-five canoes shoving off."

Instantly Phips roared: "Port watch, go below—fetch up ballast—pile it along the bulwarks."

While stones thumped into the scuppers, James and Mary Phips's twenty-first son ranged the deck, making sure every man handling a wheel lock, snaphance, or flintlock had his weapon freshly primed and that he carried slung to his shoulders a powder horn, a patch pocket and a pouch containing bullets and/or a supply of heavy buckshot.

To wide-eyed, tousleheaded youths and a quartet of sinewy younger women he issued pikes or hatchets but only after warning them to drop all the stones they could into canoes arriving alongside before resorting to the use of edged weapons. A sinking canoe, he pointed out, easily could remove more than one savage from the boarding party.

[55]

Reports yelled down from the mastheads convinced Phips that the main Abenaki attack would come from the south bank. In a ragged column groups of canoes and other captured small craft had begun moving out from the lee of a long and rocky point jutting stark against a background of dark-green evergreens. That Red Fish still was reporting only a handful of craft putting out from the Sheepscot's north bank came as considerable encouragement. All along, Phips had been aware that his greatest danger lay in the chance that the Abenakis might attack along both beams at the same time and so overwhelm a divided handful of defenders. Now it appeared that everything depended on how quickly he could drive the *High Hopes* through the Narrows' tortuous channel where, at its narrowest point, foaming rocks and reefs afforded a passage less than forty yards across.

Now painted and befeathered raiders from along both banks entered fast water and commenced paddling furiously to intercept. Distinctly, high-pitched howls and war cries became audible over the river's hissing, rushing noises.

By now the *High Hopes* had picked up respectable speed driven as she was by the ebb here constricted to something like mill-race speed and further assisted by the rising wind beating downstream. Only briefly did Phips divert attention from steering long enough to try to estimate the savages' chances of cutting him off at a point not far ahead where the channel broadened, thus causing the current to slacken considerably. It remained impossible to estimate either the Tawnies' numbers or whether they'd be able to arrive alongside. At best this was going to be a near thing.

The wind having blown away the last of the wood smoke, beardless Jack Phips, stationed forward and nervously handling an ancient Scottish Dagg horse pistol, began to make out spirals, streaks and even checkerboard patterns done in scarlet, black, ocher and blue paint on dark and predatory faces which appeared to be all glinting teeth and gaping red mouths.

Once the wild-haired and half-dressed settlers had lined the starboard rail they checked the primings to a weird assortment

[*56*]

of firearms. Phips bellowed: "Don't nobody shoot till I holler the word!"

Tilting back his head, he yelled to the Penobscot lookouts: "Come below, my brothers, fast, fast!"

Screeching tribal war cries, both Indians slid down backstays and notched arrows to bowstrings the instant their moccasins thudded on deck.

John Dale, gripping a rusty French Charleroi carbine so hard his knuckles showed white, panted: "Jesus Christ! Must be easy half a hundred of 'em."

"How many canoes comin' in from north?" yelled Phips, keeping attention on a sharp bend in the channel where ale-brown water creamed about a cluster of pointed rocks.

His brother Jack bawled over rising clamor: "Five—still better'n a bowshot off."

"All hands to sta'board rail! No matter what, see you beat off the first-comers else ye'll sure enough lose yer scalps."

The foremost canoes, in position to intercept, came surging up, their occupants yammering like timber wolves closing in on a snow-foundered moose.

Young Jack Phips now demonstrated unfitness to bear responsibility by suddenly raising a whoop and emptying his cumbersome horse pistol at the lead canoe before his brother gave the order to fire.

Charged as it was with a half-dozen buckshot the shot, nevertheless, proved unexpectedly effective. A brawny sachem bearing a yellow turtle sketched on his bony chest and another brave painted black and red were hit so hard they lurched spasmodically sidewise, upsetting their birchbark craft and spilling a pair of fellow warriors into the current, screeching like scalded wildcats.

A ragged cheer went up but Phips snarled: "Damn you, Jack! Soon's I find time I'll knock yer block off!"

Flights of turkey-feathered arrows now commenced to arch and hiss towards the brig but for the most part flashed harmlessly over her deck. A few, however, plunged, quivering briefly into the *High Hopes*'s raw decking. Boys and strong young women stared at these round-eyed, then crouched lower under the bulwarks, gripping ballast stones.

"Oh, my God!" shrieked a lanky youth who'd taken an arrow through his shoulder. He staggered about, wild-eyed, wrenching at the shaft until it broke off. Sobbing angrily he then returned to his post by the rail.

Momentarily removing his gaze from the brig's course, William Phips saw the water alongside growing dark with a tangle of splashing canoes. "Aim at them canoes all bunched together but *don't fire yet!*"

To the boys and young women he yelled: "Soon's they come a mite closer start heavin' stones."

A quick glance from a corner of his eye revealed that Abenaki craft launched from the north bank were making but slow headway; they must be hampered by some freak eddy.

When the foremost canoes weren't more than five yards off, Phips shouted: "If ye can't find time t'reload, club yer weapons or use broadaxes and pikes but don't let 'em cross the rail! Now *fire!*"

Brodbelt, Larkin, Pomeroy, his stepfather and the rest steadied barrels on the rail before loosing a noisy and very ragged volley.

Through swirling clouds of gray, rotten-smelling smoke, John Dale, while frantically reloading a ponderous snaphance, glimpsed boys and girls heaving ballast over the rail as fast as they could. Canoes overturned or began to sink; paint-streaked faces yowled and brown arms threshed wildly, raising sheets of spray.

Despite the white men's best efforts several canoes arrived alongside, discharged screeching warriors who easily scaled the *High Hopes*'s low bulwarks.

Ululating, brandishing *casse-têtes*—stone war clubs—tomahawks and skinning knives, Blue Foot's people sprang onto the deck but for the most part promptly went down under clubbed muskets, hard-swung broadaxes and peavey points.

From more distant canoes other Abenakis launched flights of

arrows, one of which struck Jack Phips's side; another pierced the heart of a fisherman from below Fort Arrowsic.

Aware that his brig steadily was gaining headway, William Phips emptied a bell-mouthed musketoon at a group of braves crossing the rail then dropped his weapon to jam the tiller hard-a-starboard thus forcing canoes into collision and permitting the brig to slide by unattacked.

Despite the arrow swaying from the skin of his side, Jack Phips and another settler managed to reload and fire barely in time to blast back a fresh batch of boarders or drop them, kicking helplessly, onto the brig's smoke-obscured deck.

The surface became dotted by heads wearing bedraggled fur or feather headdresses swimming doggedly towards the *High Hopes* for, like most tribes inhabiting the Maine coast, the Abenakis were expert swimmers even in such bitterly cold water as this.

From the bow, Fast Otter and Red Fish standing elbow-to-elbow continued to loose arrows so fast and so effectively that Blue Foot's braves, wailing, started to retreat to the rail.

Shrill, yelping war whoops became supplanted by deep-pitched Anglo-Saxon shouts once the breathless defenders bunched up and, using clubbed muskets or edged weapons, launched a concerted drive which sent the Abenakis reeling backwards over writhing or motionless figures whose bright blood was rendering footing precarious.

When still another row of screaming heads appeared above bulwarks, Phips yelled to Brodbelt: "Take—helm—keep 'er as she goes!"

"Yah-h-h! Yah-h-h!" Gripping a broadax in both hands the shipbuilder created a deadly windmill of steel and sprang at a knot of half-naked Abenakis who, screeching and brandishing tomahawks and war clubs, were attempting to rally.

No one noticed Granny Eldritch's appearance through the mainhatch until, swinging a hatchet and keening like a banshee, she sank her blade into the neck of a blue-and-black-painted warrior, shrilling: "Yon's for my Jamie, ye curs'd de'il!"

Perhaps it was the woman's wildly streaming white hair

and blazing little dark eyes which disconcerted the savages, or perhaps it was because William Phips, hunching massive shoulders behind the broadax just then literally split in half the shaven head of a huge, yowling savage. He must have been a subchief, for immediately when he fell the attackers, emitting doleful cries, dove over the rail and struck out either for the shore or towards a few undamaged canoes which now were fast dropping astern since the brig's canvas had filled and she had begun sailing downstream at a really smart clip.

Panting, Granny Eldritch tossed back her silvery mane, kicked a bloodied brown corpse and shrilled: "Cap'n, 'twould seem many o' these sons of Belial will plague us nae mair."

"Gospel truth!" Impulsively, Phips flung an arm about shoulders which proved surprisingly soft and at the same time glared defiance at onlookers who, witnessing this gesture, made the sign and spat in the widow's direction.

Once the Abenakis abandoned a patently hopeless pursuit, Phips ordered all dead or wounded savages stripped of weapons and heaved overboard.

Chapter 6

OFF CAPE ANN

ONLY AROUND DUSK of the fourth day of what normally should have been a three-day trip down to Boston did the *High Hopes*, delayed by a spell of rerigging at sea, raise the coast of Cape Ann on which only a few dim, yellow-red lights showed. Thus far the voyage had proved lonely; only one small schooner, likewise crammed with refugees, had been sighted and overtaken.

Numbly, Captain William Phips, at the helm as usual, rubbed the back of a hand across hollowed eyes before directing attention to the evening star rising, pure and brilliant out of the ocean. Could yonder brilliance represent that personal Star of Fortune in which he'd believed ever since he could remember?

He peered aloft to make sure the lookouts were alert—they were. Next, he made out the dark outlines of survivors lying huddled in exhausted slumber under the lee of the weather bulwarks.

[*61*]

A glow created by a hard pull on a short-stemmed clay pipe momentarily illumined Phips's bronzed features, thinned to cragginess and darkened by a five-days' growth of beard.

Since few passengers possessed even a single item of warm clothing a majority made their way below to the crowded, evil-smelling hold. The open Atlantic night winds could blow mighty cold even in August.

Pegeen Hammond having improvised a strip of sailcloth into a shawl, lingered in the bows, leaned on the rail and studied the scarcely visible coastline. If only she'd been allowed just enough fresh water to wipe successive layers of dirt and dried perspiration from her face and body. How she hated such uncleanliness and the less she thought about her tangled and greasy hair the better. Nevertheless, she'd managed to plait its coppery abundance into braids and secure them with leather thrums whacked from Jack Phips's deep-fringed hunting shirt. Fortunately, the young fellow's arrow wound had proved entirely superficial.

After a good wash what Pegeen most yearned for was an undershift of some description and a pair of shoes. The greasy and shapeless Abenaki moccasins she'd been wearing were uncomfortably small and lent her broad but small and well-shaped feet little protection.

Save for John Dale, that blank-eyed new widower standing lookout duty in the bows, she was alone, listening to the rhythmic hiss-hiss and rush of an endless succession of waves parting unseen under the stem.

Aside from Pegeen's own experience at Hammond's Fort, John Dale's must have been appalling. Imagine watching his wife scalped, seeing her belly slashed open before his very eyes.

Shivering under her improvised shawl, Pegeen risked a sidewise glance and saw his outline swaying gently, rhythmically by the knightheads. Phips's partner appeared to be gazing fixedly into the violet-black and star-studded sky as if in an attempt to solve an insoluble problem.

Thoughts reverting to Tom Booker, Pegeen reckoned she

maybe understood, in a small way, how low must be the First Mate's spirits. They both noticed an extra-brilliant shooting star blaze across the sky in a long arc in the general direction of Boston. A lucky omen, perhaps?

For the first time it really sank in that by now Pa, Ma, and the rest of them must now be corpses uglily decaying around Hammond's Fort—food for black bears who never were fussy about what they ate.

As nearly as Pegeen knew nowhere had she kinfolk she might turn to. If only Ma even once had mentioned her origins; as it was, she'd never even so much as given her maiden name.

Pa, an ex-sergeant in the 42nd of the Line, for some reason known only to himself had remained equally uncommunicative. All Pegeen knew for sure was that Richard Hammond of Southampton, England, had married Ma very shortly after arriving in Boston and almost at once had taken up a soldier's land grant in the vicinity of Exeter in New Hampshire. After only a short spell of farming he'd moved on up to the Maine District and had set about timbering in the vicinity of Sheepscot so successfully he'd built a big house, had been elected Captain of the local militia and otherwise was becoming an important figure in the community.

One fact concerning Ma appeared indisputable; the very few people who had known her at all well agreed that Jenny Hammond must have sprung from "quality" folk. Well-traveled settlers claimed Ma's accent had originated in East Anglia —most probably Lincolnshire.

Ma never had been one to complain save on rare occasions when she'd lament her inability to present her dour and undoubtedly virile black-bearded husband with but a single offspring—and a girl at that.

Sadly, Pegeen again pondered why Ma, although herself well-educated, never had afforded her only child more than rudimentary instruction in writing, reading and elementary ciphering. Apparently, Ma held that a fancy education didn't

[63]

work to a female's best interests; too often she'd said imperfect knowledge led only to unhappiness.

Sometimes she wondered whether Ma had kept her so ignorant in order to ensure that her daughter might never mingle with high society and so perhaps hear talk which had better remain forgotten?

The night wind could have stirred her hair in a way she enjoyed if only it hadn't been so filthy. Ah me. What will befall me when we reach Boston? Of course I'll have to set about earning my daily bread. But how? Of course I can cook and bake frontier fare better than most; again, some folks have allowed I'm uncommon skillful at spinning, weaving, cutting and sewing rough garments such as we use in the backwoods.

Surely, in a great city like Boston where they say dwell above four thousand souls, there *must* be a need for a hard-working domestic. Much as she hated weeping, her eyes filled. If only my dear, darling Thomas were alive to look out for me. With that thought a rising uneasiness suddenly gripped her for, with their wedding but a few weeks off, she and Tom Booker on a few occasions had sneaked off "into the bushes," and there, awkwardly but rapturously, had anticipated the privileges of matrimony.

Swaying against the rail Pegeen all at once became aware that for a second successive month she apparently wasn't going to be "with the flowers." Cold shudders prickled her shoulder blades and a sickening sense of panic struck her. Oh dear, oh dear, what was to become of her if Tom's seed had taken root?

With ever colder breezes beating in her face Pegeen sobbed quietly a few moments before squaring sinewy but pleasantly rounded shoulders and drawing a series of quick, deep breaths, just as Pa had done while tackling some especially knotty problem.

John Dale, standing a few feet away, noticed the girl's agitated breathing and treated her shadowy figure to a lingering glance before returning attention to the brig's course, conscious of growing pride in this vessel designed by Will and contructed through their joint efforts.

Thanks to hasty readjustments in her rigging and to the setting of her canvas, the *High Hopes* now was surging smoothly along with movements so easy they conveyed an almost soothing quality. Pleasingly crisp sounds came from under that uncommonly long and slender bowsprit Will Phips had insisted on experimenting with. Aye, he was commencing to foresee that, properly rigged and handled, this *High Hopes*, ton-for-ton, should prove one of the speediest vessels sailing the North American coast.

Peering astern, Dale noticed Luke Brodbelt had taken over the helm allowing William Phips free to pace the tiny poop deck with large head bowed as if lost in thought. His powerful, compact body was responding almost wearily to the motion.

John Dale reckoned that most likely he could fathom what was on his partner's mind. What kind of a reception might be expected in Boston?

Phips especially must dread his inevitable encounter with fancy-talking Amyas Tilton, Esquire, a young nose-in-the-air, who, nevertheless, more than once had proved himself shrewd if not sharp concerning business matters. For a long time rumors had persisted that Tilton had purchased shares in the *High Hopes* in expectation of getting even with Phips for having cut him out by winning the Widow Hull's dainty little hand.

Mary Spencer Hull Phips, Dale had heard, was a small, delicate woman with the restless motions and brilliant black eyes of a wren. Despite her usually low-pitched and melodious voice, it was bruited about that on occasion Mrs. Phips could shrill loud as any fishwife. Maybe there was something to such a rumor? A perceptive observer might detect an incongruously firm set to that pretty rosebud mouth of hers.

While the brig plowed onwards and the dim loom of Cape Ann vanished, Dale recalled how gossips had it that only because Mary was by four years Will's senior had she accepted this penniless yet strangely persuasive young braggart of a shipbuilder, come but a few years earlier from the Maine District of Massachusetts Bay Colony, annexed back in '69.

Although uneducated, uncouth, and lacking friends of importance his ambitions, too often voiced, were of a soaring nature.

After a while even his all-too-numerous critics became forced to admit that this boastful brawler and celebrated curser, who on occasion drank too much, nevertheless was uncommonly able, industrious and scrupulous about keeping his given word.

Hadn't he time and again demonstrated such amazing imagination and undeniable skill in designing and constructing all manner of vessels that he'd become sufficiently well-heeled to purchase an important number of shares in Captain Eli Greenough's thriving shipyard?

Mused John Dale, while flailing arms against the increasing chill, what an oddly assorted couple William Phips and Mary Spencer Hull must have presented when, back in '72, they'd appeared before a magistrate after having for three days in a row published "intentions towards marriage." William, muscular and weather-beaten, standing straight as the proverbial arrow and near six foot tall and Mary only four feet eight in height and verging on the plump side but with fashionably sloping shoulders and petite and well-proportioned in other directions.

Mean-minded folk continued to contend that young Phips had courted Mary only because John Hull, her late husband, a moderately successful dealer in wool and woolen textiles reputedly, but incorrectly as it turned out, had left Mary one of the wealthiest widows in or around Boston.

From all John Dale had been able to ascertain without prying, Mary Phips was making his partner a rare-fine wife—devoted, yet capable of coping effectively with her rough-hewn and often hard-headed spouse. So far so good, but how would Mary Phips react to the disaster at Jeremesquam Point?

With regard to his own immediate future, the Mate of the

High Hopes didn't feel overconcerned; he now was penniless, true enough, but no longer charged with family responsibilities. As an expert ship carpenter he shouldn't meet with much difficulty in landing a good-paying job straightaway in one of the several new shipyards cluttering Boston's shoreline from Fort Hill around North Point all the way to Mill Pond.

Yet, somehow he knew he simply couldn't linger around Boston; he'd have to sail to foreign shores and somehow free himself of memories of those grisly events in the vicinity of Fort Arrowsic.

Yep, he reckoned he'd frequent certain taverns along Mackerill and Ship Streets patronized by reformed pirates and hardbitten seafarers of all nations who, in their cups, might babble about sunken riches awaiting to be raised by bold and unscrupulous adventurers.

Everyone was aware that, during the last two centuries, dozens if not hundreds of treasure-laden Spanish and Portuguese vessels undoubtedly had come to grief all over the northern Caribbean, off the Bermudas, in the Bahamas Passage and along the coast of Florida. Certainly he'd lose nothing by keeping eyes and ears open.

He saw the Hammond girl bend over the rail, obviously weeping, yielded to impulse and went over to put an arm about her till the convulsive quivering of her shoulders slowed, then ceased.

At length he offered: "Reckon this here voyage is turnin' out to be just 'nother case of 'so far so good.'"

"That's so, sir," she agreed but kept staring at the darkly restless ocean. "Matters could have gone a lot worse in the Narrows so I'll not complain beyond that I'm almighty hungry —thirsty, too." Numbly, she resettled her canvas shawl. "But I guess we all are."

"Aye, reckon so."

"Please, sir, when we make port what *am* I to do for clothing? All I own are these rags I stand in and I've not a farthing to my name."

[67]

"Pity, but if it's any comfort, ye're no worse off than most on board. Any kin or friends 'round Boston?"

"No, sir," she admitted. "I've never traveled from home saving once to Saco and once to Pemaquid." She forced a tremulous smile. "Oh, Mr. Dale, I'm *that* scairt over the notion of venturing into a great town like Boston. I'm so young and green I daren't think on what may become of me."

He raised heavy yellow brows. "You certain-sure, Pegeen, you got no kith, kin or friends yonder?"

"Nary a soul." When she began to shiver violently, Dale slipped off a salt-stained pea jacket and placed it about her shoulders. "Maybe that'll help."

By the light of the hot August stars she peered up into wide-mouthed features the lips of which were set at a faint slant to the left downward. "Thank you, sir. 'Specially on account of I hear you've got more than your fair share of sorrows. 'Twas only this afternoon I heard tell all about Fort Arrowsic."

Said he quietly: "Reckon what chanced there weren't much worse than at your Pa's settlement. Good thing you 'scaped and warned the people 'round Monsweag."

A brief silence ensued in which could be heard monotonous faint creaking caused by the main yard's grinding against oaken parrels.

Several times Dale ran fingers through heavy, neck-length hair before tightening his arm about her shoulders. "Can't promise, but mebbe I c'n be of some help iffen worse comes to worst with you; you see, I know my way 'round the port a bit." He expected Pegeen to take him right up on that, but she didn't.

"An all else fails," said he, "reckon I might find friends who'd harbor you 'til ye can find a situation."

To his surprise the Hammond girl dropped her head against his shoulder and sniffed, "Oh-h, you're being so kind I 'most can't bear it. Nobody else has spoke much to me since I was just a little kind to poor Mrs. Eldritch."

Dale asked sharply: "D'you take her for a *real* witch woman?"

[*68*]

Pegeen dabbed at her eyes, then blew her nose with her fingers. "Don't know 'bout such matters. Pa never would allow witch talk 'round the Fort. He was almighty strict about that—and so was Ma."

"Then they were real Christians—" He broke off as the subject of their conversation, a frail and white-haired figure materialized at the head of the ladder leading to the main hold. Swaying uncertainly, Granny Eldritch sought the lee bulwarks and leaned so far out over the rail that William Phips roused from the pile of damp canvas on which he'd been dozing near the helm.

After dismissing Dale and his companion he made his way over to place a hand on the woman's bent shoulder. Gruffly, he inquired: "What's amiss, Ma'am?"

She turned quivering features and fought to control the violence of her grief. "Ah-h, sir, t-tell me how c-can folks calling themselves C-Christians be s-so unco' cruel?"

"'Cruel'? How?"

"Aye, a big, valiant brute has just slain me wee kitten crying that it must be what he termed my 'familiar' because the puir wee beastie chanced to be colored all black!"

She was shocked by the ferocity of the Captain's outburst of scorching obscenities.

"Sorry, Ma'am. Didn't mean to offend but injustice and blind superstition I can't abide; never have and never will! Mayhap ye can find another kitten once we make port."

"Mayhap I will, an our shipmates don't have me jailed without a hearing, like pairsons accused of witchcraft are in Salem and other settlements."

Awkwardly, Phips patted the woman's shoulder, inquiring softly: "That dead lad in the skiff really was yer son?"

"Aye, sir. My puir Jamie took some savage's ball i' the back even as he were shoving off."

She wept and set up a lament in that strange language rumored to be "witch's talk." Certainly, her words sounded nothing like any of the several Indian languages or dialect he was familiar with.

[69]

"Which tribe's lingo you usin'?"

"Why, sir, 'tis naught but plain Gaelic, me mother tongue. *Aiee! Aiee!* Why was I cursed to be born 'neath such an unchancy sign that I'm alone now wi' every hand and tongue against me?"

His arm supported the woman's sagging but surprisingly soft body. "Ye're wrong there, Ma'am. In me ye've a friend ye can rely on."

Quieting, Mrs. Eldritch sniffled. "Ye're a stalwart, bonny mon, sir-r, so bravely to befriend a puir body who before God, never has done anyone a harm." She tilted back a head framed in flowing silver and peered steadily into his face. "Ye'll ne'er regret this, William Phips." Her features, he realized, though angular, were finely chiseled while her small, mismatched eyes appeared almost perfectly round.

Hurriedly she continued: "Ye may be sure I'll no' risk ye embarrassment by lingering aboot Boston. Fast as I can I'll seek the Rhode Island Plantations where I've heard the inhabitants are more reasonable-minded."

"A sound idea but how'll you get there? Got any money?"

While the wind moaned gently through the rigging Granny Eldritch fumbled in the bosom of a patched gray cotton blouse, presently produced a small snuff box bearing what appeared to be an elaborate coat-of-arms engraved on its lid. By its weight he guessed the container must be of solid gold or possibly of heavily plated lead.

"Umm. This should serve to get you where you aim to turn but, Ma'am, be cautious about where you show this else ye're likely to find yer gullet slit."

When he started to turn away the fey creature checked him almost imperiously. "Wait. In gratitude I'll tell ye something aboot yer future." She started to speak in an odd, squeaky monotone. "For a' I've never been any part of a witch I confess I *do* possess the power of second sight."

Wind-stirred garments darkly aflutter, the woman covered her eyes. "William Phips, ye'll overcome the handicaps of humble birth and faulty learning, but not wi'out pain and over-comin' many dangers. I see yer Star of Fortune waxing bright, then waning, then blazing again—but to what end I canna' yet see."

Gaze fixed on the disheveled figure braced against the bulwarks, Phips spoke over the hiss and slap of waves along the brig's side. "Did ye know, Ma'am, that I'm the *twenty-first* son of my parents? Might this not have a bearing on my destiny?"

"'Twouldna astonish me. Aye, come what may, ye'll follow yer Star through thick and thin 'til Old Bones cuts ye doon for good."

"'*My Star*'! How could you know that ever since I was a little tacker I've believed in my Lucky Star?" His voice deepened and he peered fixedly out over the black water. "Why can I be so *sure* that someday I, an unlettered roughneck from the frontier, will one day serve as captain of a Royal man-o'-war?"

She cried in that strange, singsong voice: "Ye will; what's more I see ye standing before kings!"

Grinning, he raised a hand. "Thank ye kindly, Ma'am, but to be honored by a single king would satisfy my ambition."

"Nay. I see ye made much of, by more than a single monarch."

"Can ye tell me aught more?"

"Aye. Frae waters 'neath the earth ye'll raise a vast treasure but not all of it."

He gulped. "You certain-sure?"

"Aye. Ye'll not let anyone or anything stay you from it."

William Phips raised eyes to galaxies glowing in the heavens like white-hot nails driven into a purple-black sky. When he lowered his gaze Granny Eldritch had disappeared.

Chapter 7

BOSTON TOWN

ONCE CAPTAIN PHIPS started to steer among a scattering of low, glacially scored and often treeless islands dotting Boston Harbor, everybody lined the rails to peer in awe and wonderment at the scene unfolding before them. Only Phips's mother, Mrs. White, Jack, his next-younger brother, John Dale, and a very few others ever before had beheld so great a town as Boston.

Mary White, still fairly slim and straight despite having brought some twenty-six offspring into the world, appeared animated for the first time since this wretched voyage had commenced.

Absently scratching innumerable black fly and mosquito bites, Jack Phips towered over a cluster of small half brothers and sisters and identified landmarks on a shore beginning to shimmer blue-bronze under yet another blazing sun.

His big-knuckled hand swung to the right. "That tall hill

with the windmill on it is Copp's Hill; there's a considerable graveyard on it but you can't spy it from here."

Someone asked: "What's that there big mount near the center of the town? The one with some sort of a tower atop it?"

"That's Beacon Hill," Mrs. White informed, spluttering saliva because of a missing front tooth. "From that tower signal flags are flown and beacon fires lit in time of danger."

With the *High Hopes* making better speed thanks to a freshening northeast breeze, Dale identified various other landmarks.

"Off to steerboard in the direction we're headin' ye can see a fort called the North Battery which protects the entrance to the Charles River."

An almost toothless old man queried: "What be them three hillocks lyin' beyond and left of Beacon Hill?"

Eager to appear knowledgeable, Jack Phips broke in: "Them? Oh, some call 'em the 'Tri-Mounts,' the 'Three Mounds' or the 'Tramonts.' Behind the North Battery lie a mort of docks and shipyards; more are bein' built all the time."

Wincing from the flesh wound in his side, Jack pointed left, "'Way over yonder stands Fort Hill. Pretty soon ye'll see the walls of a stone fort called the South Battery."

"Master Phips, how many cannons do them batteries hold?" queried a heavily freckled lad.

"Not many," Jack admitted, "but sufficient, I reckon, to keep the French and pirates respectful."

"P-pirates?" quavered a badly sun-burned girl. "Are there many such about?"

"No tellin'," growled Seth Larkin. "Such come and go all the time—disguised, of course, but *so far* no outlaw ship has dared venture close to port."

One of the older boys sang out: "Mr. Dale, what's that there great pier which sticks so far out into the harbor? The one with derricks and all them little houses onto it?"

"That's called the Long Wharf; lies at the foot of King Street. Yonder line of half-sunk rocks and pilings which parallels the shoreline is called the 'Barricado' or 'Out Wharf.'

[73]

'Twas designed to protect Town Cove where the first settlers landed.

"'Course, nowadays Boston stretches a long way behind them docks and wharfs where you see all them masts and yards, 'round the South Battery all the way to Hudson's Point on the Charles River 'way over to yer right."

Pegeen, clinging to the foremast shrouds, experienced a sinking sensation. Mercy! Just look at all those shingled roofs and big two-story houses!

She turned to a gaunt-featured woman carrying a small boy balanced on her shoulder. "Please, Ma'am, how many church steeples do you number?"

"Three. Used to live there so I can name 'em. That there steeple showin' above King Street back from Long Wharf belongs to Old Church—the first built in Boston; folks claim 'twas back in 1630."

She shifted the child to her other scrawny shoulder. "While ye're lookin' in that direction note that great four-story wood buildin'. 'Tis the Town House where laws are made and the Gen'ral Court sits in Council. The King's Governor rules from there even if the ground floor is used for market place in bad weather—otherwise, folks do business in a big square 'round the Town House."

As the brig sped by Bird Island survivors craned necks out over the rail. A few young men and boys even climbed into the shrouds better to view the awesome vista ahead.

"Now," continued the gaunt woman, "that steeple to left of the Old Church belongs to the South Church, whilst the one 'way over towards the North Battery marks the North Church—both was built nigh on fifteen year ago. South is the newest."

"Please, Ma'am, how many people dwell yonder?" Pegeen inquired of Mistress White.

"Why, child, last I heard they number near four thousand, not countin' travelers and seafaring folk."

"Four thousand! How can so many folks dwell all in one place!"

The refugees gaped; most of them never before had beheld more than ten or fifteen buildings in any settlement.

The *High Hopes*'s company presented a pitiful spectacle; without exception they were scratched, filthy, wild-haired, badly sun-burned and half-clad in noisome rags. Nevertheless, Phips sensed that these people all the same retained a dogged, undefeated air. Possibly they'd become accustomed to hardships unknown in the Old Country while the younger ones never had enjoyed security or the basic comforts of Europe.

In contrast to the vast and empty ocean Boston's large harbor appeared positively crowded. Everywhere, it seemed, flashed the sails of ketches, sloops, snows, fishing boats, shallops and various types of coasters. In the outer harbor a pair of tall, full-rigged ships lay with topsails aback awaiting pilots.

In ever-increasing numbers terns, gulls and other seabirds shrieked and laughed as they wheeled about the *High Hopes*'s raw yellow topmasts. Lines of soot-hued shags or cormorants scudded low over the waves with snaky black necks extended.

From the poop William Phips ordered all hands aloft to shorten canvas, whereupon men and youths clambered clumsily aloft to clew up the forecourse allowing the brig to proceed at reduced speed under poorly rigged topsails and jibs.

A small boy started pointing excitedly. "Say-y, ain't that there a gibbet on yonder dock with something hangin' to it?"

Jack Phips chuckled. "Aye, Bub, that there's Execution Dock where pirates, mutineers, witches and other criminals get hanged. Take care you don't wind up over yonder."

To Phips it proved pleasant to realize how speedily this new brig sailed under reduced canvas, how readily she responded to slight pressure on her helm.

Before long he steered past North Point and the insignificant little battery on it, towards the Charles River's mouth, past Thornton's Shipyard, then Hint's and on towards an unusually tall derrick marking the end of Captain Greenough's fitting-out dock—his destination.

Enviously the *High Hopes*'s Master viewed Captain Scarlett's long and ample wharf piled high with freight. God

A'mighty! No less than four heavy, seagoing vessels lay tied up to it.

In a grating voice he ordered the recognition pennant hoisted to advise those interested that William Phips's new vessel was making port.

Phips's flaming-red features contracted when, after reducing canvas to a single jib and foretopsail, he worked the *High Hopes* towards Greenough's wharf along which scatterings of people had started out eager to learn the news. It stood to reason that among the gathering crowd there must be several shareholders in the *High Hopes*. Anticipation of what these men were going to say created a sour taste in Phips's mouth.

Because, for over a fortnight, a succession of small vessels transporting dazed, bedraggled, and usually destitute refugees from Damariscotta, Sahagadoc, Saco, and plenty of other settlements had been making port, a sizable curious crowd soon collected beneath Captain Greenough's tall derrick. A little apart and outside a small countinghouse of Flemish bonded brick stood waiting a small group of bleak-faced, well-dressed men. Even at this distance Phips recognized most of them and set his jaw as if suddenly sighting breakers along a lee shore.

Almost as soon as the brig tied up it appeared that due to the arrival of so many destitute people fleeing King Philip's fury, Boston's Town Council had made rough-and-ready preparations by providing such refugees with a frugal supply of plain food, castoff clothing, and emergency shelter in a temporarily empty warehouse.

A pot-bellied and peg-legged roundsman wearing baggy gray breeches and a grimy scarlet tunic shouldered his way alongside the *High Hopes*, raised a halbert on high and sang out: "Those amongst ye having neither friends nor means will come ashore and follow me. Those in better case must make their way at once to the Principal Clerk's office in the Town House and there leave names and the places where they may be found. God save the King!"

Pegeen Hammond, dripping sweat and possessed of nothing

beyond the torn and foul-smelling garments she was wearing decided she'd better join a group gathering about the one-legged roundsman.

It would have been difficult, she was thinking, to visualize a more sorry collection of humans than this sun-reddened group who mostly went barefoot and lacked headgear of any description. Only a few individuals were hugging even a small bundle; pinch-faced children, hungry and tired-out, whimpered; certain women, recalling recent horrors, commenced drearily to weep.

Pegeen was preparing to join the roundsman's party when John Dale gripped her arm, saying quietly:

"Avoid the Town's charity; I've seen what it's like. I've a cousin who lives or used to live hard by. Some 'holier-than-thous' claim Jim Turner's a bit of a rascal and his wife Betsey little better." He grinned. "But still they're warmhearted so I allow they'll provide you with bed and board 'til ye find employ. Come along."

Before setting off, Dale cast a quick backward glance at William Phips and made him out on the *High Hopes*'s poop, grim-faced and square-shouldered and quite alone except for the two Penobscots who, quite expressionless, were viewing the scene with restless and opaque jet eyes.

Taking Pegeen by the hand as if she were a small girl Dale led her along the dock towards a procession of drays, carts and wains raising lazy clouds of dust along Ship Street. Whips cracked, dogs barked and teamsters shouted and cursed.

Spasmodically, her fingers closed around his and she began to tremble over all this noisy confusion while he conducted her, wide-eyed and staring, past a bewildering and seemingly endless succession of warehouses, coopers', ironmongers', and chandlers' shops until finally they halted at the junction of Prince's and Back Streets—a definitely unfashionable-appearing neighborhood.

Dale made an awkward attempt to reassure his companion. "This is where Jim and Betsey 'bide. Likely later on you'll find

[77]

better accommodation but for the moment I reckon this is just another case of 'any port in a storm.'"

Through luck they discovered James Turner and Betsey, his buxom breezy-mannered and rather frowsy spouse, at home. From amid an aura of rum fumes Dale's cousin chortled, "Beelzebub's balls! 'Tis Johnnie Dale!" and then treated him to such a bear hug there seemed small doubt about its sincerity. "So the Injuns didn't part yer hair after all?"

"Didn't miss by much. I'll tell you later," Dale said curtly. "This here's Pegeen Hammond, a neighbor who's lost her whole family, same as me. Right now she's broke, frazzled out and needs help."

On Mrs. Turner's smooth, pink-and-white features appeared an expression of real concern while deliberately she surveyed Pegeen from dusty moccasins to tangled auburn hair. She decided this wench was uncommonly well-built though, like most frontier-bred females, a trifle on the wiry side. Still, there was something about those big, wide-set, dark-blue eyes of hers which invited attention.

Betsey stepped forward smiling, and patted Pegeen's sun-darkened cheek. "Any friend of Johnny's is welcome under our roof. Come inside."

Dale grinned, vastly relieved. "I'll not forget this, Betsey. From my next cruise I'll fetch you back the fanciest pearl and gold earbobs ye could dream on."

Turner laughed so loudly the hot little room resounded. "Avast! Betts has expensive tastes despite the blue-nose sumptuary laws."

"'Sumptuary laws'? What are they?" Right from the start Pegeen wanted to avoid trouble.

Dale said, "They be regulations passed by our Puritan rulers which set out just what quality and cut of clothes persons of different classes must and must not wear but only red-hot 'holier-than-thous' pay 'em much heed these days."

"Come along," said Betsey, squeezing Pegeen's hand. "Expect ye're ready to sell yer soul for soap and a good soak in a tub o' hot water. Don't act so scairty-cat, lovey, me and Jim ain't about to eat so pretty a girl—leastways not alive. Ye'll soon get used to Boston—more's the pity."

Jim Turner was of about average height, had small pale-blue eyes, thick sandy-brown hair and moved with peculiar lithe power. In his right ear he wore a heavy ring of red-gold which twinkled when he reached up into a cupboard to lift down an earthenware demijohn of black Jamaica rum.

Once they'd drained wooden piggins of the fiery stuff, laced with a little water, Turner summoned a lazy grin, "Johnny, me lad, 'tis chancy ye've turned up just when ye have."

"Why so?"

"There's a matter I'll broach later on which mayhap will interest you, maybe not. Heard that that shipyard you and Will Phips have up Monsweag 'way is going mighty well."

Dale stared into his piggin. "Aye. We *were* doin' fine till Squando's Pennacooks and Blue Foot's Abenakis took the warpath 'thout warnin' and massacred and burnt every settlement they could reach. Will and me got away by the skin of our teeth just after they'd put the torch to our yard and pile of seasoned ship timbers. Give me 'nother tot, Jim, and I'll give you an exact account."

Turner pulled together his shaggy brows. "Oh, ho! So that's why ye've turned up so sudden and raggedy-ass!"

"Aye. This ill wind may well blow me and Phips into the debtors' prison lest we can find people who'll see us through this bad patch—especially Phips."

"Wouldn't bank on that; plenty of people hereabouts despise his eternal brag and bluster."

"Maybe so, but no one can deny he *is* a master designer and shipbuilder who also *understands* the sea better than most."

A shaggy brown-and-white mongrel bitch swollen with pups waddled in from Prince's Street and, teats sagging, sought a cool corner from which she kept liquid brown eyes on the two half-clad figures slouching on rush-bottomed chairs.

Drawled Turner, tilting the demijohn: "Till you find out where ye stand or how bad off ye are, Johnny, I'll say no more

[79]

anent a certain proposition I've in mind—one which could make the both of us richer than rich."

"I ain't hopeful so can't ye drop me a pointer right now?"

Turner glanced about, waited till a cart creaking under a load of pickled alewives had turned into Back Street, then queried softly: "Ever been minded to try treasure huntin'?"

Dale nodded after taking a swallow. "What seafarin' man ain't dreamed on it now and again?"

His cousin leaned forward, looked at him hard, then said softly: "Right now I'll only vouchsafe this much. I've got me a true map about where a very rich boodle lies, but don't ask me how." He hiccoughed once and again. "Besides, I own a schooner: she's small to be sure, and likely was built by Methusaleh himself, but I allow she's sufficient sound to gain the Bermudas."

When the last destitute refugee had shambled off Captain Greenough's freight-littered dock in the roundsman's wake, the single passenger remaining aboard the brig was Granny Eldritch, who readily had heeded the Captain's injunction to remain out of sight until darkness fell. Reasonably enough, William Phips had pointed out that, most likely, her fellow survivors, for some time, would remain too preoccupied with immediate troubles to begin spreading rumors that a witch had been imported into the God-fearing port of Boston.

Aside from the two impassive and secretly fearful Penobscots, only Seth Larkin, Luke Brodbelt, and Tim Pomeroy had lingered aboard the new brig whose decking still showed marks recognizable as dried blood.

Wearily, William Phips stumped down to his cabin and combed tangled, oily brown hair into some sort of order. While pulling on his only jacket he wished he dared take time to shave but if he didn't go ashore right away those grim-faced people outside Captain Greenough's countinghouse might deem him wary of confronting them.

He snapped to Brodbelt: "You and the rest wait here till I return."

Brodbelt looked anxious. "Aye, Will, but what'd ye figger will happen to us and the brig?"

"Tell you soon's I find out."

Squaring wide shoulders, the shipbuilder swung easily over the rail and marched rather than walked towards the knot of shareholders waiting, unsmiling, in the shade of the little brick countinghouse. Then for the first time, he noticed John Dale's absence. Damn! If ever he'd needed a supporting voice that moment was at hand. However, it came as a measure of relief to note Captain Eli Greenough's craggy, mahogany-hued visage among the waiting group.

Somehow, he and old Eli gradually had come to attain considerable respect for each other's uncommon commonsense, shipbuilding abilities and unquestionable integrity.

Well-dressed as usual, Amyas Tilton, Esquire, was the first to address him in a clipped, precise accent. "Well, Captain Phips, pray permit us to offer sincere congratulations on our new vessel's maiden voyage. We all are feeling confident that the returns from this venture will prove satisfactory."

While peering down a thin high-ridged nose, his thin, pale-pink lips formed a half-smile. "Am I correct in this assumption?"

Short and rotund Zeke Dobbs, who'd made a small fortune in the West Indian lumber and molasses trade, queried: "Is your shipyard up to Monsweag fully occupied?"

Before Phips could reply, Samuel Sumner, a well-to-do dealer in ship timbers, squinted watery, red-rimmed eyes against the hot, bright sunlight and put the dreaded question: "Tell us, Cap'n, am I nearsighted or do I fail to see any part of that deckload of twice-seasoned lumber you promised?"

"Ye're not nearsighted, Mr. Sumner. There's none aboard."

"Then where is it?"

Deliberately, William Phips's gaze traversed the semicircle of anxious faces. "That lumber was burnt by the savages whilst, as a Christian duty, I was taking survivors aboard instead of loading timber."

[81]

"I've noticed such worthy considerations pay few dividends," observed Amyas Tilton acidly.

Captain Greenough growled: "Damn it, Tilton, William did what he ought. He couldn't abandon friends and neighbors to die a terrible death or get carried off into captivity!"

A brief silence ensued until Sam Sumner's grim expression relaxed a trifle. "We've all already heard terrible tales aplenty but suppose you relate exactly what chanced along the Sheepscot."

In succinct language, Phips described the Abenaki attack and the arrival of survivors which had prompted his decision to let the lumber go and wait as long as he dared for more refugees to come in. Then he added in an odd monotone: "'Tis a notion of mine that certain of those people I've saved, or their heirs, someday will render this Colony great services."

"How can you say that?"

"Because my Star tells me so."

"'*Your star*'? Stuff and nonsense!" rasped Zeke Dobbs. "Look, Will, we've all got our bellies full of boasting and beliefs which border on witchcraft. Your star, an there be such a zany thing, is about to set for good and all!"

Phips glared about in that arrogant manner which already had cost him dearly. "Think what you will, by the Almighty, I can and *will* accomplish any task I determine on, no matter what the odds!"

Turning to Greenough he lowered his voice, "Eli, I'm weary nigh unto death so must go home and rest. When and where shall we meet again?"

Before turning his back, Amyas Tilton said coldly: "There will be a meeting of shareholders and creditors in my counting-house come tomorrow morning at ten o'clock sharp. For your sake, William Phips, I count on your attendance."

Chapter 8

CROSSCURRENTS

HOW STRANGE TO RECALL all at once that, in over a year's time, Phips had not beheld this neat, ivy-draped little house on the corner of North and Ship Streets behind its trim, white picket fence. Constructed by Captain Spencer, his late father-in-law, the dwelling was of white-painted clapboards and distinguished by a pair of small leaded and diaper-paned bow windows—a sure sign of prosperity. It faced the rutted and pot-holed length of North Street.

The doorway was simple but well-proportioned and flanked by plain Doric pilasters of handsomely carved yellow pine, the white paint of which, about their lower extremities, had been grayed by mud cast by passing traffic.

Since both street-level windows were standing open against this enervating summer heat, Phips reckoned his wife must be at home. His heart lifted; dear, trusting and trustworthy Mary.

Phips was about to grip the front door's egg-shaped and

well-polished brass knob when it turned and the portal swung slowly inwards to disclose the minute figure of Mary Spencer Hull Phips staring at him in round-eyed incredulity. She caught a sharp breath, then straightened, said evenly, "Welcome home, William. Dear me! 'Pears like somebody's pulled you through a hawsehole feet first!"

"Ye're wrong, Mary, but that's about the only ill thing that hasn't happened." Phips stepped inside, automatically hung his tar-stained watch-jacket onto a pair of deer's antlers then bent over and bussed her heartily on a smooth and slightly sweaty pink cheek.

What he'd really yearned to do was to bear-hug her and give her a resounding smack on the lips, but something in her manner restrained him.

All she said was, "Expect, William, you might do with a cool drink and a bait of food?"

"Aye, that I would." Crushing fatigue expressed itself in his every movement when he followed her into the kitchen.

All at once Mary faced about, delicate pink features and chin aquiver and, eyes filling, suddenly flung herself into his arms. "Oh, dear to my heart, how fine 'tis to have you home safe! Ever since those first reports about King Philip's new uprising reached town I've been *that* fearful for you. I've prayed and prayed for you, often under the guidance of your great good friend, the Reverend Mr. Increase Mather."

"Ah, Mary! My Mary!" Easily he swung his wife off the floor and hugged her so hard she squeaked. "Let me down, dear William, and repose yourself," she cried shoving forward a ladder-back chair with a rush bottom. "But mind, right now, you're to tell me *only* about what you've the mind to speak on." Eyes brimming, she turned hastily towards the kitchen larder.

Said Mrs. Phips, pushing a damp lock of very fine black hair from her forehead: "Suppose, William, that we survey the present situation frankly." She summoned a thin smile. "Not that I enjoy the prospect."

"Nor I. Nevertheless, dearest wife, please speak first. What is in your mind?" His tone was soft, almost musical. It didn't in the least resemble the arrogant, abrasive voice he used in taverns, shipyards, and at sea.

After smoothing her hair, Mary momentarily became sufficiently unladylike to use her apron to fan herself. "Very well, William, I expect for a time you will receive a deal of praise for having sacrificed personal gain to succor all those people in danger of their lives. But such commendation will soon wear off. Then what do you think will happen?"

Frowning, he picked up a cold chicken leg but didn't bite into it. "Once my shareholders and creditors have held their meeting tomorrow 'tis a five-to-one bet they'll attach the *High Hopes*." He summoned a tight smile. "My dear friend Amyas Tilton has been yearning for a chance to shove a spoke in my wheel ever since you gave him the mitten. How long ago *was* it?"

"Near two years and a half, my love. In that connection, before gossips get to you, let me say that during your absence Mr. Tilton has attempted to act friendly and be helpful on several occasions, but he never received encouragement, of course."

Phips bit savagely into the chicken leg, spoke with his mouth full: "And what was that meaching collegian's manner?"

Mary's small and perfectly round dark eyes shifted, then steadied. "Oh, he always was as polite as pie. You know how genteel he is—a typical graduate of Harvard, you might say."

"Aye. Butter never would melt in his mouth," he grunted, but silently wished he could have attended Harvard College over in Cambridge for even a few semesters.

Said she hurriedly: "Amyas never once acted in the least forward and without fail he always expressed more than passing interest in how your shipyard might be faring."

"Like him. But, for all that, don't for a moment doubt he's still out to lift my scalp in a business way. He always was a poor loser."

Grinning, he reached forward and chucked her round little chin. "But I allow ye're well worth his enmity." He pulled her onto his knees, murmuring, "God's love, Mary, I'd near forgot how wondrous soft and sweet to the touch you are."

Mary flushed, pressed herself closer and whispered: "Beginning to feel frisky are you, William? Well, I vow after all this time I could do nicely with a bit of husbandly attention." Crimson, she wriggled free and hurried to place a half-loaf of wheaten bread before him.

"An that's the case—" He started to arise, hollow gray-blue eyes kindling but Mary shook her shapely small head. "Not now. Unless you've changed a lot, business always comes first."

He sighed and returned voracious attention to a pewter salver of cold chicken and squash pie.

"What else is in your mind?" Mary demanded, then opened the back door wider.

The day had grown so hot the steeple on the South Church seemed to waver and become animated.

"I'll go straightaway to seek out certain merchants and friends and try to gauge their—their inclinations." He was pleased to use so elegant a word but recently added to his rapidly expanding vocabulary. "Need to know about where I stand before I attend that damn'—beg pardon, dear—meeting tomorrow." Steadily he considered his wife's deceptively bland features. "I intend an they sell me out, as likely they will, to build stocks and a slipway alongside old Captain Greenough's dock. I *know* I can turn out the swiftest, soundest craft in or around Boston!"

"Aye, William, I've heard you say so time and again, and so has everyone else."

After a while Mary asked evenly: "Tell me true—just how bad was the onslaught on your property?"

"Couldn't have been worse. Though it was of all of a piece with what happened at Cape Porpoise, Falmouth, Sagahodoc, and Saco clear up to Fort Pemaquid."

From far down Ship Street arose an increasing babble of voices. From their front door the Phipses watched a town crier tramp into Ship Street all the while clanging a brass hand bell. Pretty soon they could hear him. "Hear ye! Hear ye! King

Philip is dead! King Philip is dead! Murdered by one of his own savages."

Voices called from all directions. "When? Where?"

"Ain't heard yet," the crier admitted. "But 'tis certain-sure King Philip is dead!"

Savagely, Phips spat onto dust lying thick in the unpaved street beyond his threshold.

Mary said, "May the Lord forgive him his sins."

"Forgive? Hope the Devil spits that curséd Wampanoag on a red-hot skewer and roasts him forever!"

"Now! Now, William, control yourself. Remember the Good Book directs true Christians must forgive their enemies." Gently, Mary slipped an arm about her husband's solid waist. "Oh, my dearest one, you can't have the least notion of how often I've lain awake all night tormented when one vessel after another, carrying stricken people, made port or how very often I've prayed for hours that you might be alive and safe."

He framed her face between powerful, callused hands. "Needn't have fretted yourself," said he in that peculiar tone she'd come to recognize and worry about. "I was destined to come back, so much remains for me to accomplish. My Star still will rise again. Count on it as surely as yonder sun will set tonight!"

When around noon next day William Phips approached his home, even at a distance Mary recognized his long stride and square shoulders swinging along Ship Street where small children, dogs, pigs, geese, and chickens roamed at will. Once William drew near enough she recognized that hard, almost cruel set to his mouth which she'd come to dread.

Not a word was spoken till they had seated themselves in the backyard under a half-grown apple tree—the coolest spot available.

She raised slim brows. "Well, William?"

Scowling, he spread hands in a discouraged gesture he seldom employed. "The news ain't good, not at all, at all. They've impounded the brig and all her gear. Amyas Tilton wasn't to be

[87]

shaken from demands that the *High Hopes* be seized and sold to satisfy creditors and cover the shareholders' investment."

"Anyone take your side?" The question came without emotion.

"Only Johnny Dale, who turned up from somewhere at the last minute and Cap'n Greenough. The three of us couldn't muster enough votes to accomplish anything to the contrary."

Impatiently, he passed the back of his hand over a red-brown brow beaded with sweat and unseeingly surveyed the surrounding shingle rooftops and red brick chimneys. "Yes, my love, Tilton and his followers not only have attached the vessel but aim to take that piece of shoreline on which I've been planning to build the new shipyard. Think of it, they mean to seize land you and I hold title to! So, my dear," said he grimly, "aside from this dwelling *and* your love I'm almost back where I was when I landed in Boston in '69, friendless, unlettered, and penniless."

"Oh, William, this mustn't be!" Mary burst out. "Not after you've studied, worked so hard and accomplish so much."

He plucked a long stalk of sweet grass and started chewing it. "Small profit crying over spilt milk—as Ma used to tell us boys." He straightened, looked her full in the face as a small sigh escaped him.

"Hear me, Mary, even if worse comes to worst, I *will* somehow overcome; we'll never have to accept charity! Nay, someday we'll set one of the finest tables in town and notables will vie to accept our hospitality."

Phips arose and, hands clenched behind him, tramped around the little backyard. "Well, Wife, at least one good thing has resulted from this—this setback; I'm now able to sort out real friends from those of the fair-weather persuasion."

"Good. How many do you count?"

"Enough of the first kind so's I think I can raise sufficient to pay mortgage money and keep clear title to the boatyard shore lot."

"How much money will you require—right away, that is?"

"I must lay hands on about a hundred and fifty pounds hard

money. Beyond that I needn't worry. I reckon experience and skill at shipbuilding will take care of future payments."

He stared unseeingly at the outlines of a well sweep rising in the adjoining yard. "Now tell me, Wife, where am I to find that hundred and fifty sterling?" In a rare gesture of uncertainty he hammered one brown fist upon the other.

"What about the Reverend Mr. Increase Mather? He's a true friend and well-off, or so they say."

"Aye, but he's away preaching to the Indians and I can't learn when he's due back."

Mary went indoors and brought out a bowl of radishes which she commenced to trim. Finally she said very quietly: "There's a bit of farm land over to Charles Town, mayhap—"

Phips's broad bronzed features contracted. "Many thanks, my dear, but already you've helped me so much that the sayin' goes I've married you, an older woman, only for—"

"I've heard such gossip—kind friends have seen to that," she cut in, firm little chin rising, "but I pay it no heed, William. Besides," she smiled, "aren't I only four short years your senior?"

He picked up a wide-brimmed hat of light palm fibers such as traders to the West Indies brought back and savagely fanned himself. "You're *not* to sell your Charles Town property. Is that clear?"

Mary dropped her gaze, then with deliberation she selected another radish for attention. "Very well, William, it shall be as you say."

"I've leaned on you long enough. By God, I'll raise what's needed in other directions!"

All the same, Mary Phips knew well enough that there weren't any "other directions"—at least ones which might be counted on in a hurry, therefore, tomorrow, she'd set about selling her land through a dummy and explain only after William had cooled down. Poor William! How distraught he must be under that confident air.

Imagine William's never having enjoyed proper schooling. Long ago she'd heard how he'd practically taught himself to read, write and even to cipher so accurately that any vessel he worked on, usually proved first-class from stem to stern and truck to keelson.

Since their marriage she had, quite without allowing him to suspect, afforded instruction in history, theology and last, but far from least, use of correct grammar and social deportment. If only he wouldn't devote so much time to frequenting low dens, hobnobbing and roistering among multilingual seafarers and other shady denizens of Boston's waterfront. Knowing William, she deduced he wouldn't be wasting time and more likely be acquiring knowledge which eventually might come in useful.

Casually, she inquired: "How soon do you require that mortgage money?"

"Within three days. My fellow shareholders ain't patient—least of all Tilton."

"Don't fret yourself, William. I *know* we'll discover such a sum in time to keep the shore property." She hurried on. "When you start your yard I presume you'll have John Dale for foreman and master shipwright?"

A disreputable tabby cat appeared and set about elaborately stalking a small bird feeding at the far end of the backyard.

"I fear not. Johnny's too broke up over the murder of his wife and unborn child: swears he'll go to sea and so steer clear of anythin' remindin' him about that."

"A pity," Mary commented, "but I can understand."

"I don't. Damn it! Johnny's the shrewdest judge of ship timber I've come across. Howsumever, I'm counting on his coming back once he's shed of his misery."

Phips shoved broad, naked feet back into heavy, brass-buckled brogans, discarded for the sake of comfort, and swung himself erect.

"Well, my love, my settin' here like a bump on a log will butter few parsnips so I'm off for a cruise along Fish Street. Don't know just when I'll be back so don't wait up."

He pulled on his flat-crowned West Indian hat. "Remember one thing, Mary, come what may, you're *not* to sell that land 'crost the river."

Chapter 9

A COURSE FOR THE BERMUDAS?

THE *Saucy Betsey*, a sloop some 38 feet overall and of 42 tons burthen, lay tied up to Haywood's Wharf, a short, ramshackle affair situated near Town Cove's noisy and bustling northern extremity.

Dusk deepened rapidly as Dale and Phips started picking a route among a jumble of barrels, bundles of pipe staves, casks and cases stacked on splintered planking. The former, swinging along on slightly bowed legs, commented: "Mighty fine of ye, Will, to understand why I've let you down right now and have come to view the magnificent craft I'm supposed to navigate."

"Where to?"

Dale hesitated until they had side-stepped behind a row of tar barrels. "So far, we're keepin' it dark but I'll tell you, and only you, we intend for the Bermudas."

Phips slowed his stride, uttered a low whistle. "The Bermudas! You must be daft! Those pinpricks on the ocean lie nigh eight hundred miles away."

"Hell, you know of successful voyages longer than that made in lesser craft; wager *you* would manage all right."

"Mayhap someday I'll be forced to try it, but not yet, Johnny, not yet. When d'you expect to shove off?"

"Come tomorrow's morning tide."

Moodily, Phips surveyed the familiar aspect of Town Cove with its ranks of towering masts and geometric patterns of yards seen against a background of shops, warehouses, smithies, and a rope walk or two. He noted with interest that no less than four oceangoing ships were making ready for sea; as many other big vessels were discharging cargo, screamed at by big gray-and-white harbor gulls and dainty black-capped terns which went flapping by after the day's scavenging to settle for the night upon the barricado's lime-splashed rocks and rotting pilings.

Dale, with a wry grin, indicated a small and poorly painted sloop lying near the wharf's end. "Behold, my friend, the little beauty I'm supposed to navigate. Big fellow loafin' on her poop's my cousin, Jim Turner. Ever met him?"

"No, but if he's the same James Turner I've heard tell about I'll be interested to meet him."

Dale paused, queried uneasily: "Why? What have you heard?"

More and more lights commenced to glow among structures lining the waterfront. Phips said, "May well prove only a packet of lies, but I've heard tell of a James Turner who's supposed to have sailed along of Cap'n Bannister."

Dale's dark eyes rounded in the deepening dusk. "Bannister? You ain't meanin' that bloody pirate who ranges 'round Jamaica and the Bahamas in the *Golden Fleece*, are you?"

"Aye. Bannister's a bad 'un and, by all accounts, one of the worst."

Dale looked aside, "Then I'm certain-sure Cousin Jim ain't the fellow you've heard about. Jim may be tough and wild and over ready to brawl but I'll take my Bible oath he's never been a pirate."

Phips said evenly: "Fair enough. A while back you said Turner's a married man, didn't you?"

"He and Betsey both say so."

"Um. 'Twas with them you've left Captain Hammond's daughter to lodge?"

"Aye. They took her in, for all the poor wench hadn't a farthing to bless herself with."

A few yards short of the *Saucy Betsey*'s stern, Phips looked his companion steadily in the eye. "Johnny, you and me have planned, worked, and sweated together for nigh on ten years; you've proved a true friend and I'll never forget the way you stood up for me so fierce at the creditors' meetin', but I ask you fair and square, isn't there *anythin'* I can do to keep you from embarkin', half-cocked, on this loony treasure hunt? Why'n't you wait a bit and help me get the new yard going, then, maybe, we'll go off together on some better-found gold huntin' expedition." He lowered his voice. "I'll confess, Johnny, I been thinkin' somewhat in that direction. Been listenin' to all manner of tall tales told along the waterfront but so far I've yet to hear one which holds nigh enough water to suit me."

Dale shook his big yellow head. "Ye're generally right, Will, but, damn it, for a while I've had a bellyful of shipbuildin' and frontier life. What I need, bad, is to back off, forget those things we both know about and make a fresh start." Impulsively, he gripped Phips's shoulder. "Listen to me, Will, an this adventure succeeds, I'll give you my oath to return here straightaway with my share o' the loot and we'll enter partnership once more and maybe go treasure fishin' whenever you say." He peered anxiously through the deepening afterglow. "How're you farin' moneywise?"

"Not near so well as I'd hoped but I've promises of credit—sound ones. Guess 'tain't for nothing I'm known to turn out faster and sounder vessels for less money than any builder around here. Come now, John, won't you stay with me?"

"Sorry, but I'm dead-set on tryin' my luck in the Bermudas."

During their conversation, Phips had been running experienced eyes over the little vessel's frayed rigging and stained, often-patched yellow-brown canvas. Her black paint was blistered and had scaled down to expose bare wood in many places; moreover, one of the flukes on her only anchor had almost rusted away. "Wish to God you were settin' out in somethin' better than a ramshackled tub like this."

"Oh, hell, Will, like the singed cat, the *Betsey*'s better than she looks at first glance. Come along, I'll make Jim Turner known to you."

A moment later Phips was clasping hands with a stocky, ginger-haired and bearded individual of about his own height. Turner, he noticed, had large and widely separated but heavily bloodshot eyes of the palest imaginable blue. Wearing a thick gold ring in his left ear, he fairly exuded good nature. In fact, the man resembled a buccaneer less than anyone could have imagined.

"Welcome aboard, Cap'n Phips. Heard a lot of talk 'bout you one way and another."

Once the visitors squatted on gear littering the tiny poop deck, Dale's cousin grimaced: "Aye, ye're right. My standin' and runnin' gear ain't all they might be, but I reckon 'twill serve. Besides her hull is sound as a sovereign and she don't leak overmuch. Wish I'd sufficient hard money to slip her and have her strakes scraped and recaulked but I ain't got it, so needs must when the Devil drives. Me and Johnny will have to trust to luck."

"Hope you won't need it. Remember, ye'll be enterin' the cyclone latitudes and season ere long. So you're intending for the Bermudas?"

"Yes, but pray keep that to yerself. Don't want to invite competition, ye might say."

The sound of nearby voices and the dull, rhythmic *thump-thump, thump-thump* of oars against thole pins became more noticeable while they descended to the captain's cabin—if so tiny a hutch might be so dignified—there barely was room for three grown men to seat themselves.

"Ever took an interest in treasure huntin', Cap'n Phips?" Turner queried casually when for a second time rum had been poured and watered only a trifle.

"Mebbe, mebbe not," Phips evaded, licking his lips. "Fellow can hear plenty of fanciful yarns spun in the ordinaries. Mighty few sound like they might have somethin' to 'em."

"All the same not a few treasures *have* been found on land and beneath the sea I know about. I've even seen one dug up down in—" Abruptly James Turner fell silent by taking a long and noisy gulp.

Phips's heavy, straight brows joined themselves. "Cap'n Turner, just what leads you to believe this ain't some sort of wild-goose chase ye're takin' John on? Most treasure hunts turn out to be just that, and have cost many a venturer his last penny if not his life. Spaniards ain't exactly friendly or merciful."

"Ye're right in that, but this is a different matter; Bermuda's a British Crown Colony." The *Saucy Betsey*'s master pulled up his shirt to expose a wide leather belt or surcingle which he untied and from it plucked a slim oblong of yellow-brown parchment secured by heavy red tapes.

"Cast an eye over this—" He flattened a heavily wrinkled chart. Turner allowed his visitor to inspect the strip of vellum just long enough to make out the crude map's markings.

Gripped by a sudden powerful and unfamiliar exhilaration, Phips stared hard and in an instant memorized every detail of importance. "How'd you come by this?"

While refolding his chart Turner winked solemnly. "From a shipmate dying of a fever. Gave it me in gratitude for having saved his life in battle. We was cruisin' off Grand Abaco in the Bahamas at the time."

Turner didn't feel called on to add that he'd provoked the chart's previous owner into a brawl when the other had got so drunk he couldn't tell the point of a cutlass from its pommel.

On taking possession of the deceased's seachest he'd discovered among other oddments a leather pouch containing a few gold sovereigns, escudos, louises, moidores and other coins along with the well-folded chart he now was restoring to its covering.

The *Saucy Betsey*'s master smiled like a friendly mastiff. "Aye, sir, 'twas a lucky day Cousin Johnny came on with you on the *High Hopes*."

"Lucky, why?"

"Well, you see, Cap'n, I'm none too sound a navigator whilst Johnny is reputed one of the best."

"Ye're right, he's all of that." Phips's tone grew incisive. "What're you payin' him?"

Deliberately, Turner finished his rum. "Nothin' but me and Johnny here agreed to share and share alike in whatever we come acrost." He cocked a quizzical brow. "Say, Cap'n, ain't you that Billy Phips who singlehanded cleared out the Bower Anchor's bar last week and whipped the tar out of the Bristol Bruiser?"

Amid semidarkness emphasized by the feeble flicker of a whale-oil lanthorn, Phips nodded. "Aye. Must have been feelin' my oats a little."

Turner offered his hand. "Then I'm double-proud to make yer acquaintance."

Four days after the *High Hopes* had been impounded and moved to Amyas Tilton's wharf, Pegeen Hammond began to feel something like her old self, physically at least. For one thing she'd regained weight and with it a measure of her usual boundless energy but still remained in no way reassured concerning the future.

Before the sun was well up, Pegeen, having borrowed a patched but demure gown of grisette cotton and a pair of over-large cowhide shoes with runover wooden heels, drew a deep breath and, on her hostess' advice, started seeking employment along Prince's Street—away from the noisy and disorderly waterfront where anything could, and often did, happen to a lone and handsome young female.

To begin with she felt so frightened she kept her gaze on the ground but took courage when, as the day brightened, more and more people appeared. Barrow men began hawking a variety of wares vying with strident pedlars carrying trays of goods slung before them. Two-wheeled carts heaped with garden produce, hay wagons, fish carts and lumbering wains creaked along under loads of assorted barrels, crates, puncheons and wooden cases of all shapes and description. Blacksmith shops began to give off their ringing, not unmusical clangor. Dogs barked and chickens strayed confidently among slowly turning wheels.

On the corner of Hanover and Anne Streets, Pegeen, sheltering in the entrance to a cobbler's shop, finally plucked up sufficient courage really to look about and notice brawny women lugging baskets of produce on their way to Market Square. Mostly these were very plainly dressed in somberhued garments of such workaday material as frieze, drugget, linsey-woolsey, dowlas, homespun, or in ribbed Hampshire kersey.

Some pedestrians, sailors by their rolling gait, wore knitted wool caps, grimy canvas shirts and loose-legged petticoat breeches. More numerous were workmen and mechanics mostly shirtless and clad in deerskin jerkins, pants of leather or duroy and heavy woolen stockings.

Now and then some well-to-do citizen strode by with his tall walking stick tapping dusty cobbles. As a rule such wore high-steepled, broad-brimmed black felt hats with a brass or silver buckle securing a band in front.

Because of the heat only a few mandilions or short, hip-long mantles were in evidence worn over sober-hued doublets of serge, buckram or flannel. A surprising number of ministers of the Gospel passed by readily distinguishable by wide and long white linen falling neckbands.

While proceeding along Anne Street towards a glover's sign under which she hoped to find use for her skill with a needle, she flattened herself against the front of a dyer's shop to watch, wide-eyed, a file of sturdy town watchmen march by under shouldered halberts, steel burgonets and breastplates dully agleam. Lord, how these soldiers were sweating in long-sleeved woolen shirts, baggy brown breeches and thick-ribbed hose of the same color.

To Pegeen's vast astonishment she noticed quite a few people, apparently servants, busy at various occupations, whose skin was black as pitch.

On reaching Market Square she suffered a severe shock on discovering Red Fish and Fast Otter slumped in the public stocks beside a pillory and an apparently well-used whipping post. Both bore a placard reading COMMON DRUNKARD slung to his neck. They looked so miserable she wished she could do something, at least give them a drink of water, but she didn't dare to attract attention.

Heart hammering, she entered the glovemaker's tiny shop to suffer the first in a long series of disappointments.

It soon became apparent that honest employment, no matter how menial, simply wasn't to be found largely because several shiploads of indentured female servants recently had made port. For an uneducated, unskilled but personable young female absolutely no situations were to be found except as "barmaid" or "chambermaid" in a less-than-reputable tavern or boardinghouse.

For three eternal days Pegeen ranged the town, invariably to return in the evening disappointed on sore and blistered feet. Although bone-weary and badly discouraged she nonetheless was thankful that thus far her pregnancy remained apparently unnoticed.

During the evenings and early mornings she attempted to repay in a small way the Turners' hospitality through tidying their dwelling which, apparently, hadn't enjoyed a thorough cleansing in a considerable time. Also, she made herself so useful about the kitchen that Betsey, clad only in a shapeless nightrail and slippers, took to lolling in a comfortable armchair continually predicting that someday Pegeen undoubtedly would make some man a first-rate goodwife.

"Aye, dearie, clever housekeepers like you are scarcer than hen's teeth. Young girls nowadays think only of pleasure and dressing up so's in the evening they can go strolling about the

Common land with their gallants turned out like fashionable Marmalet Madams.

"Aye, 'tis wonderful what good food and a bed rest will do for a girl. Who'd have thought when Johnny Dale fetched you here all bedraggled and burnt to a crisp by the sun you might turn out so—so—well, luscious and pleasing to look on."

Pegeen flushed. "Oh, dear Mrs. Turner, how ever can I thank you? You and the Cap'n have been so wondrous generous and kind. If there's aught I can do to prove my gratitude you've only to tell me."

For a moment Pegeen was puzzled by the contemplative manner in which Betsey Turner studied her over a leather jack of beer. Finally the handsome, big-bosomed woman heaved a sigh. "You bein' the honest type I'm sure you mean what you say. Mayhap an opportunity to prove it will turn up afore long and I'll be *that* glad to have you for company once Johnny and Jim set sail. Aye, we'll have ourselves a fine time else I'm a great fool—which I ain't."

"Are they really set on departing tomorrow?"

"Probably not. Jim allows he's in need of a sextant; says he's heard talk of one can be bought real cheap over to Charles Town. So I reckon he'll ferry over and take a look at it tomorrow."

"And—and where will be Mr. Dale?"

"At the Mermaid's Mirror." The older woman sniffed. " 'Tis a low-class ordinary if ever there was one but I guess Cousin John can't afford no better right now."

Betsey motioned with her mug, "Set you down, Ducky, and rest yer poor tired feet."

Pegeen smiled gratitude and slipped off those big and shapeless shoes she'd worn ever since the Indian moccasins she'd appropriated on the brig had fallen apart. The tiny kitchen's smooth stone flooring felt really fine on reddened soles when she crossed to a wooden bucket and drank deep from a gourd dipper floating on its surface. Lord's mercy! She was *that* weary from tramping all over town and fending off amorous advances.

"You look plumb tuckered out. Whyn't you stretch out and

treat yerself to a little rest?" Betsey Turner suggested. "Later, maybe, we'll see iffen we can alter a spare dress of mine so's 'twill set off that pretty figger of yours to better advantage. Come tomorrow night, me and Jim intend to dine a pair of old shipmates of his from the Spanish Main so I want you should look real pert, Ducky, and help us show 'em rascals a fine large time so you can't go on wearin' that there homely grisette gown with all the sweat marks."

Pegeen's large dark-blue eyes filled—she'd met with so little kindness since the raid. "I'll be eager to please, Ma'am."

Whatever Betsey Turner's failings, she proved an expert semptress and converted a reasonably new challis gown of hers so bright-blue that Puritan neighbors looked askance at its exciting hue. There could be no doubt that her handiwork fashioned a garment which made the most of Pegeen's firm but graciously curved body. She intended to set it off with a knot of emerald-green silk tied into the girl's freshly washed and naturally curly auburn locks and an inexpensive enameled locket suspended from a black ribbon.

"Put it on. A girl must get the 'feel' of a dress 'specially when it's of such costly material."

Pegeen hesitated and while stroking the garment summoned an uncertain smile. "Please, Ma'am, I'd rather not wear this."

"Land's sake, why not?"

"Well, Ma'am, I've neither an undershift nor petticoats fit to wear under so fine a dress. My Sunday gown and all my underpinnings got lost in the raid."

A throaty chuckle escaped Betsey Turner. "La, Ducky, you've no call to wear aught but Adam's livery 'neath this pretty blue dress—'tis so tight small clothes would only spoil its fit."

"But, but I couldn't do that. 'Tisn't decent."

"Boston ain't the backwoods," Mrs. Turner said sharply. "Not indoors at any rate; however, I'll favor you with the loan of an over-the-head undershirt of lawn edged with a mite of lacework; 'tis what the Frenchies term a 'chemise,' or so I'm told."

Going crimson from brow to bosom Pegeen stared at the floor.

"Now toot along and wash real clean before you try on the dress then we'll see if it needs adjustments here and there." Mrs. Turner spoke kindly, encouragingly.

"But, but—"

"'But me no more buts,' Ducky, and do like I tell you." She fixed the Hammond girl with penetrating eyes, "That is if ye're *really* minded to try to repay our hospitality."

Next morning James Turner, sure enough, took a sail-ferry over to Charles Town to look at the sextant he'd heard about, but when the sun dipped low over the Charles and Pegeen came limping home Jim hadn't returned.

"Drat that rogue!" Betsey called pettishly from the back-yard where she was taking in washing done by Pegeen. "Never can count on him when I need him around. Still," said she briskly, "there's no cause to fret; likely he'll turn up soon account of those sailor friends of his comin' to supper. He gave me money to buy a flagon of fine Spanish wine. Afore we sit down to sup you'll cut some chunks of that red Dutch cheese real neat—should go fine with biscuits and smoked eels."

Already Pegeen had been instructed when to serve the cold joint of mutton, pickled pig's trotters and pot of fresh-baked beans which, along with a bowl of corn-meal mush, would constitute the main course. A big pompion pie hot out of the bake oven and fresh whipped cream would serve for a sweet.

Even when the dusk deepened and the town gradually had quieted there still was no sight of, or message from, Captain Turner. Pegeen began to pray silently, fervently that burly, still sad-eyed John Dale might drop by; he sometimes did around this hour.

"Hope nothing harmful has overtaken the Cap'n," was all she could find to say while setting out pewter trenchers, knives, and two-tined forks on the kitchen table.

Betsey unconcernedly poured herself another beer from an

earthenware pitcher. "Don't fret yourself; like a bad penny, Jim's bound to turn up any time now. Ducky, go light that taper on the mantelpiece whilst I sample the wine and make sure I ain't been cheated." She took a long swallow, smacked her lips and winked. "Umm. 'Twill do; 'tis mellow as a satisfied bridegroom."

Pegeen knew that moving about like this devoid of under-pinnings—the chemise had not been forthcoming—must be shameful. Yet unfamiliar sensations caused by this incredibly soft fabric caressing her skin were nevertheless definitely stim-ulating. She'd have felt a heap easier about her appearance if a barely noticeable bulge between her hips hadn't been created by abundant pubic hair.

From Back Street a man's singing drifted through Jim Turner's half-opened front door:

"O, I once taught school down on the Cape
Where they do thin's up in purty good shape.
They make their livin' by catching mackerel
But I'd just a lief teach school in Hell.
Hadn't been there but a very short spell
Afore I was courtin' old Zebedee's Sal—"

A smile widened on Betsey's full red lips as she fluffed a fancy little apron. "That there must be Jethro Radcliffe. He mayn't be much to look at but all the same he's got a mighty fine and heart-movin' singing voice. Wonder who he's got in tow? One will get you two 'twill be someone can play the Spanish guitar."

"Heyo, Betts, we're here!" Through the doorway sidled a gaunt, deeply tanned and lanthorn-jawed individual with pre-ternaturally long and heavily tattooed forearms. He'd a close-shaven bullet head upon which perched a round fur hat; it put Pegeen in mind of a kitten crouching on an Indian gourd.

His companion who, indeed, was carrying a battered guitar slung to one shoulder, wore small golden earrings and was so dark-complexioned and had such short and tightly curling jet hair Pegeen at first sight mistook him for a black fellow. Before long she ascertained he was a Portuguese mulatto from the Cape Verde Islands.

The narrowness of Jethro's bony chest was accentuated by a sweat-stained blue-and-white striped cotton jersey and a greasy black neckscarf. Swaying somewhat, he continued his song:

"Now Zebedee was a fisherman bold
And Sal was his datter just 'steen old—"

For a moment Betsey acted flustered. "Come on in quick, shut the door and finish yer ditty in here else you'll have my pious neighbors complainin' again. 'Specially that mugiferious old biddy who dwells across the street."

Jethro grabbed Betsey, kissed her right on the mouth, then hugged her so tight he heaved her substantial figure clear off the floor.

Smiling broadly, she slipped an arm about him. "How d'you fare these days?"

"Like always, Honey. Old Jethro's ever ready for a fight, a frolic, or a footrace."

Pegeen caught her breath and stared, round-eyed and be-wildered when Jethro shoved forward his swarthy, slightly built companion. "Joe Silvestro ain't so much at singin' but he sure can strike some purty measures on that git-tar of his. And he can dance lively, too. Say, Betts, who's this high-tittied dolly ye've got here?"

"Pegeen Hammond—a young friend who's biding with Jim and me for a space. She's escaped from them terrible Indian massacrees up Pemaquid and Sheepscot way. Her family didn't."

Betsey went over to slide a plump arm around the girl and shoved her forward. "Come on, Ducky, smile. Remember, the gents are friends and ain't about to lift that pretty red hair of yours."

"'Pegeen'?" Jethro drawled. "Say, ain't that a Irish name?"

"I—I've always believed so, sir," Pegeen stammered and, flushing furiously, attempted an awkward half curtsy while

[*103*]

declaring herself mighty pleased to meet friends of Captain and Mistress Turner's. From the way both men stared Pegeen felt certain-sure that they already must have guessed that, save for shoes and stockings, she stood jay-naked under Betsey's pretty, tight-bodiced blue gown.

Jethro peered about. "Well now, I swan, you and Jim have found yerselves a real snug harbor. Yep, real snug. Iffen I could find me such a place I reckon I'd give up seafarin'—which is a dog's life at best. Ain't that so, Joe?"

"*Sí*. Me like land more better."

Making a wide gesture, Betsey said, "Set down, boys and make yerselves comfortable. If ye're minded to shed footgear go right ahead—this stone flooring's real cool on tired feet, ain't that right, Peg?"

"Oh, yes it is. Don't you think so, Mister—sorry, I didn't catch your name—"

"Me Joe. No spik good Eenglesh—mebbe you teach, heh?" Eyes clinging to that small bulge in the bright blue challis gown on a level with the girl's hips, Silvestro unslung his guitar and started to seat himself on a stool but suddenly slipped a sinewy brown arm around her, clamped leathery lips smelling strongly of garlic onto her mouth and held them there a long moment despite her weak struggles.

Without protest, Betsey allowed herself to be swept into Jethro's arms and fondled under her skirt.

"Shiver my strakes, Bets, yer still like a bloomin' ripe peach! How in blazes d'you keep yerself lookin' so—so appetizin'?"

Utterly bewildered, Pegeen didn't know what to do so endured another of the Portuguese's moist kisses and cruel pinchings of her unprotected thighs before she twisted free and, under the pretext of fetching wine, started for the kitchen. When, agile as a cat and giggling, Silvestro caught her, she dealt him such a slap that his head was tilted sidewise and he lurched backwards hissing furious, unintelligible curses.

Jethro laughed. "Easy, Joe, don't try boardin' so dainty a craft all of a sudden. Easy does it."

It proved amazing how quickly the swarthy seaman recovered and, grinning whitely, held out a pink-palmed hand on the palm of which had appeared a pair of pine tree shillings. "Me sorry. For you. Silvestro mean no hurt. Him fine fellow, pay good, see?"

Betsey Turner kept her voice low but incisive while following Pegeen into the kitchen. "Don't get huffy, Ducky; remember yer promise. Ain't you been enjoyin' a free bed and feedin' high for nigh on a week?"

Eyes streaming, Pegeen backed up against the food cupboard. "But, Ma'am, that—that dark fellow offered me money! I'm not a loose woman! I'm decent."

"Not a loose woman!" hissed her hostess while the visitors, grinning broadly, listened from the doorway. "The hell you ain't! You ain't married, yet can you truthfully deny ye're in the family way? Don't try to cozen me. I knew it by a certain look about yer eyes the minute Johnny Dale fetched you into my house."

Pegeen's lips writhed. "Please, Ma'am, you don't understand. Tom and I were to be wed very soon and would have been hadn't the savages—"

"Forget yer excuses, you shameless hussy. Fact remains you let yourself get tumbled by a fellow you weren't married to. So, since you ain't a virgin no longer, what's the odds who lies with you next?"

"But, but I *loved* Tom and was to be his wife!"

"Silence! How dast you stand there wearin' my dress and shoes and try to go back on yer given word?"

Betsey's manner underwent abrupt alteration. She summoned an ingratiating smile, "Come now, you may be just a simple backwoods girl but I deem you no fool, so come along and act agreeable to Joe—he ain't about to eat you alive."

Struggling in a mental hurricane Pegeen followed her now lively, chattering hostess back to the fore room and made no effort to avoid pinches and groping fingers while pouring wine and setting out cheese and biscuits.

Jethro threw back his head to continue the chanty he'd been singing on arrival:

[*105*]

"—Oh, I had Sal once
And it felt so nice
I says to myself
'I'll shag you twice'—"

"Sorry, Ma'am, I forgot the smoked eel," Pegeen muttered and scurried back into the kitchen. Heart pounding like an Abenaki hand drum, she fled into the warm darkness of the Turners' untidy backyard.

For a girl reared on the frontier it was no problem to vault a low fence and drop into the adjoining yard in which a watch dog immediately raised frantic alarm. The brute being chained, she paid no heed, only clutched tight and hampering blue skirts thigh-high before darting through a gate and running blindly along a shadowy, ill-smelling alley in the direction of Ship Street.

Since a few people were still about Pegeen, panting like a hard-run hound, sought the shadows of a doorway and hurriedly smoothed her garments.

Sweat-bathed and hopelessly bewildered, Pegeen Hammond struggled to regain a measure of self-control and take stock of her situation. She succeeded after a fashion, perhaps because she'd inherited something of Captain Richard Hammond's levelheaded disposition.

It didn't take long to decide that only Captain William Phips or John Dale could help her out of this fix. Trouble was, she'd not the least notion where in this great town the *High Hopes*'s former Captain abided.

On the other hand, she recalled Mrs. Turner's having mentioned that John Dale had put up at some tavern called the Mermaid's Mirror, an establishment she'd noticed during her wanderings about town. Wasn't it somewhere along Mackerill Street?

She guessed she might find it, provided she kept to side streets and hid whenever anybody came along. At this hour, long after nine o'clock, most Bostonians, of the God-fearing sort at least, had been abed for some time. But Pegeen even hid from occasional roundsmen patrolling the streets with staff and lanthorn.

A bell in the steeple of the Second Congregational Church on North Square commenced booming ten resonant strokes drowning out the noises of a brawl and a woman's shrill screaming from some ordinary located on a side street when, breathless but less terrified, she recognized the Mermaid's Mirror's faded swing board.

Pegeen hurriedly straightened her hair and, perspiring like a logger on a summer's day, set her jaw before pushing open the public house's door to find herself in a long, low-ceilinged and smoke-veiled room. In it groups of roughly dressed men, nearly all seafarers by the looks of them, sprawled about heavy tables drinking, casting dice, singing off-key or bickering in voices grown loud and raucous with liquor.

For a few moments no one noticed the presence of this handsome young woman in the tight blue dress, then someone sang out, "Heyo! You seekin' company, Sissy?"

"N-no," she gulped, wishing she weren't so all of atremble. "I only seek a friend of mine."

Three or four men lurched erect. "Then ye've come to the right place. In here we're all right friendly."

Her string of misfortunes appeared to have ended when, through stratas of rank-smelling smoke, she recognized John Dale singing in concert with a trio of bearded, mahogany-faced companions in leather jerkins and petticoat breeches.

Dale vented a startled obscenity, then got to his feet and advanced waving a leather jack of beer. "Damn my soul to Hell if 'tain't me lovely li'l shipmate, Pegeen."

"Oh, Mister Dale, sir!" She choked. "For the dear Lord's sake, please help me. I'm in terrible trouble."

"In trouble, eh?" chortled a red-bearded longshoreman who'd a great blue powder burn disfiguring one cheek. "What *hev* you done, Johnny? Been dandling this wench?"

"Always handy wi' the dollies, ain't you, Johnny?" yelled another. "Where on earth you come acrost so fine a armful? B'God, she's purtier nor Judy Earle's speckled pup."

"C'mon lass, gi'e us a buss."

A gap-toothed fellow reached out to pinch her bottom

while Dale was fetching her to his table. "Ain't much to this pullet, Johnny, but ye sure can feel what there is 'cause she ain't wearin' nothin' under her gown."

"Avast!" Dale dealt his boon companion a slap which must have loosened the fellow's few amber-hued teeth. "Listen, the lot of you! This lass is decent, an old friend and neighbor. Lay off!"

Red-eyed, Dale shook his yellow head several times as if to clear it, then peered at her through drifting tendrils of tobacco smoke. "What in tarnation brings you here at such an hour? Why ain't you along of Jim and Betsey?"

Peegeen tried to muffle sobs. "Oh-h, I'm so—so ashamed I scarce dare confess what's chanced."

"Such bein' the case," said he, "come along up to my room where ye c'n talk out."

The powder-burned fellow fetched a resounding belch. "Wal, I swan, you never was one to waste time. Pot boy! Draw 'nother round! Once ye've done wi' her, Johnny boy, send word and we'll draw lots for the next turn."

At the cost of painful sly liberties taken with her buttocks, Pegeen Hammond followed Dale's stocky outline up a narrow flight of stairs on gritty treads worn thin through use.

Dale's quarters proved to be a malodorous hutch of a room scarcely large enough to accommodate a shapeless single cot-bed and a three-legged stool. However, it appeared palatial once he'd ignited a mutton tallow-dip candle from a whale-oil bull's-eye lanthorn burning yellow-red in the hallway and had bolted the door.

Dale beckoned for her to sit beside him on the sagging bed then said: "Speak up, Peg."

Lord, how Dale's hungry expression reminded her of poor dead Tom whose corpse must be rotting beside the Sheepscot.

"Oh, please Mr. Dale, hold me tight. I-I feel so lone, so helpless." She burst into such a wild flood of tears they darkened the front of Mrs. Turner's blue challis gown.

Chapter 10

THE SAUCY BETSEY

IF JOHN DALE expected Jim Turner to kick up a bobbery on learning that his partner intended bringing a female passenger aboard the *Saucy Betsey* he was disappointed. To the contrary, the dingy little 38-foot sloop's master only fingered his heavy gold earring and agreed without demur. In fact, Turner appeared highly amused over the way Pegeen had thwarted his spouse's lubricious scheme.

"I ain't nowwise took aback; Betts always has been a trollop at heart; a body can't never tell what she'll get up to next." He broke out laughing. "'Tis high time she gets hoist by her own petard and cheated out of the earnings of a toothsome morsel like Peg. Lord! That girl would stir life into a stone saint."

Dale's dark, slightly straddled eyes narrowed as he snapped: "Forget that. Pegeen's to be a workin' *passenger*, no more and no less. Understand?"

Jim frowned. "Private property, eh? But she must pay some sort of passage money. You know how flat broke I am."

"You know damn' well she can't. You'll have to be satisfied with any fare I can scratch together which will be a piddling sum at best." Steadily, he peered into his cousin's bacon-brown features. "It's that or—"

"Or what, Johnny?"

"Or ye'd better start lookin' for another navigator."

Turner's earring gleamed when he nodded. "Ye've got me by the balls, Coz, and that's a fact, so I'll settle fer two pounds, which won't be near enough to feed a lusty wench the likes of her."

"Guess maybe I can raise twenty shillings but not a penny more."

James Turner spat over the rail into gray and refuse littered water, then grinned and offered a callused, tattooed hand. "Needs must when the Devil drives so we've agreed, Johnny me lad."

"Needn't look so put-upon—two pounds is plenty considerin' the sort of accommodation the poor creature will have to endure."

"Where'll she bed?"

"In a hammock slung between our bunks in the cabin; reckon there's just enough space. God send the weather stays favorable for 'tis a far piece to the Bermudas. On that subject did you come across a decent chart over in Charles Town?"

"Sort of. One I found ain't exactly new, but 'twill serve our purpose I reckon."

"I want to see it."

The water-stained square of paper proved to have essential data recorded in rough fashion.

On his way back to the Mermaid's Mirror it occurred to Dale that during the voyage the Hammond girl likely must need certain mysterious items of female gear. What about that? Since, literally, he was down to his last ha'penny, the widower figured the only chance of raising Pegeen's passage money and her necessaries would be to touch Will Phips for a loan although everyone knew his boyhood friend must be almighty hard up, too.

While avoiding a towering load of hay drawn by a yoke of fawn-colored oxen, he wondered if he really was smart to go off on such a chancy treasure hunt. Possibly, but all-too-vivid memories of the horrors of Fort Arrowsic remained. Besides, if he really got to share in a treasure he could rejoin Will. Lord! If only he weren't so damn' boastful he'd get farther ahead but one fact loomed large in his former partner's favor: far and wide William Phips was known to be scrupulously, almost ridiculously honest and, thus far, at least, his word always had proved as good as his bond, whatever the cost.

As expected, he found Phips supervising the construction of a gundelow in Captain Greenough's shipyard. On such a hot day as this the stench of layers of gull droppings whitening the office's shingled roof proved especially noxious once they went indoors.

Heavy brows merging, Phips listened without interruption to his old friend's terse explanation as to why Pegeen Hammond—aside from her departure from the Turners'—must leave Boston and seek fields of green and pastures new where no one could possibly have heard of Captain Richard Hammond of Sheepscot or of his family.

"You certain-sure she's pregnant? Mary says some women can dissemble fine in that direction an such a need arises."

Dale shook his big, straw-hued head. "She's in the family way, all right. Peg seemed mighty shamed yet, funnily enough, kind of proud about admittin' she'd tumbled with her intended a few times just before they were due to get spliced."

Phips put down a ruler and drawing pen, looked Dale steadily in the eye, said almost wistfully: "John, ye big lummox, why can't you alter your mind? I've come across some likely backers over in Roxbury and Charles Town, small potatoes to be sure, but useful right now." His voice arose to its familiar, confident pitch. "Never doubt I'll soon have a shipyard going great guns. So why go rantum-scootin' off on this daft treasure hunt along of an unhanged pirate? Turner's been one.

[111]

I've asked about him and I'm sure. Even if he *is* yer cousin he'll slit yer gullet once ye discover anythin' of value."

Dale's gaze wandered out of the countinghouse and came to rest on a double rank of raw pine pilings rising stark and forlorn out the muddy gray beach beyond Greenough's shipyard. Where in Tunket had Will found money to make even this much of a start?

"Thanks for yer warning. I'll watch out, but somehow, like I said before, after what chanced up home I've got to quit New England for a spell."

His wide features lighted. "Who knows? Mayhap Jim and me *will* discover a treasure on the Bermudas. An we succeed I'll speed back to Boston." His voice swelled and his fingers dug hard into Phips's sinewy forearms. "Then, by God, we'll build vessels which will be the envy of all New England. Oh, by the bye, Peg allowed the other day she spied Fast Otter and Red Fish in the public stocks for drunkenness."

Phips jerked a nod. "Heard about that so I paid their fines. Fine divers are hard to come across." He turned towards the din of hammering and sawing. "Right now they're workin' yonder, where I want them." Frowning, he picked up a ruler. "Tell you somethin', private-like, Johnny; if I can't secure sufficient credit to suit my purpose I just *might* go back into the West India trade and earn what I need. Happens the *Star of Boston* I once owned is for sale."

"You could do worse than go to sea for a spell."

Phips cocked his head to one side in a characteristic motion. "You still dead-set on sailin'?"

"Aye. Figger on catchin' the turn of the tide 'round seven tomorrow morn."

Phips slowly got to his feet. "All right, be bullheaded, but I don't like the look o' that sloop of Turner's at all, at all! For one thing, she's just too damn' small for such a voyage. God help you if a line storm finds you in the Gulf Stream. For my money the *Saucy Betsey*'s a drowning cage if ever I've spied one and I've seen aplenty."

"Yer wrong, Will. Her hull's sound. I've tested her planking and timbers all over with my sheath knife."

"Hope ye're right. Howsumever, listen to me about one thing." Phips's voice assumed a grating quality. "Havin' a young and good-looking wench aboard a tiny craft like the *Betsey* ain't going to ease matters."

From a small ironbound strongbox William Phips produced a canvas pouch and deliberately counted out forty-five pine tree shillings.

"Want a receipt? You should have one, I expect."

"Why for?" Phips snapped. "Your word's enough for me. Didn't the two of us grow up together? You're loyal and honest even if you ain't too bright concernin' money matters and things like treasure seekin'. Come morning I'll be down to the slip and see you sail."

The sky above Town Cove was showing a lovely pearly pink hue when William Phips made his way out to where the *Saucy Betsey*'s five-man crew were making ready to castoff.

To Pegeen, standing on the main hatch and looking more than a little forlorn, he called, "Ye're a decent wench no matter what's happened and like me you've got plenty of backbone. Don't trust *anyone* too far and ye'll make out all right —I'll risk hard money on that!"

Turning to the sloop's Master he added harshly: "Turner, I hold you responsible that no mischance befalls either Jack or your passenger—else you'll find a fistful of teeth rammed down yer gullet."

Turner, not in the least daunted, sprang easily onto the dock snarling: "Before you try that, Billy Phips, ye'd better bet just where ye'll wake up, if you ever do! Damn you for a fortune-huntin' braggart! You ain't all that smart; I, too, could have married a rich widow."

Barely in time John Dale jumped into separate the furious pair.

Chapter 14

STRATEGIC RETREAT

IT DIDN'T SEEM REAL that more than a month had elapsed since the day the *Saucy Betsey*'s mildewed sails had driven through an opening in the embarcadero to pick a devious course among the rocky islands studding Boston Harbor. For all William Phips became fully occupied with the business of recruiting competent workmen, erecting stocks and ways while at the same time endeavoring, vainly it seemed, to raise sufficient sums to complete the new shipyard, he retained in his mind's eye a clear-cut memory of that sorry little sloop's departure.

Johnny Dale had been at the tiller with Pegeen Hammond hunched over and weeping beside him. Of James Turner there had been no sign—likely he was drunk and snoring below.

Before using his key to Captain Greenough's countinghouse he paused long enough to cast a wry glance at the pitiful supply of construction timber he'd thus far been able to assemble. It accomplished nothing, he told himself grimly, to dwell on the fact that two men on whom he'd most relied for backing suddenly had proved unable to make good their promises.

Moses Tinsley suddenly had been taken ill of a strangury from which he had died forthwith and Jonas Dunster had lost his store, warehouse, and the living quarters above it in another of those many fires which afflicted any town the majority of whose buildings were wooden. Thanks to the prolonged drought, Boston had become a gigantic tinder box.

Uncommonly low in spirits for one of his resilient nature, Phips entered the comparatively cool brick countinghouse, sought his drafting table and stood staring blankly upon plans for a sizable brigantine Eli Greenough was about to lay down.

While stripping off his coat he again wished that Jack Dale hadn't remained so pigheaded about going off the way he had. But suppose he proved an exception to the rule and returned a rich man? Damn! Such booty would come in mighty handy.

He continued to stare at the drawings.

The fact that at present he was standing next to bankruptcy couldn't be blinked aside despite a modest loan from the Reverend Mr. Mather and proceeds from the sale of Mary's Charles Town property—over which he and Mary had their first real row. Even so, the fact remained he still stood short nearly two hundred pounds which was needed to complete and equip a boatyard in even the crudest fashion.

He stared through dusty window panes at the stocks on which rested the frame of a gundelow that included not a few notions of his. A derrick creaked and complained while swinging heavy timbers into position. Saws rasped and wooden caulking hammers set up a monotonous, dull *thump!* as they payed oakum into a seemingly endless succession of seams on a small pink careened nearby.

He sighted No-me-tha—Red Fish—crouched and blowing a fire kindled beneath an enormous cast-iron cauldron of caulking tar and Tookaw—Fast Otter—lugging an armful of firewood across the debris-littered ground.

Both Penobscots were wearing short *wamuses* or hunting

shirts so frayed and ragged they suggested coarse and dingy lacework dangling above tar-stained sailcloth breeches.

For all the hard times they'd experienced since quitting the *High Hopes* both redmen looked to be in fair condition.

He leaned out of a window and called down in Abenaki, "Greetings, how fare you, oh my brothers?"

Fast Otter yelled up, "Not bad, Augpac, our brother; work hard—bellies full. When you take us to lands where people speak our tongue?"

"Soon maybe we'll sail from Boston together."

"*Wagh!*" shouted Red Fish, lean features lighting. "How soon?"

"Before long, oh my brothers, so work well and stay away from rum."

Phips almost told his blood brothers of a project he'd been mulling over ever since he'd heard about Tinsley's untimely demise and Dunster's getting burnt out, but he thought better of it. Instead, he unlocked a drawer containing drawing instruments, then filled a bowpen to complete the design for an improved forefoot. Instead of sketching he remained bent over the drawing table straight dark brows knit, gnawing his nether lip—a trick he'd acquired while considering critical decisions.

Umm. What about Captain Youngblood's offer to sign on as Chief Mate for a prolonged cruise to the West Indies? Captain Youngblood's offer had been temptingly liberal: fifty pounds cash money plus the privilege of lading a private cargo and of trading on his own account till he could buy back his old *Star of Boston.*

What most tempted him was the fact that Silas Youngblood —for all his surname—was old, over fifty and moreover was suffering badly from the lung sickness. Doubtless he entertained hopes that, with a bitter New England winter in the offing, a long cruise in warmer climes might help restore his health.

The dull *thump!* of an inbound sloop-of-war's cannon saluting the North Battery prompted Phips to look out over the slate-gray Charles. What he saw evoked a series of curses so loud and inspired that a pair of longshoremen working below glanced up in admiring awe.

Rounding Merry's Point, outward bound, sailed the *High Hopes*—his *High Hopes*. Properly rigged now, with her standing rigging taut and newly tarred and wearing a fresh sheet of clean white canvas, she presented a rare fine sight.

For over a fortnight he'd been aware that her new owners—mostly stockholders in the original company—had rechristened his brig *Endeavour*—a commonplace name quite unworthy of her. His only consolation was that at present she was captained by Sam Sumner, not a bad sort. Sam could be trusted to fetch her back and pay him his due share—if anything remained on Jeremesquam Point worth salvaging. Umm. Could any of those precious twice-seasoned ships' timbers possibly have escaped the holocaust? Possibly, for no Indian would understand its value.

Aboard the passing vessel he knew were his tough old stepfather, John White, his Mother and two half sisters, plus another baby on the way and she not aged a half-century. In their company were a handful of settlers returning to Monsweag and points along the Sheepscot.

He noticed that the Penobscots also were watching the brig plow towards the Outer Harbor. Fast Otter, whose stiff roached crest rose half a head taller than the twin blue-black braids of his companion, gave no indication of his reactions before returning to his duties at the tar kettle but Red Fish grabbed up the stub end of spar and, like a war club, shook it furiously at the passing vessel.

At the end of the day's work comparative stillness descended along the waterfront and over the stark black tangles of masts, derricks, gantries and stocks so suggestive of a burnt-over forest.

Phips, carrying his well-worn jacket over one arm, knocked, then entered Captain Eli Greenough's musty-smelling office and found the nearly toothless old fellow studying drawings he'd completed during the day through spectacles perched on his beak of a nose.

"Evenin', Eli. What d'you make of 'em?"

"Aye, I've been studyin' 'em, careful-like. Wal, now, they do seem purty good, though I ain't nowise sure about the way ye've altered the angle o' the rudder's counter-top axis. Still, I allow you generally know what you're about—so I warrant 'twill improve her steerin' a mite."

"Glad you think so because I've a couple of other notions which may increase her speed."

"Such as?"

"For one thing the mainmast ought to be moved aft by about two feet. Then there's a new steeve and length of the bowsprit to be considered. Don't fret yerself, I'll have 'em figgered out afore I leave."

Captain Greenough's shaggy gray brows shot up. "'Leave'! What in Tunket air you talkin' about?"

Phips mopped his brow. "To tell the truth, Eli, I've been thinkin' on my present state, and I figger my future don't look over-bright. You've heard the two men I'd been countin' on for sizable loans ain't nowise able to make good?"

"Yep. Heard about Tinsley's bein' took off sudden-like and the fire over to Dunster's. Poor feller. Allow him and his family will be in for mighty thin times come winter." He scratched at silvery bristles covering his chin. "Can't you reach anyone else?"

"No. I've tried everybody I know." Phips's laugh grated. "Most are only sympathetic, so I stand far short of the money I need or can earn around Boston, but somehow I'll make 'em eat their scorn and false pity. May I roast in Hell forever if I don't! Aye, Cap'n, despite everything, I'll grow rich and powerful and famous." His voice resounded in the little office like a bronze gong. "Howsumever, I'll ne'er forget yer friendship and confidence durin' these dire days."

The younger man's color mounted. "An you could, Eli, old friend, I know ye'd grant further credit—you've already been more than generous. 'Thout yer loan I'd never have kept

[*118*]

title to yonder piece of shoreland." He glanced through dusty panes at the beginnings of his shipyard.

"That bein' so, what have you in mind?"

"I aim to take a shortcut towards raisin' money to equip my yard, first-class."

Tilting back his head the master shipbuilder peered up from cavernous black eyes. "Mayhap you will, and again you mayn't. Why must you always aim so mast high, young feller?"

"Because I must follow where my Star leads me."

"Harrumph. What's yer notion?"

"Heard of Silas Youngblood?"

"Aye, if he's the same as owns the schooner *Sea Horse*— Say, didn't you re-fit her just afore you traipsed off to the Maine District?"

Phips nodded. "Maybe you ain't heard but Cap'n Young-blood's health ain't all it might be."

"Yep. So I hear. What of that?"

"Keeps coughin' blood and what with winter comin' on I allow he figgers a long voyage amongst the West Indies in a warm climate might do him a world of good."

Eli Greenough pushed spectacles farther back on his grizzled head, looked disapproval. "Take it he's offered you a berth?"

"Aye, as Chief Mate and with a right good lay in the cruise's earnings."

"Presume, too, Youngblood's granted you a right to ship merchandise for your own account?"

"Aye, when opportunity offers I'll be allowed to trade on my own. And besides"—Phips lowered his voice and bent forward—"he kind of hinted he's heard of a treasure which just might be hunted along the way."

"Pha! Didn't mention anything specific, did he?"

"No."

"Then that talk was only bait."

"Maybe so."

"Knowin' you as well as I do, Will Phips, I reckon you're calc'lating Youngblood ain't likely to last out this voyage so you'll stand a fair chance of winding up Captain of the *Sea Horse* and likely turnin' a pretty penny."

Laughter escaped Phips which made the office reverberate. "B'God, Eli, you always were smarter than a barn full of owls and have hit the nail square on its head."

"Soft soap will get you nowheres. Has Youngblood told you where he intends?"

"Aye. The farthest port of call will be Bridgetown in Barbados but first we'll put into Norfolk, Virginia and pick up a load of horses some of which—if we're lucky in the weather —we'll carry over to New Providence in the Bahamas and sell the rest in Port Royal, Jamaica, where they'll fetch a higher price—if any survive."

Captain Greenough pulled a browned clay pipe from his desk and methodically proceeded to pack it from a deer's bladder pouch. "A word of warnin', Will, and mind what I say. When you reach the Bahamas and Jamaica don't let yourself get beguiled by mouth-waterin' yarns about sunken treasures. Such are stock-in-trade 'round pirate and pirateer havens. I know 'cause I've put in there plenty of times. Go carousin' and in every tavern ye'll meet a mort of fast-talking rogues of every nationality who'll cozen you into viewin' or maybe buyin' a dirty piece of parchment purporting to show exactly where such-and-such a wreck lies with a emperor's ransom in silver, gold, emeralds, pearls aboard, all ripe for the taking.

"Me, I've known many a levelheaded man who's lost his last shirt and sometimes his life chasing such glitterin' moonshine. Wanting to get rich quick is a great failin' in human nature."

Phips nodded gravely. "Aye, Eli, I've heard aplenty wild yarns right here in Boston. Folks blame me for spendin' so much free time along the harbor front but 'tis only to hear what's goin' on abroad. I listen, sure 'nough, but may I be dipped in dung if so far I've heeded treasure talk serious-like. Right now all I aim to do is to fetch the *Sea Horse* safe back here gunnel-deep under a likely cargo, then buy a schooner I've in mind. I'll show these lily-handed, nose-in-the-air, stay-at-home merchants how to win wealth greater than they've ever dreamed on!"

Equably, Captain Greenough advised: "If I were you I wouldn't toot my horn so loud till at least I own one to blow. Now, listen. You'll be well advised to fetch home all the muscovado sugar you can find hold space for; also plenty of rum but *only* of the best quality, which likely you'll find in Barbados. If ye've any spare change left over, you'd be smart to buy a few niggers, but *only* clever ones, docile and fit to serve the rich folk of this town. An you're interested I can tell you which tribes make the best house servants: Mandingos, Fulahs, and Yarubas are among 'em."

Slowly Phips shook his head. "Thanks, but I don't aim to enter into the slave trade. Somehow, Eli, the idea of holding human critters in bondage goes dead against my grain. Pa felt the same way; he'd never buy an enslaved Injun no matter what."

From the west sounded the first faint rumble of an approaching thunderstorm. The twenty-first son squared muscular shoulders, thrust forward his big jaw. "Nevertheless, someday my favor will be courted by the high and mighty, both here and in foreign parts. Anyone tries to block my purpose I'll outwit or batter to the ground!"

All Eli Greenough said was: "When does Youngblood plan to clear port?"

"In around ten days' time." His voice softened as he placed a hand on the older man's shoulder. "Have no concern, my good, true friend, as I said, my plans for the brigantine will be completed before then."

Captain William Phips, somewhat wearied, was stumping along Ship Street when the first rain in many weeks commenced to patter and raise miniature explosions in fine dust lying inches deep in the road. Quickly the fall increased to a drumming, lashing downpour. In all directions joyful voices greeted this phenomenon. People ran into the street and, after momentarily lifting faces against this torrential downpour, ran indoors to reappear carrying bowls, tubs, kettles, buckets, even chamber pots—any container able to catch this pure and precious fluid. Very few wells in Boston's low-lying areas weren't more-or-less tainted by brackish flavors. Like many another, Phips made no effort to seek shelter, only reveled in cool rivulets purling over foul-smelling skin.

Suddenly, a livid, root-shaped bolt of lightning crackled out of the purple-black sky and struck somewhere on Copp's Hill and an almost immediate terrifying crash of thunder caused nearby window frames to rattle and householders to go scurrying indoors. Almost immediately another flash illumined the town with unearthly brilliance all the way from the South Battery to Beacon Hill and beyond.

Splashing through puddles swiftly forming ankle-deep along North Street he gained the unassuming entrance to his home. No light was shining through its diaper-paned windows which didn't disturb him; at breakfast Mary had announced she'd intended spending a day or so in Roxbury, a pretty little nearby hamlet, where a female cousin lay ailing. In a way, Will experienced relief over Mary's absence. He loathed being reminded, even tacitly, of so many obligations in her direction, wife or not.

Shoes squelching softly, the big figure pushed open a picket gate to his tiny front yard but halted abruptly and peered through torrents of silvery, pelting rain at what he first took to be a large dog cowering beneath one of the two boxbushes Mary had planted to flank the entrance. Still another flash revealed that yonder was not a dog but a small, dark-haired woman swathed in a streaming black cloak.

"What're you about?" He bent and hauled the disheveled figure into the clear.

"Please, Captain Phips, be kind enough to unhand me," whimpered the apparition. "'Tis me, Betrag Eldritch!"

"Can't be! Yer hair's blacker than pitch whilst hers was snowy and your skin's nigh as dark as a blackamoor's."

Again a bolt, striking somewhere near the Second Church, permitted Phips to realize that the irises of this bedraggled creature's deepset eyes *were* of different hues.

"By Satan's cloven hoof, ye're Granny Eldritch. But how can you have altered yer appearance so complete?"

"By means of barbers' dye and walnut juices." The woman wrung hands in terror. "Mercy, what a drefu' tempest. Since the fall of dark I've been hidin' nearby awaitin' yer retairn. Ye were so long comin' I was afeared ye might ba' gone to sea or been cast into debtors' prison."

She commenced to tremble so violently he took her arm growling: "Small gain standin' in this rain, welcome though it be. Come along."

He used a massive brass key and shoved open the front door. Next he clumped back into the kitchen where he used bellows on coals glowing faintly under a covering of ashes.

Once a thread of flame sprang into being, he employed a paper spill to ignite a bull's-eye lanthorn slung from a beam. Even in the lanthorn's clear radiance of the whale-oil he barely was able to recognize the supposed witch for, thanks perhaps to darkened hair and skin, many lines had been erased from her features. Mrs. Eldritch appeared younger, almost handsome in a queer, fey fashion.

"Mistress Eldritch—"

"An it please ye, Cap'n, for the sake of safety I've took back me maiden name of Cameron."

"Then Mistress Cameron 'twill be. Why have you sought me out?"

"I ken none else from whom I might beg a wee loan—just passage money down to Providence in Rhode Island Plantations where I'm told the Quakers are more kindly disposed towards Dissenters than the Puritans of Massachusetts Bay Colony."

"How have you managed to survive?"

Her gaze wavered to the floor. "Why, sir, I've flogged a cairngorm-and-gold brooch and a few wee silver baubles.

"After we landed I was that fearfu' someone off yer vessel might recognize me and raise the hue and cry straightaway so I journeyed inland till I found shelter 'mongst a band of

[*123*]

savages camping near a hamlet called Weston. They were kind to me after their fashion."

"You were smart to quit this place." After using a dish clout to wipe the wet from his face he tossed it to his guest. "Terror of witchcraft so increases hereabouts all manner of poor, friendless wretches are being taken up and jailed on the stupidest of charges. 'Tis said this madness rages even worse in Salem Town. Avoid that place as you would the plague."

Eyes intent, Betrag Cameron crouched on a footstool and watched him replenish the kitchen fire and then from the pantry cupboard take out a half loaf of bread, a bowl of corn-meal mush and a cold half joint of mutton. These, together with a crock of ale, a firkin of butter and a pair of pewter plates, he placed on Mary's well-scoured kitchen table.

"Help yerself, Granny. You must be even hungrier than me, and that's plenty."

Tears suddenly mingled with moisture beading the apparition's mahogany-brown features. "May the gude Laird bless and presairve ye always, Cap'n."

In pitiful eagerness Betrag tore off a chunk of bread, then voraciously reached for a thick gobbet of mutton.

Phips also began to cram his mouth with food between pulls at a jack of luke-warm ale. He poured a measure into a wooden noggin. "Here, wet yer whistle, Ma'am."

Although rain continued to pound furiously upon the window glass, lightning and thunder gradually receded in a southerly direction until the storm degenerated into a simple, steady downpour without any wind behind it.

At length Phips sighed and settled back wiping his mouth on the back of a broad, bronzed hand. In renewed curiosity he peered at the strange figure on the opposite side of the hearth. An odd effect was created by her shadow cast black and gigantic upon the white plaster wall behind. "Ye said ye're minded to seek refuge amongst the Quakers?"

"For a space," Betrag admitted, still chewing hard. "Aye, for, like you, I'm fated to follow my Star. Would I could read me ain future near as clear as I can yours."

He used a forefinger nail to dislodge a shred of meat from between strong, ivory-yellow teeth. "The future, eh? Aye, let's speak on that later, but first things first. What's the fare required to carry you down to Rhode Island?"

She shoved a damp strand of hair from before those strange, mismated eyes; her angular features quivered. "Is ten shillin' too much?"

Nodding he went upstairs, unlocked his seachest and selected coins from a slender canvas bag.

Over the rain's steady drumming he said to the weird figure warming hands at the fire: "Here. Take this as a gift, free and clear."

Across a circle of amber radiance cast over the littered table the two peered steadily at each other a long moment before she cried: "I canna find wurruds sufficient to thank ye, Cap'n, but I'll try tae repay ye in me ain fashion."

Betrag Cameron then drew a series of slow, shuddering deep breaths, went over to crouch and peer fixedly into a cluster of rosy-gray, throbbing embers. Presently she commenced to speak in a low-pitched monotone, the like of which William Phips never had heard. Intently, he listened to words which became indelibly engraved upon a very retentive memory.

"I see you, the twenty-first son of Mary and James Phips, destined by the stars in their courses and the Five Sisters o' Kintail to stand before kings!"

Phips settled onto his chair, thrusting callused bare feet towards the hearth. "'Kings,' Ma'am? Why, to stand before even a single monarch would satisfy my wildest ambitions."

Betrag spoke sharply: "'*Kings*,' I said. Now be silent else ye'll spoil my vision."

"Pray proceed. What else do you see for me?"

She stooped lower over the coals. "I see you soon engaged in a design wherein the Fates decree delay and disappointing rewards." Her voice strengthened until it sang like bass notes played on a viola. "In the thirty-seventh year o' yer life, despite jealousy and the evil intent of powerful enemies, as I've already said, ye'll discover and win a vast treasure—a veritable emperor's ransom."

"'Treasure! A vast treasure' you said?"

Phips jumped up, gaze fixed on the back of the Cameron woman's wildly disordered hair.

"Aye, but ye'll not win the whole of it."

Despite quickened breathing he noted a rising inflection in that unnerving, singsong voice.

"In the forty-first year o' yer life, William Phips, a king will send ye in a position of great trust somewhere beyond the seas."

"Which king? What seas?"

Her hand flickered sidewise in a snake-quick gesture. "I see ye struggling amid the evil endeavors o' rich and high-born nobles contemptuous o' yer common birth and fearfu' o' yer ability."

As if fatigued beyond endurance, the Cameron woman's frail body commenced to sag and her voice faded to an undertone so faint he was forced to bend low over her.

"I see ye holding a high public office, great in power, adventure and danger. Ah-h! I can see no mair."

Barely in time his arm shot out to encircle her before she could collapse among the coals.

"And then? What *then*? For God's sake, Ma'am, let me know how I'll end!"

Uncertainly Betrag raised sunken, lackluster eyes. "Would that I could, but more, neither yer Star nor the Five Sisters o' Kintail will disclose."

Chapter 12

GULF STREAM

TO BEGIN WITH, life aboard the *Saucy Betsey* went surprisingly smoothly despite the presence of a comely young girl among a crew of five widely disparate men. All the same a female's presence on this 38-foot craft evoked minor complications which accomplished little towards simplifying a dull and uncomfortable daily routine.

On the first night out John Dale told Pegeen she must sleep as best she might in a hammock woven of West Indian fibers which was slung in the sloop's tiny hutch of a cabin between narrow transom bunks occupied by Jim Turner and himself.

Since the cabin's roof rose but a scant two feet above deck level and the depth of hold was less than six feet there wasn't much room to move about. Nor was there space for anything resembling a forecastle, so the three deck hands somehow had to find shelter under a half-deck built under the bows and sleep in coffin-like boxes built between the sloop's side and a thin plank bulkhead. They were forced to enter their bunks through a hole cut in one end, much like squirrels crawling into a hollow tree.

When the sloop had been at sea about a week, Dale noticed that Pegeen's initial cheerful and helpful nature appeared to be changing. Privately he wondered if this weren't attributable to the fact that her pregnant condition was becoming noticeable to even a hopeless dullard. Sharply, she now slapped aside groping hands and employed language such as never had been heard in the vicinity of Hammond's Fort except perhaps by some drunken trapper.

Nevertheless, the strong auburn-haired girl continued to haul and heave and soon became able to reef and handle canvas with the best of them—in fact more effectively than a leather-faced and aging one-eyed French buccaneer from Tortuga named Victor. He was suffering from an old wound in the side which never had healed properly. For all the Frenchman's evil countenance, his manner towards Pegeen remained considerate beyond an occasional absent-minded pinch of her thigh or bottom.

Often at night she overheard Victor talking to himself in his own language and at such times noticed how the quality of his voice softened and altered so much she wondered whether he hadn't once been at least somewhat of a gentleman.

Then there was Moog, a wiry, quick-moving, generally silent and phlegmatic half-breed Mohawk, disfigured by a broken and oddly twisted high-bridged nose. This fellow was on board only because Turner had got the mixed-breed sufficiently drunk to induce him, for a pittance, to scrawl his totem mark on the *Saucy Betsey*'s Articles.

From the start it was apparent that the Mohawk had been eager to quit Boston without attracting undue attention. Nevertheless he not only proved a first-rate deck hand and helmsman but also seemed uncomfortably ready to use the heavy-bladed skinning knife he carried in a fringed sheath slung to his belt of braided rattlesnake skins. Privately, Pegeen suspected its wickedly blue-white blade had displayed a different hue plenty of times. Other members of the crew must have shared her opinion for they left Moog to himself as much as possible.

The third deck hand was a good-natured loutish and vacant-eyed youth answering simply to the name of "Dennis." In his late teens, Dennis was awkward, but with ease could heft burdens two ordinary men couldn't have moved.

To Pegeen it appeared those empty gray-green eyes of his followed her too intently whatever she was about. It came as a considerable relief that a single hard slap delivered early during the voyage had sufficed to deter advances, for the time being at least. Nevertheless, she remained uneasy over the way he stared and kept wetting his lips when some duty required her reaching upwards high enough to disclose an unusual expanse of smooth and sturdy brown legs or when she set about rigging a tarpaulin across the cabin's companionway to secure privacy before disappearing to attend to natural needs in a heavy wooden bucket.

It was only to be expected that Pegeen should do the cooking as best she might over a sandbox installed on the little sloop's main hatch cover. This she was glad to do after sampling Dennis's culinary efforts.

Although the sky did gray over on occasion the wind continued out of a favorable quadrant so, according to Dale's calculations, the *Saucy Betsey* ought to be approaching the Bermudas at an unusually smart clip.

More than once the very immensity of these endless expanses of dark blue, white-flecked and empty water overwhelmed the young woman reared as she'd been where forests crowded in on all sides and a body never got to enjoy a really wide view. Only once had a sail been raised and then only briefly as a tiny speck on the horizon.

One day John Dale explained this appalling lonesomeness. Most vessels, said he, on clearing Boston shaped an easterly course for Europe north-northeast for Canada; otherwise they pointed bowsprits towards the Caribbean or west-southwest for ports in the Southern Colonies.

As day followed eventless day, the wandering of big, yellow-haired John Dale's hands and the nature of his kisses became bolder, especially after supper when the crew had begun to drowse and snore about the untidy deck.

As for Jim Turner, he usually went below about the same time, there to smoke and devote attention to an apparently inexhaustible supply of Jamaica rum till sleep overcame him. During the day Dale's cousin would range the deck clad only in breeches and that wide belt of waterproofed leather which he never removed.

Weather permitting, Pegeen and Dale then would sprawl side by side in the stern on a pile of old sails with Dale steering by use of callused toes hooked over the smooth tiller handle which left him free to hug her close and bestow long, moist caresses that aroused pangs of pleasure in both of them.

Until such moments Pegeen hadn't realized how poignantly she missed Tom's clumsy but energetic attentions and therefore responded more and more wholeheartedly, largely through inclination and also because she felt it wise to comply, for, very clearly, she understood that, pregnant, destitute, and otherwise friendless her only hope lay in maintaining Dale's goodwill.

The only one whose attitude really alarmed her was that of rangy, gap-toothed Jim Turner, the only man larger and more powerful than her paramour—especially after he'd been applying himself to the rum jug. On one occasion he muttered obscenities while slipping a hand up her petticoats to toy with her pubic hair and cup ever-swelling breasts. All the same, thus far she'd managed pleasantly but effectively to thwart his advances. She didn't dare to protest audibly for fear of provoking a quarrel which well might prove disastrous.

Nevertheless, she reckoned that, sooner or later, a clash was inevitable, especially since Dale, having shaken off most of his depression, was becoming more observant and possessive.

Chapter 13

LINE STORM

THE *Saucy Betsey* must have sailed nearly across the Gulf Stream when, one especially torrid morning, Moog lifted his ruin of a nose and commenced to sniff loudly like a deerhound trying the air for scent.

Victor, the ex-buccaneer, also appearing uneasy, studied the cloudless, brazen-blue sky and tested the atmosphere at intervals. Only Pegeen and simple-minded Dennis remained unperceptive.

"What ails them two?" Turner complained. "Act like they was smellin' 'bout for a hot wench."

Dale frowned. "Like me, they sense a change comin'; weather's chancy 'round this time o' year hereabouts."

Once the last breath of breeze had died out the *Saucy Betsey* wallowed, gaff swinging and creaking uselessly. She rolled monotonously among oily low combers created somewhere far below the horizon.

For her part Pegeen noticed that those seabirds she had loved to watch circle and swoop so gracefully about the masthead had disappeared. Only a few dainty little gray-black stormy petrels remained to skim from one patch of golden Sargasso weed to the next. Porpoises also vanished and the silvery flitting of flying fish no longer continued to delight her.

The temperature mounted till the men, aflame with sunburn, went about their trifling labors naked save for improvised loincloths. Pegeen, uncomfortably aware of her relentlessly distending abdomen and swelling breasts, bemoaned the fact that she, too, couldn't strip to the waist. All the relief she could obtain was to wear nothing under a smelly and sweat-drenched gown of calicut cotton.

After the calm had persisted for five days with the sloop making no perceptible progress, Jim Turner posted Dennis, armed with a cudgel, to guard the ominously hollow-sounding water butt.

Nerves already frayed, tautened still more under a stifling oppressive atmosphere. Once darkness closed in, everyone excepting Pegeen and the helmsman lay sprawled naked about the deck, like corpses on a battlefield.

To go below meant added torment but Pegeen was thankful to have the cabin to herself for a while where she could wash privately after a fashion and comb the worst snarls out of her greasy, tangled hair.

Lacing fingers beneath her head, she blinked sun-swollen eyes, tried to foresee the immediate future and found it not reassuring. Something warned that that long skein of evil fortune, which had commenced to unroll outside of Pa's stronghouse an eternity ago, was far from reaching an end.

What sin could she have committed aside from those all-too-brief dalliances with her intended? Why should the good Lord punish her so unrelentingly? She knew she wasn't truly a bad girl—what she'd done and was doing with John Dale had to be done to remain alive. What was wrong about that? Nobody in their right mind wanted to die till their time came and she was only eighteen.

If only Tom's seed wasn't sprouting within her. Tom, dear Tom, so infinitely tender in his rough way. She only hoped he'd died swiftly and hadn't been dragged off to perish inch by inch at some Abenaki torture stake.

As she lay swinging back and forth in foetid gloom a doubt arose that John Dale wasn't too sure about just where he was sailing. Were this so then only an agonizing death through thirst and starvation awaited her.

Although she felt drowsy she fumbled under the bag of rags and spun yarn she used for a pillow until her fingers encountered the handle of a heavy oaken belaying pin. Swing and dip, swing and dip; the hammock's monotonous swaying eventually took effect and she slept.

Pegeen had no notion how much time elapsed before she roused to a realization that the sloop's motion had altered and gusts of cool, clean air were beating down the companionway.

This change in the *Saucy Betsey*'s movements also allowed her to sense rather than perceive that someone was coming below only an instant before a hard hand was slapped over her mouth. By the reek of rum on her attacker's breath and his weight she knew this must be Jim Turner.

"Lie still, be accommodatin' and ye'll suffer no harm— otherwise—" She winced under the prick of steel between her breasts.

Harsh bristles scored her cheeks before Turner's mouth clamped down on her lips, half-smothering her. Once he'd worked her shift above her hips he wheezed over increasing sea noises: "Get down on my bunk. Can't have us no fun in this contraption."

"All right, but p-please don't hurt me. I-I'll treat you fine." Pegeen swung trembling legs over the hammock's edge at the same time trying to free her weapon. If only she dared to scream; surely Dale and the deck hands by now must have roused with the sloop fairly under way. But the Captain's knife point was digging deep enough to start a hot trickle running down her belly so she lay flat on the Captain's narrow bunk, locked her legs and put up a perfunctory struggle.

While the *Saucy Betsey* commenced to heave and roll as if some Titan's paddle had started to stir the Atlantic the companionway darkened again and dimly she heard John Dale's voice snarl, "What the—? Leave her be, ye mangy son-of-a-bitch!" Gripping Turner by the hair, he hauled his cousin reeling onto his feet.

"Got—knife!" Pegeen yelled, then, freed of Turner's weight, lunged upwards and groped for the belaying pin while the two grappled and lurched about under the sloop's accelerated plunging and rolling.

Aware that Turner was much more powerful, Dale sensed his one chance lay in pinioning Turner's knife hand till he found an opportunity to drive a knee into the Captain's groin—a difficult maneuver since both were reeling about in nearly complete darkness.

As in the grip of a hideously realistic nightmare Pegeen tried to dodge the struggling bodies until she succeeded in freeing the belaying pin. The *Saucy Betsey* gave a violent, twisting roll, momentarily separating the antagonists and Dale was flung backwards hopelessly off-balance. His head struck a stancheon so hard myriad white-hot stars exploded before his eyes and his knees buckled.

"Teach—damn' whoreson—cross me." Turner bent and set his weight behind the knife's point but failed to drive home the blade because Pegeen, gripping the belaying pin with both hands, had brought it down with all her wiry young strength. Captain James Turner collapsed, never to regain consciousness; since such is impossible for a man the top of whose skull has been crushed in.

Pegeen grabbed her hammock's hook to steady herself, then, still clutching her weapon, managed to drop onto her knees and try to test Dale's pulse. Indescribable relief flooded her. His heart seemed to be beating strongly, regularly.

First off, she somehow must restore Dale to consciousness before Turner came to. How? Water in the face, of course, and a big drink of liquor. So wild and unpredictable had the sloop's movements become she found it impossible to stand or even to maintain a steady crouching position. Nevertheless, she worked her way up the companionway into a furious welter of flying spray.

Victor and Moog she barely made out clinging to the tiller handle and attempting to steady the struggling vessel.

Out of the wind's lightless tumult Victor bellowed: "Where are the *officers?*"

"Both bad hurt! Dennis, fetch water from—butt."

Even by the light of a bull's-eye lanthorn it proved difficult to estimate the seriousness of Dale's head injury which, like most scalp wounds, was bleeding freely. After she'd awkwardly bound up his head with a strip ripped from someone's shirt and had poured a dipper of water over his face, Dale commenced to regain consciousness.

"Wha—what happen'?"

She told him briefly while giving him a swig of rum to speed his recovery.

"Moog!" he gasped. "Tighten tiller-lashin's run afore—wind! Comin' on deck right away."

The sloop's sickening plungings presently diminished a trifle.

He heard Pegeen gasp. "Can't find pulse in—Cap'n's wrist."

He crawled over and got a shadowy look at the top of James Turner's head but that was enough. "Bastard's skull is stove in. He's dead. How come?"

"I did it." Pegeen's voice barely penetrated the tumult. "He was set to stab—kill you. See? Knife's still in—hand."

"Why, you've killed him."

"Hope I don't come to regret it."

"You won't." Dark blood continued to trickle over Dale's forehead as, dizzily, he hauled himself erect. "Come below one of you. Cap'n fell; skull's cracked wide open."

"He dead?" Dennis called down over the wind through the shrouds.

"Yep. Come down—help lug him on deck."

Pegeen grabbed his arm. "The map he keeps in cincture!"

[*135*]

"Hold on a minute, Dennis. Must make sure he's truly dead."

It took longer than expected to unknot the greasy thongs securing Jim Turner's wide belt.

"Tie it about me." When she'd done so he called up: "Cap'n's sure 'nuff dead. Come help heave him on deck."

Just before the body slid limply over the sloop's bulwark, Moog's knife slid from its sheath long enough to cut off the dead man's right ear—the one with the gold ring—and slip it into his waistband. The mixed-breed also made silent note that Captain Turner's belt had disappeared.

Chapter 14

REEFS

STRANGELY ENOUGH almost immediately after Turner's body had splashed alongside the winds' force appeared somewhat to decrease but great, crashing combers grown steeper so filled the air with fine spray it became difficult to breathe. Towards daylight the storm's velocity picked up again, but this time came screaming out of the west. Quickly, boiling rollers veiled in spindrift swept every movable object on deck overboard.

The sloop shuddered and rolled half-over time and again while her company, relentlessly battered and buffeted, clung to lifelines and struggled for breath.

Long since the mainsail and both jibs had been reduced to rags and tatters, leaving the *Saucy Betsey* to wallow and squatter helplessly like a badly wounded wild duck.

By hauling herself along her lifeline, Pegeen got sufficiently close to Victor to cry, "We going—sink?"

The old buccaneer spewed up a lot of water before feebly shaking his head. "Just might live—if—don't grow worse."

By clinging for dear life to the tiller handle beside Dale, the girl felt safer although suffering savage blows whenever the rudder lifted clear of the water. At long last it seemed the sloop, unaccountably, was encountering less violent seas. Long since a series of thundering combers had carried away the only small boat lashed over the main hatch; rope ends writhed about the deck like demented brown serpents.

Thanks to an endless succession of scurrying lead-hued clouds, dusk descended early.

Without warning the main boom's sheet tackles parted and started that heavy spar to flailing in vicious semicircles above the deck forcing the crew to cower flat, half-drowned, lest they be knocked overboard or get crushed into bloody pulp.

Impenetrable dark had fallen when a grinding *crack!* warned that the mast had snapped and been carried away.

"This does it!" Dale yelled above wind so powerful it ballooned his cheeks and almost drove words back down his throat.

Chilled, battered and hopelessly confused, Pegeen, despite darkness, managed to hitch her lifeline about a cleat and doggedly kept on struggling to breathe.

Sometime during the night an unearthly quiet ensued although mountainous waves continued relentlessly to pummel the waterlogged sloop like a bully belaboring a helpless child.

Dale shoved his mouth close to Pegeen's ear. "We in eye of storm. Seen it happen—Bahamas."

"How long we—stay afloat?"

"No tellin'. Miracle we alive come daylight."

Some whim of the storm sent the inevitable backlash, which proved of brief duration, roaring off on a southerly course. When, before very long, a gorgeous scarlet and gold dawn broke, it revealed the *Saucy Betsey* still afloat but riding so low on the surface that waves swept over her like a half-tide rock.

Later, John Dale reasoned that one explanation for the

wreck's unreadiness to sink must lie in the fact that Jim Turner had economized by stowing inadequate ballast. Presently he realized that Pegeen had managed to lash herself to the rail and now, terribly bruised, was sitting half-awash in water which kept sluicing endlessly over the canting deck.

Next, he made out Moog's figure crouched under the forepeak and secured to the barrel windlass by a rope's end. Of Victor and Dennis he could see no trace.

"You hurt?"

He had to shout several times over the tumult of waves boiling about the wreck but, eventually, Pegeen's sodden head lifted and she peered at him, blankly it seemed, until her bluish lips formed the ghost of a smile.

"All over. Seems like."

Once the seas had lessened a trifle, Moog cast himself loose and came crawling aft.

For all his head was throbbing like a hand drum, Dale got onto hands and knees to peer over the remains of the bulwarks and realize that, in all directions it seemed, reefs were spouting like a vast pod of whales, also that the waterlogged sloop was being propelled straight towards a cluster of jagged, foam-smothered rocks.

All the same he found a fragile reason for encouragement on recalling that no reefs ever had been charted or reported to exist anywhere between the coast of North America and the Bermuda Islands.

Chapter 15

CAPTAIN ABRAM ADDERLY

THAT SPLINTERING TANGLE of timbers and cordage to which the *Saucy Betsey* had been reduced settled so low it began to bump and grate over more and more unseen obstacles while being thrust deeper into an apparently limitless maze of foam-crowned coral heads.

There seemed only one consolation to the situation; the farther the wreck blundered among the reefs the less grew the force of seas whose strength was being dissipated among the rocks. Shortly before darkness descended again, the wreckage quit drifting and came to rest on a horseshoe-shaped and low-lying reef.

Moog, who appeared in better shape than either of his companions, gripped the mast's jagged stump and, struggling erect, leered in a direction which by the sunset must be southerly. Presently he uttered a grunt and pointed to the eastward. "No sure—mebbe see land—mebbe only shadow."

Dale, his throat afire from all the salt water he'd swallowed, croaked: "Better be land. Can you pray, Pegeen?"

"Do my best. But I—so sinful, won't count for much."

"Bosh! How're you feelin'?"

She was lying propped up on the remains of the afterdeck.

"I'm feeling better," she lied. Her body was one huge ache, scratched, battered and bruised over nearly its entire surface. "No bones broken, I think, but I'm terrible hungry and thirsty and my belly got whacked bad—hurts something fierce. How's your head?"

"Like after a big carouse." He tried to grin. He'd been burned to an angry shade of crimson after his shirt had been torn off and so Jim Turner's cincture was in plain view. He felt more than a little lightheaded once the wreckage had grounded and remained heaving sluggishly up and down. "One good thing—so far we've seen no sharks. Reefs must be keepin' 'em offshore."

Pegeen only nodded.

Gradually the wind died out and the darkening sea flattened sufficiently to permit the men to lash a shredding of canvas to an oar which, miraculously, had remained jammed into the *Saucy Betsey*'s broken forepeak.

"Too short—not much good," grunted the mixed-breed.

"Better 'n nothin', that's all. Well, maybe come daylight we can rig us a raft." He found a measure of consolation in the fact that his sheath knife somehow had remained attached to his belt and that his cousin's map presumably remained lashed about his middle, although God alone knew in what condition it might be. Everything depended on what ink had been used. Ordinary ink long since would have washed away but, hopefully, the map might have been rendered with waterproof India ink or a West Indian mixture of turtle oil and gunpowder.

Crabwise he traversed what remained of the deck to put a scraped and bleeding arm around Pegeen's equally lacerated shoulders. She sighed, then her tangled head came to rest against him.

Moog, a few feet away, lay slumped with arms and knees

retracted into a foetal position. All three slept like the dead until the mixed-breed roused them at dawn, grunting: "*Is* land!"

Knuckling swollen, red-rimmed lids Dale made out a faint bluish smear upon the horizon and, more important, a tiny triangular patch of brownish sail headed in the wreck's general direction.

Without command Moog snatched the rag of canvas off an oar, climbed the mast's splintered stump and began frantically to wave.

If only a tin foghorn or a conch shell bugle or a bell remained—anything capable of attracting attention. Should the men in that far-off boat fail to notice such a low-lying piece of wreckage the three of them would be dead long before this murderous sun went down.

Again and again it seemed that the distant vessel—she looked to be a sort of shallop equipped with an extra-tall mast and stubby bowsprit—hadn't spied the wreckage for the little craft kept veering off first in one direction and then another.

All of a sudden Dale sensed that her helmsman must be picking a course among this deadly maze of coral heads, reefs and ledges.

Eternities seemed to elapse before the shallop arrived within hailing distance, by which time the bleary-eyed survivors could tell she was manned by four people. A barrel-chested black-bearded figure was at the helm; a very thin young fellow and a pair of dark-faced youngsters in their early teens completed her crew. None wore shirts and evidently their hair hadn't felt scissors in a very long time.

Expertly, the helmsman guided his craft into a clear space between two lazily creaming boilers before bringing her into the wind.

"Lucifer's liver!" Black-Beard called through cupped hands. "I've come across some sorry pieces of flotsam in my time but none to pair with yours. Anyone fit to catch a line?"

Dale swayed erect. "Reckon so."

Presently the homely, red-brown shallop lay riding gently alongside.

"And who might the likes of you be?" Black-Beard demanded.

Dale gave abbreviated information.

"Who's the fee-male critter?"

"Mistress Dale—my, my wife."

Moog only blinked.

"Thank ye kindly for your help, sir. How might you be named?" Dale queried while the girl's stiffened fingers sought to secure a few buttons clinging to the front of her dress.

"Ye kin call me Abram—Cap'n Abram Adderly." He jerked a broad thumb at the thin young man. "This here lout is Mark, my oldest boy; t' other lads belong to neighbors. We was fixin' t' set pots for lobsters along of yonder old wreck when I spied yer signal. Laws, laws!" he grunted and spat noisily into the sea. "You're sure disappointin'. Ain't even tuppence's worth o' salvage here for my trouble. Better climb aboard. Mark, you and the other younkers lend a hand and help make these castaways welcome to the bountiful joys o' Bermuda of which there ain't many."

The survivors, having swallowed scoops of warm, brackish-tasting water and gnawed on iron-hard sea biscuits, collapsed, inert on the shallop's floor boards amid a tangle of lobster traps and crudely contrived fishing gear.

Captain Adderly continued to talk as lonely people will while, with consummate skill, conning his speedy little craft towards a low-lying and barren-looking island which appeared to form the tip of a chain of islets extending in the general direction of the Gulf Stream.

"Aye," the Bermudian drawled, "us sure was lucky we didn't get hit full-on by that rage of two days back. Such a tempest can raise plain and fancy hell hereabouts, 'specially if one catches a vessel cruisin' offshore.

"Funny thing; they say these here Islands first settled by a passel of colonists headed for Virginia but a great rage blew up and their vessel—the *Sea 'Venture* I think she was named—was drove onto a reef off the East End. They claim her commander, Sir George Somers, or 'Summers' as some say, on purpose drove his sinkin' ship 'twixt two rocks so she *couldn't* go down; every last soul aboard got safe ashore."

He scratched under a wide-brimmed hat of fraying palm fibers. "I've fetched in plenty castaways but can't recall many in worse case than the three of you."

He turned deeply tanned features towards Pegeen. "How you makin' out, Sister?"

Face ablaze in the pitiless sunlight, she murmured, "Guess I kind of hurt pretty much all over, but it isn't too bad save for some pains down here." She touched her lower abdomen and too late wondered whether the Bermudian had noticed its perceptible roundness. Silently but fervently she blessed John Dale for that unexpected lie.

"Now, Mrs. Dale, just rest you easy and hang on a space longer. Me, Mark, and the lads will have you safe ashore within a hour."

Adderly continued: "My dwellin' ain't much to look on but we do make out, somehow. Wish we could fetch a wise woman to 'tend yer wife but we've scarce any neighbors closer 'n Mangrove Bay and there ain't many even there. These Islands are kind of lonesome." He waved a knobby brown hand indicating a heavily wooded island lying at some distance off the right. On it shone a single white roof.

"Life on the Bermudas at best is rough and not always ready, as you'll soon discover. Plenty of times we'd die of hunger if 'tweren't for cahows, wild pigs, fish, and turtles."

"And," put in Mark, a gaunt but alert-appearing youth whose small and restless gray eyes peered like an English sheep dog's beneath an enormous mop of sun-bleached brown hair, "such pickin's as we find in wrecks."

"That's no lie," the bearded man admitted. "And, every so often we may go trading or"—he winked—"cruise, privateering-like, 'mongst the West Indies. Sometimes we're lucky and fetch back worthwhile trade goods."

"Ever seek treasure?" The New Englander was at pains to sound casual.

"Some have, or so 'tis said." Abram Adderly's gaze shifted over the shimmering emerald water. "Some even believe there's a hoard of Spanish gold buried somewheres on the West End. Aye, venturers have come now and again to seek it out."

"Ever find?" Moog spoke for the first time, eyes hooded.

"No. Near's I know they've all sailed away emptyhanded. Now suppose you tell me more about that tempest—how far back did it hit?"

Dale told him, then hitched himself onto his elbows. "These really *are* the Bermudas?"

"Yep. Didn't you intend for here?"

"Aye, but with one thing and another my navigation wasn't overexact."

Adderly's manner changed. "Ye can navigate?"

"Sure I can—granted decent instruments."

He watched the Bermudian's bloodshot eyes for a moment come to rest on Jim Turner's cincture.

"How'd you earn that long gash in yer scalp?"

"Struck a stancheon hardish durin' the storm."

Moog, still chewing a raw fish, listened, battered, copper-hued features impassive. In his pocket he fingered Turner's gold earring but his brooding gaze so seldom left Pegeen's disheveled figure it gave Dale occasion to consider what attitude the half-Mohawk might take under present conditions. How much did he know about what really had occurred below-decks?

The shallop now entered relatively smooth water closer to land. No longer did reefs boil and spout in all directions.

Captain Adderly evidently hadn't exaggerated: if his craft was typical the inhabitants of these Islands indeed must be poverty-poor.

The New Englander already had noted the complete absence of ironwork; cleats, blocks, and tiller mounting. All had been carved out of some reddish wood which looked like Bermuda cedar—a wood widely admired among shipbuilders for its toredo resisting and enduring quality. The shallop's leg-of-mutton sail and running gear were seriously dilapidated.

While the shallop continued inshore the sun grew hotter and hotter until it caused Dale a giddiness which didn't help him to observe his surroundings.

Pegeen, it appeared, had sunk into a semistupor; she lay staring blankly at her feet with flaming, swollen features shaded only by a tangled matting of auburn hair.

For a while the New Englander attempted to concoct a convincing yarn concerning the *Saucy Betsey* and her company, but the effort proved too great; gradually he succumbed to exhaustion and only aroused himself when the little sloop's keel grated upon a small, sandy beach.

Chapter 16

IRELAND ISLAND

CAPTAIN ABRAM ADDERLY'S DOMICILE—if so ramshackle a structure could be thus dignified—mostly had been
crudely built of stone and rough-hewn cedarwood save for
one section constructed from well-planed planks undoubtedly
salvaged from wrecks.

It soon became apparent that the Bermudian only recently
must have quarried a number of sandstone blocks. Apparently he had added to the original wooden shack a sizable room
intended to serve as a combined dining room, living room and
kitchen. Its dazzling whitewashed roof had been fashioned
from thick slabs or "shingles" of sandstone.

When Dale admired the whitewashed roof his rescuer
drawled: "'Tweren't just for looks we done that. Ye see, all
over these islands fresh water's mighty hard to come by because there ain't no springs, creeks or ponds anywheres so we
have to catch rain on the roof and store it in cisterns like that."

He indicated a large, oblong structure sunk level with the ground and with a rounded brick top. Stone troughs from the roof evidently conducted rainwater into it.

At both ends of this stone section wooden lean-tos equipped with bunks accommodated the children and a miscellany of ribby dogs, fowls, pigs, and goats.

In one corner the Captain and his shrill-voiced wife occupied a salvaged fourposter bed casually screened by a faded brocade hanging. Save for a pair of handsomely carved and gilded armchairs of French origin the furniture consisted of a plain wooden bench, a greasy plank table and a few unpainted cupboards and seachests. There being no wardrobe a pungent collection of ragged and mildewing garments dangled from pegs let into the wall.

Captain Adderly's house stood amid a grove of sea grapes and cedars above a shelving beach facing a great, bright blue-green bay which usually sparkled in the sunlight.

Nearer the water's edge stood crude stocks in which lay a half-framed ketch of about 150 tons burthern. Close by was a sawpit and platform but with very little cut lumber in evidence. From the number of cedar logs awaiting attention it would appear that a severe lack of labor must exist hereabouts. Beyond these logs loomed a large stack of grotesquely tangled driftwood.

As it turned out, Mrs. Polly Adderly's bark was far more dangerous than her bite; no sooner had Pegeen been half-dragged and half-carried up to her home than she shooed three young children out of one of the lean-to ends, and with shrill curses ordered them to bed down under a worn-out whaleboat —much to the disapproval of a sow and a litter of squeaking black-and-brown piglets.

Altogether, Abram Adderly's get numbered seven, four boys and three girls ranging in age from fifteen-year-old Mark, the rail-thin, shock-haired youngster who'd come out in the shallop, to Wee Helen, aged about a year.

Without delay Polly, mumbling to herself all the time, stirred a fire under a cast-iron kettle and presently ladled out big wooden bowls of conch stew—a dish Dale soon came to despise because it was served so frequently.

Adderly said: "You and the Injun feller can bunk in the east lean-to; 'tain't no palace but 'twill serve to keep the wind and rain off you. You'll have to get used to the land crabs. Kill 'em whenever you get a chance. They bite something fierce, worse 'n sand flies, mosquitoes and bedbugs but not so often."

The big-bearded Bermudian, seemingly ready to please, lifted some dry garments off their pegs, adding casually, "Want me to take care o' that fine leather belt of yours? Dry it out and oil it up some?"

Dale managed a grateful smile. "Thanks, but I never part with it; contains a magic stone given me by a Pequot powwow. 'Tis supposed to bring me good luck—"

A low chuckle escaped Adderly. "Wouldn't say it's been overuseful of late. Say, didn't you now speak of a Pequot?"

"Yes. What about that?"

Adderly's gnarled brown forefinger briefly explored a graying thatch. "Why, 'round thirty, thirty-five years ago a passel of such redmen was fetched down and sold for slaves. Got themselves captured in some war up in the Massachusetts Bay Colony."

Unexpectedly Moog spoke: "Pequot War not fought much in Bay Colony, most in Rhode Island, old men say."

"Yep. That's right." Dale dipped his newly bandaged head; it was aching dully. "'Twas back in '37 almost the whole Pequot tribe got massacred or enslaved when Connecticut-trained bands led by a Cap'n John Mason took their main town by surprise. How did these savages work out as slaves down here?" Dale continued rubbing ointment into his bruised and swollen scalp.

Adderly bit off a chew of tobacco. "No good at all for field-hands; being proud warriors they'd liefer eat dirt and die 'fore they'd till and hoe ground. However, they took right pert to seafarin' and made jim-dandy fishermen, whalers, and boat-builders."

He turned to Moog. "You been a ship's carpenter maybe?"

[149]

"No. But me fine sailor." The disfigured mixed-breed pointed to Dale. "Him fine shipbuilder, fine navigator."

"Now ain't that elegant!" The Bermudian smiled so broadly the corners of his mouth all but touched his ears. "Funny, a hunch told me I'd do well to succor you people. Been tollin' on the *Dove*—that's the ketch you see near the water's edge— for nigh on a half-year, help's so scarce. What I need is—"

The black-bearded fellow broke off, for in the coral stone section of the house had sounded a scream so agonized John Dale felt hairs squirm on the back of his head.

Chapter 17

THE MAP

A WEEK after Pegeen's protracted, agonizing, and nearly fatal miscarriage, Captain Abram Adderly used a mangled left hand to scrape a beading of sweat from his forehead before putting down a pod auger and backing down a rough ladder leaning aginst the *Dove*'s half-planked larboard beam.

Once on the chip- and sawdust-littered sand he strode over to John Dale whose body, stripped to the waist, glowed a bright red-brown since in these latitudes even a winter sun could prove merciless especially when shining through a high cloud overcast.

Abram spat, grunted: "Come along, Jack. Time's come for 'a walk and a talk'—and I don't mean it the way a feller invites a girl into the underbrush." Red-rimmed hazel eyes flickered to that sweat-marked brown leather cincture invariably secured about the New Englander's muscular waist.

When Dale nodded, the Bermudian led off along a short,

rock-studded beach, one of many indenting Ireland Island's eastern side. He ended by indicating a driftwood log. "Now, my friend, let's sit us down and talk 'thout interruptions."

Carelessly, he eased a long-bladed knife out of its sheath, rested it across his lap. "Been noticing how handy and knowledgeable you are about shipbuildin'; since we see eye-to-eye on most matters mebbe we'll talk about going shares in that craft we're working on, on account of I can't pay you."

His gaze became direct, thrusting. "However, I ain't never gone shares with a man I can't trust all the way."

This brought Dale up sharp, slightly straddled brown eyes growing alert. " 'Can't trust'? What ground you got for such a remark? Have ever I lied to you?"

"No, not about anythin' important, but you ain't been tellin' me the *whole* truth, neither."

The shaggy-bearded Bermudian picked up a pebble, tossed it towards a flock of dainty gray-and-white sandpipers dipping and running along the tide's edge.

"What's your meaning?"

Abram looked squarely at Dale. "You ain't never told me you came to Bermuda a-treasure huntin', now have you?"

"No. That I've not. What makes you figger I have?"

"Why else would you and your people risk venturin' 'way out here in a miserable little cock-boat like the one I found you in?"

Dale's tawny mop of hair dipped. "Ye're right about that, Abram, only hopes of finding a treasure could have made me coon-cub-crazy 'nough to risk navigatin' such a tub towards a pimple on the face of the ocean like the Bermudas."

Adderly fingered his bushy black beard. "Since I've bin right so far, I'll hazard you keep a map of some sort hidden in that there wide leather belt. Correct?"

Dale's pale yellow teeth gleamed briefly amid broad, sun-darkened features. "Funny. Only last night I was figgerin' I'd show it you come this evenin'." His voice took on an edge. "Before you feel tempted to slay me for it."

Adderly's hand started towards his knife's hilt but as quickly fell away. "I'll admit I bin' plannin' on something like that. 'Twould be easy, there bein' no constable west o' Warwick Tribe."

"Yep. Ye're even sharper than I figgered on, Abram."

The Bermudian deliberated, fingers remaining to his left hand drumming against his knee. "Very well, but before we strike a bargain I aim to take a long look at yer map and see what's on it."

"Fair enough, but before I show where the loot's supposed to be buried what are the chances of keepin' this matter to our-selves—aside from Pegeen and Moog?"

Almost savagely Adderly growled: "Damn' fine."

"Good thing you didn't try to kill me for my map—'twouldn't make no sense to you," Dale commented.

"Why?"

"Account of Turner, my later partner, explained the true meanings behind certain marks." Dale paused. "Too bad he perished durin' the tempest."

Frowning, Adderly fused beetling brows. "Meanin'?"

"That to murder me 'thout understandin' what those marks mean would lead you to no treasure."

"You got a mighty tellin' point there," the Bermudian ad-mitted. "What course d'you suggest plottin'?"

"To start off, I don't see sense in splittin' the plunder more ways than's absolutely necessary. Do you?"

"'Course not."

Dale peered blankly over darkening Great Sound at the low and distant loom of Spanish Point and several rocky islets short of it. Finally he drawled, "Suppose you've been wonderin' over Moog, too? How much he knows."

"I have. What *is* he anyhow?"

"A good A.B. and what us New Englanders term 'a mixed-breed,' him bein' part Mohawk Indian and part white. Alto-gether he's a tough, unpredictable character who, though he keeps pretty silent, don't miss much."

Abram queried: "How much he know?"

"Only the general nature of what I've got in here." A

callused and tar-stained forefinger tapped the cincture. "Ain't nowise certain what he might be plannin' on."

The Bermudian sighed, pulled out and methodically loaded a well-blackened short clay pipe. "No point worryin' on that score. Easy to get him out of the way; kill him or sell him into slavery. You know? There's not a few North American savages held in bondage on these Islands right now."

"Might do that to some other redskin but not Moog—he's part Mohawk. That's not to say he just mightn't meet with a bad accident if and when we locate the treasure." A mirthless chuckle escaped the New Englander. "Always provided Moog don't scrag us first."

Adderly paused with tinder box poised, uttered a rasping laugh. "B'God, Jack, ye're a man arter me own heart. We're a bloody rough lot in Bermuda—West End 'specially."

"Don't act surprised, Abram, life on the New England frontier ain't a bed of roses, either; a man can't even be certain he'll wake up wearin' his hair come next sunup. Ye'd understand that, had you been on Jeremesquam Point last summer.

"Since we'll likely to need help in findin' and unearthin' the treasure suppose we offer Moog an eighth share? He'll keep mum, cause he's got no one to blab to lest he comes across some fellow Injun he can trust—which ain't likely from what I've seen."

"We'll have to chance that," Adderly said after momentary deliberation. "How can we use him?"

"Since I don't know for sure *which* cove is the one we want, why don't Moog start fishin', casual-like, close off the tip of this Island and see if he can spot a wreck which could be the *Santa Ana?* An he succeeds, 'twould give us a better idea 'bout where we'd ought to start searchin'."

The Bermudian looked suspicious. "Then you *don't* know where to go lookin'?"

"No. You've my word on that. Map gives no name or clear indication except that a certain cove lies somewheres near the end of this island."

"All right, I'll let Moog knock off work a mite early. Can he swim?"

"Better'n a salmon. Then there's another fact you'd better know."

Gently, Adderly's fingers again closed on his knife's handle. "Such as?"

The New Englander slipped out his own sheath knife and deliberately commenced to whittle an Indian prayer stick out of a piece of driftwood. "Pegeen knows about the map. For a fact, 'twas only through her I thought to strip this belt off Turner's body afore we heaved it overside."

"How come he died?"

"Like I said, his head got stove in durin' the great tempest," Dale stated without batting an eye. "She'll *have* to be in the know." Noting a scowl on Adderly's leathery forehead, he added: "Don't fret, whatever share Pegeen gets will come out of my portion."

"Fair enough," grunted the Bermudian. "Still, I don't fancy so many people being in on this."

"No worry; she'll keep her trap shut tight nor any oyster, you can lay to that."

"Why?"

"A winsome young female like her can't be sure about her future an I'm not 'round to look after her. Besides, she'll come in useful; she's smart and as handy around a vessel as most boys and she ain't a bad cook."

Successive flocks of cahows, departing from burrows for nightly foraging, raised an eerie unearthly clamor. Early explorers had deemed this to be the cries of devils, so originally they had named Bermuda "The Isle of Devils!"

After a pause, Dale said, "Best we get this straight; you and I are to go equal shares in the *Dove*—treasure or no treasure?"

Adderly reared back, snorting, "An we don't come across the plunder why in hell should I grant you a even interest in my ketch?"

"Because my labor and skill at shipbuilding and navigation are well worth it. That's why. With Moog's help we can complete as fast and handy a craft as ever sailed out of Bermuda and in half the time it'd take 'thout our help. Also she'd be twice as fine a vessel and you'd be saving money. I've learned how scarce and costly good labor is in these parts."

Snapped Abram: "What's a master carpenter or joiner earn?"

"Two pounds a day paid in tobacco," came the instant reply. "Sawyers get paid by the hundred foot they cut. But I want to know if you recall the names of any treasure fishers?"

"One was a feller named Blount, came seekin' the wreck of a vessel he called the *Saint Anne,* or somethin' like that. Found her remains all right but there weren't no treasure aboard—least so he claimed."

Puffing on his evil-smelling pipe Adderly continued: "Then, not so far back, came a feller name of Southwood; claimed he was an astronomer. Him and his party hunted till he got discouraged and went away growlin' that mayhap 'twas just as well the treasure weren't found on account of 'twas guarded by fire-breathin' dragons and that if a body even did clap eyes on the loot he'd get blinded for life. Often wondered why Southwood searched so hard *on land.* All the rest worked on the wreck."

Dale knew, but didn't feel ready to reveal something Turner had confided during a drunken moment. Apparently the *Santa Ana* had been driven aground so close to Ireland Island that her captain had decided to have her treasure rafted ashore for safer hiding.

Dale cast loose laces securing the scuffed and oily cincture then, seeking a flat rock, smoothed out a ragged rectangle of badly wrinkled yellow-brown parchment. Its markings, though apparently rendered in waterproof India ink, had grown badly faded and faint.

"Well, Abram, there she is. See what you can make of this."

Surf thundered dully among reefs and boilers, cahows swooped and raised their unearthly clamor. Abram Adderly sank onto sinewy hams to peer at the parchment as a man dying of thirst stares on a cup of water.

[*156*]

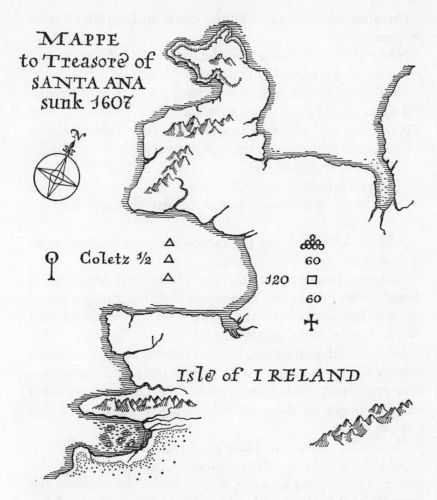

MAPPE
to Treasore of
SANTA ANA
sunk 1607

Coletz ½

Isle of IRELAND

"Umm. This here does show somethin', but what in Hell do them markin's mean?"

"That's for me to know and you to guess about."

Adderly planted a black-nailed thumb on the square.

"What do this box signify? What's the meaning of them things like piled cannon balls?"

A faint smile twitched at the New Englander's scarlet-brown features. "I ain't too sure, Abram, and that's God's truth. While we're guessin' suppose you tell me what you make of that cross below the box, and the meanin' of those numbers?"

On purpose, no doubt, Turner never had explained their purpose.

"Only that the treasure must be hid on land. Ye've proved yer point, so rest easy—I can't do nothin' 'thout ye."

Dale thought, 'Till after we locate the loot. Aloud he said, "In good time I'll speak about what I've kept secret. Now suppose you say where to look for the cove marked Coleta with a kite or something of the sort alongside it."

"What's Coleta stand fer?"

"Coleta is Spanish for cove."

"And could that ½ and those three triangular reefs identify it?"

Adderly kept studying the ragged rectangle of parchment obviously trying to memorize it.

"Offhand I can't answer that but I'll try to locate the cove though 'twon't prove easy on account of this here map is pretty crude and mayn't be accurate." He got up while Dale refolded his parchment, pulled at his beard, then said, "Got me a idea. Suppose I hold jollification, say to celebrate me and 'Manda's tenth wedding day, and invite certain folks who off-and-on have speculated on hidden treasure? Given sufficient drink someone might let drop, all unknowing, a tip which might come in handy."

"So you've been married that long? Don't show it much."

Adderly chuckled. "Funny thing, most people livin' to-gether in these parts are only married under the common law but me and 'Manda got spliced legal-like. Expect you and Peg likely will join up one way or the other someday."

When Dale made no comment the Bermudian drew several whiffs on his malodorous pipe—Bermuda-grown tobacco being plentiful but far from aromatic.

"Suppose you know that whilst Peg was ravin' sick she let the cat out o' the bag, 'llowed you and her ain't married."

Dale's squarish features stiffened. "Yes. I've been told so. What of that?"

"Nothin'! Plenty of couples don't bother to get hitched

either way so there'll be small gossip if you start knockin' together a shack for the two of ye."

On a small, sandy cove fringed by yellowwood trees and ash-green cedars lying a scant hundred yards south of Abram Adderly's ramshackle home, John Dale a few days later started a hut.

What he built was a rough but sturdy affair contrived out of driftwood planks and cedar boards laboriously cut by Moog and himself in Adderly's sawpit. Its roof of yellow-brown dried palmetto fronds was skillfully thatched by friends and neighbors.

Nearly completed, the shelter was just large enough to accommodate a rough plank table, a few stools, and a corded bed barely wide enough to hold a couple of larger-than-ordinary people.

While twilight deepened Pegeen remained near the water's edge awkwardly repairing a fish net ripped by a shark.

Sounds of hammering prompted her to glance over a bare brown shoulder and watch the mixed-blood and her "husband" hammer into place hinges of heavy leather supporting the door, the hut's only entrance.

So this, Pegeen told herself, is to be the very first home of my own. How different from that log cabin Tom had been raising. 'Twill serve for a time but I'm damned if 'twill satisfy me overlong."

Blankly, Pegeen Hammond peered over the Great Sound. How lonely it was here—beautiful to be sure, but so very empty; seldom could a body sight even a single boat let alone a ship. In the whole encircling panorama only three small white roofs were visible among distant undulating and dark-green hills.

True, it had been quite as lonely around Pa's farm but in a different sort of way. Along the river towering evergreens had crowded in on all sides so close they'd masked all but a very few signs of human habitation. In only a few spots around Pa's fort could a body see above a quarter-of-a-mile in any direction.

Tying knot after knot, Pegeen fell to wondering how many folk who'd lived around Hammond's Fort would recognize her nowadays for, during the weeks following her recovery, she'd filled out considerably, especially around her thighs and bosom —which was surprising, considering the monotonous and primitive diet on which she was existing these days.

For a girl barely nineteen her features must have hardened beyond her years, she guessed, as well as her body, for with all the work expected of her from dawn till dusk she'd grown downright tough and muscular.

Over raucous cries of myriad seabirds she heard Dale's deep voice and turned to look. The door now was in place and Jack was fitting a crude wooden latch while Moog, hunkered down alongside, was using his wickedly long sheath knife to carve something out of cedarwood, possibly a catch for the door.

After a few final knots Pegeen was relieved that at long last she no longer was conscious of that dull pain which persistently had gnawed at her lower abdomen. Lord, she must be strong as an ox to have survived not only the seemingly interminable agony of her miscarriage but the well-intentioned yet primitive midwifing of Abram's wife and skinny old Betty Lusher, the Adderly's nearest female neighbor.

For three whole days and nights, they'd told her later on, she'd hovered at death's door repeatedly calling out for somebody named Tom.

Pegeen's nether lip crept between her teeth as it did always when thoughts of Tom Booker entered her mind.

Strange, wasn't it, she should cling to a conviction that, somehow or other, Tom had managed to survive the Abenaki onslaught. Possibly he still lived as a miserable, ignoble captive? Was she clinging to this belief because she'd lost their child?

Naturally, word of her ravings had got about till everyone in the West End knew that when John Dale had declared himself and Pegeen to be man and wife he'd been lying in his teeth.

One evening she noticed the big shipwright sitting slumped

on a log bench and staring fixedly into the sky. Could it be, she wondered, that Jack might be thinking of his lost wife? She went to sit beside him. When she took his hand he kissed her gently. "Reckon we'd better plot a course for ourselves." He'd begun slowly to rub his wide jaw as he did when thinking extra hard. "At sea 'tis held risky to keep cruisin' too long by dead-reckonin' and since it's plain that the two of us are alone and penniless in a damned savage world something had better be done about it."

She made no reply, only kept clear, dark blue eyes intent on his rather small and slightly straddled ones until he said, "Peg, I sense you've got reasons why you don't want us to wed, legal-like, no more than I do."

"What makes you say that?"

"Well, to tell the honest truth I figure neither of us is truly in love with each other. Right?"

Pegeen's deeply sun-burned features flushed while her frowsy auburn head inclined. "That's true, I suppose. What do you think we ought to do?"

"From all I see most couples around these parts live together mostly under the common law. Suppose we do the same?" He looked hard at her. "But if a child should come along we'll get spliced all shipshape and legal."

Using a big toe, she traced aimless circles in the sand before breaking into a slow, wide smile. "What you say makes sense, Jack."

"Good. That bein' understood, I undertake to protect and provide whilst you keep house; we'll share-and-share alike whatever comes."

What he said next came as a distinct surprise.

"Now, Peg, should you ever take a real fancy to a fellow you *might* come to love I'll not break with you, so long as you ain't brazen about it. Me, I reserve the same privilege an I feel so inclined but don't fret on that score. So far I ain't spied ary female fit to hold a candle to you."

Owl-eyed, she said evenly, "sounds like a reasonable arrangement, but in all honesty, Jack, you've got to realize nowadays I don't truly understand myself. So much of what I've always believed in has gone caterwampus I must order my thinking along new lines."

"Ain't a bit surprised; I ain't none too sure of myself, neither, so we'll agree to remain partners till one of us feels a change of heart."

Chapter 18

JOLLIFICATION

AS A DOUBLE CELEBRATION of Abram and Amanda Adderly's tenth wedding and the "roof wetting" of Mr. and Mrs. John Dale's new home, the big-bearded Bermudian held the jollification he'd planned on. Saving for the Fred Lushers, who lived on the opposite end of Ireland Island near Mangrove Bay, all guests arrived by sail or rowboat.

Pegeen, wearing an ill-fitting calico gown but with auburn hair freshly washed and dressed, experienced a thrill of real pride in showing off how she'd contrived to furnish this windowless one-room shack. In it stood a table of cedarwood and a small New England-type chest of drawers; a pair of still-empty shelves above it had been fashioned by the "bridegroom." There was also a handsome European-made bedstead looted from some wreck.

In lieu of chairs, a pair of stump stools equipped with smooth-planed boards to form a back rest did duty for the time being. Pegeen's special pride, however, was a battered but gaily painted Spanish seachest boasting a handsome and now well-shined brass lock more than capable of containing the couple's scant apparel as well as possessions of value—thus far, they weren't numerous.

The "bride" had contrived a few decorations out of pink coral branches and pale lavender sea fans; the hut's floor of fine white sand was clean and even through vigorous use of a palmetto frond sweep.

Everyone of the twenty-odd guests of all ages acted in high spirits; a jollification like this all-too-seldom took place to break the incredibly dull monotony of existence in so sparsely inhabited a locality.

No less than five families complete with toddlers and nursing babies disembarked on the beach alongside that cradle in which the ketch was nearing completion. She was, the neighbors noted, being constructed entirely of cedarwood, in defiance of the Somers Isles Company's recent regulation to the contrary— so rapidly was this favored wood becoming depleted.

As was the custom in this rugged place, guests brought along baskets of food and jugs that gurgled invitingly; some were filled with palmetto wine fermented from the heart tops of such trees.

Long since, Dale had found this drink preferable to rum-bullion, a harsh punch largely based on skull-popping West Indian rum. Pegeen favored palmetto wine, having discovered that a cup or so helped her understand the extraordinary speech and even prompted her to like some of these hairy, uncouth and largely illiterate islanders.

The Tom Gilberts, prominent and influential in the West End, brought along a pair of slaves: one a shiny and very black Negro, the other a sickly looking, pale-skinned Carib Indian about whom Moog commented in lordly contempt: "Him not real redman; him true slave, weak like squaw, never warrior."

Once a huge driftwood bonfire commenced to blaze and crackle children of all ages screeching, raced about and yelling so loud that cats, dogs, and livestock took to the underbrush.

Many were fascinated by a bright red-and-yellow bird which, perched on Captain William Davis's ragged shoulder, screeched and, to their wonderment, uttered wonderful curses in English, Spanish or French.

A pair of Abram Adderly's half-grown goats, sacrificed for the occasion, had been spitted and set to roasting over pits of glowing charcoal along with scrawny fowls, a few ducks, and a great number of cahows—those succulent native birds still so tame and numerous that boys easily could club dozens to death in an hour.

The real gastronomic treat for the occasion, however, was Irish potatoes imported not so long ago and still quite a rarity. Dropped into a cast-iron cauldron of boiling seawater along with a mess of spiny lobsters and blue-fin crabs these proved to be the real tidbits. Fish, especially fancied for flavor such as dolphins, giltheads, amberjacks, groupers, yellowtails, and other varieties were being broiled on low grates.

Once the sun went down the company set-to using clasp knives or fingers to render food into eatable portions.

When liquor began to take hold and the men got "hot"—as the local phrase went—Dale paid close attention to what such tough Captains as Will Peniston, Graham Veale, William Davis, Tom Gilbert, and his one-eyed brother John, were saying.

Once everyone had gorged to repletion, the younger children, uniformly grubby and shaggy, clad in rags and tatters, straggled off to curl up like puppies on the warm sand wherever they chanced to be overcome by sleep. Older youngsters, whooping and yelling tirelessly, played rough and noisy games.

Gradually the females drifted aside leaving their men free to drink, lollygag and smoke around the bonfire which, replenished, was sending lazy spirals of sparks into the purple-black sky.

Dale, having stuck to palmetto wine, remained reasonably sober but felt concerned over the quantities of rumbullion Abram Adderly was downing until he noticed that for once the Bermudian actually was watering his punch.

Soon it became apparent that in general wrecks were of two

[*165*]

basic descriptions; first, vessels which, storm-driven, had met their doom among the cruel tangles of banks and reefs which, off the West End, extended six miles or more in certain directions.

Secondly, there were vessels which even in fair weather had been lured to destruction through false beacon fires lit by certain West Enders on a tall, pointed hill near Eli's Harbor. Farther, cows and horses wearing lanthorns slung to their necks were set to grazing along the shore, successfully counterfeiting the movements of anchored vessels. Such practices had been employed so successfully that the height in question already was becoming known as "Wreck Hill."

Taking care to slur his speech, Dale queried of Captain William nicknamed "Bloody Bill," Davis: "Are the reefs off the East End as dangerous?"

"Not by a jugful," chuckled the huge, hairy fellow, whose round red face was framed in ginger-hued whiskers. "That's why most ships headed for these waters make for Saint George's rather than risk puttin' into Mangrove Bay."

While using a frayed yellow fingernail to pick decaying front teeth, Adderly turned to bittern-thin Fred Lusher. "Say, Fred, didn't I spy you fishin' a lot off the end o' Ireland last spring?"

"Aye. That I was."

"I bin' wonderin' why, since you know as well as the rest of us the best fishin' grounds lie out to the sou'west." He drained his cup. "Don't tell me you was just out cruisin' fer pleasure."

Lusher squirted tobacco juice at the fire, accurately since he lacked front teeth. "Naw. 'Twas because, a spell back, I got took in for a while by a tale about some Spanish galleon gone down off the tip of Ireland Island, God knows how far back. Well, I located the wreck; she lies 'bout half a league off Whipray Cove."

Drawled Captain Tom Gilbert: "You dove on that there wreck?"

Dale cupped an ear over the fire's crackling.

"Aye. Me and the boys worked it a considerable time but

didn't come up with anythin' worth our trouble. Her timbers were too scattered and deep-covered with corals."

"How close to shore does this here wreck lie?" asked Captain Davis.

"Like I said, only half a league, so 'twould ha' been no great trick to raft her cargo to land. Whether she'd any treasure aboard I've no notion. Anyhow, seems those Spanishers built a shallop and set sail for home."

Dale suggested: "Think maybe the Dons took along their riches?"

Bloody Bill Davis belched comfortably, then relighted his pipe from a coal lifted with fingers so thickly callused they seemed impervious to heat. "Doubt it. Their escape vessel must ha' been too small and cranky to risk carryin' treasure."

"Maybe that's why treasure seekers have explored around Ireland off and on," Captain Veale commented.

Adderly inquired thickly, "When'd last party come searchin'?"

"Perhaps eighteen, maybe twenty years ago."

"Anybody ever look about Whipray Cove?"

"They say some did, but found nothin'."

Whipray! A dazzling light burnt in Dale's imagination. *Whipray!* Might that queer, kite-shaped mark beside the word Coleta on Turner's map be a crude representation of a whipray? A covert glance at Adderly convinced him that he too had noted the reference.

The talk ran on other wreck sites, mostly unexplored. These were the remains of French, Flemish, Dutch and Portuguese vessels, but a great majority were of Spanish origin. This, Captain Lusher pointed out, was only reasonable since from time immemorial *flotas* from New Spain, after clearing the West Indies, invariably bore northwards to sight the Bermudas as a sure fix before commencing their long and perilous run to Cádiz.

Big Tom Gilbert, swaying before the bonfire like a tree about to be felled, held a mug poised before his mouth. "T'my mind all treasure-seekers are ijits," he bellowed. "Sensible folk

who aim to prosper, stick to tradin', shipbuildin' or privateerin' and end up a sight better off than rampagin' 'bout the
seas in hopes of raisin' silver and gold which, likely enough,
never went down where they think."

Despite precautions, John Dale was feeling pretty high when
he noticed Moog slumped against a nearby skiff and apparently
plunged into a drunken stupor; this likely was the case. Everyone knew an Indian never could hold liquor worth a thin damn.
However, since the mixed-breed lay sprawled within easy earshot of the bonfire the New Englander lurched over, used a
bare foot to stir Moog, who only mumbled before collapsing
even flatter onto the sand whiffling loudly through his big
broken nose.

On the evening following the jollification, Abram Adderly
followed by a nondescript cur set off for the Dales' shack.
The whale-oil lanthorn he lugged shed a clear bright light only
because its glass, for once, had been wiped.

Advancing, he discovered John and Pegeen seated close together on a half-log bench planted outside their door.

"Well," Abram observed, "I'd say you young folks look
right companionable."

"Aye. We're makin' out, aren't we?"

The girl's wide and ready smile flashed in the lanthorn's
rays but she'd noticeably aged beyond her scant nineteen years.
"Can't complain, Abram, and remain truthful."

Dale brought out a stool and a jug. "Sit you down, friend,
here's a measure of leftover rumbullion. Lord God, what a
jollification."

The bushy-bearded Bermudian nodded. "Ain't that God's
truth! Since I came to 'round midday all the hammers of Hell
bin poundin' my skull." He pointed to the door. "Need to
talk private-like; midges won't torment us so bad inside."

"Reckon you've come for a real good look at my map but,
before I get it out"—Dale was speaking slowly and softly—
"we'd better make certain-sure exactly how we stand 'mongst
ourselves."

"Fair enough. A well-charted course makes for safe cruisin'."

Once the Bermudian had set his lanthorn on the table the three, sweating mildly under the humid heat, stood in awkward silence, their shadows distorted by the rough texture of the palmetto frond roof.

Finally the New Englander said: "Is it clearly understood I'm to own half a share in the *Dove;* win, lose, or draw, and without regard to findin' treasure? We go half and half in that, too."

Pegeen watched the other's hairy sinewy throat contract a few times before he mumbled, "We do."

Once they'd sat down, Dale said, "One thing more, you give your solemn word, Abram, that if somethin' bad happens to me all my share is to go to my—'wife'?" and in any event she's to receive a third part in the treasure."

Adderly frowned. "Don't like such a idee; 'tis bad luck to bring a female direct into a business venture of any sort."

"Nevertheless, that's the way it's going to be or count me out."

"All right, have it your way, but I still don't favor such a notion."

What the New Englander failed to mention was that also he'd promised Pegeen she might sign on aboard the *Dove* as Second Mate if she so wished; secretly, however, he was determined to do everything possible to dissuade her from going to sea.

The Bermudian took a gulp from a coconut shell mug, "Peg's yer responsibility. What about Moog?"

"Don't fret. Out of my share I'll grant him a decent allowance of whatever's found, but he'll have no interest in the *Dove* beyond his pay."

Adderly drained the last of his rumbullion then wiped his mouth on the back of his crippled hand.

"It's up to you to keep the redskin in order. Me, I don't like the look of him and that razor-sharp carver he wears."

"I'll do that but Moog's well aware neither of us trust him so far as you can heave a bull by the tail. Howsumever, we

[*169*]

need his help, 'specially if and when we start digging. Besides, I know he's a first-class seaman."

Pegeen started to feel better once the two men had struck hands and Dale had started to cast loose thongs securing his cincture.

After the New Englander's powerful work-scarred brown hands had flattened the map and weighted its corners with pebbles, he abruptly dashed out of doors and ran a wide circle through bushes hemming in the shack; small use making it easy for anyone to eavesdrop. Moog, least of all.

Reassured, Dale returned indoors and planted a tar-stained forefinger on a symbol which, until last night, he'd figured might represent either a tadpole or a kite. "After what Cap'n Davis let drop, ain't it likely this thing represents a whipray?"

The Bermudian's shaggy black brows merged while his pale eyes shone in the whale-oil lanthorn's glow. "Seems likely. Reckon we'd best scout careful-like around that place marked Coleta which you say is Spanish for cove."

"Where is this cove?"

"Well, at a quick guess I'd say Whipray must be about the third in from the tip of Ireland Island."

"What kind of measurement would a Spaniard use?"

Dale glanced at Pegeen's radiant features. The girl's smooth golden-brown forehead wrinkled momentarily. "Of course, I don't know for sure, but d'you recall, Jack, how, back home, in rough country, distances were measured in strides? Pa used to say such strides averaged about a yard in length."

"B'God, Peg, mayhap you're on the right track! But what does that ½ figure mean? If we were to pace 120 strides 'twould be interestin' to see where we fetch up?"

Excitedly the Bermudian broke in. "If what you say is so then mebbe them figures marked 60 might mean distances measured likewise."

His elation faded when Pegeen commented, "Fair enough, but before we can get anywhere we first have to find that pile of cannon balls or round stones and the location of that cross."

Cheekbones accentuated by the lanthorn's glow, the three

stared blankly on one another until Dale said, "If we hunt careful-like, we'll find 'em, I'll bet on that. Main thing right now is to let nobody suspect what we're about."

"Ye're right," Abram grunted, red-rimmed eyes fixed on the map. "Now here's what I think: lots of folks, youngsters 'specially, like to search the beaches lookin' for ambergris and useful things which sometimes come driftin' ashore. Should any of such folks mark me or Jack rangin' 'round Whipray Cove durin' work hours they might start imaginin' things. God knows there's precious little 'round here for people to think about."

"True, but what're you drivin' at?" Dale queried.

"Suppose Peg wanders aimless-like about the island's end and not only 'round Whipray like maybe she was beachcombing for ambergris. Maybe she can spot them three pointed rocks and see how far out in the Cove they lie—if they are any there. An she's lucky then the three of us can go out afore sunrise and maybe locate them other landmarks."

"'Ambergris'?" Pegeen said, "I keep hearing talk about it. Just what *is* ambergris?"

The Bermudian looked mildly astonished over such monumental ignorance. "Why, Peg, 'tis a substance worth considerably more than the same weight in pure gold. Come across a lump big as yer fist, lass, and ye'll be rich."

"Much found around here?" Dale queried.

"No. Only barely 'nough to keep idle people on the lookout."

Pegeen began setting out wooden plates for a cold snack.

"What does ambergris look like and why is it so precious?"

"Looks like a chunk of pearly-gray beef gristle. Some eddicate fellers say it's somethin' sick whales puke up or shit out."

Dark-blue eyes intent, Pegeen peered across the table. "But wherein lies its great value?"

"Because 'tis used as a base for the rarest and finest perfumes in all the world fit even for you." Adderly leered at the handsome, buxom young woman. "'Tis also supposed to make a old man, an he drinks a decoction of it, feel randy as a spring

[*171*]

cockerel." He snickered. "Reckon yer husband won't need a swig of ambergris for a good while yet. Like me."

Adderly raised his refilled mug. "Well, friends, here's to swift findin' of the loot!"

Chapter 19

THE CACHE

EARLY NEXT DAY Pegeen hurriedly braided sun-bleached bronze-hued hair and secured it beneath a faded blue bandanna before picking up a wicker market basket. In no great hurry, she started off along the beach below the shack where she found Jack and Abram already sweating over the ketch. As she passed, frowsy and barefooted, they treated her only with brief nods.

While passing she noted that, as a part of the ketch's bow, a sturdy support had been rigged to accommodate an overlong bowsprit Jack was insisting upon.

Casually swinging her basket, Pegeen skirted a series of coves and inlets serrating Ireland Island's western shore—no point indicating to a chance observer the direction she really intended to follow.

At a leisurely rate the girl pretended to search tide-bared stretches of sand for scallops and even waved to a pair of shock-haired Adderly boys who, naked as jay birds, were diving for conchs and spiny lobsters.

Once a hillock obscured the Adderly's cottage and its untidy surroundings, Pegeen turned left, cut across to the peninsula's western shore and soon started wading knee-deep along a succession of small, sandy beaches separated by bush-crowned ridges of gray-white Aeolian sandstone. She took care in traversing such outcrops whose edges often proved painfully sharp. By now she'd learned that cuts inflicted by such rock took a very long time to heal.

Unhurriedly, Pegeen worked northward, stopping every now and then to haul a promising bit of driftwood above the high water mark.

At length she crossed a small ridge and, breath quickening, sighted Whipray Cove. She judged the ebb must have started sometime ago, so, if Abram Adderly's reasoning had been sound, she might soon be able to watch waves begin to break over three, pointed rocks rising near the center of this especially lovely emerald-blue cove.

Driving before her a half-wild nanny goat and a pair of sportive black-and-white kids, Pegeen made her way down to the beach and started to wade seawards. Long since she'd hiked her shapeless calico skirt about her thighs then tucked its hem into her belt.

She debated whether, in this isolated spot, to risk stripping completely, but decided against it, not on the grounds of modesty but simply because the sun's heat already was growing too intense for complete exposure. She continued to splash along, thigh-deep, keeping her attention on the Cove's center.

No rocks yet had become visible out yonder. Perhaps the tide remained too high? With warm wavelets lapping her buttocks, Pegeen began collecting scallops with delicately striped brown-and-white shells and depositing them in her basket. There always remained a chance that a child might appear foraging for palmetto berries among the tree and bush covered high ground hemming in Whipray Cove.

Let's see now, she mused, those rocks seemed to lie near the outer center of this cove, but how far out? Thwarted for the time being, she watched the sparkling maneuvers of a flock of delicately shaped snow-white birds whirling and diving on terrified smallfry near the Cove's entrance.

Wouldn't this tide ever go out? Pegeen waded ashore, set down her basket, then settled onto a wave-smoothed driftwood log, sensuously enjoying its warmth against her wet bare bottom and allowed her thoughts to run backwards.

From now on, how would matters likely proceed between her and Jack? In tenderly rough fashion he was considerate and undemanding beyond gratifying her surmounting need for physical satisfaction. If only memories of Tom would stop haunting her.

What she liked least about her present situation was being so utterly dependent upon her "husband." As a case in point, what about that agreement granting her no *outright* share in the future; only whatever Jack might feel pleased to give her?

A flock of dainty, gray-and-black golden plover skimmed by, piping plaintively, then settled on the beach and started to tip and run about feeding on minute sea worms. Weren't such delicate birds fitting inhabitants for this lovely, lonely little piece of Heaven on earth?

Pegeen selected a flat pebble, then expertly skipped it out over translucent water just as she'd once flung such a stone over the Sheepscot's dark-brown current.

All at once she sprang to her feet, aware that near the Cove's center a dark, pointed object ringed with foaming water had appeared. Then, moments later, a second point appeared roughly twenty yards to the right of the first; when a third dark triangle showed among gentle swells rolling in from the ocean, Pegeen's heart started thumping as it had not since her run from Hammond's Fort.

Tilting her face skyward, she flung wide her arms and yelled at circling seabirds: "Oh Lord, I thank Thee! I thank Thee!"

Pegeen waded out until a very deep trough in the bottom forced her to halt with warm sea water licking and swirling about her breasts. Since she couldn't swim a stroke she had to stay where she was. She faced about and studied every detail of the shoreline intensely, for, somewhere off to the left, should lie a cairn of cannon balls or rounded stones. Soon she discovered that because of low trees, bushes, and tufts of tall beach grass she could from this point discern absolutely nothing of significance.

What about that cross? She peered to her right but could spy nothing faintly resembling a crucifix among a grove of yellow-wood trees.

The girl calculated she at present was standing some thirty yards short of the three rocks so, since the trough remained too deep to cross, she commenced wading back to the beach and at the same time tried to count her strides towards the high-water mark but quickly discovered this to be impossible—swells kept throwing her off balance. Nevertheless, Pegeen waded inshore in as straight a line as possible at right-angles to the line of rocks and kept on peering to either side, but sighted neither a cross nor a cairn nor any indication that such might ever have existed.

Dripping, she decided to hunt for the cross first. Possibly a few fragments of it might remain? No. Since the *Santa Ana* had been wrecked some sixty years ago commonsense warned that such a hope must be frail.

Doggedly the bronzed young woman circled and got badly scratched by underbrush in the process. Whenever her bare feet trod cactus she spouted obscenities she'd never dreamed existed a year ago.

She met with no better luck in locating a group of rounded objects inland and to the left of these pyramid-shaped black rocks now half-exposed and speckled with barnacles.

Midday heat rendered Pegeen so giddy she had to seek shade. She felt better once she soaked her bandanna and, employing a pad of wet seaweed for extra protection, tied it back into place. After lowering her sodden skirt she headed for home in a morose mood. Home? Did that rough built shack really constitute a home? Perhaps not, but she reckoned she'd better deem it such a while longer, but not for keeps, no siree. Pegeen Hammond felt destined to preside over far more luxurious establishments; on this subject she entertained a forceful if inexplicable conviction.

While skirting the third beach down the shore from Whipray Cove, she noticed a sizable patch of bright-yellow Sargasso weed in which an object seemed entangled. Likely 'twas only some dead bird or a piece of flotsam.

What she discovered on splashing out was only an ugly shapeless blob of greasy-looking matter about the size of a turnip and giving off faint, iridescent hues. Picking it up she was repelled by this lump's slimy texture. What in the world could it be? The remains of some sea creature ground to bits among the reefs? No. The blob's texture didn't resemble that of any fish she'd encountered. Possibly this might be part of a giant octopus or a squid?

All at once she remembered something. Could this disgusting lump possibly be ambergris? Of course not. Not for nothing had Pegeen Hammond been born under what Captain Phips would have termed an unlucky star—hadn't recent events demonstrated as much? But what if this slippery mess she was holding between callused hands really was ambergris?

After a considerable spell of soul-searching she decided to keep mum, even to Jack, for, if only half of what she'd heard concerning the value of this repulsive substance was correct, dazzling possibilities blazed in her imagination. Aye, by the great jumping Jesus, as Jim Turner would have put it, she'd find a secure hiding place and wait till perhaps she could sense that direction in which the Wheel of Fortune might turn.

Neither Jack nor Captain Adderly acted overly impressed that she'd spotted the three rocks so readily, but dwelt on her failure to identify other fix-points shown on Turner's map.

This prompted a number of furtive explorations, which revealed neither a cairn nor the remains of a cross. Only then was it decided to take Moog into their confidence. The half-Mohawk, Dale figured, most likely had an Indian's eye for ground and might notice significant details which readily might escape European observation.

Patiently, the four continued to range about growths of wind-twisted cedars, yellowwood trees and scrub on low heights enclosing Whipray Cove.

On the fifth survey the half-breed drew attention to a number of yellowish, sea-rounded stones of volcanic origin scattered and half-buried about an area in which outcroppings of weathered gray sandstone predominated.

Still not daring to hope, John Dale planted a stick at the approximate center of that scattering of volcanic stones.

Adderly fingered his swart beard. "Well, 'ppears like the redskin just might be puttin' us onto somethin'!"

"So far, so good," Pegeen agreed, "but this don't do us much good till we can find some trace of the cross or that square with 60 drawn to either side."

Next afternoon the New Englander zigzagging patiently through the scrub above Whipray Cove, noticed a bronze nailhead barely visible amid shaggy bark on the trunk of a largish yellowwood. Peeling off the bark he discovered a second nail hard driven into the wood about two feet to the right of the first.

Hands commencing to quiver, he probed the trunk's covering, found a third bronze nail roughly embedded and equidistant to the left. Next, he located a fourth nailhead about a yard below the other three and raised a whoop so loud the others came arunning. Once they recognized the cross-shaped pattern of the nailheads and understood the implications they capered about, babbling like idiots and slapping each other on bottom and back. Moog raised an eerie, ear-piercing scalp yell.

Spring being well advanced dusk lingered, permitting Adderly and Dale to take a bearing on that branch marking the cairn.

"Now, lest I ain't much mistook," stated the Bermudian, "if we measure sixty strides in this direction from yonder stone pile, then take sixty paces from this tree towards the stones we ought to come on the place where that square we've seen nothin' of is supposed to be."

Pegeen asked: "But what about that '120' on the beach?"

Adderly said: "I think we'll find that the square lies about a hundred and twenty paces above high water. So after we've run a line from the cross and the cairn the box ought to lie where a line from the beach cuts across it."

Dale nodded. "You're making sense, Abram. Let's first run a line between the fix points and see what happens."

After Moog had paced sixty strides from the cairn and Dale had done the same from the cross they ended up face-to-face but, search as they might, discovered nothing whatsoever unusual in the sandy gray ground.

The New Englander marked the meeting point by planting another stick. "Now suppose us fellows each takes one hundred and twenty strides up from high water at right angles to those three rocks?"

The result proved encouraging; one hundred and twenty paces from the beach brought all three men close to that point where Pegeen stood waiting besides Dale's stick marker. But nothing significant was noticeable.

Moog fingered his battered nose a moment before grunting, "Mebbe not mean much, but me notice land here lower by a little."

Pegeen was first to sense that if their calculations were correct at the moment they should be standing approximately on the site of that hollow square on Jim Turner's map. Moog was right; they were standing in a slight, rectangular depression all but concealed beneath beach bushes; but conceivably this was only a natural declivity. However, it had grown so dark it was impossible to investigate further at present. Besides, in order not to attract attention, they'd fetched along no digging implements, which was just as well since "gold fever" was so addling their judgment that despite previous precautions they would have risked digging in broad daylight.

As luck would have it, a full gale accompanied by vicious rain squalls arose during the night, rendering it impossible for small craft to venture out. Such weather also discouraged aimless wandering about.

The oddly assorted quartet now dug with frenzied intensity. In order more efficiently to drive her spade into the sandy soil Pegeen had donned a pair of her "husband's" brogans. From a stake driven into the depression's center they dug trenches three feet deep, fanning outwards along varying quadrants.

Sweating like a June bride, as Will Phips would have said, Abram suddenly commented: "Say, this hollow's kind of squarish and about the size of a biggish vessel's main-hatch cover."

Before long his comment became substantiated; a number of iron nails, badly rusted but still recognizable, were turned up.

Presently Moog uttered a low whoop and held up a section of decayed but expertly joined wood. In Abram Adderly's opinion the wood was mahogany which, he explained, shipbuilders in the old days had used lavishly in the construction of vessels in New Spain.

"Aye. That hollow square *could* represent a hatch cover and this"—he fingered the section of rotting wood—"could be a corner of it," conjectured the New Englander. "What with these nails 'tis my guess that whomsoever buried somethin' here rigged a hatch cover to protect the hole before buryin' the whole business."

With renewed energy the four dug furiously until Adderly, plying his shovel along the edge of the deepening pit, suddenly straightened screeching, "My God! *Look*! Look at this!" He held up a dully gleaming gold coin.

It was a crudely shaped oval and obviously hand-struck but this piece-of-eight nevertheless was stamped with a cross separating the Royal arms of Spain. What really interested the half-naked and wild-eyed treasure hunters was that here was gold, *gold*, GOLD!

Pegeen started to weep. Dale, Adderly, and then the half-breed by turns kissed and caressed the find. Then the searchers plied their spades again and turned up only fragments of coarse red pottery.

Expectations soared when four smaller gold pieces—half-doubloons—and a dozen or so silver pieces-of-four reales came to light, but after that, dig where they would nothing more of interest was turned up, beyond a woman's gold ring set with a small emerald.

Rain squalls continued to flail them but without even pausing to gulp a mouthful of food the diggers, hands blistered and backs aching, dug deeper. Dale's spade next turned up four links of a gold chain of sufficient weight and length to encourage the nearly exhausted diggers to extend their area of search.

When darkness finally closed in they stood, with bleeding hands, panting and trembling. Only then did they start for home avoiding each other's eyes.

At daybreak the diggers extended the circumference of the dig and deepened their hole till they encountered bedrock. Only then did an inescapable, stunning fact sink in. Parties unknown already must have rifled the cache.

Only Moog appeared unaffected.

Pegeen cried a little, then limped away and sat down staring blankly out to sea as if seeking an answer to some vital but insuperable problem.

Adderly, spouting wild curses, briefly went berserk and rushed about slashing at the underbrush with his spade.

As for Dale, he drew a series of deep, deep breaths then began to laugh harshly and ended by digging up from its hiding place the bag containing the sum of their pitiful find and fondled all the coins. So this was what Spanish silver and gold looked like? Oddly enough, he experienced an inexplicable certainty that, before he was done, he'd caress many similar coins.

Chapter 20

COMPACT

THAT EVENING the Bermudian fetched a half-gallon of black Demerara to the Dales' hut; that he'd already been sampling the liquor was only too apparent.

Silently Pegeen filled two coconut shell tumblers, then poured herself a half-measure.

"Take care, Peg," Dale warned sharply. "This stuff can raise blisters on a billy-goat's arse."

Abram Adderly proved in a vicious mood; his talk a pointless flow of profanity.

After a while the big New Englander snapped: "Easy, Abram, no point tryin' to drown your sorrows. Better face facts."

"Where's that goddam Injun?"

"Dunno. I ain't spied him since we got back."

Pegeen kicked together embers smoldering in the outdoor fireplace she usually cooked on.

Dale sighed. "Tell me, Abram, what sort of price d'you figure those coins and the other bits and pieces might command?"

"Dunno. Everythin' depends where they're offered. I'll hazard on these Islands you might, after plenty of sharp bargainin', touch 'round sixty-seventy pounds, nowhere near enough to finish the ketch the way you and me have been plannin' on." The New Englander spat into trampled sand at his feet. "No use blinkin' that fact. Peg, fix us another tot."

Once she'd disappeared inside, Dale looked hard at Adderly while sparks floated upwards and acrid smoke momentarily drove aside swarming mosquitoes. "You know why, all along, I've been wantin' to build the *Dove* extra-sturdy?"

"Sure, all along I've known why you set such powerful deck braces and cut deck plankin' extra thick," grunted the Bermudian.

That Jack had been right about the strength of Demerara rum, Pegeen was ready to concede after only a couple of swallows: the firelit scene had started to shift and waver. Half-mumbling she inquired, "Why did you do so, Jack?"

The New Englander finished his drink. "Hadn't counted on explainin' till we found out 'bout the blasted treasure but now I will. Those braces and planking are sufficient strong to bear the weight of three or maybe four light carriage guns to a broadside."

Adderly goggled. "But that ain't possible in a craft of her size!"

"Take it easy, Abram; what we'll mount won't go heavier than 6-pounders—plus a pair of swivel guns mounted on the rail. Properly handled, they will let us beat off vessels of the same tonnage, short of a regular man-of-war."

A pair of curs slunk out of the underbrush, squatted and stared across the fire, eyes yellow-green and extra luminous since the night was very dark. Dale felt relieved, were Moog in the vicinity these animals wouldn't have come, since dogs here, as elsewhere, detested Indian scent.

Adderly queried: "I still want to know why you figger you need such armament on a common trader?"

Pegeen arose and went over to sit by her "husband," masking a serious effort to shake off the effects of the drink. Something warned that a conversation was about to ensue which might well affect the course of the future she'd determined upon.

Dale said: "Think a minute, Abram, and you'll see that, properly armed and carrying a largish crew we could touch at plenty of ports and islands and cruise in waters most traders our size wouldn't dare visit for fear of being prized by privateers or any pirate who raised our tops. See my point?"

"Aye. Go on."

"Since, over the years, you've voyaged plenty about those latitudes I trow you could name many rich little ports itching to do business which they daren't transact for fear of pickaroons, privateers, and buccaneers."

"Aye. For a long spell I been hankerin' to trade with islands like Redonda, Antigua, Marie Galante and Les Saintes."

The Bermudian's hoarse voice gathered force. "Satan's codpiece! when I think on the prices British goods would fetch down there I'm agreeable to armin' the *Dove*."

Pegeen tilted dregs out of her shell onto the sand, deciding she despised the taste of rum. "But cannons, powder, and shot and other weapons come dear, don't they?"

"Ye can bet yer pretty tits on that," Abram growled. "Armaments don't come cheap anywhere, least of all down to Saint George's. Them East Enders are the worst pack of thieves this side of Hell. They'd sell their sisters to a Moor were the price right." He cast a penetrating glance at the deeply tanned and full-blown girl across the fireplace. "Why's a female like you interested?"

Pegeen evaded by saying a trifly thickly, "How much d'you figure it'd take to arm the *Dove* the way Jack wants and to buy a set of sound sails?"

"More'n I like to think on. Anyhow, since the treasure ain't to be found what in Hell's the use our gabbin' 'bout what might ha' been?"

Once his jug had been emptied, Abram Adderly swayed onto enormous callused brown feet. "Well, g'night, folks, reckon I'd better get home afore I have to crawl back to 'Manda."

"Grand idea," solemnly agreed the New Englander. "Tomorrow we can start figurin' on how to shave costs."

Once Abram had lurched out of sight, Dale passed an arm about Pegeen, kissed her with unusual ardor. "All evenin', girl, you been lookin' better and better."

Liquor-warmed, she pressed urgently against his hard body. "If that's the way you're feeling why don't we turn in?"

"'Turn in'? Why not here? 'Ain't no one about."

"Ground's a poor substitute for a bed." Pegeen fought down a suspicion that her distaste for love in the open stemmed from recollections of those few precious times she and Tom had lain together among the alders back of Hammond's Fort—mosquitoes or no mosquitoes.

Pegeen Dale, as finally she was learning to call herself, by now had become sufficiently artful to let her partners worry for a few days, and was in no hurry to seek a deep hole in the rocks in which lay the supposed ambergris.

Before starting supper tonight she sought the boatyard, arrived in time to see the two men donning ragged blue-and-white jerseys.

She announced with convincing diffidence, "Think I've lately found somethin' maybe valuable. Come look at it." Without pausing she led them into the hut.

"Before I show you what I've found," said she evenly, "let me remind you I was present when you two struck partnership in the ketch: share and share alike."

"True. What of it?"

"Is that contract still binding?"

Dale shot a hard look at the Bermudian, who said: "What's that to you, Sis?"

Pegeen chose words with care. "Since our highfalutin hopes

about the treasure have come to naught, I figure you both have done a bit of second-thinking."

Dale said, pulling a strip of sun-dried skin off his forearm, "Of course. We'll have to cut corners outfittin'."

Deliberately, Pegeen seated herself on the log bench, picked up a palm leaf and fanned herself. It was fun watching these brawny fellows squirm. "How much money is needed to arm and finish the ketch the way you wanted?"

Adderly sighed, used his crippled hand to scratch his crotch. "Near two hunder' pounds, but what's that to you?"

Well aware that what she was about to say likely might mark a turning point in her life, the girl said softly: "If I can find the money you need would you grant me a third share in the *Dove* and her earnings?"

"Holy Jesus!" The Bermudian towered above the seated girl hands working spasmodically by his sides. "You've found 'nother part of the treasure and kept mum. Speak up, you bitch, where've you hid it?"

Dale interrupted harshly. "Don't go off at half-cock, Abram. I know Pegeen better 'n anyone. Whatever she is or ain't, she's no part of a cheat!"

Adderly's discolored and gapped teeth exposed themselves in a grimace. "That's as may be. Then how else would she come by wealth of that sort?"

"Won't tell till you promise me a third share."

Adderly shouted, "To hell with that! I ain't splittin' hard-won profits with no silly female."

Dale hesitated. "That's 'way too stiff a price."

Pegeen, having learned something about haggling, pretended to deliberate. "Well, then, suppose you grant me a quarter-share, fair and square, then maybe I'll find the money you need so bad."

Silence ensued in which the bicker and screams of clouds of seabirds wheeling endlessly above Ireland Island sounded unnaturally loud.

Finally Adderly said sullenly: "An you make good your talk, a quarter-share in all ventures will be yours but, damn yer eyes, an you try cozening me you'll find yer pretty throat slit so neat you scarce won't notice it."

Pegeen's chin went up and she glared at the Bermudian. "Keep your bargain and I'll keep mine. Do I have your word of honor, Jack Dale, I'm to enjoy quarter-share in the *Dove* and any profits earned by her?"

"I so do. Now speak up. Where is the money and how'd you come by it?"

She told them about the ambergris, disappeared into the hut and brought out a small, leaf-covered basket silently praying her trove would prove to be what she believed.

It did.

Part III

TIDES OF INTRIGUE

Chapter 21

H.B.M.S. SALEE ROSE

THE AFTERNOON of April 8, 1685, proved unusually hot and humid, but on occasion sudden rain squalls caused frothing whitecaps to erupt amid a tangle of reefs through which a big-nosed and monosyllabic Pequot Indian slave-pilot was conning H.B.M.S. sixth-rate, *Salee Rose.*

The twenty-first son of James and Mary Phips had put on weight during the eight years since he'd quit shipbuilding in Boston to establish and expand a lucrative trade with the West Indies. No fat, however, was visible on his wide, mahogany-hued features, torso or on long legs sturdy as topgallant yards.

Employing a hoarse bellow instead of a speaking trumpet, Captain Phips ordered Union Jacks hoisted to all topmasts plus his wholly unauthorized commodore's pennant. He then instructed Francis Rogers to prepare to salute a brace of small stone forts guarding the entrance to a narrow channel affording access to the spacious and blue-green waters of Towne Harbour on the north side of which showed the white roofs of Saint George's, capital of the Bermuda Summer Isles.

Beetling brow merged, the *Salee Rose*'s Captain reflected that, disappointed though he now stood, nevertheless he'd made good his perfervid boast: "Some day I'll command a King's ship." But what a scarecrow of a Royal vessel this command had become what with her dark-blue paint grown patchy and blistered through long months under a merciless sun and her standing rigging badly in need of tarring or replacement. Her canvas had deteriorated into veritable Joseph's coats of patches and panels varying from pale gray through yellow to deep-brown. Sadly, his *Salee Rose* didn't begin to approximate the Royal Navy's minimum standards.

Catching up a dented brass speaking trumpet, Phips ordered topsails braced in compliance with his pilot's instructions and winced over the slovenly way the saluting cannon's crew slouched to stations. But what else could one expect of such a collection of blackguards, scrapings of Caribbean parts who, as a rule, had signed Articles only a few jumps ahead of the law.

He glanced at his helmsman, and once more rejoiced that Fast Otter had survived an epidemic of especially virulent smallpox which, in Port Royal, had killed Red Fish and had decimated the miserable crew he'd signed on at Deptford nearly two years ago. What a bunch of mutinous, murderous bastards they'd proved themselves!

Sailing slowly, H.B.M.S. *Salee Rose*, 180 tons, sixteen guns, and manned by a complement of forty-five officers and hands, left the labyrinth of reefs astern and pointed her stubby bow-sprit towards a pair of insignificant-appearing limestone forts guarding opposite sides of the harbor's entrance. Union flags stirring above them were badly faded and frayed.

Phips turned to Francis Rogers, his saturnine First Officer, an intelligent and versatile individual too tactless and straight-forward for his own advancement.

"Well, Mr. Rogers, and what d'you make of this so-called 'Isle of Devils'?"

"Can't say, sir, but to my mind 'Isle of Devils' don't seem so fit a name. This is as pretty a place as I've sighted in a long while. Look at all those pretty little islands and the rounded hills couched in greenery behind 'em."

"That may be, but bear in mind the saying 'handsome is as handsome does.' Over the years I've heard a deal of wild reports concerning the inhabitants of these islands. Plenty of 'em are reputed to be wreckers, privateers, or downright pirates and as for greed, 'tis claimed most Bermudians would try down a mouse for its fat."

Through a verdigris-greened brass telescope Phips narrowly inspected the forts while the bronze-skinned pilot ordered helm shifted two points to starboard.

"Notice, Rogers, flags on both batteries are flying at half-mast."

Lieutenant Rogers attempted levity: "No doubt lamenting the ruin of the last virgin in these islands."

Fabric creaking audibly, the little sixth-class entered the channel. Out of courtesy Phips ordered the colors lowered to half-mast while preparing to salute the port.

"Fire number one!" Phips bellowed, "and for Christ's sake, Rogers, see our salutes are fired exactly one minute apart."

Discipline ashore also must be indifferent; all the *Salee Rose*'s six salutes had boomed and started echoes rumbling among a group of low hills rising back of this tiny colony's capital before the batteries first spouted smoke in acknowledgment of a Royal ship's arrival.

When he noted how tortuous was this channel, Phips felt justified in having paid a pilot well for all the *Salee Rose*'s pay chest was so near empty its iron bottom easily could be discerned.

Even though the *Salee Rose*, Algerian-built and captured from Barbary pirates only a few years earlier, had proved a handy sailer, transit of this channel remained hazardous. Time and again, the impassive big-nosed Pequot at the last moment avoided obstacles till he'd conned the ship to a sheltered anchorage off Gallows Island. There, he ordered topsails and jibs struck and the ship's remaining anchor which when dropped trailed a wake of silvery bubbles visible a long way due to unbelievably clear, light-green water.

Following considerable delay a portly claret-complexioned quarantine officer was rowed out, to puff up the Jacob's ladder. Sweating hard, he offered a slack salute in the quarterdeck's direction only because this was a King's ship.

Next, he clambered to the quarterdeck on which Captain Phips, Lieutenant Rogers and Mr. Charles Salmon, the King's round-faced treasury agent stood waiting in wide-straw hats and mildewed white linens.

"Why do you fly your flags at half-mast?" Phips demanded.

"Why, sir, them flags is lowered on account of we've just got word His Majesty, King Charles II, is dead."

King Charles dead. It seemed as if someone suddenly had rammed an icicle up Phips's backside, chilling his innards, God above! Weren't things already bad enough? No. Not by a damn' sight, if the monarch who'd loaned him this little man-of-war indeed was dead. Phips burst into a torrent of livid obscenities. His Star of Fortune seemed to be paling, faltering in its course.

Nevertheless a glimmering of hope remained in that King Charles, having no legitimate heir, but plenty of bastards, probably would be succeeded by James Stuart, the late King's brother and former Duke of York who, William Phips well knew, kept abiding interest in naval matters.

Aye. Even before the *Salee Rose* cleared England, back in '83, the Duke had been devoting considerable time, money, and energy toward restoring the Royal Navy to its usual size and efficiency.

Once canvas had been brailed up and port formalities observed, Phips went ashore, his main purpose being to gauge the local state of affairs. From the Port Captain he ascertained that Sir Richard Coney, the Somers Island Company's present Governor of Bermuda, was a sadly frustrated official; this lovely, peaceful-appearing little colony actually was seething with political, economic and religious unrest. According to him, the Somers Island Company, having ruled under Royal patent since 1612, had so misgoverned the colonists they were petitioning the Crown to revoke the Company's Charter and re-charter Bermuda as a Crown Colony in order to conduct their affairs in a more liberal and profitable a fashion.

Wearily, the Port Captain explained: "Sir Richard's an able man but the poor devil's hands are tied since the locals won't obey his orders and the Crown refuses to send troops to enforce Company regulations.

"Can't blame the locals too much," the Port Captain continued. "The colonists here now number betwixt four and five thousand and are strictly forbidden to import goods from England save through the Company's magazine ship—that's the official supply vessel which comes here but once a year to off-load and take on cargo.

"Captain, you should read the sky-high prices Company agents place on essential imports!" The official scratched a purplish wart on the side of his nose. "Matters have become so touchy we're all hoping the new King soon will cancel the Company's Charter before a real rebellion breaks out."

As was his custom on arriving in a hitherto unvisited port the *Salee Rose*'s Master invited the Port Captain on board, lounging in a cane chair and comfortable in loose shirt and pantaloons of blue-and-white striped cotton, he put a few pertinent queries and stored the answers in his ample and retentive memory.

Once the guest had stripped off his jacket Phips surveyed the Towne Harbour the glistening waters of which were dotted by a good number of very small, cedar- and palm-grown islands. The little town itself was dominated by Signal Hill, on which stood a wooden tower.

Without comment Phips decided that Saint George's, as a trading center, didn't amount to a hill of beans compared to many ports studding the coast of British North America or such thriving havens as Georgetown, Barbados, or Port Royal in wicked Jamaica, which, for time out of mind had served as a refuge and refitting base for the King's ships as well as buccaneers, pirates, and privateers.

Even Government House appeared unpretentious to say the least and long unpainted.

Aside from a government stone dock the rest of the wharfs were wooden, poorly maintained, and the New Englander rated, significantly devoid of freight. Otherwise, only a few warehouses, a rope walk, and a half-dozen boatyards were to be seen.

On this sultry morning only a few little sloops, skiffs, shallops, and sailing barges traversed the harbour. Perhaps a dozen small native merchantmen lay at anchor off Saint George's Towne. However, one immediately attracted and held Phips's interest. Umm. What was there about yonder ketch's lines which set her apart? What about that overlong bowsprit and the pronounced rake to her masts? Such weren't often seen about the Caribbean except on North American vessels. Again, there was a noticeable lack of tumble home to her sides.

With his pipe's stem Phips pointed. "That big ketch yonder, friend, is she from New England?"

"If you mean the *Dove* ye're mistook, she's Bermuda-built and from the West End. Comes here now and then to water and take on supplies."

"Who owns her?"

The Port Captain fanned away a halo of flies. "Why, sir, 'tis a sort of partnership they say. One of the owner's local, name of Adderly; t'other's a furriner who got wrecked off Ireland Island quite a while ago."

"His name?"

"John Dale—or so he claims."

John Dale! Sharp, tingling sensations pricked at William Phips's fingertips, as usually they did when he was suffering a surprise of the first magnitude. Joy gushed into him in a soul-warming flood. God's glory! Somehow, Johnny must have survived Turner's insane project.

He only half-listened while his companion went on; "'Nother peculiar thing 'bout yonder *Dove* is that Dale's wife serves as Second Mate; he's the First. 'Tis said although she's good to look on she's a capable navigator and tougher then tripe when it comes to driving a bargain."

"The hell you say!"

"Aye. 'Tis even rumored Mistress Dale has slain two men by her own hand."

Once he'd signed requisite papers, Phips joyfully watched the Port Captain depart, then took a few turns about his quarterdeck.

All in all there seemed to be little room for doubt but he decided to check up, Dale being a fairly common surname around Massachusetts Bay Colony. So he ordered his gig readied and, taking her tiller, steered for the *Dove* which must be taking on supplies since a battered lighter lay alongside with half-naked, black figures unhurriedly passing freight on board.

Even at a distance Phips found no difficulty in identifying a tall, bandy-legged figure superintending the loading.

A host of all-but forgotten memories returned: the time he and Johnny, as youngsters had speared a huge hair seal which in its death throes nearly had sunk their canoe in icy waters. Then there was that bull moose they'd tracked through snow and had killed with bows and arrows; also plenty of bloody fist fights fought over some long-forgotten trifle.

He snapped at his oarsmen: "Put yer backs into it! Pull faster, ye lazy bastards!"

Cupping hands he stood up and in carrying tones shouted: "*High Hopes* ahoy! *High Hopes* ahoy!"

Under the shade of a wide-brimmed straw hat, Phips grinned at the way Dale jerked spasmodically erect before running to the rail yelling, "Phips! My God, Will, is it *really* you?"

"None other and pray note, Johnny, m'lad, I *am* in command of a King's ship!"

On gaining the ketch's deck Phips peered about. "Where's this female I hear ye've taken into partnership?"

"Gone to the West End along of Abram Adderly." An almost impish grin on Dale's features. "When you get to see our Second you'll get the shock of yer life."

"Why so? You ain't married a black woman?"

"No. Recall that red-haired wench who sailed along with me and Jim Turner? The survivor from Hammond's Fort?"

Phips's jaw fell then he burst out laughing. "Not Richard Hammond's brat?"

"Aye. Pegeen's growed into a lusty and strong-minded female creature. What's more she's become I'll leave for you to discover."

As was the custom in warm latitudes, meals aboard a small vessel were cooked on a sandbox and consumed on deck. Digesting a supper of turtle steak and amberfish, pawpaws, beans and rice, and plenty of good English beer, Phips and his host shucked shirts and settled down in canvas armchairs to reminisce and enjoy a cool evening breeze.

Phips found it fine to be alone once more with his former partner and presently deduced that Pegeen and Adderly had gone to Mangrove Bay in the West End to dispose of smuggled goods landed there in defiance of Company regulations.

Phips peered over the rim of a pewter beer mug.

"So ye're made Pegeen Hammond yer wife?"

"Aye, Will, but only under common law—accordin' to local custom. At any rate, over eight years Peg and me have got on tolerable well."

"Eight years, eh? Expect you've a flock of young 'uns to pester you."

Dale shook his big head, bleached silver-yellow by tropic sunlight. "Wrong. But t'ain't *my* fault we're childless 'cause I know Peg now and again has tumbled with other fellows."

"What! You give her leave to do that?"

"Same as me. From the start we agreed on that since we ain't ever been in love like the poets write about." He reached for the pipe he'd let go out. "Likely you know Peg lost her intended same day my dear Jenny and our baby got killed. Reckon some people can love like that only once."

"I understand. Don't know how I'd manage without Mary. But why ain't Pegeen ever been got in the family way?"

"Reckon 'Manda Adderly made sense when she claimed

when Peg miscarried, she got tore up inside so bad she can't ever conceive.

"Ashore, Peg's real lively in bed but at sea, being as she holds shares in this vessel, she takes her duties serious. She's sea-smart, can navigate and keep watch better'n most men."

Darkness having set in, a scattering of yellow lights began to glimmer along the rim of Towne Harbour.

Someone forward called: "Ahoy, Mr. Dale, our skiff's comin'."

Chapter 22

GET TOGETHER

MOMENTS LATER Phips experienced a not unpleasant surprise when Pegeen Hammond, followed by bushy-bearded Captain Adderly's lanky figure, lightly vaulted the ketch's rail and dropped onto the deck. Under other circumstances Phips might have failed to identify this shapely though muscular young woman, save for those ruler-straight brows, large dark-blue eyes and abundant auburn hair braided tight under a blue bandanna surmounted by a wide-brimmed straw hat.

"Captain Phips!" Pegeen hesitated, then rushed forward and flung arms about him and, eyes suddenly filling, bestowed lusty smacks on his leathery cheeks. "This is wonderful!"

The King's Captain hugged her so tight she gasped and cried out. After letting her go he chuckled; "I suppose, Peg, you figgered Old Scratch long since had claimed me for his own?"

"Oh, no, sir!" she cried in rich, slightly husky tones. "John, Abram and I often heard tell about you in the West Indies.

Why, once or twice we made port only hours after you'd sailed. Down yonder a lot of captains admire and envy your success in trading and wonder about your treasure-seeking 'ventures."

"In those parts you can hear any amount of such claptrap."

The *Salee Rose*'s Master slapped Adderly so hard on his back the Bermudian swayed.

"A pleasure, sir!" he gasped. "Weren't you the one what fished the *Mariposa* wreck to small avail?"

"Aye."

"Better luck next time."

"Well, if 'tis any consolation, I've met with bigger disappointments." He surveyed the *Dove* lying darkly mirrored by the harbor's glassy water. "For a small ketch ye go well armed." Her gunports showed as well as the swivel gun mountings on her rails.

Somehow it didn't surprise the twenty-first son that Pegeen, squatting on a transom, took several hearty swigs from a foaming mug of ale before unconcernedly igniting a black, finger-thin seegar.

Pegeen found Phips considering her in open curiosity. How much had the former Captain of the *High Hopes* learned about her? Was he aware she'd murdered Jim Turner and had pistolled a brace of buccaneers? Had Jack told him about her miscarriage? That, since then, she'd not only lived with him but had slept with other men? Could he surmise she now thought no more over beheading a chicken or slitting the throat of a goat destined for slaughter than of sewing on a button?

She needn't have worried. All William Phips perceived, by starlight and the glow of a smoky lanthorn set on the companion hatch, was a strikingly handsome young woman whose restless eyes were lustrous but had lines about them which oughtn't to have been there. Her mouth, he noted, still turned up at its corners and that dimple in her chin he'd admired so long ago still was present.

From around a fire throbbing on a tiny nearby island African voices floated across the water. Their chanting was rich but unintelligible and endlessly repetitive.

Salee Rose's Captain commented at length: "Am I mistook or didn't you fail to discover the treasure shown on Turner's map?"

Dale spat over the rail. "Oh, we located the right spot, only someone had found it before us."

"Any notion who might have been the lucky party?"

"Naw," growled Adderly. "It just weren't there."

"You've cruised about the West Indies considerable, Johnny?"

Dale nodded. "Aye. We've done plenty tradin' that way and when chance offered maybe a mite of privateerin' 'gainst the Spanish, French, and Dutch. Haven't done too poorly, either."

"Privateering, eh? Reckon that would explain why you'd carry six carriage guns on a vessel of your tonnage. Presume you always could produce a letter of marque if need arose?"

Abram Adderly chuckled. "Of course, Jack's always held we should privateer legal-like and *never* attack a British vessel no matter how temptin'—same as old Harry Morgan who always carried a commission of some sort. He *never* was the out-and-out pirate his enemies claim."

"Tell me, Jack, you ever considered returning to Boston?" The question included Pegeen.

"No. Peg and me like livin' in the Bermudas. Ain't over-many Crown officials here, no witch hunts or Puritan preachers to make life a misery."

"You intend settling here, for keeps?"

Pegeen said quickly: "For the present. Right now we own a warehouse and a shipyard on Mangrove Bay. We put in here only to recharge our magazine, buy shot, fresh sails, cordage and such-like."

Pegeen leaned forward, boldly rested a hand on Phips's knee. "Suppose, Captain, you sail your long boat around to Ireland Island and pay us a visit? We've a house which ain't much to look on but 'tis comfortable all the same. The West End is mighty lonesome, sometimes weeks or months pass without our sighting a big vessel."

Phips went over to the bulwarks, piddled, then returned

buttoning his front flap. "Whilst ramming about the West Indies I heard you've all tried fishing for treasure."

"Who doesn't?" Dale settled comfortably into his canvas armchair. "Whenever we heard likely information 'bout a wreck we'd go look for her. Sometimes we'd find her but, by Christ on the Cross, *always* someone has beat us to it!"

Phips drew hard on his pipe. "What else would you expect of a wreck that's easy to find? I know. Been my fate, too. Soon after we parted in Boston, Jack, I fished on a promising wreck lying not far out of New Providence in the Bahamas. Found her all right but raised only sufficient plunder to carry me to London where influential friends bought me a Royal Navy commission and secured the loan of a ship to go hunting a great wreck named the *Vice-Admiral*."

Dale queried intently: "Meet with any luck, Will?"

"No, damn it. Found nothing to reward my backers. So I expect to meet naught but trouble when I return to England."

Following an uncomfortable pause, Dale changed the subject. "I trust Mrs. Phips is hale and hearty?"

"Aye. In fair weather and foul my Mary's remained staunch and healthy. You see, my fortune's ain't always been so poor as right now. I've made enough to build us a fine brick house on Green Lane."

From among the shadows Pegeen ventured: "You must be away from home a good deal, sir?"

"Aye, and since we've no get of our own that don't make it easy for Mary. All the same, she stays reasonable, does charitable work, and makes a home for Johnny, my brother Jack's little son. Mayhap I'll take him for a ship's boy when next I intend for the Spanish Main."

"You'll head for Jamaica?" Dale suggested.

"Could be. I'll sail soon as I win a new set of backers, a better-found ship and build some special diving tackle I'm bearing in mind." He broke off. "You've touched at Port Royal often during your voyaging?"

Drawled the *Dove*'s Master, "Sure enough, for supplies, rum and frolicks and maybe to listen to news and gossip along the

[203]

waterfront. *You* know, Cap'n, a smart trader don't get far in those latitudes lackin' knowledge about what might be goin' on elsewhere."

Phips slapped his thigh. "Now ain't that gospel truth. Speaking of news; by chance, you heard anything about that galleon I spoke of called the *Vice-Admiral?*"

"Yep. Reckon every seafarer from Barbados to Antigua and Havana has heard yarns about the tremendous treasures she was supposed to be carryin' when she went down, but so many have searched for her in vain, like you, 'tis reckoned she's a will-o'-the-wisp, like many another."

Surprisingly Phips shook his head. "Nonsense. *That* wreck is real! I know because—" He broke off short.

Dale started to speak but kept quiet; why blurt out that, in Port Royal during the *Dove's* most recent cruise, he'd got pretty drunk with a certain English seafarer named Tom Smith. Embittered and in his cups Smith had confided rather convincingly that he'd located the *Vice-Admiral's* remains and with his own eyes had beheld many great guns lying among piles of coral-coated pigs, sows, and bars of silver and gold scattered amid rocks and sea plants.

Dale asked casually: "Tell me, Will, down in Jamaica you ever hear of a feller calling himself 'Tom Smith'?"

Pegeen sensed a subtle alteration in Phips's manner as he tapped sparks of dottle from his pipe. "Aye, just missed meeting the fellow meself. Heard tell he told Governor Molesworth down in Kingston some yarn 'bout having found the *Vice-Admiral*. At any rate the Governor credited Smith's story sufficient well to despatch the *Bonetta*, a King's ship under command of Captain Edward Stanley, to hunt for her. Since Stanley had aboard a pilot who swore he could find the site without Smith's help the Governor did poor Tom the dirty and the *Bonetta* sailed without him, expecting no doubt to pocket Smith's share."

Phips snorted. "One thing I can't abide is bad faith. I've never cheated anyone and so help me God I never will!"

Dale crushed a moth crawling over his cheek. "Ever since I've known you you've never tricked an honest man."

Pegeen murmured, "In that case, Jack, suppose you tell the Captain 'bout our talk with Tom Smith."

Fervently if silently, Dale cursed his "wife's" interference but, to his astonishment, Adderly spoke up. "Sure. The three of us all talked with Smith and somehow came to believe he really has seen a wreck and he's positive it was the *Vice-Admiral*'s."

Tense beneath a casual manner, the twenty-first son prompted: "What did Smith claim?"

"Said he'd surely spied a broken hull lodged betwixt two towering rocks, cannons and heaps of silver sows, and pigs and even a few gold bars, swore he'd recognize the right spot 'cause, nearby, a chimney-shaped rock lifts just clear o' the surface."

Phips hunched forward, elbows on knees, peered steadily at the Bermudian. "Tell me, *if* Smith truly sighted sunken treasure why in Hell didn't he drop anchor, calculate a true position and start diving straightaway?"

Dale intervened. "Don't wonder you ask. Well, Smith explained whilst he and his companions were arguing over what to do next a storm blew up so hard their only anchor line, which was rotten, parted and *you* know, Will, a nest of reefs ain't no place to get caught in lackin' sound ground tackle. They'd no choice but to hoist sail and run for their lives.

"When the storm let up, Smith's boat had been driven so far none of her crew had any clear notion of where they'd been.

"'Though Smith's been back twice seeking a chimney-shaped rock, he's never spied it. All the same, he swears he'll find the *Vice-Admiral* again on account of he's more or less sure of the latitude."

Phips's gaze quickly shifting from one dimly seen face to the next. He said, "Since you've been straightforward with me I'll tell you something in exchange, something which ain't generally known. I was commissioned by His late Majesty to expressly search for the *Vice-Admiral*'s wreck off Hispaniola in this vessel but I've failed, Goddam the luck!"

Abram Adderly suggested: "Sounds like you aim to try again?"

"Aye, that I intend but with King Charles dead, God alone knows what the future holds for me." His voice deepened. "All the same, somehow I'll win the new King's patronage and with a better ship and trustworthy crew I'll succeed, by Jesus, *I will succeed!*"

Softly Pegeen ventured: "Cap'n, from what you say and all we've heard, there must be other parties determined on finding the *Vice-Admiral?*"

"Small doubt about that," Phips snapped. "Likely they won't but should such rascals raise this treasure or any other in British waters lacking the King's license they'll wind up dancing a floorless hornpipe on Execution Dock. Treasure fishing in British waters without a warrant ranks the same as piracy."

"So we've heard," Dale stated, "but plenty of men, some of 'em honest skippers, stand ready to take a chance." That he, Pegeen, and Adderly might belong in that category he didn't feel called upon to mention. Few colonial seafarers were eager to share hard-won riches with His Majesty.

"Well, friends, think on what we've talked about and I'll do the same. Come aboard my ship tomorrow and I'll show you some of the gear a serious plate fisherman has to have along." He grimaced. "Not that what you'll see is the best yet contrived or near stout enough, but 'twill serve to lend you a notion of what's needed." Through the starlight he peered at his former partner. "Once you've taken a good look, Jack, I hope you'll consider maybe coming along on my next voyage which, by Lucifer's smoking prong, is going to make all concerned rich beyond belief!"

Long after the *bump-bump* of the visiting gig's thole pins faded, the *Dove's* afterguard remained on her poop, talking in undertones. The ketch's crew, Moog included, lay sprawled and snoring about her deck for, long after sundown, the tiny fo'c'sle remained hot as any bake oven.

Adderly, slouched against a roll of sails awaiting repair,

turned to Pegeen; over the years he'd grudgingly come to respect her opinion, for all she was but a female.

"Peg, in the light of what Phips let drop, what course d'you figger we might follow?"

"Can't answer right off," she evaded. "Need to consider so important a matter for a while. What's your opinion, Jack?"

Dale scratched his yellow shock of greasy hair. "Like you, I don't jump to quick conclusions, but I sure didn't fancy what Will said 'bout hangin' unlicensed plate fishers."

The Bermudian snorted: "Ever once hear of anybody gettin' his neck stretched for poachin' a wreck in English waters?"

"No, but I sure don't aim to be the first. Tell me true, Abram, how much more d'you calculate my friend knows about the *Vice-Admiral?*"

"Why do you ask?"

"He acts so sure of himself. But then, he's acted sure of himself even when he wasn't. What's your opinion, Peg?"

"Haven't any—yet—but I sense Cap'n Phips is holding something back."

"Why?"

"At this time he'd be a bloody fool to spill the sum of his knowledge to anyone who isn't in on the matter with him."

Dale spoke as if thinking aloud, "True enough, but ain't it possible he figures we might have private information he lacks?"

"Why so?" Adderly grunted.

Pegeen spoke up. "Think, Abram, think! *We* have gabbed with Tom Smith himself whilst all Will Phips knows is what he's learned secondhand—provided he's tellin' the truth. I suspect Tom Smith also was holding something back when the Governor of Jamaica hired him to lead Captain Stanley to the wreck. Stands to reason Smith wouldn't have aired his whole knowledge till the *Bonetta* had come pretty close to the wreck. Would *you?*"

"Hell, no," Dale admitted. "Molesworth and Stanley were goddam fools to bilk Smith the way they did and put their trust in another man. Wouldn't be oversurprised if we learn facts Phips and Stanley ain't even heard of. For example they mayn't be aware the *Vice-Admiral* went down a damn' sight closer to the Abroxes than to Handkerchief Shoals—as most people believe."

Pegeen yawned noisily: "What is the King's portion of treasure trove?"

Dale said, "Generally a quarter-share. Why'd you ask?"

"Just wanted to be sure; even a quarter of the *Vice-Admiral*'s treasure could build a whole fleet of battleships or a great palace!"

Adderly scratched flea bites along his sides. " 'Tain't right. Why make His Majesty the compliment of a great fortune when others risk money and their very lives whilst all he's got to do is to sign a warrant at no cost to himself."

Silence settled over the little poop deck in which the eerie shrieking of cahows homeward bound sounded unusually noticeable.

At length Dale demanded: "Well, Abe, what're you thinking?"

"Why not strike out on our own? We've got us a stout, well-armed ship and Moog, given a little time, can find us sufficient good Injun divers for our purpose. We now know Phips is homeward bound, emptyhanded, so he'll have to win new backers. Yep, the new King, too, won't be in any great a hurry to grant a failure a license or a warrant; 'twill likely be a good while afore Phips can start treasure-fishin' again; we'd have a good start on him an Smith's tips prove out!"

"What's yer opinion, Peg?" Dale put a hand on her arm, and gave it a squeeze.

"I'm for outfitting and making for Port Royal as fast as we can, though I may change my mind if we can't learn more exactly about where the *Vice-Admiral* went down. Mayhap, Cap'n Phips will let slip something more tomorrow. Failing that I'm for trying to find Tom Smith, go even shares with him and start fishing the wreck straightaway."

"License or no license?"

"Don't you think 'tis a worthwhile risk? British men-of-war are mighty scarce 'round the West Indies—nowadays especially."

Chapter 23 ·

HIS EXCELLENCY'S PRISONERS

THE SUN WAS LOWERING by the time the *Dove* had completed watering and taken aboard adequate supplies for an extended cruise when Captain Adderly and his partners had a pair of oarsmen pull them over to H.B.M.S. *Salee Rose*.

Once the man-of-war's crew noticed a young white woman in the gig they lined the rail, cheered, and offered lewd suggestions when Pegeen, skirts billowing and legs flashing, nimbly gained gangway.

The moment John Dale's yellow head showed above the bulwarks Fast Otter raised such a tremendous war whoop persons on nearby vessels hailed them to learn what was amiss.

While waiting for Captain Phips to appear the visitors looked around and with half an eye noted all manner of strange gear. Thought Dale, it was typical of William Phips he should appear on deck securing the well-polished brass buttons of a navy-blue frock uniform coat worn above a waistcoat of scarlet silk. The twenty-first son even had tucked a lace-trimmed handkerchief into a deep cuff turned back in lemon-yellow.

Said Phips almost stiffly: "I'd have had the gangway manned in yer honor, Jack, but I'm fed to the teeth doing country dances with the Governor and Company officers."

Pegeen also had gone to some trouble over her appearance. Her naturally wavy auburn mane had been combed into a queue and secured by a bright-green, swallow-tailed ribbon afforded an effective contrast to a blouse of yellow linen and a full, dark-green skirt sufficiently brief to expose an eye-catching length of calf and largish feet shod in neat, silver-buckled brogans.

Although her features glowed an unfashionable golden-brown and bore a sprinkling of freckles, her straight little nose, lively dark-blue eyes, and well-shaped mouth might have attracted appreciation in any moderately smart gathering about London.

Phips ordered a dark-faced foreign seaman to distribute palm-leaf fans, then led the way to the shade of an old topsail stretched above his quarterdeck. He paused. "Shall we refresh ourselves now or wait till you've inspected my diving tackle?"

Adderly, wearing a frayed straw hat, grunted: "Right now, an it pleases you, sir."

That "sir" from a Bermudian constituted a courtesy which escaped neither Pegeen nor Dale.

"Oh, before we go below"—Phips voice changed to a crisp British accent—"permit me to present my First Officer, Lieutenant Francis Rogers."

"Servant, Ma'am." Mr. Rogers, a sparsely built, horse-faced individual whose steel-gray eyes reminded one of sword points, jerked a curt bow in Pegeen's direction.

Blushing for the first time since she could remember, Pegeen bobbed a graceless curtsy. How long had she not yearned to acquire something of the manners of people of breeding and fashion, to learn how such talked, dressed and behaved? From whence came such hankerings? Possibly because Ma, reputedly, had been born into polite society?

"Mr. Rogers," Phips announced, "is the smartest navigator you'll encounter in a month of Sundays, along with you, Jack, an you ain't forgot yer old skills."

Francis Rogers grinned, then, in broad West Country accents, changed the subject. "Ever since we dropped anchor I've been admiring the lines and rig of your ketch, Captain Adderly."

"Aye, your *Dove* stands out," Phips commented. "Looks like some of the craft me and Jack built up to Jeremesquam in the old days." He then led them to a pile of rusted, salt-whitened diving gear. "Those tongs, grapnels, crowbars, scoops, and picks and rakes are for use only in shallow waters."

Mr. Rogers pointed. "Yonder's a saw-toothed sledge. That contraption was designed by the Cap'n to be hauled along by small boats for objects fathoms deep. It can rip loose promising coral-covered objects later to be raised by block and tackle." He hesitated. "Sir, shall I explain 'bout your diving tub?"

"Not now. I still ain't satisfied with its design." Features lighting, Phips faced his visitors. "This much I will tell you. An I build my bell the way I want 'twill allow divers to work an hour or more below the surface."

Fast Otter now appeared, and grinning, gripped hands. Then, briefly Pegeen Dale and the Penobscot dwelt on that unforgettable voyage down the Sheepscot.

"Where's Red Fish?" Dale queried.

"Him died of smallpox."

Fingering his ragged black beard, Adderly queried: "Cap'n, sir, 'bout how many divers are needed to fish a big wreck?"

"Not less than six; more, if she lies really deep."

"Deep?" Dale prompted eying the jumble of gear.

"In eight fathoms or more."

Pegeen put in: "What kind of divers d'you most favor, Captain?"

"The best and most enduring are white men, provided they're willin' to work for a small wage—and mighty few are. Next best, but hard to find, are redskins from back home —like Fast Otter. They're used to cold water, strong tides and currents; much tougher than Carib Indians although some of 'em, like Lucayans from Venezuela, are used to pearl diving and can prove pretty strong. As a rule most ain't sufficient tough to last long; generally, they go deaf or die of lung fever."

Inspection completed, Phips led the way back to the shade of his quarterdeck where sat waiting a rotund, jovial, spectacled individual who, disdaining the discomforts of European dress, was taking his ease in a purple-and-yellow banyan—a sort of loose dressing gown—and an absurd round hat of yellow straw. The apparition shook hands before "making a leg" to Pegeen, declaring himself charmed to make the acquaintance of so lovely a young lady.

After roaring for refreshments Phips said: "This popinjay is Charles Salmon, who, like the singed cat in the adage, ain't so bad as he looks. For a fact he's the finest cartographer I've ever run across. Too bad he's also agent for the Royal Treasury, aboard to make sure I don't attempt to hornswoggle the King of his share in the treasure we've not found."

Dale immediately sensed something underlay this statement but nevertheless felt attracted to this colorful personage.

With becoming diffidence, Pegeen ventured: "Don't believe, sir, I've ever beheld a truly well-drawn chart. Mr. Salmon, would you be sufficient kind to show me an example of your skill?"

Phips, while fanning himself, studied John Dale, decided he must take him along on his next venture so, to bait the hook, drawled: "That's a flattering invitation, Peg. Charles, suppose you fetch up the map you made of the north shore of Hispaniola?" He lapsed into broad New England accents when the cartographer disappeared below. "You two bein' old friends, I'll confide that *somewhere* on Salmon's chart is shown the *Vice-Admiral*'s approximate position."

Compared to Jim Turner's crude map, Mr. Salmon's handiwork proved to be a thing of beauty decorated as it was with sea monsters, puffing cherubs and tritons.

"Are all charts for the Royal Navy drawed so fine as this

one?" Dale queried, at the same time attempting to memorize salient points. Pegeen and Adderly also praised the chart at sufficient length to register notable markings.

Phips said suddenly: "Well, that's enough to convince you Charlie Salmon's a master draughtsman."

The cartographer was rolling up his handiwork when the anchor watch sang out that a rowboat flying an official flag was pulling for the *Salee Rose*.

Frowning, Phips said: "Jack, in view of what you've seen and heard what about joining my next expedition? You'd make a heap of money."

The New Englander avoided Phips's eye by glancing out over Towne Harbour's sparkling blue-green expanse. "I'll mull that overnight, Will. When do you sail?"

"Day after tomorrow an all goes as planned." Phips sought the taffrail and peered down upon the untidy figures of a man in chains and a woman huddled in the rowboat's middle.

"What sort of cat's meat you bringing?" Phips demanded the steersman, a slovenly fellow wearing the uniform of an ensign in the Governor's bodyguard.

"A pair of prisoners, Cap'n. Troublesome rogues 'e Govenor wants should stand trial in England for treason."

"Jailbirds!" The *Salee Rose*'s Captain broke into language so foul it commanded Pegeen's admiration. Over the years she'd become remarkably proficient in that direction.

As if he'd not sufficient troubles already! Awkwardly, the prisoners scrambled up to the gangway; the manacled man, a gaunt, lanthorn-jawed starveling glared defiantly about.

"Sir! Sir!" shrilled his companion, a bony-faced woman with wild-streaming hair and intense, staring black eyes. "I protest! This arrest is illegal! Me and Harry Bish are being transported for no crime—only for protesting 'gainst the Company's oppression and its encouragement to impious faiths."

Phips paid no heed beyond scanning this noisy harridan. "Name?"

Said the official: "Sarah Oxford. The other trouble-maker is Henry Bish."

"On what charges am I to transport them?"

"Like I said, for treason 'gainst the Crown, sir. This precious pair have been ranging these islands encouraging armed rebellion 'gainst the Company and our new King who they hold to be a secret follower of the Pope of Rome."

The Ensign spat over the rail before presenting a thin sheaf of documents. "Here, sir, are Governor Coney's orders to transport these prisoners home for trial. Look sharp, sir, lest they raise a mutiny 'mongst yer crew."

With other impending troubles it seemed too much that a pair of dangerous rebels had been foisted upon him. Still, as an officer of the Royal Navy he'd no alternative but to respect Governor Coney's warrants.

There was one more blow awaiting him the next day. Mounting his quarterdeck at daybreak he discovered that the *Dove* had vanished.

Chapter 24

LITTLE TOWER HILL GAOL

WILLIAM PHIPS couldn't bring himself to realize that a few hours earlier bailiffs suddenly boarded the *Salee Rose* in the Thames and had summarily placed him under arrest. Then they had hurried him away to a noisome cell in the "Nagg's Head," Little Tower Hill Gaol.

Still shaking with outrage, Phips tramped back and forth blaspheming so loudly a turnkey peered through a barred wicket let into the cell's massive oaken door and ordered silence lest the prisoner wanted to test the bite of a lead-tipped cat-o'-nine-tails.

Unshaven, bronze-red features suffused, Phips briefly snarled defiance but ended by controlling himself. He even found a measure of encouragement through suspecting some weighty reason must lie behind this swift and quiet incarceration.

The immediate cause for his confinement, he finally ascertained, was that once they'd been turned over to the authorities, in London, Henry Bish and Sarah Oxford had sought a solicitor, complaining they'd been illegally arrested and deported from the Bermudas. To substantiate their suit both prisoners had produced copies of Governor Coney's deportation order; apparently they contained a number of legal errors.

Peering between heavy bars the twenty-first son dully viewed the progress through rain squalls of a variety of wherries, ferries and dingey sailing barges plying the lead-hued Thames and bumboats circling anchored merchantmen and warships.

What a miserable soul-chilling contrast to those sunny skies and sparkling waters he'd taken for granted for so long.

Scowling through the bars, the New Englander admitted to himself that at least some of Granny Eldritch's predictions had been realized. He *had* stood before a King and *had* commanded a Royal vessel but that was all.

Again he visualized himself received by saturnine and long-nosed Charles II. Thanks to coaching by Lord Albemarle and tough old Sir John Narbrough—the same who'd won fame and a small fortune through trouncing the corsairs of Barbary—he reckoned he'd comported himself at least creditably.

To start with, His Majesty, in patient disinterest, had listened to this brawny New Englander elaborate on a scheme for raising incredibly enormous wealth from the *Vice-Admiral*, a Spanish galleon reputed to have gone down somewhere off the northern coast of Hispaniola.

How high had his hopes soared on learning, weeks later, that His Majesty had been persuaded by Albemarle and others to issue not only a Royal Patent authorizing a search but also to lend for this purpose H.B.M.S. *Salee Rose*.

In return, Charles II had stipulated it was up to other shareholders to arm, provision, enlist and pay the *Salee Rose*'s complement.

Grimy hands clenched behind him, William Phips resumed pacing. How to terminate this unjust and time-wasting ignominy? Lord Albermarle, he'd learned, to his impotent fury, was away from London no doubt visiting one of several country estates. Who else among his backers might hold sufficient rank to be of real assistance? What about the Earl of Sunderland? Possibly. Despite foppish dress and an affected mode of speech, Sunderland was no weakling or foolish when it came to making money.

Aye, he'd appeal to Sunderland.

He fumbled in the baggy canvas knee-breeches he'd been wearing when the bailiffs had pounced on him. Finding a rough-edged silver piece-of-eight he pounded on the door until a turnkey shuffled up, key ring jingling.

"Wot the 'ell is it now, ye noisy barstard?"

Phips held up the coin bright amid the musty gloom.

"See this?"

"Not being blind as a bat, I do. Wot abaht it?"

"Fetch me a quill, ink, a sheet of foolscap and sealing wax and it's yours; more than ye'll earn, honest, in a fortnight."

By the light filtering through the window bars he started to write, as always gnawing his lower lip.

To the Right Honorable the Earle
of Sunderland.

Secretary of State
Right Hono'^{ble}
I received by the order of the Governor of Bermuda as
by his Warrant appeares Henry Bish aboard his Maties
ship the Salee Rose and to deliver him to your Honor
which I have done accordingly, since which time the s^{d}
Henry Bish hath arrested me, Wm Phips, and am now in
custody in the Bayleyes hands in the Nagg's Head belonging to His Ma^{ts} Little Tower. On my restraint I doe and
am inforced to hinder his Ma^{ts} business, Pray be pleased
to take some Order that I may be discharged. And as in
duty bound I shall ever pray for your Honor and remain
at Your Honor^{s} Command.

William Phips
From the Nagg's Head on Little Tower Hill
3rd August 1685

He lay open-eyed, fingers laced under a tangle of greasy hair while thoughts, like defeated troops, straggled across his mind. Would that ill-favored turnkey actually deliver his letter or would he consign his appeal to the fire? Ever practical, Phips sensed that, in all probability, his plea wasn't likely to reach Lord Sunderland's attention.

The prisoner sighed, listened to the squeak and furtive scurryings of a multitude of rats. One seemed to be sampling the contents of the cell's malodorous and long unwashed earthenware chamberpot.

Especially galling was the recollection of the way John Dale had let him down. Evidently, the man he'd encountered in Bermuda had become decidedly different from the youth he'd grown up with.

To a certain extent he had to hold himself to blame. Only a great dunce would have directed Mr. Salmon to display his chart and expose considerable information concerning the wreck of the *Vice-Admiral*.

He ought to have sensed what was in the wind when Dale and Adderly mentioned their conversation with Tom Smith.

Aye, and what might Tom Smith be doing—Smith who with his own eyes apparently had seen the great treasure ship.

Come to think on it all three visitors had stared hard under pretext of admiring Mr. Salmon's handiwork. He could picture them back in the *Dove* helping Jack Dale—who'd always been handy with a drafting pen—create a facsimile of Salmon's chart.

Experienced navigators, Adderly and Dale *must* have noted the wreck's presumed latitude—27:20 11 °—and months ago in Bermuda had burned that position into their memories.

The New Englander commenced restlessly to pace back and forth to the discomfiture of swarming rodents. That others might beat him to the prize was intolerable.

How would Mary accept news of her husband's imprisonment? Staunchly, beyond a doubt, just as she'd stood by him during all those troubles with the law when the *Salee Rose*'s villainous first crew had run riot the length of Boston's waterfront.

Chapter 25

OTTAVIO GALLUCIO

THE LONGER WILLIAM PHIPS stumped about his all-but lightless cell the more poignant grew his despair. Surely, something more serious than improperly drawn warrants must lie behind his imprisonment? He reviewed, step-by-step, the *Salee Rose*'s disappointing cruise and ended by deciding that, beyond a doubt, the one responsible for his disgrace must be John Knepp who, with Charles Salmon, had sailed in the sixth-rate as a Commissioner from the Treasury.

Certain it appeared that Knepp, on returning to London, had placed against Captain William Phips a report which Ananias himself might envy. The worst of it was that as a Treasury official Mr. Knepp's word undoubtedly would stand against that of a brash New England sea captain.

While listening to the coughing and hawking of prisoners rousing in adjacent cells, Phips thought back to certain blazing-hot days last year when he'd ordered the *Salee Rose* to wood and water at an insignificant port called "Porto Plata," known to English seamen as "Spanish Wells" and situated on the northeast coast of Hispaniola hard by Cape Francis.

He'd visited the place not only for supplies but to transact a surreptitious traffic in hides, rum, and sugar in exchange for European shoes, cloth and hardware, not to mention highly illegal powder and shot in defiance of severe Spanish prohibitions.

Having accomplished the day's traffic with His Honor, Don Pedro Fuentes, Alcalde of Porto Plata, and reluctant to return at once to the *Salee Rose,* he left crumbling *cabildo* (customhouse), *calabozo,* (jail) and red-roofed dwellings of the little port behind to wander inland and once more explore the intriguing liana-hung and flower-decked tangles of a rain forest. He carried a fowling piece on the odd chance of encountering some edible bird or beast as a change from the monotonous fare aboard ship.

While traversing a dense thicket in which vines dangled from tall cedars and silk-cotton trees like the remains of ragged, gray-green sails, he heard a voice calling in English: "Help! For God's sake, help! They mean murder!"

Roaring like the Biblical Bull of Bashan, Phips plowed through snarls of interlaced vegetation.

The very size of him caused a pair of scrawny, wild-haired rag-clad *mestizos* to vanish into the scrub with the ease of snakes.

Sprawled on the ground and trembling violently lay a white-haired, pitifully thin and leather-faced ancient.

"*Gracias, amigo,*" he quavered. "Much thanks! Take me away, maybe they come back."

"Where?"

"My hut not far off."

Lifting the scrawny figure clad only in tattered pantaloons, Phips carried him along a barely passable trail to a miserable little palm-thatched hut standing in a small clearing. The scarecrow meanwhile continued to babble in heavily accented English mixed with Portuguese and Spanish.

"How come you speak English?" Phips queried while knotting a rag over a shallow wound on the ancient's shoulder. "You from an English colony?"

"No, me Genoese; *piloto*. Sometime me steer Engleesh sheeps."

Once he'd reconnoitered the clearing and heard only the grunts of foraging pigs Phips returned to the gaunt figure, found him clutching his wound and attempting to beat away clouds of flies.

"Who are you?"

"Me Ottavio Gallucio—very poor, but you not be sorry you help."

While the New Englander was easing the bony old man onto a pile of withered palm fronds a pert, yellow-and-black bird resembling a thrush hopped into the hut and from brilliant, yellow-rimmed black eyes peered briefly about before returning to the torrid sunlight.

Phips wondered why anyone would want to attack so pitiful a creature. "Why did you yell for help in English?"

A faint smile curved lavender-hued lips. "Me learn Engleesh ship is een Porto Plata. If me call een Spaneesh nobody help."

"Anything you want?"

"*Sí*, meester—water, drink."

After he'd gulped from a calabash cup the old man's sunken, bloodshot gray eyes wavered up to meet the New Englander's hard dark ones. "*Por favor* give name to thank."

"Cap'n Phips."

"Saint Christopher preserve you, *Capitano*—may you always sail under lucky stars."

Phips peered intently into the wrinkle-seamed and mahogany-hued features. "You *believe* in lucky stars?"

Gallucio grimaced. "In youth me believed in such stars. But only bad luck follow."

Phips placed a hand under the ancient's shoulders and, while raising him for another swallow of coconut water, noticed a few pitifully worn feminine garments strung to a liana rope. So this miserable old fellow did not live alone? He stood up, head making crackling noises among dangling palm thongs and picked up his fowling piece. Time he was returning to Porto Plata.

"No! No!" quavered Ottavio Gallucio. "Please no go till Félicia, my woman, come back from hunting fruit."

"How soon will she return?"

"No sure. Fruit close by all picked." Imploringly, Ottavio raised shriveled hands splattered with chocolate-hued freckles. "For love of God, robbers maybe come back, kill me!"

"But why would they? You've nothing here of value I can spy."

"Stay! You not be sorry, no sir."

Squatting on a low stool, Phips used a fiber fan to disperse persistent swarms of small, blue-black flies which settled to drink at the corners of the old man's eyes but since Ottavio Gallucio didn't seem to heed these pests he soon quit.

Phips then produced that small silver flask he customarily took ashore when engaged in trading—often, its contents had oiled the wheels of progress. Out of a clump of ferns a strange, guinea-pig-like agouti thrust its head but noticing the figures it at once retreated.

Rum, watered with coconut milk, sufficiently restored the old pilot to struggle up on an elbow. "*Mil gracias.* You only good man me meet in long, long time. Me grateful. Come back tomorrow, me tell great secret. Maybe make you most rich. *Oíga!* Félicia returns."

Out of the dimness of the jungle materialized a bent gray-haired Indian woman whose flat and wizened features were lumpy and mottled by insect bites. Félicia paused, ready for instant retreat on sighting this tall stranger.

"*Para!*" called Ottavio. "*Es amigo.* Saved me from *bandidos.*"

Timidly, Ottavio's companion advanced, horny bare feet making not a sound.

"Félicia, make the señor welcome."

Withered breasts swinging low under a loose blouse, the old creature bowed, exposed yellowed stumps of teeth in an ugly smile.

"*Buenos dias*, señor."

"Good day, ma'am," he returned in passable Spanish.

"Will the *bandidos* return?"

Ottavio quavered. "Perhaps no, *Capitán*. Surely you come tomorrow, early?"

"I'll come back first moment I can, count on it." Phips meant what he said. Why should a figure so completely destitute-seeming be assaulted? And that mention of stars!

Next afternoon he wandered past Porto Plata's weather-beaten brick *cabildo* and, in apparent aimlessness, sauntered through a grove of giant mahogany trees and out of the sun-baked port and by a circuitous route returned to Ottavio Gallucio's squalid hut.

He discovered the ancient sufficiently recovered to have seated himself under a lofty satinwood tree. Gnarled nut-brown legs outthrust, the old man appeared incredulous when Phips held out a small canvas sack.

"Here's a chunk of boucan for you, old man, some ship's bread, coffee and sugar."

"Bless you!" Tears commenced to zigzag down among the wrinkles. "You a saint—even though Engleeshmans."

Once Félicia had mixed rum and coconut water, Phips seated himself on a stump, slowly revolved the cup between tanned broad hands.

"Leave us, Félicia," the ancient directed. "Go seek riper papayas than last ones." Once the disheveled old woman had crept off into the jungle Ottavio lowered his voice. "Please walk circle about hut, make most sure none can listen."

Once his visitor had obliged, Ottavio's silvery head doddered a few times before he said, "Because of your great goodness, *Señor Capitán*, me tell very precious secret."

Ignoring a variety of insects incessantly buzzing about, William Phips hunched closer, strained to catch every word.

"Know, *Señor Capitán*, me not always poor like now. Once was famous *piloto;* fight many battles, win much moneys. Was man of importance but lost wife, family, everythings in great earthquake in Nicaragua.

"*No importa*." Exasperatingly, he paused, sucking with toothless gums at a slice of boucan. "In *año* 1642 or maybe 1643 me apprentice *piloto* on great galleon, *Nuestra Señora de la Concepción*." Red-rimmed eyes sought Phips's wide-set ones. "Her name holds meanings for you?"

"None at all. What was the *Nuestra Señora de la Concepción?*" He repeated the name to memorize it.

"Ship of Vice-Admiral of *flota* for that year. Commanding was *Señor Don Juan de Campos*."

Like a crack of nearby thunder the designation exploded in Phips's imagination. *The Vice-Admiral* by God!

"What d'you say was this ship's name?" He had to make sure.

"*Nuestra Señora de la Concepción*. Een Porto Bello, Havana, and Vera Cruz me watch lower into her treasure rooms riches beyond belief."

Phips, trembling a little, bent over the frail figure to offer more rum and coconut water.

A burning question presented itself. Ottavio's assailants of yesterday must have suspected he knew something, but how much did they have to go on? What could have led them to seek out the old pilot? Such rascals certainly wouldn't be above torturing him to extract information about the wrecked galleon's position before knives forever sealed his lips. Hell's roaring bells! This old fellow might not live to see tomorrow's sun.

Like flaming arrows a pair of scarlet macaws sped, shrieking, over the clearing and disappeared almost instantly among the treetops. In the jungle an ax in the far distance started to thud a dull, irregular rhythm.

"What about this wreck? I sail early this evening so if you've anything to say, for God's sake speak up."

The old man summoned a feeble smile. "Bend lower, *amigo*. Me tell how with these eyes saw wreck of *Concepción*, lying on ocean floor."

"How long ago?"

"Me not sure; mebbe eight, nine, even ten year. Me already

[*224*]

old but risked life to sail and paddle out to Ambrosia Bank alone."

" 'Ambrosia Bank'?"

"*Sí*, ees tangle of reefs shape' like deep horseshoe."

Eyes riveted on Ottavio's almost skull-like features, the twenty-first son listened as never before.

"You sure it was the *Concepción*?"

"*Sí, Señor Capitán*. Me recognize carvings on stern, saw masts, cannon cover' by corals, sea plants but so thick hard see much. Another drink, *por favor*."

Gallucio swallowed, his voice gained in strength and clarity. "Wreck lies broken in two among big reefs, bottom rough, jagged."

"How deep does the galleon lie?"

Despite furious poundings of his heart, Phips held his breath: so much, so much depended upon this.

"Me not able judge sure but me think most of wreck lie een four, five, or six fathoms—Engleesh measure."

"Did you dive on her yourself?"

"*Sí*. But me all alone and big wind come on quick, quick. Me bring up only sword easy to break off; five big emeralds on hilt of solid gold."

"You still have it?" Tales were well enough but 'twould be ultimately convincing to handle a tangible piece of evidence.

The old man sighed and, closing his eyes, shook his head. "No. Long ago bad peoples me rob of sword in Puerto Rico, but stupid peoples think me still have part of treasure. The *ladrones*—thieves—yesterday were such."

At a soft crackling in the underbrush the New Englander sprang up and, cutlass ready, plunged into the foliage only to return almost at once wearing a taut grin and silently cursing a wandering donkey for having even momentarily interrupted the ancient's discourse.

"Only a stray burro. You brought up nothing else?"

"*Nada*, no could stay. Storm blew. Me een small canoe sixty miles from Porto Plata."

"Only *sixty miles*?"

[*225*]

"*Sí.* To find Ambrosia Bank sail north-northeast from Porto Plata. On way you sight bad reefs called *Los Abreojos.*" The leathery lips twitched, "Een your language means 'keep eyes open'—*Los Abreojos* ees trap for unwary; beyond lies Ambrosia Bank."

It seemed as if all the world were standing still, that nothing existed beyond the old pilot's wrinkled brown features.

"What's the latitude?"

The old pilot cackled. "Me wonder why you, navigator, not ask before. Me not tell; come back, me take you straight to wreck *sin duda!*"

Recalling what Tom Smith had described as a chimney-shaped rock, Phips queried: "Does any sort of landmark identify Ambrosia Bank?"

"*Sí.* When *Concepción* go down, tall, thin rock show forty, fifty feet above high water, near center of horsehoe. But"—his eyelids fluttered—"when me go back alone me find tall rock broke down close to surface; little stump only remaining."

"Can you account for this?"

"*Sí.* Earthquakes big, little, some under ocean often shake Hispaniola. Five years back big quake raise great waves, destroy many ships, villages, and lives. Could even swallow *Concepción.* Has happen' some wrecks."

Hot and humid as the day was, chill rivulets started to course down Phips's back. The *Vice-Admiral* swallowed! As from afar he heard the old pilot add, "Tremblings maybe knock' down last of tall, thin rock; not count to find eet."

"An you get well enough paid; could you steer me to the wreck?"

A cackling laugh escaped Ottavio. "Me not accept a single *peso.* You save remains to my life. I go, me show, but not now. Not good time—hurricanes come soon now. Your ship too small, too weak. Once there, you must fish very fast, *amigo.* Once tales get out *Concepción* found, all buccaneers and corsairs een Eendies hurry that way."

Phips felt tempted to insist on an immediate attempt but,

exercising a caution which always had swayed major decisions, he ended by keeping quiet. Besides, Gallucio was right: the *Salee Rose*'s canvas and rigging were dangerously worn and small new leaks starting all-too-often and God knew that second crew, picked up in Jamaica, weren't proving at all reliable. What could be expected of such rascals once gold, ingots, pigs, and sows of silver, caskets of jewels and the like started coming on board? The prospect wasn't reassuring. Mutiny, murder and sudden death inevitably must follow.

Having reached a decision—the most difficult of his career—Phips deliberately poured the last of the rum and coconut water.

"And so, *amigo mío*, what should I do?"

"Return England—get big, strong sheep weeth many cannons. Get good crew; trusty officers and men. Come back next spring and Ottavio Gallucio take you to *Concepción*—eef her wreck remains."

"I'll take your advice but how can I be sure you'll still be around? Remember those *ladrones*."

The old man said simply: "Future in hands of God. Soon me draw map, show latitude, useful landmarks. Eef danger come, me leave map, sealed proper, with Don Pedro Fuentes, Alcalde of Porto Plata. Me say ees Will—he must deliver *only* to you, *muy amigo mío*. Félicia will be told."

Abruptly, Phips was recalled from the past by a resounding tramp of feet advancing along the corridor. Keys rattled, then helmeted guards flanked the cell's entrance and with halberts saluted the arrival of a well-dressed officer in company with that self-same bailiff who, the day before, had arrested him aboard the *Salee Rose*.

"Stand up, you Colonial oaf," he rasped. "This here is Mr. Graham, Lieutenant-Governor of the Tower. He bears instructions concerning you."

Long years later Captain William Phips would be able to recall every detail of that interview in the Lieutenant-Governor's moldy-smelling and chilly office. Once its door had closed on the bailiff, Mr. Graham had become cordial to the point of def-

erence. He even treated the prisoner to a glass of sherry before producing a neatly folded document. "Fancy you'll rather
enjoy reading this."

The New Englander's grimy hands, tipped by overlong
black nails, began to shake while he moved to an arrow-slit
window and, gnawing his lower, lip read:

> To Mr. Graham about Phips
>
> White Hall 4: August 1685
>
> The enclosed letter from Captain Phips, Commander of his
> Majesty's Frigate the ROSE having been presented to the
> King, His Ma^{ty} thinks fitt that Bayl bee given on His
> Ma^{ty's} behalf for Captain Phips for soe much as relates to
> his bringing over the prisoners: of which I am directed to
> give you notice that you may take care it bee done
> accordingly.
>
> I am,
>
> WILLIAM BRATHWAYT

Incredulous, Phips was forced, moving his lips, to read the
order twice. By God, so he had retained a few influential
friends in this gloomy, hostile land, otherwise why should His
Majesty himself have despatched such instructions to the Little
Tower? From no lesser a personage than Lord Sunderland
could the King have learned about the imprisonment of an un-
important colonial sea captain.

All that mattered to the twenty-first son was that he soon
would be free again to follow the course of his Star.

Chapter 26

WILL'S COFFEE HOUSE

SHOULDERING A PATH through dense and noisy traffic on Russell Street on his way towards Will's Coffee House, William Phips reckoned he cut a very different figure from that miserable-appearing wretch who, only yesterday, had marched, proudly erect, out of the Nagg's Head, Little Hill Tower prison.

To recapture modish speech and mannerisms painfully acquired a couple of years earlier while seeking the late King Charles's favor, was proving unexpectedly easy, moreover his landlady unaccountably had preserved and cared for the wardrobe left in her charge. Apparently styles had altered scarcely at all, so the cut of his garments remained reasonably fashionable.

It lent him additional confidence that his new black peruke was curled exactly right and secured into the prevalent mode by tortoise-shell hairpins. No shoemaker's artistry, however, could disguise the broad and ample proportions of feet shaped in moccasins: also, he *must* remember to slow his rapid, loose-kneed frontiersman's gait. To stride quickly simply wasn't done about London Town. To accomplish this he took to regulating his pace through the use of an ivory-tipped walking stick.

Sauntering along, the New Englander paused now and again to peer with curiosity into shop windows. A succession of frowsy street girls sidled up offering companionship, Phips being extra well-dressed and standing nearly a head taller than the average Londoner. What with his clear, deep red-brown complexion and large and wide-set gray-blue eyes bright as polished steel buttons he seemed worthy of persistent solicitations.

A sharp contrast this, he reflected, to the narrow, dark and sordid byways and purlieus of Port Royal down in tropical Jamaica. All the same, progress across Covent Garden was not without hazards; at any moment a second-story window might bang open and a voice would screech "Ware below!" even as the contents of a slop jar or chamberpot was emptied in the general direction of a cobbled kennel serving as the street's only drain.

Phips, however, arrived at Will's Coffee House without damage and, to his huge relief, at once sighted Sir John Narbrough's angular and weather-beaten figure seated in a corner with a man he failed to recognize.

The famous scourge of the Barbary pirates got to his feet and offered his hand, a courtesy hitherto denied the New Englander. Narbrough introduced his companion as Sir Richard Haddock, a fellow Commissioner in the Royal Navy. An impression crossed Phips's mind that this narrow-faced gentleman, so pallid and smooth-shaven, to an absurd degree resembled the fish from which his surname was derived; further, he'd a colorless overhanging upper lip, and a deeply receding jaw while his round black eyes, though bright, appeared devoid of expression.

Once the big New Englander had seated himself, Sir John, smiling all the while like a friendly mastiff, ordered bottles of claret, then tugged absently at bristly gray mustachios.

Phips scarcely could hear over the hubbub of voices, the clink of glasses and the cries of vendors hawking wares along Russell Street.

Sir John Narbrough had almost to bellow, "B'God, Will, 'tis fine to behold ye turned out in style again. Still, perhaps you'd best see about that jabot—its lace should be from Bruges, which is modish at present, rather than Alençon, which is not. How does your finery suit you after so long an absence?"

Phips started to speak huskily but regulated his voice to a fashionable drawl. "Too demmed tight but I expect I'll again grow accustomed to it. Please Sir John, can you tell me a little about our new monarch?"

"Dick, here, can oblige better than I."

The three put heads together over the table while Sir Richard gave a brief but shrewd sketch of King James II who he implied at the moment was not popular with a majority of his subjects; certain tax laws he'd caused to be ennacted had not been well-received. Furthermore, although nominally a Protestant, almost everyone knew King James was a secret but fervent Catholic, so much so there was talk about replacing him with a bona fide Protestant ruler. A candidate most mentioned was a dour Dutch prince called "William of Orange" who, moreover, possessed a legitimate claim to the Crown of England through having married Mary, James the First's eldest daughter. Nor, stated the Naval Commissioner, did many Englishmen enjoy their new Sovereign's patent admiration for boundlessly ambitious Louis XIV of France to whom James II remained indebted for great sums of money advanced to secure for James succession following his brother's demise. Phips listened intently, hardly touched his wine.

Eventually, Sir John broke in. "Enough on the subject. Suppose, Captain, you describe for Sir Richard's benefit this project of yours which caused Sunderland to have you freed."

Phips obliged in lowered voice, dwelt on some reasons why he felt positive he would be able, if properly outfitted, to locate the *Vice-Admiral*'s wreck and raise her enormous treasure.

"Well, Dick," mumbled Narbrough. "How does all this strike you?"

"Reasonable, more than reasonable I might say. However I forsee trouble in one direction."

"And that is?"

"You first must win Royal permission to dive."

"True, but what of that?"

"Captain Phips is a New Englander, and therefore deemed a blue-nosed Puritan, a breed which His Majesty despises as the Devil loathes Holy Water."

Phips, flushing, snapped: "But, damn it, sir, I've never been more of a Puritan than I had to be if I wanted to live and do business around Boston. In fact, I've ever had small use for such self-righteous bastards as now rule Massachusetts Bay Colony and who persecute anyone who disagrees with 'em, especially anyone even suspected of witchcraft."

Briefly, but with effect, he spoke of Granny Eldritch's sufferings.

Sir Richard brushed an imaginary speck from lace frothing at his cuff. "Be that as it may, Captain Phips, the King hates Puritans of any description, so it should be our aim somehow to arrange for either the Duke of Albemarle or his Grace of Sunderland to present you to His Majesty with a view that you may arouse his greed with your tales of manifold riches to be won at small cost to himself. He is so deep in debt he just might listen. John and I are much too small fish to gain the Royal ear."

Sir John Narbrough said: "Suppose we adjourn to my lodgings to conduct a more detailed summation of our problems?"

Since the veteran lived in nearby Bow Street, the three soon reassembled in an untidy apartment in a room which, with difficulty, might have been designated as a study.

Sir Richard stretched long, bony legs in front of him and, steepling fingers under his nose, fixedly regarded the New Englander. "I like your proposition, Captain. You must command a sound, well-armed ship?"

"Aye, sir, but when I sail, knowing those seas as I do, I'd

prefer to command two strong vessels. Plenty of guns will be required to protect the riches I will raise."

Sir John Narbrough chuckled. "You say 'will' and not 'if'?"

" 'Will' because I alone possess knowledge which will ensure success!"

Sir Richard raised a be-ringed but none-too-clean hand. "I will now mention a possibility which possibly may wreck this venture from the start. 'Tis privately known that since His Majesty fears a landing of Protestant forces from Holland he will not, short of dire necessity, despatch a ship of the Royal Navy from his realm."

Narbrough's balding gray head inclined. "All too true and 'tis best not to forget we face another hindrance in Mr. Samuel Pepys, Secretary to the Lords Commissioners of Admiralty. Why he hates the Duke of Albemarle so bitterly is of no moment; the fact remains that he does, and is in an excellent position to nullify our project."

A medley of street noises beat through the open windows as Sir Richard scratched under an untidy brown periwig. "The question remains, even should Lord Albemarle manage some- how to gain and approach the King's ear, how are we to nullify Mr. Pepys's enmity?"

Phips commenced to stride back and forth, lace at his wrists and knees swaying. Finally he faced the Commissioners, as- sumed something of his old arrogant manner.

"Wasn't it through Mr. Pepys's good offices I was released from prison?"

"In part, yes," Sir Richard Haddock admitted.

"But why?"

"Because Pepys has heard a good deal concerning your treas- ure hunting scheme which was furthered by His Late Majesty. Were it not for his consuming hatred of Albemarle I hazard we might count on Mr. Pepys's influence. As Secretary to the Admiralty, he would have much to say whether or not a license might be granted us."

"In that case," Phips said slowly, "wouldn't it be a smart

[233]

move for you gents to get me an appointment with Mr. Pepys without the Duke of Albemarle having anything to do with it?"

A rasping laugh escaped narrow-faced Sir Richard Haddock and he surveyed the burly figure in fashionable raiment with something approaching respect. "That point, Captain, is well taken. Wouldn't be surprised if Pepys might not bring His Majesty around, if only to do Kit Monck out of money which would find its way into the Royal Treasury."

Phips stopped pacing. "In other words, Pepys, to spite Lord Albemarle, might act in our favor with the King?"

"Aye, that's pretty much the hang of it," mumbled the veteran Admiral, then rang for bread, cheese and ale.

Chapter 27

LORDS OF ADMIRALTY

ALTHOUGH BY NOW FAMILIAR with the uncertainties of life at Court and allowing for the innumerable intrigues forever under way in Whitehall Palace, William Phips commenced to despair when days then weeks elapsed and there came no summons to appear before Mr. Samuel Pepys.

Characteristically, he used the interval in making preparations for a return to Porto Plata. For one thing he devised, and with his own hands helped build, an improved diving bell patterned on designs obtained from a Swedish naval engineer who'd fallen on hard times.

Also, he scoured the navy yards for the best obtainable raising tackle. Best of all he was successful in dissuading his old First Officer, horse-faced, shrewd and extremely capable Francis Rogers, from accepting a lucrative post aboard an East Indiaman. He also kept an eye on Fast Otter and other North American Indian divers who had sailed aboard the *Salee Rose*.

Did it constitute a poor omen that his appointment, when it finally arrived, should fall on a really foul autumn day?

Apprehensions mounting, he nevertheless boldly entered a large and gloomy new building in which the Royal Navy was being administered since the old Admiralty House had been destroyed during the Great Fire of 1666.

Eventually he was escorted down a moldy-smelling corridor until he encountered Mr. Pepys in a small, low-ceilinged office, and to his dismay discovered the Secretary was not alone. Also present were a quartet of big-wigged officials including Sir John Narbrough and three gentlemen he correctly assumed must also be Naval Commissioners.

Later, the New Englander retained only confused impressions of addressing Mr. Pepys—a solid, square-jawed figure with eyes coldly gray and penetrating as rapier points.

Incredibly, he never had felt surer of himself than while frankly describing the *Salee Rose*'s recent cruise and at the same time supplying sound explanations, but no excuses, for its disappointing results.

Aware that the Secretary's expression remained anything but friendly, Phips enlarged boastfully on his wide experience and many voyages around the West Indies. In desperation he then enlarged upon the probable efficiency of his unique diving tub and of certain other specially designed devices capable of raising coral-encrusted objects from an ocean's floor.

To his pained surprise, Phips noted some of the faces, ranged beyond the table before which he stood, were not lighting up in the least. So, in rising despair he described—but, in part only—his encounter with Ottavio Gallucio and the priceless secret confided by him.

In hopes of arousing a glimmer of interest he even repeated what the old Genoese had told him concerning those fabulous riches he personally had seen being lowered into *Nuestra Señora de la Concepción* some forty years earlier. Such was his fury being unable to alter the stony expressions on those imperturbable faces he all but blurted out the name of the reef

[*236*]

and the approximate latitude in which the *Vice-Admiral* lay—but he didn't.

Employing a none-too-clean fingernail, Mr. Pepys at length scratched his chin and looked Phips straight in the eye. He spoke crisply but softly: "Your glowing discourse has held much of interest to us, Captain. We also have received commendable reports of your reputation for honesty, uncommon sea-sense and ingenuity, but such a venture as you propose for the present is not practicable; we must bide our time."

In dazed incredulity, Phips glared speechless, for once, into the Secretary's pale features, and later wondered whether a muscular tremor had caused the lid of Mr. Pepys's left eye to flicker or whether he was being tipped the most fleeting of winks.

Chapter 28

HENRY CHRISTOPHER MONCK,
2ND DUKE OF ALBEMARLE

AT BEST A WRETCHED PENMAN, grammarian and speller, Captain William Phips lately had taken to employing a secretary, one Arthur Davies, lent through the kindness of Sir John Narbrough—himself a most indifferent correspondent.

The day being uncommonly dark, coals glowing in a minute fireplace seemed only to emphasize the bone-penetrating chill pervading Phips's quarters in the Crown & Dove Tavern.

When a knock sounded on the door, Davies admitted a footman wearing Lord Albemarle's livery. He touched his hat, and bowing, offered a small, crested envelope. "Sir, my Lord invites you to read this instanter."

The twenty-first son read: *Don your best finery and hasten immediately to Newcastle House. His Majesty has deigned to receive you at this afternoon's levee.*

As usual the courtyard fronting Whitehall Palace was crowded by carriages, gigs, coaches, and vehicles of all descriptions. Some were quite plain and colorless, others were re-splendent with bright paint and giltwork and, more often than not, bore a coat-of-arms embellished upon their doors. Coach-men wearing expensive liveries cursed grooms struggling to re-strain the plunges and curvettings of hot-blooded carriage horses. In another part of the forecourt saddle horses, hitched to a series of rails, fidgeted, snapped, and kicked out of sheer boredom.

Lord Albemarle led the way bearing an impressive number of decorations and orders glittering on his dark-blue, long-skirted coat. Captain William Phips tramped in his wake, wear-ing a modishly cut suit of plum-colored velour devoid of orna-ments.

The oddly contrasting pair were granted immediate admit-tance whereupon a resplendent figure bearing a tall, gold-topped staff and wearing a towering black peruke appeared and the twenty-first son heard himself presented to the Lord Cham-berlain.

The air in a long succession of anterooms was stifling and redolent of stale perspiration given off by chattering swarms of courtiers which not even powder and French perfumes could disguise. The Lord Chamberlain gestured the visitors to halt, entered the Presence Chamber and promptly reappeared, and bowing, intoned, "Gentlemen, pray enter."

James II, King of England, Scotland, Ireland and France, for, stubbornly, he had clung to that empty title, occupied a huge and ornately carved armchair set on a red-carpeted and two-stepped dais.

Over a gleaming parquet floor, Lord Albemarle's rotund figure advanced, knelt and delicately kissed the King's long and bony hand.

William Phips of Jeremesquam, heart pounding like a kettle drum, followed suit but without grace and found himself gazing into the long-nosed and jaded-appearing features of his Sovereign framed in a massive full-bottomed wig the sable curls of which rippled halfway down to a golden waistband. The King's complexion was sallow and a galaxy of dull-red pimples remained visible despite a heavy layer of pale-brown face powder.

In his most unctuous tones Lord Albemarle murmured: "Your Majesty, I am honored beyond all deserts that you should receive my friend, Captain Phips from your Colony of Massachusetts Bay."

The King settled back in his armchair and treated his American subject to undisguised and unnerving scrutiny. Deliberately, weary but penetrating black eyes set too close together traveled from Phips's slippers, buckled in cut steel, to that periwig Monsieur Albert had assured was curled and trained in the very latest mode.

At length King James drawled: "On occasion we have heard accounts of you, Captain Phips; some unfavorable but more to the contrary. What is it you would of us?"

Lord Albemarle stepped to one side, smiled encouragingly, while Phips, struggling to keep his speech measured and even, recited the plea he'd rehearsed countless times dwelling on the incredible richness of a treasure reposing not so far below the surface as to render salvage operations too difficult or impossible.

From James II's impassive expression Phips guessed His Majesty might have perused Mr. Pepys's report on his speech before the Lords of Admiralty.

Albemarle murmured: "Sire, we have formed a company to undertake this search and if successful in obtaining your assent we guarantee Your Majesty's share will prove enormous." He paused for emphasis. "And at no cost whatever to the Royal Treasury."

The King's enormous wig swayed to a slight nod. He produced a lace-trimmed handkerchief from a very deep cuff and fanned himself indolently. "If we agree we will expect to be paid one-tenth of the gross profit earned." He smiled faintly. "'Gross.' You will note that it was not for nothing we were reared in Scotland. If there is aught else you have to say, Captain, speak up. We find your accent and curious turn of speech, well, unusual."

"I trust my Yankee accent does not grate on Your Majesty's ears; 'tis peculiar to the Colony of Massachusetts Bay."

"Come on, man speak up; time presses."

"Why, sir, Your Majesty, I mean," Phips stammered. "An you intend to favor our enterprise it would be well to issue our license with all despatch."

The King considered the suitor in mild astonishment.

"Why so?"

"Because, Your Majesty, news of the wreck's approximate position is now known, so there can be small doubt but that at this very moment, expeditions are being fitted out in Europe and in the West Indies to plunder the *Vice-Admiral*. 'Twould be a cruel shame to deprive the Royal Treasury of riches rightfully belonging to the Crown."

"Humph! 'Twould avail such rascals nothing lacking our permission to fish in British waters where we have been informed the wreck is believed to lie."

Albemarle advanced, knelt before the dais. "Be that as it may, Sire, we beg you to favor us without loss of time."

Briefly the King fingered a long blue jaw. "We will deliberate this matter. My Lord Albemarle you will be informed of —er—a possibly favorable decision in due course. You have our permission to withdraw."

Once the suppliants had backed out from the Presence Chamber, Lord Albemarle slipped an arm about his taller companion's shoulders—a gesture not lost upon an anxiously waiting throng of courtiers. This, plus the fact that His Grace of Albemarle seemed to be wearing a smug expression caused rumors to spread with incredible rapidity among London's more select clubs, taverns and coffee houses.

Later on, more than a little drunk, William Phips found occasion to wish that Mary, Jack Dale, and Betrag Eldritch might have witnessed his audience.

Chapter 29

31st JULY, 1686

SIX GENTLEMEN, more or less elegantly attired, arrived at Newcastle House to dine in Lord Albemarle's privy dining room where silver, napery, and crystal glittered in lavish display under a towering chandelier of Venetian glass supporting sufficient candles to reveal the room's least details. Behind each chair stood a footman wearing the host's handsome blue-and-gold livery.

Short and stocky Lord Albemarle's florid, roundish features beamed and sweated above a jabot of sparkling Valenciennes lace and a gold-laced coatee of burnt-orange velvet. Weather-beaten, flat-faced Sir John Narbrough with the fiercely flaring gray mustachios had contented himself by wearing navy blue and white.

Lord Falkland, whose gray, narrow features and huge hooked nose suggested a bird of prey, was costumed in emerald green; rings set with large precious stones flashed to his least gesture.

Sir James Heyes, youngest of the company, was built much like William Phips, but on a smaller scale. His scarlet tunic offered an effective contrast to the brawny New Englander's well-cut coat of dove-gray satin.

"Gentlemen, I have requested the pleasure of your company in honor of a birthday."

"Whose?" Mr. Foxcroft, the only commoner present saving Phips, wanted to know.

"Why, that of our Company!"

So intense a silence descended that a drop of candle wax falling onto a salver caused a clearly audible *ping!*

Although hampered by a great scarlet seal, the host, grinning, pulled out from his coattail's pocket a scroll of parchment. At the sight of it, shivers rippled across Phips's back like a cat's paws striking a placid millpond.

Albemarle heaved his squat figure to its feet and held the document on high. "Here, Gentlemen, is our Company's patent, signed by His Majesty and duly executed by the Lord Privy Seal authorizing us to seek, delve and fish for treasure in British Territorial waters!"

Everyone leaped up, pumped hands, embraced and pounded one another's shoulder blades. When Sir John Narbrough used granite-hard fists to thump Phips's back, hot tears filled the twenty-first son's eyes.

The Duke donned a pair of square-lensed spectacles and looked about, blinking. "I now will read in part the patent granted to your humble servant, as representing our Company of Gentlemen Adventurers:

"'He is granted ownership of all such wrecks as shall be found by him in the seas to the windward off the north of Hispaniola. Also is granted to him, and through him to his associates, possession of all such riches, bullion and plate whether ingots of gold, bars or pigs of silver or valuables of what other kinds whatsoever as shall be found within such wrecks.'

"I might add that His Majesty is pleased to be satisfied with only a tenth part of whatever treasure is recovered."

Revelry ensued and before servants set about replacing the first set of guttering candles, shareholders were reeling like storm-tossed pilot boats. Mr. Foxcroft lay beneath the sideboard grunting like a richly dressed hog and dour Lord Falkland felt prompted to fence with Sir James Heyes, fortunately using lighted tapers instead of rapiers.

Henry Christopher Monck draped an arm about Phips. "Well, my lad, at last seems we've brought the matter off, despite the best efforts of lovable Mr. Pepys and his coterie."

The New Englander, forgetting all but an overwhelming sense of relief, impulsively gripped the King's favorite in a bear hug much as he would a friendly sachem in the Maine District's backwoods. "Ask what you will, Kit, even my life. You shall have it."

The Peer giggled drunkenly, gasping: "For God's sake, Will, leave me be ere you crush in my ribs." He steadied himself, said abruptly, owl-eyed: "Come to think on it, Will, there *is* something I'll ask of you."

"Great or small, consider the favor granted. What would you of me?"

Above retching noises made by a guest who seemed to have forgotten that an excess of wine can flow in opposite directions, Albemarle said thickly: "Cousin of mine—Marquis of Cranbury—has a second son, the Honorable Frederick Delacorte, who has been overindustrious in sowing a harvest of wild oats. Fact, the young fool's squandered what little wealth his father's allowed him and now stands so plunged into debt the debtors' prison's gates yawn for him.

"In short, my Cousin needs to see the Honorable Freddie out of England in a hurry. Cranbury hopes that, granted opportunity, the youth may redeem himself, for his elder brother George is of sickly disposition so Frederick soon may inherit the title."

Phips laughed, infinitely relieved that no more serious request had been put forth. "Why, sure, Kit, I'd be pleased to sign on the fellow an you desire so. Consider it done; but how is this noble sprig to be treated?"

Sobering a trifle, Albemarle said, "You are not to promote my Cousin's son till you see fit; the Honorable Freddie first must learn to discharge duties as a common seaman."

Phips experienced a dampening of his ebullient mood. Would this popinjay turn out to be a trouble-maker? Bitter recollections of that unruly rabble he'd shipped aboard the *Salee Rose* returned. Still, since he'd coped with a whole pack of mutinous scoundrels, didn't it stand to reason he could, with the use of only the little finger of his left hand manage a single, insubordinate fellow? Mercifully, William Phips at the moment was unable to read the future.

Chapter 30

DEPTFORD—SEPTEMBER 1686

FOLLOWING ISSUANCE of the Company's license many moves held in abeyance were now put forward. Lord Albemarle, following the considered advice of William Phips and Sir John Narbrough, ranged along the Thames until they discovered and thoroughly examined a pair of vessels which appeared suitable.

One, a small frigate named the *Bridgewater*, was fairly new and stoutly constructed, having originally been built for the Royal Navy. However, for some obscure reason she never had been accepted and commissioned. Of about 200 tons, this stout, yellow-painted ship mounted twenty-two 12-pound carriage guns and had proved remarkably fast and handy during trials held off the Downs.

The New Englander felt pleased with her beyond all expectation. Moreover, his new command's rigging was sound and her two suits of sails recently had been cut from canvas of the best quality. Her four anchors of varying weights had been expertly forged: in short, save for a vessel designed and built by himself, the *Bridgewater* was all he could ask for.

Even the frigate's new name Phips took as auspicious; tactfully, she'd been rechristened the *James and Mary* in honor of the King and his consort. Could it be anything but an encouraging coincidence that his *own* parents had borne identical Christian names?

Yes, *James and Mary* surely should bring that luck he was going to need in large quantities.

Never one to risk all his eggs in one basket, Lord Albemarle, at Phips's request, also purchased for the Company a stout little sloop of fifty tons mounting ten small guns which the New Englander in gratitude named the *Henry of London* for Henry Christopher Monck, and saw to it that dependable and resourceful Francis Rogers would command her.

Further, as a hedge against possible disappointment off Porto Plata, Phips insisted that the expedition ship an ample supply of trade goods the sale of which might help defray costs should unpredictable misfortunes thwart his search for the great galleon's remains.

Phips's sleep remained troubled through fears that Ottavio Gallucio might not still be alive when the *James and Mary* dropped her hook off Hispaniola. Also, he suffered agonies over a possibility that some expedition might have forestalled him or that a submarine cataclysm could have engulfed the wreck.

Anxiously, he watched the diving tub on which he'd lavished so much ingenuity and toil lowered into the frigate's mainhold along with diving gear fashioned according to his design and specifications.

Personally, he checked the quantity and quality of the *James and Mary*'s sea stores and saw to it Captain Rogers took similar precautions aboard the *Henry of London*.

In the "great cabbin" aboard his new command, Phips dictated a final letter to Mr. Davies:

My dear Wife; I scarce can contain my pleasure that promises I have made which many deemed to be but outrageous boastings at last are about to become realized.

Hold your head high, dear Wife; for I now stand on the threshold of a triumph which will 'rouse the admiration and envy of the whole world.

The only flaw in my present situation lies in the fact that I must sign on an ill-mannered young nobleman named Frederick Delacorte only because I am so deeply beholden to His Grace of Albemarle.

Protested Mr. Davies: "In heaven's name, sir, ease off. My fingers are so cramped I scarce can hold the pen."

Once the secretary had flexed and laid out a fresh sheet of foolscap, Phips resumed:

I rejoice you did not witness the arrival at dockside of the Honorable Frederick, second son to the Marquis of Cranbury. He drove up in some friend's fancy coach clad in purple finery. Moreover, this sprig of the nobility had the effrontery to appear lugging beneath his arm a spaniel wearing a silk ribbon tied to its silly head.

Haughtily, this young fop of about twenty-five demanded to be shown his cabin and appeared thunderstruck when I informed that he was no passenger but only an ordinary seaman; also that I had received strict instructions he need expect no favors and if he failed in proper discharge of his duties the boatswain would be free to kick his arse and even use a cane an he protested.

Spiritedly the popinjay defied me till one of his familiars reminded him of a pack of bailiffs hard on his heels eager to clap him into debtors' prison. Thereupon the Honorable Frederick shuddered and passed his little dog into his friend's keeping.

Tomorrow our principal shareholders will collect at Deptford to bid us Godspeed. I would you could be present.

[*248*]

From afar I kiss your hand—pray note how polished a
courtier your frontier ruffian of an husband has become—
and remain your ever-affectionate

WILLIAM

On the *James and Mary*'s cramped quarterdeck Captain
William Phips clad in the same elegant garments he'd worn to
a farewell breakfast given by his backers and admirers stood
between a pair of light stern chasers.

Gently, a breeze beating down the traffic-studded Thames
ruffled a snow-white ostrich plume curling about his high-
crowned hat's brim and set varicolored signal flags strung casually to various stays and shrouds to flapping. Sunlight glanced
bravely off the gilded hilt of a dress sword presented by his
Grace of Albemarle.

Now that the little frigate's anchor had been heaved, foul
with evil-smelling mud and smartly catted, freshly set topsails filled, yards swung about and the ship gathered way.

On Admiralty Dock sounded a series of cheers when, from
James and Mary's maintop, was broken out the red cross of
Saint George on its white field while on the mizzen gaff jerkily appeared a Union Jack. Another such fluttered to the foretopmast, the yellow-painted private man-of-war glowing in
the brilliant sunshine, presented a memorable picture.

To Phips's pleased astonishment when his flags were broken
out a third-rate H.B.M.S., *Carlisle*, fired a six-gun salute. That
a Royal ship-of-the-line should accord him such recognition
seemed noisy proof that King James's favor was accompanying
the Company's expedition.

Immediately he yelled for Tom Armstrong, his one-eyed
Master Gunner, to acknowledge the courtesy. Other Royal
vessels moored in the clay-colored stream or undergoing repairs in adjacent dockyards, joined in creating such a tumult
that clouds of gulls resting on hulks rotting along the river-
bank wheeled, shrieking, into the sky.

Francis Rogers on green-painted little *Henry of London*
also returned salutes.

For the twenty-first son the scene almost escaped reality; here he was actually commanding a squadron—of only two vessels to be sure. Since in reality he wasn't commanding vessels of the Royal Navy this might not be the propitious moment to break out a commodore's long red pendant secreted in his seachest.

Turning to First Lieutenant John Strong, a big-boned, long-faced Yorkshireman with whom he'd trafficked, more or less aboveboard, for a long time down in the West Indies, he said: "Order gun captains to answer salutes with reduced charges—no use wasting powder we damn' well may need later on!"

The Yorkshireman might have been deemed handsome except that a buccaneer's pistol ball had carried away the top of his right ear and a galaxy of bluish spots of burnt powder grains dotted his lanthorn jaw.

The cheering faded while the *James and Mary*'s topmen shook out gallants and royals and picked up speed.

Watching the shore cluttered with docks and shipyards slip by, he turned to chubby and red-faced Mr. Hans Sloane, reputedly a competent physician, diarist, and cartographer.

"Take a good look," he invited. "May be some time afore we cruise this river again."

"Captain, you've just read my mind. Wonder how many of our company will live to see England again."

"Aye. God and the Devil alone can answer that."

Starting for his quarterdeck's ladder he noticed the Honorable Frederick Delacorte, wearing rough clothes, standing apart. He was gripping the rail and staring mournfully at the shore. The starch seemed to have departed from his back and from his unsteady stance the young fellow must have been drinking hard.

Phips thought back to that occasion on which Albemarle had queried: "In what capacity did my Cousin's son sign Articles?"

"As ordinary seaman; but should this lily-handed carpet knight prove diligent and reliable I may allow him to assist

Mr. Waddington, the Crown's treasury accountant and assayer."

Once Woolwich had been left behind, Phips ordered ornamental signal flags struck, then started for his "great cabbin" which wasn't great at all, only a small, sparsely furnished merchant captain's quarters, but he noticed several deck hands struggling with the Honorable Freddie who had just then managed to break loose and come charging up the quarterdeck ladder, scarlet-faced and gibbering. "Won't tolerate such goddam filthy quarters, such vulgar abuse!"

Phips blocked his path. "Shut up, and go below, you snot-nosed whelp!"

"H-how dare you, you a low-born Colonial, address a—"

The Captain's fist caught the younger man flush on the jaw causing a *smack* loud as that of a sail too suddenly filled. Lord Albemarle's cousin slumped inert onto the quarterdeck.

Phips beckoned the Boatswain. "Tug this dainty carcass below. When he comes to, warn him if he ever again approaches my quarterdeck without orders I'll snap his silly neck!"

Part IV

OFF HISPANIOLA

Chapter 31

PORTO PLATA AGAIN

ON THE 15th December, 1686, the Company of Gentleman Adventurers' frigate *James and Mary* weathered Cape Cabron and stood into that passage which separates that peninsula from Water Key. With confidence in Mr. Charles Salmon's chart, lying unrolled before him, Captain William Phips hailed the helmsman: "Bear two points to starboard!"

"Two points starboard it is, sir!"

Slowly the bowsprit and well-filled jibs swung in the general direction of Porto Plata, presumed to be lying some fifty nautical miles to the southwest.

All in all, Phips was pleased because events thus far had gone well, save that, from the start, the *Henry of London* had proved to be a deplorably sluggish sailer. Continually, he'd had to order his flagship—as rather grandiloquently he termed her —to shorten sail to keep the sloop in sight.

Yes. Everything had gone according to plan when the little

expedition had put in to wood and water at Carlisle Bay in Barbados, where crews had remained orderly.

The Honorable Frederick, outwardly at least, not only had appeared reconciled to his lot but successfully had defended himself against the toughest of deck hands. Also, he'd appeared surprisingly eager to learn navigation.

Once Barbados barely lay astern, a howling, blinding gale had struck during which the *Henry* had become lost to sight and there could be no telling where she might have been driven if, indeed, she had remained afloat.

Captain Rogers, of course, carried instructions to rendezvous at Mona Island or, failing that, in Samana Bay on the northeastern coast of Hispaniola. But the *Henry* had not appeared at either meeting place; only hope remained in the fact that Francis Rogers was among the very few who knew that Porto Plata was to be this expedition's ultimate destination.

Phips's other principal worry lay in the probable difficulty of convincing the Governor and other authorities in Porto Plata that although this vessel mounted twenty-two cannon she was arriving with no hostile intent and only wanted to trade while taking on water, wood and other supplies.

While at a leisurely speed, the *James and Mary* was skirting Hispaniola's northern coast, four of the ship's company stood by the port bulwarks watching the surf-rimmed tan-green coast slip by. Heavily forested, it looked hilly at many points and in the distance loomed the bluish peaks of conical mountains which, according to Master Gunner Armstrong, were extinct volcanoes.

"Come tomorrow," the bandy-legged Armstrong predicted, "we ought to raise the tall, lone mountain behind Porto Plata— a blessed handy mark if ever there was one."

He turned to Fast Otter, stripped to the waist and wearing a red bandanna knotted about his dark and narrow head.

"Figger we'll find the *Henry* already there?"

The Penobscot shrugged wiry, copper-brown shoulders. "Mebee, mebee not. Me not *shaman*."

The Honorable Frederick Delacorte who, long since, had

become known simply as "Fred," peered over a long succession of gloriously bright-blue rollers and the diamantine whitecaps cresting them, then turned to dumpy Mr. James Waddington—Assayer and Accountant for the Royal Treasury and, for the time being, also acting supercargo. "Sir, what lies yonder?"

"I've never been this way before." Mr. Waddington turned to the Master Gunner. "How about you?"

"Looks like Cape Francis or *Francisco* as the Dons term it." The Honorable Frederick watched a school of silvery flying fish explode from ultramarine waves, then scatter over patches of lemon-yellow Sargasso weed.

Deeply sun-burned, horny-footed, and with long light-brown hair bleached to a honey-yellow, his single garment a pair of tar-stained canvas breeches, the Marquis of Cranbury's second son certainly would have been unrecognizable to friends about London or around the Home Counties.

To his astonishment he was commencing to tolerate his present situation and pondered prospects for improving it. By degrees he was learning to appreciate loud-mouthed and incredibly profane Captain Phips's sure sea-sense and also the rough-and-ready fairness with which he administered discipline.

All the same he still wasn't ready to forgive that blow on the jaw dealt before he'd even had a chance to adjust to the brutal existence aboard a man-of-war. There'd be plenty of opportunities later on to level the score.

As newly appointed assistant to the supercargo, he ought, once the wreck was located, to be in an admirable position to convert confidential knowledge to advantage.

The Honorable Fred drew several deep breaths, "How big is Porto Plata?"

"'Tain't much; may be two thousand folks of all breeds. Tomorrow you'll see what there is provided the place ain't been wiped out by pirates or leveled by an earthquake."

"Earthquake?" The Honorable Frederick lifted tawny brows.

"Aye. They suffer a lot of 'em in these latitudes."

Mr. Waddington sighed at the prospect of descending into the frigate's furnace-hot hold. "Come along, we'd better break out cotton yard-goods from number four hold. Skipper likely will want some, first thing."

When they sought the main companionway the Honorable Frederick cast a lingering upward glance at figures occupying the quarterdeck busily surveying the distant coast through spy-glasses. All went barefoot and were wearing broad-brimmed Jamaican straw hats, soiled loose shirts and baggy breeches.

Dominating the group was William Phips's burly figure, next tallest stood the Yorkshireman John Strong, First Lieutenant; noticeably shorter was Mr. Sloane, Surgeon and amateur cartographer; shortest of all was irascible, red-haired Second Lieutenant Hubert Maddox from whom the new assistant supercargo was acquiring the rudiments of navigation and seamanship.

Before descending into the stifling and evil-smelling 'tween decks, the young nobleman glanced over his shoulder at the sparkling ocean and noted yet another school of those great green turtles which, over a long voyage, would supply the only fresh meat for a ship's company. What an indolent life such creatures led—drifting aimlessly wherever currents chanced to carry them—a pity humans were doomed to a different fate.

Phips closed the lid covering his telescope's eyepiece with a soft snap, pointed to a steep cliff rising sheer from the headland's end. "Yonder's Cape Francis."

"An that be the case," observed Mr. Strong, keeping an eye on a great albatross gracefully circling the frigate's tops, "come daylight we ought to be dropping anchor off Porto Plata."

Studying his superior, he watched the New Englander begin to finger his broad jaw as generally he did when perplexed or uneasy. "What's on yer mind, sir?"

"I'm wondering what we'll find when we make port."

Privately, he was conjecturing on who the Governor of Santiago Province might be—the post had stood vacant during his last visit—and whether Don Pedro Fuentes still might be *alcalde* and occupying the port's less-than-imposing *cabildo* of adobe brick.

Above all, was Ottavio Gallucio still alive and able to supply crucial details omitted during his original disclosures?

What if he arrived to find a Spanish man-of-war at anchor or, worse still, competitors under various guises? All he said to Strong was: "I'm concerned over whether I can convince the Governor and port officials we're but peaceful traders only bent on an exchange of merchandise." He heaved a gusty sigh. "I'd give my left ball to be sure what's happened to the *Henry*. Wonder if Rogers, in such a damnably sluggish sailer, mayn't be heading straight for Porto Plata?"

John Strong shook his battered head so hard his hat's brim fluttered. "Knowin' Rogers like I do, I vow he'd never, willing, miss a rendezvous. I'm fearin' we must count her lost, else she'd sure-enough have turned up in Samana Bay."

"What will you do to hoodwink the Spaniards?" asked Mr. Sloane.

On broad, bare feet Phips took a turn about the quarterdeck. "First thing is to make us look more like an ordinary merchantman; trim sails and rigging careless-like. Send most of the cannon below and leave gun ports open to prove they're empty."

"Sounds like sense."

"How long since you've put into Porto Plata, Will?" queried the Surgeon.

"Nigh on two years—a damn' sight longer than I've counted on. Yep. The Dons may have patched up the largish battery they've got defending the harbor's mouth—will have, if they finally have found a Governor with a mite of spunk."

When a lookout sang out, "Sail ho!" his gaze swung sharply upwards.

"Damn! That's the third since sunup. Lookout! What d'you make of her?"

"Looks like another little lanteen-rigged coaster, sir; bearin' away towards the nor'east."

"All the same, I don't like it," growled Phips. "Never have sighted so many craft hereabouts this time of year." His man-

[259]

ner altered, became brisk, "Mr. Strong, better start sending guns below lest some nosy revenue boat heads this way. Next, I want gallantmasts sent down to prove we're ready to trust the natives and don't aim to tip-and-run if things go wrong."

"What about divin' and fishin' gear?" the Mate wanted to know.

"The diving bell and the rest are to go below hatches right after the guns. Call all hands and get busy."

By sundown, back-breaking toil had transformed the *James and Mary* into what appeared to be a slow and slovenly merchantman showing many empty gunports and fairly crawling along under sloppily set canvas.

Phips commenced to feel better but as dusk deepened a rosy, throbbing glow lit the western sky and gnawing doubts assailed the "Commodore." Somewhere below the horizon a vessel was burning.

Chapter 32

FÉLICIA

WAS IT PURELY BY CHANCE that a flotilla of piraguas fishing northeast of Porto Plata, on recognizing a European ship, at once should hoist patched brown sails and scud away towards Porto Plata at top speed?

The private-armed frigate *James and Mary*, plowing along over lazy, bright-blue rollers flew only a single frayed Union Jack from her mizzen's gaff; halyards, braces sagged, and rope ends trailed over her side while her longboat was being towed on from the bight of an unseamanly long painter.

Secretly, the Honorable Frederick Delacorte enjoyed the "Commodore's" barely suppressed frustrations over his command's appearance but all the same he'd grudgingly admired Captain Phips's address made at sunrise.

"Remember," he'd grimly warned all hands, "success depends on gulling the Dons into taking us for a simple merchantman. Make one mistake and we'll all end up in some filthy prison for God knows how long. Dress as you please and carry out orders in slack manner.

"Everyone must keep reminding himself we're *only* here to trade, which likely won't be difficult since I suspect only few of us will be allowed on shore at the same time. For good and sufficient reason the Dons fear the presence of any sizable gang of English or Colonial sailors. Above all"—his hard, gray-blue eyes swept the deeply tanned men lined up below the quarter-deck—"keep yer traps shut whenever Spanishers are on board, and stay peaceful despite any and all provocation."

It came as a shock to Phips that when his frigate stood in towards the port to note that the brick-and-tabby battery protecting the entrance to Porto Plata's fine harbor *had* been repaired and the snouts of no less than fifteen heavy pieces of ordnance were peering through recently rebuilt embrasures.

Aye, somebody possessed of energy must be in control, were one to go by the fact that not only the *cabildo* but also the customhouse or *casa de moneda*, had been freshly whitewashed; their roofs no longer were palm-thatched but had been done over in dull orange tile which must have felt uncomfortably hot on the feet of buzzards accustomed to roosting on them.

There were other evidences of energy on someone's part. One of the mission church's towers was nearing completion although its mate remained a sorry stump and a short stone pier now jutted into the harbor's azure waters over which planed ungainly brown pelicans looking like creatures from some pre-historic era.

"Salute the port!" Phips bellowed for, as the frigate bore down on the battery, a swarm of white-and-yellow-clad figures were running onto gun platforms. A Spanish flag rose jerkily on a flagpole, so, after the "Commodore" had ordered his vessel brought nearly into the wind, three salutes started echoing among rounded foothills encompassing a tall, lone mountain rising behind little Porto Plata.

Second Officer Maddox, glass trained on the battery, called sharply: "They're running out guns!"

Thrice the Union Jack dipped as if anticipating a friendly

reception; the frigate meanwhile came into easy range of the battery with her cannon unmanned. Under orders, her crew waved and shouted obscene greetings.

All the same Phips felt his throat closing. No telling what the political situation ashore might be—news of some fresh hostilities might have reached here. Hell and damnation! At this point-blank range a few broadsides from the battery would put an abrupt period to all his hopes.

An officer in a long yellow coat appeared on the parapet and shouted something unintelligible; all the same Phips calmly ordered his best bower anchor lowered near the center of the harbor's entrance.

Topsails slatting uselessly, the frigate lost way, then gradually rounded into the wind.

The crew held their breaths and cursed feelingly. Who knew for sure whether at any minute devastating broadsides might not blow them all into bloody tatters?

For William Phips ensured a period of dreadful uncertainty, alleviated only when, from the stone pier extending from the *cabildo*, a small boat put out flying the yellow-red-yellow flag of Spain. In its stern slouched an unshaven official wearing a flat, plumed hat and a dingy yellow tunic. His plump body swayed rhythmically to the efforts of ragged brown oarsmen pulling in leisurely fashion towards the anchored and helpless merchantman.

Once the government boat arrived alongside and whitely grinning Indian rowers had tossed oars, a Jacob's ladder was lowered and lines cast to the boat's crew.

To the Honorable Frederick, loitering as near the gangway as he dared, it came as a revelation to witness the transformation in the "Commodore's" manner. Clad in a simple blue-and-white suit, the New Englander was all smiles and his gestures were deferential as, in fluent but poorly-accented Spanish, he bowed and invited the official to board.

Pleasantly, he received a bald, fox-faced, mahogany-complexioned official who turned out to be one Colonel Ramirez, Commandant of the port's defenses. The Spaniard's manner, however, remained suspicious, bordering on the contemptuous when shown into the "great cabbin" where Mr. Waddington, acting as Phips's personal aide in addition to his duties as supercargo, poured out choice wines.

Hands lounged about the deck idly coiling rope or calling insults, fortunately unintelligible, down to the boat alongside.

Anxiously, Mr. Sloane and the Second Officer lingered on the quarterdeck sweating profusely from more than the heat of the sun. What might be taking place below? On the main deck the Honorable Frederick, along with most of the crew, experienced mounting misgivings as time dragged by. At the end of about an hour Phips and the Spaniard reappeared, chatting amiably in what appeared to be a relaxed mood. Phips indicated a pair of boxes placed in the gangway, and made a careless gesture. "Here, *Señor Coronel,* are trifling gifts—a case of choice French brandies as token of esteem for you and your subordinates. Kindly present the other case to His Excellency, the Governor, with my compliments. By the way, I don't believe I know that distinguished gentleman's name."

"*El Gobernador* is Señor Don Henrique Montalban." The Colonel's smile faded. "Don Henrique is most able but possibly overenergetic for such a climate as this."

"With the greatest of pleasure I anticipate an opportunity to present my respects. Oh, one more thing: Is my old friend, Pedro Fuendes, still *Alcalde?*"

To Phips's infinite relief the gaunt Colonel replied in rapid Spanish, "*Sí, Señor Capitáno,* and prepared to trade, with discretion, for foreign goods. He, I, and *el Gobernador* not long ago reached an understanding on such delicate matters. We must trade or perish since little of the supplies we need so badly ever arrive from Spain or the Tierra Firma."

A series of cautious hints revealed that no vessel resembling the *Henry of London*'s description had been sighted in the vicinity of Porto Plata.

Should Ottavio Gallucio have died and his wishes respected, then Don Pedro Fuentes should have in his possession that "Will" promised by *Nuestra Señora de la Concepción*'s pilot.

Burning impatience to settle that point rendered Phips almost dangerously precipitate in initiating further inquiry.

Colonel Ramirez was persuaded to linger long enough to inspect certain cases of extra-tempting trade goods hoisted on deck from among cannon and fishing apparatus in the hold. Judging by the expression on the Spaniard's saddle-brown visage he judged he'd correctly foreseen the sort of supplies these people needed the most.

Having had considerable experience in the Spanish West Indies, Phips anticipated no prompt reaction, well aware that, from the beginning, the all-powerful *Casa de Contratación* in Seville had forbidden, under terrible penalties, including death, importation of any manufactured goods of non-Spanish origin.

When a second day passed without word from the *cabildo*, Phips suspected this energetic Governor had smelt a rat.

As further reassurance to the authorities, the twenty-first son ordered the frigate's topmasts sent down and all yards lowered, pointedly placing his vessel in no condition to escape quick destruction by the battery. This maneuver proved so successful that, next day, a customs official arrived alongside to indicate obliquely that a certain amount of trade just might be permitted but under no circumstances would more than ten of the merchantman's crew be allowed ashore at one time.

Soon piraguas, canoes, and scows started rowing out, laden deep under piles of erotic-smelling hides, mahogany and logwood, hogsheads of crude brown sugar and casks of smoked pork and beef to be hoisted inboard by a crane rigged to the mainmast.

Traders departed with cases of cutlery, yard goods, hats, shoes, harness, and medical supplies, and, only after dark, a small supply of firearms and ammunition. Transactions purposely were protracted as much as possible; haggling continued for hours on end in hopes the *Henry of London*'s topsails yet might appear on the horizon.

Towards the end of the second day's trading, Phips, together with Mr. Waddington and his new assistant, the Honorable Frederick Delacorte, were rowed ashore. Presently the

[265]

Captain wearing his second-best suit called on the Governor, Señor Don Henrique Montalban, whom he sensed was not only astute but unscrupulous. Indeed, Phips decided, it wouldn't be beyond this official to seize the helpless merchantman on some trumped-up charge once trading had been completed.

Reluctantly quitting the *cabildo's* comparative coolness and scattering dozing pigs and chickens the New Englander sauntered out into torrid heat and circled the market place where nearly naked Indians and ragged peons drowsed in patches of shade.

As might have been expected, the *Alcalde* was not in his office but enjoying a siesta in his own dwelling.

Fat little Don Pedro Fuentes appeared all graciousness and somehow managed to retain a measure of dignity despite slippered bare feet, a sweat-stained yellow banyan and shapeless turban.

The Mayor declared himself delighted beyond words to welcome the distinguished *Capitán* Phips back to Porto Plata; he clapped hands and ordered wine cooled in an olla of sweating red clay. Next he waved his guest to a rattan armchair, picked up a fan and collapsed rather than sat with sweat-stained shirt gaping over a rotund brown belly.

Talk, seemingly pointless, veered back and forth in the dimly lit apartment, yet the visitor ascertained that quite a few foreign vessels, all small, had visited Porto Plata during the past year or so. Ah? And of what nationality had these been?

Don Pedro ruminated, "Most claimed their home ports to be Jamaica or some other British West Indian colony; a few said they had come all the way down from New England and the Bermudas."

At that last remark Phips ceased fanning at a halo of flies. "Señor, I know you to be a busy man, but can you recall the name of any boat hailing from Bermuda?"

"I am not a clerk," the *Alcalde* snorted. "Possibly such information may be found in the *Casa de Aduana*. I only know that since Señor Montalban arrived here very few foreign vessels have been permitted to enter the port. You have been accorded a rare privilege but only because we stand in desperate need of certain trade goods."

Rare indecision racked the twenty-first son. Despite pointed hints, this obese little man avoided mention of a document destined for Captain William Phips. Still, he had no certainty that Don Pedro ever had received such a "Will."

Employing consummate tact the New Englander finally inquired whether a document addressed to him ever had been received at the *cabildo*.

A blind man could have sensed the change in Don Pedro's manner; small black eyes became opaque although an oleaginous smile continued to crease the *Alcalde's* chubby features. It held no meaning when he held raised hands in righteous indignation.

"But of course not, *Señor Capitán!* You affront me! Had I received such a paper as a man of honor I would immediately have presented it when first we had the pleasure of again doing business."

For a moment Phips considered mentioning Ottavio Gallucio but then it occurred to him that possibly the old Genoese remained alive. Accordingly he dropped the subject and turned the conversation towards business matters.

The big New Englander waited until twilight before seeking Ottavio Gallucio's hovel by a circuitous route on the far outskirts of the port.

Seldom had Phips's heart pounded more fiercely than when he glimpsed beyond a stand of new banana plants the hut's sun-bleached thatch roof.

Assailed by mosquitoes, he stood, carefully studied the clearing in which a pair of ribby black pigs and equally scrawny chickens listlessly were hunting food. About him reigned deep silence broken only by the chirping of insects and the first calls of night birds. No stirring of air concealed minor noises. The leaves of the lianas drooping from gigantic ceiba and cottonwood trees remained quite motionless.

He felt encouraged when a light sprang into being behind the door, but of the man he sought nothing was to be seen. The old Indian woman Félicia's bent and rag-clad figure emerged to shoo the pigs into a noisome little sty.

"*Buenos tardes,*" Phips called softly. "One hopes you and your master enjoy good health."

The old woman started violently. "*Señor Dios!—El Capitán Inglés!*" Incredulous, she peered at him from eyes so sunken they suggested sockets in a death's head.

From beneath his arm Phips offered a package of food.

"And how is my friend, Señor Gallucio?"

"*Aye de mí!* Don Ottavio went to Heaven eight months ago. God rest his soul."

Phips's stomach turned over. "You *are* sure he is dead?"

"He lies buried there." She indicated a low mound topped by a cross consisting of two sticks bound together with rags.

"Let us go inside, Félicia. There is much need to talk."

Because of his imperfect Spanish and this simple woman's lack of intelligence, quite some time was required to ascertain that Ottavio Gallucio had, indeed, died of natural causes: also, that Don Pedro Fuentes had been lying in his teeth. Félicia swore by all the Saints in the calendar that she, herself, had placed a sealed document purporting to be a Will bearing Phips's name into the Mayor's own hands, together with instructions that it must be delivered to the Englishman the moment he reappeared in Porto Plata.

Phips broke into hysterical curses. Of course the *Alcalde* had embezzled the old Genoese's information for his own use.

The wrinkled old creature timidly placed a hand on his. "One knows what you think, *Señor Capitán;* it was most stupid for Ottavio to trust *el Alcalde.* No?" She peered up into the New Englander's bronzed features with something like a little smile curving an almost toothless mouth.

"Praise God, my sainted master as he lay dying came to understand the *ladrón's* true nature, so sent him a false map which, *sin duda,* he will deny ever having received. My master foresaw that when Don Pedro would swear he had nothing for you, you would come here, *entiende?*"

"So all he entrusted to the *Alcalde* was a worthless drawing?"

"*Sí, Señor Inglés.*"

"Did my friend draw a true map?"

The world seemed to stand still while he awaited a reply.

"*Pero sí.* When Don Ottavio knew he was nearing the grave he remembered you, his protector, as a son, and made a second map with additions of much importance to the one you already have. This he placed in an olla tightly sealed and coated by tar so that wetness could not spoil it."

"Where is this jar?"

Félicia tottered to the grave and pointed towards the foot of the mound. "There. I buried it in the dead of night; no one can know."

"Bless you!"

Impulsively, Phips bent and kissed the old woman's mottled bony hand.

Lights in Porto Plata were winking out. Rays shed by a gibbous moon only faintly illumined the clearing when Félicia offered a spade with a broken handle. Surprisingly soon its blade grated upon a small, pitch-smeared earthenware jar.

Chapter 33

RENDEZVOUS

IF ANY OF THE WATCH on deck wondered why the Captain should return around midnight, go below directly and lock himself in the "great cabbin" there was no comment, even on the part of the Honorable Frederick standing anchor watch. Only he wondered, for, as a rule, Captain Phips, on returning on board, invariably made a tour of the deck to reassure himself that all hands were awake and alert. Might it not prove rewarding to solve this minor mystery?

Carefully Phips chipped off the hardened tar sufficiently to remove the jar's lid. Breathlessly, he reached inside, plucked out a grease-stained sheet of foolscap, then smoothed it on his chart table.

Next, from that ironbound chest in which was kept the ship's money, he brought out and unfolded the original rough drawing given him by Ottavio Gallucio. Through swift comparison it became evident his new acquisition was invaluable. Scrawled in a shaky hand appeared a sprinkling of remarks, soundings, cosines, and cross bearings which should go far towards locating the *Vice-Admiral*'s grave.

He noted, for instance, the presence of two hitherto unmarked shoals identified as simply *North Riff* and *South Riff*. God's love! A navigator unaware of these hazards readily might pile up his vessel since, according to Ottavio's crabbed notations, neither shoal was visible except at extremely low tide. There was no indication of any chimney-shaped rock.

A simple cross and the initials N.S.D.L.C. seemed to indicate that the remains of the great galleon lay near the center of a great horseshoe-shaped pattern of reefs marked *Banca de Ambrosia*. A few soundings indicated that most of the "riffs" composing this bank, even at low water, lay only a few feet below the surface, a fearsome, invisible menace.

Turning up his lanthorn's wick, Phips, brows knitted and lips tight, studied the depths of water inside the horseshoe. It probably would be unsafe to anchor a ship of his frigate's draft *inside* the horseshoe. He'd have to send his divers in small boats, a troublesome complication which couldn't possibly have been foreseen.

How could his precious and ponderous diving bell be conveyed inside and could it be profitably employed on so uneven a bottom? Umm. This would explain why Ottavio had marked "a safe anchorage" to the southeast of Ambrosia Bank.

Measured in nautical miles, a course, north-east-by-north, was indicated out of Porto Plata; also recorded was the distance from the tip of Cape Francis to that safe anchorage south of the deadly horseshoe.

A blue-green dawn was illuminating the stern's transom windows by the time Phips had memorized all details and had started making a copy when Mr. Strong, Officer of the Deck, called down the companionway: "Ahoy, sir! Lookout reports square-rigger standing in."

For a man of his formidable proportions, William Phips could move with amazing speed; in no time he'd double-locked both the new chart with his calculations and notations into the ship's ironbound pay chest. Then, hollow-eyed through sleeplessness and with stubble darkening his jaw the New Englander climbed to his quarterdeck, to find Mr. Strong peering intently through his telescope. His Second Officer, Mr. Maddox, was perched on the fore crosstrees. He was also using a glass to study a tiny speck on the brightening horizon. Several possibilities, mostly unpleasant, offered themselves.

Anxiety mounted when, in the battery, a drum commenced to rattle and half-clad gun crews straggled onto the parapet.

Damn! Could this be a Spanish man-of-war or a competitor possibly more heavily gunned than the Company's frigate?

Nerves tightening, Phips sought the mizzen crosstrees and focused his spyglass, the most powerful on board. It revealed the distant vessel to be a square-rigged three-masted sloop. Next, he discerned a flash of color at her maintop which seemed mostly blue.

Moments later the hope that there was something familiar about the yonder craft brightened into a certainty. The approaching vessel was flying a Union Jack and was his long-lost consort.

An almighty sigh failed to express the "Commodore's" indescribable relief.

Mr. Maddox yelled across from his perch: "Sir, that's the *Henry*, else I'll swim across the harbor with a anchor 'twixt my jaws!"

The Honorable Frederick joined in the general cheering but wondered how the Dons were going to welcome a second British ship. Would they panic and send them all to the bottom?

The little sloop was so sluggish a sailer that an hour passed before she came near enough to salute the port and fire three guns in greetings to the *James and Mary*.

Mercifully, the heavy, stone-faced battery remained silent. It did not even return a single salute.

Once Captain Francis Rogers and William Covell, his First Officer, had been rowed over, the two captains embraced with a fervor seldom displayed by male Anglo-Saxons. Then they sought refreshment in the "great cabbin." The Honorable Frederick would have given a finger to be able to go along; so much could be learned when everyone's guard was down.

By degrees the flagship's officers heard how, off Barbados, a screaming gale for three eternal days had driven the *Henry* helpless before it and had carried away her foremast, therefore much time had been lost in rigging a jury mast.

Captain Rogers said over a mug of jealously guarded English ale, "You can't credit how miserable I was when I realized we couldn't possibly rendezvous at Carlisle Bay. Therefore I shaped a course for Mona Island, our second meeting place.

"We were well on our way when a big Dutch privateer steered to intercept, so I was forced to square away and stand northwards. Luckily, the Dutchman wasn't much of a sailer either, so, after a two-day chase I succeeded in escaping under cover of darkness."

Curious, but not critical, John Strong queried: "Couldn't you even reach Samana Bay?"

"No, we'd near exhausted our water so I had to put in to a promising-looking key. There I careened to stop a bad leak started during the big gale. After we'd caulked the sprung seam, I took on a deck load of green turtles and made for here as fast as I could move in this damned crawling howker."

Everyone jumped at the report of a gun fired from the battery. A cannon ball reputedly had splashed squarely into the space separating the English ships. Phips jumped to his feet rasping: "Jesus Christ! What in Hell ails these fornicating Dons?"

The Second Officer's suspicion proved well founded. His Excellency refused to permit two British ships to remain in Porto Plata at the same time. Captain Phips was ordered to submit immediate explanations.

Flattering deference, plus subtle hints of considerable remuneration sufficed for the "Commodore" to convince Señor Don Henrique Montalban that Captain Rogers was only an old acquaintance, an honest trader who, purely by chance, had sailed from London at the same time.

[*273*]

His Excellency listened, suspicion written broad across lean and saturnine features. "One would not be so impolite as to discredit your reassurance, *Señor Capitán*, for thus far your conduct has been nothing if not straightforward. Nevertheless, I cannot permit two vessels belonging to a foreign power to— er—trade in Porto Plata at the same time. Either you or the other English vessel must depart within twenty-four hours."

Patiently, Phips pointed out that the *Henry of London* was very short of water and supplies and badly needed an opportunity to stop dangerous leaks. As for the *James and Mary*, she could not possibly be readied to sail in so brief a time. Had not all her upper spars been sent down? Was not her standing rigging at this very moment being tarred and replaced? Besides, there remained considerable trading to do; the resultant profit would stand to mutual advantage.

The New Englander delicately flicked a drop of sweat from the tip of his nose. "Besides, Your Excellency, prices on merchandise I retain on board might be reduced a trifle were my permission to trade extended for a few days. During this time my ship will be prepared to depart in company with Captain Rogers—on his return."

"On his return! What is your meaning, *Señor Capitán?*"

The twenty-first son's imagination seldom had proved more nimble than when he stated blandly, "I believe, sir, this awkward situation may be relieved by the fact my friend's ship is out of salt—a commodity which is in short supply here." This was true and the Governor must be aware of it.

"What is your meaning, *Señor Capitán?*"

"I propose that, providing it meets with your consent, Excellency, tomorrow Captain Rogers's sloop will sail for Turks Island there to careen and take on a cargo of salt. By the time he returns I shall be ready to sail. Both of us will depart, leaving behind satisfied friends, I trust."

"And when might this English sloop return?" The Governor's manner was dubious.

"With luck and good weather, within a week, Your Excellency. But should Captain Rogers encounter delays he might be absent a trifle longer."

The Governor's hand smacked a document lying before him. "*De ningun manera!* He must return within seven days! Should my superiors hear of your presence for such an unreasonable length of time they would be extremely annoyed. I would be held answerable."

Phips bow was profund. "In that case I will sail even if my friend does not appear within a week." Inwardly he was chuckling. He would have been delighted to settle for even a three-day respite.

Chapter 34

SUBTERFUGE

ALTHOUGH MORE than usual humid heat pervaded the "great cabbin," its door remained firmly bolted and two armed seamen stood guard outside but at sufficient distance to prevent their distinguishing what might be going on inside.

William Phips concluded the logical thing to do was to place all cards on the table and confide the information he'd so recently obtained.

Sweating heavily and stripped to breeches and wide-open shirts, he, Rogers, and their First Officers, Strong and Covell, bent over a copy of Ottavio's second chart—from which Phips had omitted only a few important details. There was no use in taking chances.

Phips informed Francis Rogers: "I can't lend you this map but Hans Sloane will make a copy you can keep."

He stared hard at Captain Rogers with whom he'd shared so many dangers and disappointments aboard the *Salee Rose*.

Body odors and rank tobacco fumes were not in the least diluted by a faint breeze beating in through the stern ports. By the lanthorn's reddish-yellow glare the assemblage resembled figures cast in bronze.

Phips then described his interview with the Governor and stated the agreement arrived at.

"Goddammit, Will," Rogers growled, "how dare we sail off leaving you with half your guns dismantled and your top hamper down?"

"I don't like the risk either," Strong agreed, "but we've no option if the Dons are to remain cozened."

"You've got plenty of salt in the *Henry?*" Phips asked.

"More than enough."

"Even so, to be convincing, I'll send over some of our supply. When you come back the Governor has to be convinced you really went to Turks for salt. But under no circumstances return in less than a week's time."

"Why not?" Covell asked.

"I need more time here."

"Why? Haven't you about done trading?" Rogers wanted to know.

Phips planted a forefinger on Ambrosia Bank. "Study those soundings in the lagoon formed by a horseshoe of reefs and see what you make of 'em."

All three men bent and looked hard for several minutes. Finally Rogers said: "That'd be a dangerous place for a ship drawing any amount of water to lie, even in fair weather."

"Always provided a channel could be found into it," Covell added.

Brows raised, Phips considered the hairy bronzed faces about the chart table.

"Well, and what does this mean in your opinion?"

Rogers replied: "No master in his right mind would risk anchoring in the lagoon. He'd have to lie somewhere outside."

"Aye," said Strong. "Likely at that spot Gallucio has indicated and operate out of small boats."

"True enough," admitted Rogers, "but what boats have we

[277]

got large enough to carry the powerful crane we've got to use, not to mention the diving bell?"

"None," Phips said. "Nothing anywhere near sufficient stout, and I daren't chance buying a coaster or anything else suitable—not in these waters."

Strong tugged at the remains of his ear, looked at Phips. "So what's the answer? Look somewhere else?"

"There's no time—season's too far advanced. Reckon we'll have to make our own crane boat and in short order."

"How in Hell can that be done?" Covell queried. "There's no boatyard we can use."

Phips allowed them to stew a moment. "Notice those big dugouts which bring out heavy trade goods? Well, something like that might serve."

"But where are you going to get one since you've got good reason to fear of alarming the authorities?" Rogers wanted to know.

"We'll fell the right kind of tree and hollow out a giant piragua," Phips announced, as if this would be the easiest thing in the world. "It can and will be done during the week you'll be away. I promise you that."

Francis Rogers stroked his sparse beard, bony, horselike features contracting. "Very well, have a try, but I doubt you can manage it. In any case, there remains one matter we'd better decide right now. How much are the crews to be told?"

"I always hold that honesty within reason is rewarding. Let them be told we're going close to the *Vice-Admiral.* Don't figger they'd have the intent or means to betray us. Agreed?"

Shaggy heads inclined.

Without seeming to, Phips surveyed with care the tall young man before him. Barefooted, he was wearing a floppy hat of native straw and work-stained cotton pantaloons. He in no way resembled that gaudy individual who back in Deptford had minced on board lugging a spaniel. His pale-brown wavy hair now dangled to his shoulders and a short reddish beard darkened his ruddy complexion. The Honorable Frederick Delacorte had filled out considerably Phips realized; noticeable muscles corded his arms and torso. His large and very dark-blue eyes appeared clear and steady, but one of them recently had been blackened and a tooth was missing from his lower jaw; life belowdecks could not be easy.

"What's on yer mind?"

"Well, sir, I trust you have been satisfied with my efforts to prove myself useful."

Phips said nothing.

"Please, sir, believe I earnestly have endeavored to accommodate myself to a life so different from everything I have ever known."

"Well, I hear you ain't exactly been in the way, especially of late. What d'you want of me?"

"Sir, I've been helping Mr. Waddington and he deems it fit to confirm me as his assistant supercargo. Will you allow this promotion, sir?" Intently, he peered into Phips's hard gray-blue eyes and held his breath; so many events, so much of the future lay in the "Commodore's" reaction. Of course, by now he knew that Phips had usurped that rank; by Royal Navy standards he would be a bogus commodore.

Phips said, "You ain't done badly, Fred. Shouldn't wonder, before this cruise is over, you'll maybe amount to something. I'll think on the matter."

"Thank you very much, sir."

"No need, till I confirm your promotion." Even while speaking Phips wondered over the persistence of small, nagging doubts he'd always entertained regarding the dependability of the Marquis of Cranbury's second son. Yet he had nothing definite upon which to base this uncertainty. Beyond question this young fellow had plenty of brains—too many, perhaps.

"Anything else on yer mind?"

"Why, sir, I beg permission to transfer to the *Henry*."

"Why?"

"Aboard her, sir, I can more quickly master the art of navigation."

And possibly more concerning the wreck's position, thought

[279]

Phips. Aloud, he said: "Any other reason why I should let you go?"

"Yes, sir, the red Indian, Fast Otter, has taught me much about diving and because there are only two other divers in the sloop and one is sickly. I thought mayhap I might prove useful in such a capacity."

Phips faced the applicant. "Fred, I'll confess I've never cottoned to you or your sort. Frankly, I don't understand you, still, maybe I'll gamble on my judgment which I have all my life. I need somebody aboard the *Henry* who can keep a sharp eye out, and his mouth shut and, if I've the need, give me a full and true account of all that happens aboard the sloop."

A dazzling white smile lit the Honorable Frederick's handsome, ruddy features. Vehemently, he burst out: "You won't regret this, sir. You can count on me to the death."

"Ain't asking you to die," Phips said. "'Twould serve no useful purpose." Sharply he added: "Don't get notions I mistrust either Francis Rogers or Billy Covell. Go along, learn more seamanship and make yourself useful under water."

The Honorable Frederick was turning away when Phips's voice checked him. "Think 'tis only fair to warn you I'll tell Rogers and Covell they're free to kill you like a dog an you make a single suspicious move."

Chapter 35

BETRAG OF SHEEPSCOT

THE NIGHT AFTER THE *Henry of London*'s weathered topsails disappeared over a Prussian-blue horizon, William Phips lay sweating on his bunk, torn by numerous uncertainties. Would the old pilot's map prove valid? Had Ottavio's memory failed as well it might considering his age? What if Rogers and Covell, heading nowhere near Turks Island, actually discovered the site? Would they return to Porto Plata or start fishing on their own? What if they discovered rivals already diving on the wreck? If, *if*, IF!

All along, he'd experienced a vague dissatisfaction over Francis Rogers's failure to rendezvous in Barbados or Samana Bay. He grunted, rolled over, listened to the squealing and scurryings of rats in the strong room below.

Faint guitar music came beating across the harbor. Another fiesta must be in progress. The Dons, it seemed, celebrated countless Saint's Days and other holidays.

Maybe he'd been smart, after all, in accepting the risk of sending still-unpredictable Honorable Frederick Delacorte along with Francis Rogers?

In his mind's eye the "Commodore" projected Ottavio's second map and the presence of "boilers" absent on his first rendering. It seemed a good thing Francis Rogers had been warned concerning them. Certainly it would be tempting fate to risk either vessel within that tight semicircle of reefs where the *Vice-Admiral* had met her doom.

First thing tomorrow he'd better get cracking about hollowing out a great piragua since not even his longboat was capable of carrying many men or supporting the heavy equipment he'd designed. Small boats effectively might be used to drag rakes or grapnels but this would be the limit of their usefulness.

How *did* one go about fashioning a dugout? It was one of the few forms of shipbuilding he knew little or nothing about. Praise the Lord, Indians should know plenty about making such a craft.

He numbered among his crew a pair of Pegwackets from the Maine District. But where was there to be found a tree sufficiently massive? From what he'd thus far observed only a gigantic silk-cotton might serve his purpose.

Come first light he'd pretend to go fishing and reconnoiter the coast westward well out of sight of traffic entering or leaving Porto Plata and that battery perpetually threatening the *James and Mary*.

Once more Phips's Star seemed to brighten when, only a few miles down the coast, he sighted a stand of enormous trees which appeared to tower halfway towards the zenith of a brazen-blue sky.

Accompanied by the pair of long-limbed Pegwacket divers nicknamed "Franko" and "Blanko," he ordered his gig beached in a cove which, to his experienced eye, appeared designed by Nature to suit his purpose.

Inside of an hour he'd located a tree Blanko approved of. He sent the gig back pulling at top speed to fetch tents, food, axes, adzes, gouges, saws, and other essential tools. Mr. Strong also was to send along anyone claiming experience in canoe building to Frigate Bird Cove as Phips had named the place for easy identification.

Next day, especially nimble seamen were sent aloft to lop off branches sparing only such as might cushion the great trunk when it toppled over. From dawn till dark, Phips—naked to the waist—drove his men, chopped, used adz and gouge as hard as ever he had on Jeremesquam Point.

By the end of three days the piragua which, in a sentimental moment, he'd christened the *Betrag of Sheepscot*, was taking shape. She promised to be excessively heavy and no thing of beauty but the *Betrag*, properly rigged and ballasted, should be able to support a ponderous crane and carry one hell of a load although drawing only three feet of water.

Chapter 36

THE SEA PLUME

ON THE 7th of February, 1687, a full gale howled out of the southwest, raising vast, tumultuous gray waves which went rolling in lacy, frothing patterns off towards the horizon. So viciously blew the wind that hands laboring to send up the *James and Mary*'s topmasts and upper yards had to take care lest they get blown overboard.

In the late afternoon, Mr. Strong, ginger-hued hair blowing free, stumped up to the Captain, bellowing: "A square-rigger's working towards the lee."

One of Phips's heavy brows elevated itself. "How big is she?"

Strong's powder-blued features contracted. "Can't say, still too far off, but I'll risk my bottom doubloon 'tis Francis Rogers out yonder. He's making such wearisome progress he can't make port before daybreak lest this wind slackens."

By the last light of day, Phips's powerful glass revealed the *Henry of London* laboring amid clouds of spray towards Porto Plata. He watched his consort all at once turn and flee out to sea but was not alarmed. Francis Rogers was not one to risk reefs in the dark.

Once rain-lashed darkness closed in, Phips invited Dr. Sloane and Mr. Waddington to dine in the "great cabbin" where all three, to dull consuming anxiety, got mildly drunk on taffia, a liquor much favored among the French Islands.

"Damn this Frog popskull," growled Phips. "Tastes smooth as a kitten's ass and bites like a bloody bulldog."

It was ten of the morning before the *Henry* saluted the battery, dropped anchor and promptly sent her gig over to the flagship, rowed by Fast Otter and, of all people, the Honorable Frederick Delacorte. Captain Rogers and Billy Covell, his First Officer, sat slouched in the gig's stern sheets.

When the party from the sloop commenced clambering on board, Phips experienced sinking sensations because of the uniformly somber and lugubrious expressions worn on those weather-beaten and sun-burned faces.

Once the returning officers silently slumped onto seats in the "great cabbin" Phips rasped: "So what went wrong?"

Hatchet-faced Francis Rogers spoke up, his manner despondent, his voice dull. "Following your chart, we located Ambrosia Bank all right, and, playing safe, anchored well to the south of it. For the next four days we sent in all our small boats which roamed everywhere inside the lagoon. Let me tell you, Will, the boilers in there are something fierce."

His gaze strayed and he made an almost imperceptible movement of his head to Fast Otter, standing in the background impassive as a bronze statue, held a shapeless canvas bundle between naked brown feet.

The Honorable Frederick, also lingering in the background, grinned to himself and paid very strict attention.

"Aye, sir," Covell gloomily amplified, "we sent down divers in all directions but though blessed by fair weather they found nothing of interest." He spread gnarled hands in a wide gesture denoting helplessness.

Rogers, slumping deeper into his seat, growled: "On the fourth day a strong wind set in and threatened to blow us onto the reefs so I deemed it wise to clear out while I could and come back to make a report."

The twenty-first son's lips tightened. "Nevertheless, we'll go back to Ambrosia Bank. I believe, I *must* believe the wreck lies there somewhere!" Shaking his massive head he drew a tremendous, slow breath. His eyelids drooped. Rogers make a quick motion, whereupon Fast Otter pushed the bundle under the chart table and instantly stepped back.

When William Phips opened his eyes he sat bolt upright in astonishment. All four men from the *Henry of London* were grinning like happy idiots—red-rimmed eyes alight.

"Here. Look at this!" Rogers held out a delicate specimen of underwater vegetation—olive-green with bright scarlet threads veining its long and gracefully shaped leaves. Phips immediately recognized it as a sea plume, a rare and exquisitely lovely sea growth.

"What are you crotch-festered bastards up to?" he shouted.

In surging erect his foot encountered the bundle beneath him. Cursing, he stooped and hurled onto the table what resembled an irregular, whitish-gray lump of coral but with certain unnatural proportions.

"Damn you, Francis! An you're foxing me at a moment like this I'll surely spill your guts! Where'd you find this?"

Covell, grinning like a horse collar, as they'd say Down East, said, "We were homeward bound in the gig after a long day's search when I chanced to look down and spied this sea plume. Fast Otter, tell what happened after that."

The Penobscot's jet eyes took on a peculiar glitter. "Me dive for feather. Me see it grow from mouth of big cannon all covered by coral. Me look about, see cannons, many more cannons piled like waterlogged timber. Me dive deeper, see many queer-shaped things, scattered about bottom. It so much dark have time bring up only few lumps—'dowboys' like divers call 'em."

Covell offered Phips a short-handled hammer. "Suppose you tap yon hunk of coral."

"By God, you're all swine to torture me like this." Phips's

hand shot out, brought the hammer crashing down on that odd-shaped chunk of coral, then emitted a screeching Abenaki war cry. Limestone, coating the object, had shattered the dowboy and a small torrent of silver coins fell to the deck and began to roll about. Wild yells made the "great cabbin" resound like a hard-struck bell; not the least of these was raised by the Honorable Frederick.

For a long instant the New Englander stood in a frozen attitude, hard gray-blue eyes starting from their sockets. Head whirling, he flung arms upwards shouting: "Praise Almighty God, *we are all rich men!*"

Everyone pranced like colts and beat one another's shoulders, all the while laughing like lunatics.

Finally, Phips regained a measure of composure and glared at Fast Otter. "There are more dowboys like this?"

The Penobscot's jet eyes shone in rare emotion and his craggy, copper-hued features flushed a richer hue.

"Yes, Augpac," the Penobscot stated. "Me see many little hills much covered by corals."

Phips choked, eyes streaming: "Then—then the *Vice-Admiral—must* be down there!"

A general babble reassured him.

Flashes from the past created a mental maelstrom in which struggled the twenty-first son: Betrag, the burning shipyard, Charles II, James II, Albemarle, Jack Dale, Ottavio, Mary, Charles Salmon taking soundings, Samual Pepys's inscrutable wink. Terrifying storms, endless burning calms, hunger, heat, thirst, bloody encounters, prison.

As from afar he heard Francis Rogers say: "Only I and maybe Billy Covell maybe can sense your feelings right now, but—" His exultant expression faded.

"What's wrong?"

"Whilst we were on Ambrosia Bank we sighted sails of vessels cruising below the horizon on three occasions. One set looked like they might belong to a sizable ship."

All in an instant, Phips's jubilant manner vanished. "So word *has* got about! Tomorrow we clear out of here!"

Chapter 37

SOUTH RIFF

THE *Henry of London* at two of the morning raised anchor by starlight and silently set just sufficient sail to carry her out to sea. Moments later the *James and Mary* followed apparently completely unnoticed by the battery.

Taking no risk that some little coaster might lie anchored among shadows under the land, Phips at first ordered his ships to set an easterly course as if returning to Samana Bay.

Once well clear of Hispaniola, the "Commodore" ordered helms put about and ran westward to rendezvous with the *Betrag of Sheepscot* which John Strong by this time should have sailed some five miles offshore, had his big lateen sail proved adequate.

Shortly before daybreak a pinpoint of light revealed the giant dugout's position and another load of anxiety slipped from Phips's shoulders.

In short order the *Betrag*'s yard was lowered from the crane shaft and no sooner was she taken in tow by the flagship than a course to the north-northeast was shaped with every rag of sail that would draw set.

Daylight found both ships so far offshore only the peak of that conical mountain behind Porta Plata remained in sight— a pale-blue triangle on the horizon.

After a reasonable interval a large and jagged reef identified on Gallucio's map simply as *The Rock* was sighted and afforded infinite reassurance.

Before long the foretop lookout reported the so-called *Copper Wreck*—a vessel only recently come to grief. How forlorn she appeared lying with only bare ribs protruding above the water to provide a roost for innumerable sea birds.

Next was sighted what Ottavio had labeled the *Genoese Wreck*, but of her scarcely anything remained visible.

Phips's elation and that of his officers soared. Thus far the *Nuestra Señora de la Concepción*'s apprentice pilot had listed no misleading positions or erroneous compass bearings.

Since Francis Rogers recently had sailed these waters Phips had himself transferred to the *Henry*.

"What's your opinion now?" Phips demanded, lowering his spyglass on detecting several completely unnoted reefs creaming lazily in various directions.

Rogers, after momentary consultation with Covell, scratched receding black hair. "To stay on the safe side, I venture we'd best head due east for a spell. An our navigation is sound we should be sailing along latitude 27: 20 11 south and before dark we should sight South Riff and the buoy I left marking Gallucio's 'safe anchorage.'"

Sunset was drawing gold-red streaks across the sky when Rogers who'd climbed to the main crosstrees, yelled down: "Rest easy, Will. I spy the South Riff and short of it my yellow marker!"

Chapter 38

THE LAGOON

TILL LATE INTO THE NIGHT the twenty-first son and his principal officers toiled to complete operational plans based on Francis Rogers's and Fast Otter's information. All possible contingencies seemed to have been explored, yet everyone sensed many imponderables must remain.

Dawn found both Company ships swinging comfortably at anchor well away from a scattering line of lazily foaming reefs and about two miles distant from the only known practicable entrance to Ambrosia Bank. This, for the sake of convenience, had been named the Vice-Admiral's Channel.

Both crews set about raising diving gear on deck. Small boats ranged about, permitting leadsmen to take additional soundings and mark the position of especially dangerous boilers.

On signal the *Betrag* rehoisted a badly cut triangular sail and, convoyed by sharks, made for the Vice-Admiral's Channel.

All boats carried on their floor boards a plentiful supply of small buoys painted in varying designs, red, blue, yellow and white. Divers impatiently began smearing themselves with foul-smelling grease believed capable of repelling sharks, moray eels, barracudas, and other predators. Against deadly Portuguese men-of-war and highly poisonous jellyfish there was no known precaution.

More or less according to plan, small boats escorted by shrieking sea birds, dispersed towards assigned areas and the great piragua soon dropped anchor near the mile-wide lagoon's center.

Accompanied by Rogers, Covell, and Fast Otter, Phips set out for the lagoon in the flagship's longboat propelled by a gentle breeze which sent it scudding over water so pristine it proved well-nigh impossible for even trained observers to gauge depths with any degree of accuracy.

Once inside the lagoon the sail was lowered and through his water glass—a bucket-shaped contrivance fitted with plate glass for its bottom—Phips not only could see the bottom clearly but also myriad fishes of all shapes and sizes speeding about like piscatorial rainbows; silver, sky-blue, golden-orange, brilliant green, scarlet.

All at once Phips turned to Captain Rogers. "Why ain't we sighted nary a shark in here?"

The *Henry of London*'s Master's leathery features creased into a flat smile. "You won't spy none, either; them devils generally stay outside the reefs and damn' seldom venture into shallow, sheltered waters like these."

Flying fish skittered away before the longboat riding so deep in the water she showed but scant inches of freeboard. Fast Otter grunted, pointed to a tiny buoy. The passage of years had not in the least dimmed the Penobscot's vision. "There found sea feather."

Emotion shook Phips. At long last his goal actually lay in sight. Even before the longboat's grapnel anchor went bubbling down, he pulled off shirt and breeches. When next he peered through into his water glass, directly beneath him lay the barrel of a great cannon blurred through forty years' of growth of limestone and coral, but still entirely recognizable!

"How much water here?"

"About four fathoms," Rogers told him.

"A good depth to work in."

Surprisingly, Phips turned to Fast Otter. "Tookaw, my Brother, you who discovered the sea plume must make the first dive. I'll follow close."

The Penobscot actually smiled; was it not he who had taught Augpac to swim under water defying even the Sheepscot's numbing, icy currents?

Body shining with grease and naked save for a tiny loincloth stained with urine the Penobscot selected a ballast stone from among those littering the longboat's bottom and leaped overboard. Trailed by silvery bubbles, he went flashing through incredibly pellucid water towards a pair of cannon tubes lying among several piles of weed-covered and roughly rounded objects.

Covell advised: "Better use a sinkstone, Will. 'Twill ease you down and conserve yer wind and strength. We'll rig recovery lines for 'em later on."

Nine times Phips pumped air deep, deep into his lungs, then exhaled half of his last breath before swinging legs over the thwart and disappearing into the shimmering and silent green world below.

As often as he had dived, Phips still could thrill over glories peculiar to the depths. He avoided certain flaming scarlet growths since fire corals, if even brushed by bare skin, could cause painful burning sensations.

Below, he could see Fast Otter's sinewy brown figure extended, arrow-like, behind his sinkstone. Increasing pressure on his eardrums made Phips wish he'd not, in his excitement, forgotten to clamp the usual bamboo clip over his nostrils.

Heart pounding, he made for the muzzle of a cannon slanting upwards and sighted more cannon lying jumbled together like

[292]

logs in a jam. Beyond them loomed what appeared to be the barnacle-encrusted fluke of a large anchor and, still farther away, what he'd so long dreamed of beholding—clusters of roughly rounded objects too large and irregular to be either roundshot or ballast stones.

A faint glimmer to his right started him swimming towards it with slow, easy strokes—long ago he'd learned never to move hurriedly under water. His fingertips tingled on realizing this glitter came from gold bars some eight inches in length and as thick as his middle finger.

When, spasmodically, his fingers closed over the nearest bar his heart gave a great leap, but there only remained time to grab another before surfacing. Ear-splitting yells and screams arose when he dropped the two bars into the longboat.

They shouted even louder on sighting in Fast Otter's grip a gem-studded golden goblet and marveled that it appeared as clean and bright as if it just had left a jewelsmith's shop. Experienced divers, however, were aware that although coral and other calcareous growths readily attached themselves to pewter, iron, bronze, brass, and other base metals, such never grew on gold.

More frenzied whoops arose as divers, working out of other boats, commenced to surface clutching weed-coated pigs, sows, and dowboys—terms descriptive of variously sized coral and limestone sheathed bags and pouches.

Cannon were visible through crystal-clear water but there was at the moment no sign of the low mound Fast Otter had taken to cover the wreck's stern.

A serious question now plagued the twenty-first son. Since a treasure ship's strong room invariably was located in the stern directly below the Commanding Officer's cabin, how come these pigs, sows, and dowboys had become scattered so far and wide about the lagoon?

That veteran treasure fisherman, John Covell, explained. It seemed likely, said he, as in other instances when a galleon struck, her bottom had been ripped out so, while she reeled helplessly about the lagoon, ballast and precious items of cargo had become strewn among tall spires of fanged coral and staghorn pinnacles rising between level stretches of shimmering white sand.

Nevertheless, it came as a shattering blow for Phips to perceive that most of the lagoon's floor appeared much too irregular to permit efficient use of his laboriously devised diving bell. For such a contrivance to operate efficiently, its base must rest more or less on the level in order that air, brought down in casks or jars to replenish the original atmosphere, could not escape the tub's circumference.

With time the essence for success this would present a major setback. Now it would prove impossible, lacking the bell's reserve of air, for divers to work submerged beyond two or three minutes, at the most, instead of forty or more.

Both ships carried only a longboat and gig but at judicious intervals Phips had managed to quietly come by three fairly sizable native dugouts. His mainstay, however, must be the *Betrag*.

For underwater work he counted on three tough North American Indians, three rather sickly Carib divers, and four somewhat hardier Lucayan pearl fishermen from the Venezuelan coast.

On the other hand, he had only six white divers, including himself and the Honorable Frederick. The latter, although lacking previous experience, rapidly was improving in efficiency.

The day after he'd found the gold bars Phips, following a consultation with Francis Rogers, established a routine which, subject to minor variations, would be followed indefinitely.

Following a painstaking survey Phips felt it safe to move both ships through the Vice-Admiral's Channel and anchor them just inside the mile-wide semicircle enclosed by those murderous tangles of reefs and boilers.

This change of anchorage facilitated swifter arrival alongside of small craft heaped with reeking and shapeless loot of all descriptions.

At daybreak small boats and dugouts set out carrying all-but naked divers, already greased, and fed early enough to forestall the possibility of cramps.

Day after blazing hot day the lagoon remained calm, at worst only ruffled by mild winds.

Dotting the lagoon's blue-green surface at almost any time could be seen the heads of a dozen swimmers. As expected, the best and most enduring divers were Fast Otter and the other two North American Indians. These wiry individuals could remain submerged around three minutes using picks, hammers, and short crowbars to dislodge promising bits of debris which, dumped into baskets of iron rods built according to Phips's design, were hauled up to the *Betrag* and the other tenders.

When some especially bulky or ponderous object, such as a chest, a cask or a cannon, had to be recovered, the *Betrag* was signaled, then her big crane's gaff would swing out and a block and tackle with hook attached would be lowered and secured to lashings already rigged by divers.

In order to give his crew more experience in the difficult and often risky business of dislodging objects under water, Phips delayed working that tall mound of debris sighted by Fast Otter during his initial dive and which the Penobscot felt certain must enclose the wreck's stern.

To discover the wreck's richest hoard too early might invite trouble—even mutiny. Such rough characters as he had shipped just might become maddened by the possibility of keeping vast riches for their own use, especially if gold and jewels soon were brought up in any quantity.

Meanwhile he intended casually to reconnoiter Fast Otter's tumulus while playing down its possibilities.

To the Honorable Frederick Delacorte, now remarkably muscular and tanned to a rich, mahogany hue, it came as a considerable surprise to discover that a heavy brass or bronze cannon was deemed more desirable than many bags of silver pieces. Strangely enough, so far, much the largest part of the recovered riches proved to be of silver and only a few items of gold were being brought up.

During midday hours, when danger of sunstroke became acute, divers and crew members alike sought shelter under old sails rigged over the equipment and loot strewn on the decks of both vessels. As a rule little conversation took place unless some especially promising piece of salvage had been raised. All hands were too weary and sprawled in the shade with eyes closed, breathing slowly.

Carib divers were tiring rapidly; two on occasion had begun to spit blood towards the end of a day's work. Fishing normally was resumed in midafternoon and more dripping baskets hauled aboard the tenders. Sometimes these contained shellfish, crabs, and small, brightly colored fishes hidden among a colorful variety of marine flora.

When darkness really closed in, diving teams, who always worked in pairs in the interests of safety and integrity, returned to their ships to enjoy the best food available and imbibe liberal rations of Jamaica rum or taffia.

At length the day came when Phips, accompanied by Maddox, another powerful swimmer, openly descended to examine the tumulus believed to cover the *Vice-Admiral*'s stern section which turned out to include nearly two-thirds of the vessel's length overall. Forty-odd years' growth of coral and coatings of limestone had so blurred the wreck's outlines it proved difficult to determine details.

Swimming slowly, they found the main deck had remained more or less intact and still supported a few heavily encrusted cannon behind gun ports. Curiously enough, this part of the wreck appeared a popular haven for large fish, squids, and octopuses of considerable size. Whenever possible these last scurried away, apparently terrified by invasion of their domain.

Over decades the hulk, responding to pressure from strong prevailing currents, had assumed a 15° list to starboard against which a high sandbank had formed—an effective protection and preservative. A small sheet anchor and several cannon lay to port of the wreck along with a multitude of other unidentifiable objects spilled in heaps and dotting the clean white bottom, half-smothered under lush sea plants.

On his third dive, Phips became convinced that the highest bulge in this shapeless mound must contain the wreck's stern-castle and the most precious part of the *Vice-Admiral*'s cargo. Accordingly he ordered a scarlet buoy anchored at that spot. About this marker he planned to initiate searches in a series of widening, concentric circles.

Even more bitterly, he now resented those towering coral crags and pinnacles rendering his precious diving bell quite useless. Much priceless time now must be expended in penetrating, exploring and working the strong room—or rooms—if Gallucio's account had been accurate.

Therefore, he'd no alternative but to attack the tumulus through conventional means. Swimmers still would have to descend, work briefly, then surface gasping and spitting blood more often now.

Nonetheless, divers, spurred on by the lure of untold riches, made such good headway that, at the end of two days, Phips ordered the *Betrag* anchored alongside the scarlet buoy. Soon her cargo boom commenced to winch up sections of the galleon's side until a gap was opened wide enough to permit swimmers to fetch up cannon and other objects of considerable size and weight.

Late one afternoon Fast Otter took Phips aside and muttered, "Me find—break into main treasure room."

Chapter 39

THE HONORABLE FREDERICK

ONE EVENING the Marquis of Cranbury's second son drew his rations, solid and liquid, before seeking a secluded spot on the *Henry of London*'s forepeak, there to extend his scratched and bone-weary frame on a pile of cordage. Lord, how his ears, eyes, and lungs ached! Especially his eardrums. A deep, fire coral scratch along his thigh smarted as though branded there.

All the same he smiled as he finished a mug of taffia and watched the moon rise into a violet-black and star-jeweled sky. Only subconsciously did he notice a sullen obbligato made by rollers endlessly surging among reefs and boilers along the great horseshoe's outer limits.

If only there was someone to converse with beyond the uncouth characters around him. How delightful it would be to exchange spicy items of gossip or to listen to the quick whispering of cards and the clink of coins upon a gaming table. Even more, he yearned for the sound of softly ardent feminine voices and to frolic with some delicate, sweet-smelling fine lady, or, failing that, even a common barmaid.

Closing his eyes, the Honorable Frederick Delacorte readily could visualize the delicately pointed and piquant features of Lady Agnes DeVere. Had he really got her in the family way or had the minx been tormenting him with an illusion in hopes of personal advancement; almost everyone around Court was aware that his elder brother, George, slowly but surely was succumbing to lung fever.

From aft came the sounds of hammers cracking or chiseling incrustations from the day's take. Both as a diver and as an assistant accountant, representing Mr. Waddington aboard Captain Rogers's command, he was exempt from this occasionally exciting drudgery but often took part in it.

Ah. When would he next sleep in a soft, clean bed smelling of lavender? When, once more, would he have a valet to shave him and lay out a selection of modish garments? When might he eat and drink like a gentleman again? No telling, but should certain plans mature, it shouldn't take over-long.

Lying on moldy-smelling cables, he once more puzzled over the fact that silver items formed the great bulk of what was being raised daily. Surely, somewhere in the wreck *must* lie a hoard of gold coins, ornaments, church services, and the like— not to mention precious stones and jewelry.

Where would such priceless plunder lie concealed? At the first practicable opportunity he'd undertake cautious investigations which might, with luck, assure a rosy future for one Frederick Delacorte.

To his secret astonishment, the Honorable Frederick, despite everything, was finding himself far happier than he'd ever been during his brief and checkered career. No matter how weary, he'd remain on duty supervising the cracking and removal of calcites coating the day's salvage.

Every item had to be dumped before his writing table to be listed and described before being transferred aboard the *James and Mary* for further examination and a more detailed description by Treasury Agent James Waddington.

A rough evaluation of irregularly shaped lumps of coins, annealed by action of salt water, and odd pieces of plate was arrived at by being weighed on scales operated under Waddington's watchful eye. Each and every weight duly was recorded by Charles Kelly, a jolly, plump young fellow who once had served as the Duke of Albemarle's page boy.

Long since, the ever-watchful Honorable Frederick had noted that the most valuable plunder usually was contained in small, rather than in large lumps of debris. Therefore, whenever he dove he selected the smallest dowboys, pigs and sows to shove into his iron basket.

Only the day before, while chiseling free a piece of debris, he inadvertently cracked a calcareous shell covering what might have been a cannon ball and then all but lost the last of his breath on perceiving that here was no shot but a calcified pouch. His heart gave a great leap when onto the bottom of clean white sand dropped a small handful of glowing green stones!

Emeralds, by God! Thinking fast, he noted his diving mate fully occupied with a half-buried bag. Even though close to suffocation, he lingered long enough to insert four of the largest stones into his rectum. God above! What power, what luxuries, would such baubles not ensure?

Certainly it would the height of folly not to preserve a few choice items for his own account. Twice, he'd watched Indian divers swallowing sizable pearls and had pitied such stupid fellows: evidently, they failed to realize that pearls too long submerged, lost most of their luster; besides, action of their own gastric juices would rapidly and completely dissolve these precious articles.

He dropped the remaining emeralds into a copper cup at the basket's bottom designed to receive small items, then shot upwards, lungs close to bursting.

John Covell, in charge of this dive, almost crooned while caressing the glowing, verdant stones. He then looked about, puzzled. "How come these beauties should be by themselves?"

The Honorable Frederick suggested: "Possibly they might

have been the possession of some passenger who never placed them in the strong room, which, let's hope, hasn't yet been discovered."

This explanation sounded so reasonable even shrewd John Covell appeared satisfied as, with great care, he stowed the find in a small strongbox carried for that purpose but heretofore seldom used.

Chapter 40

STERNCASTLE I

FOLLOWING SEVERAL DAYS of exploration and ransacking of the *Vice-Admiral*'s shattered hull—much to the annoyance of sundry large and small fishes and octopuses—it became evident that probably not one but three strong rooms had been built into the towering sterncastle of the *Nuestra Señora de la Concepción*. Also, that the first two rooms to be plundered had yielded chiefly silver—enormous quantities of it— in the guise of coins, bars, ingots, table services, church ornaments, personal jewelry sometimes set with gems of varying sizes and description. But of gold, comparatively little had been discovered beyond occasional coins and bars; moreover, very few precious stones were fished up.

At an evening conference held in the "great cabbin," John Strong brought matters to a head. "Silver is fine, sure enough, but where in Hell is the gold and the jewels? Should have found plenty more before now."

Phips exchanged glances with Rogers and Covell, then grinning faintly, said, "Any of you ever swim down into the hull?"

Covell nodded. "Yep. I worked as far aft as possible, but all the same figgered I'd not reached the poop itself."

Mr. Sloane raised sun-bleached brows. "And why not?"

"Because the sides are stove in so bad just aft of the second treasure room you can't work farther aft. A tangle of ribs and timbers thick as trees bar the way."

Francis Rogers shot Phips a quizzical look, then, receiving an almost imperceptible nod, continued: "That's mighty bad news because them timbers bar the way to what must be the principal strong room under the Admiral's cabin. 'Tis there the bulk of the gold and precious stones most likely were stowed."

"Christ above! That's it!" burst out Maddox.

"But," remarked Strong, "if access is blocked as bad as Covell says, how are we to gain the Admiral's treasure room?"

"We'll have to clear away sand and rubble covering the sterncastle and try to enter through its stern ports," Phips remarked, as if the matter was simple and could be accomplished in a trice. "We'll need light to work by so we'll have to break the stern wide open before starting to rip up decking in the Commanding Officer's quarters." Grimly, he added: "The greatest riches of all *must* lie under it."

Early next day all small craft were ordered to congregate about a scarlet buoy marking the tumulus covering the galleon's extreme end. Divers, saving those engaged in the forward strong rooms, were ordered to take a much-needed rest for, without pause, they had been diving almost continually for ten days, inspired by greed beyond their strength.

White divers, for the most part, and American Indians such as Fast Otter and Franko and Blanko appeared to tire less than Caribs and Lucayans. Several had given out temporarily and lay coughing weakly and hemorrhaging from their ears. Some had grown entirely deaf.

All hands on the expedition had lost weight and some had suffered "a touch of sun" which caused nausea and splitting headaches. The Honorable Frederick was among these, but continued to work like a man possessed, for, every now and then, he managed to add another precious stone to his small "private collection" skillfully concealed deep in the *James and Mary*'s foul-smelling bilges.

Furiously, crews set to attacking sand and debris heaped about the sterncastle and small boats endlessly towed scoops and rakes back and forth, gradually reducing the tumulus. Divers sawed through and attached cables to obstructing timbers and stubborn sections of planking, which then were torn free and raised by the *Betrag*'s crane.

Gradually, ornaments decorating the galleon's stern became exposed. Phips, swimming down to see for himself, noted the battered, gilded head of some saint, exposed from the mouth upwards, his blank eyes seeming to stare at him reproachfully. Above swirling sand also had appeared the paws of a lion rampant clawing the wood as if impatient to reach the surface.

By dark the upper part of triple stern ports had been exposed. To everyone's astonishment not a few diaper-shaped glass panes were found intact.

Tomorrow, rejoiced the senior officers, it should prove possible to breach the stern sufficiently to enter the quarters once occupied by Vice-Admiral Don Luis Villavincencio.

If workers previously had toiled with unrelenting intensity, their efforts now became almost frenzied. Rotting wood was levered and torn out until a jagged aperture gaped like the fanged mouth of some vast marine monster. Through it master divers cautiously penetrated a dim gloom. They groped and ranged about until they located a large trap door let into the deck of the Vice-Admiral's quarters. When finally this was forced open, Phips, Covell, and Fast Otter risked swimming downwards and almost choked on beholding a huge jumble of chests, casks and boxes reaching nearly to the deck beams above.

Some containers had burst, exposing a thick and maddening layer of gold coins lying agleam on the main strong room's still sound decking.

With incredible speed word got about that the gold hold finally had been located and penetrated. That evening all save those on duty, chattering and chortling, gathered on the *James and Mary*'s main deck to watch Waddington and other officers knock calcareous growths from oddly shaped objects. Kegs, obviously containing specie, gold bars and ingots were set aside for later examination and appraisal.

There were many salvers and plates, beautifully chased as a rule, elaborately-fashioned cups, goblets, ewers, and pitchers. What most intrigued the round-eyed, sun-burned, and universally shaggy onlookers were a number of solid gold artifacts of Indian origin. Among these were several squat and bow-legged, but expertly sculptured little idols bearing elaborate headdresses, slanting eyes, and exaggerated organs of reproduction.

Into boxes hurriedly fetched from the flagship's hold, were dropped lengths of heavy gold chain, elaborate ceremonial breastplates, necklaces, bodkins and delicate bracelets of extraordinarily fine workmanship—workmanship largely unappreciated by the scarred and weary men grouped about the cluttered deck.

"Will, b'God," cackled a seaman, "reckon that pub I've had me eye on now is as good as mine!"

For the most part, however, onlookers only stared in incredulous wonder on these first gleanings from the great strong room and cursed because work could not be resumed before daylight.

An insignificant little sow, on being cracked open, exposed a handful of maddeningly bright and gleaming gems. Wild, exultant yells rang for minutes far over the placid lagoon and the loudest to shout was William Phips.

Long ago, veteran divers had observed that coins and objects of silver when found in close contact with iron somehow remained almost perfectly preserved while such other pieces, lying apart, became annealed or survived only in varying degrees of disintegration.

Gold objects, once scrupulously weighed and listed, hurriedly were packed into small, ironbound wooden kegs and chests and promptly lowered into a small treasure room situated beneath the "great cabbin" along with jewels and a few pearls which appeared successfully to have resisted more than forty years' immersion. These last, being sorted in a rough-and-ready fashion, were placed in leather pouches, then secured in the large ironbound chest kept under constant guard in Phips's quarters.

One evening John Covell gloomily lingered on the *Henry of London*'s poop, having supervised a transfer of treasure to the *James and Mary*. He hated to see it go aboard the flagship, yet knew Phips to be right—it would be extremely unwise to risk any appreciable amount of plunder in a vessel so very slow and feeble as his command.

Covell stared over sunlit waters awhile, then studied the divers on the deck below where they sprawled as limp and inert as seriously wounded men.

To Rogers he growled: "Ain't there no end to this? We've been fishing nigh on a fortnight and always there's more riches begging to be raised. You, me—everybody knows that."

Rogers's horselike head inclined as, wearily, he said: "As God's my judge, I never believed I'd see the day when I'd tire of fishing up treasure, but now—" He indicated a Lucayan Indian breathing painfully and with threads of blood trickling over his bony, yellow-brown chest. "Yonder lies another who won't be going down for a long while—if ever. Even the red Indians are beginning to weaken. By God, Billy Phips better ease off else we'll lose every damn' one of our plungers. Resting one day a week ain't near enough respite."

This was true; although William Phips, through an odd quirk of superstition, had decreed no work should be done on Sundays, the balance of the time he was pushing men, both above and below the surface, to the limit of endurance.

Noting the mounting weakness of his divers, he, Covell, Maddox, and the Honorable Frederick, therefore, spent more and more time under water.

Although discovery of an especially rich collection of native artifacts of pure gold caused fresh endeavors, these finds failed to revive and restore strength to the Lucayans and Caribs. Even Fast Otter and his fellow North Americans were slowing down perceptibly.

Realizing already he had aboard a treasure sufficient to satisfy the greediest of kings and shareholders, brought new worries to plague the twenty-first son. When it came time to sail for home, what about his crews? Unless restrained by shrewd precautions and harsh discipline, they well might mutiny and attempt to take over the frigate—a danger certain to intensify as more huge quantities of riches disappeared below decks.

Near daybreak of the fourteenth day on Ambrosia Bank, a lookout, invariably on duty in the maintop, cupped hands, yelled: "Deck there! A sail! Sail ho!"

Phips, bleary-eyed, sweat-soaked, and long unshaven, roused from exhausted slumber and clumped on deck.

"Masthead! Where away?"

"Nor'-west-by-nor', sir."

"How rigged?"

"Looks square, sir. Can't count her masts so she must be bearing straight for us."

Moments later Phips hailed again. "How does she look and sail?"

"Full-rigged and headin' this way."

Beelzebub's balls! This was what he'd been dreading for a long time; some powerful pirate or privateer, hearing he was at work on Ambrosia Bank was closing in for easy pickings! Thinking faster than ever before, Phips sprang into action.

Chapter 41

RISKY BLUFF

FURIOUS ACTIVITY prevailed on the lagoon. The *Betrag*, all boats and canoes immediately were ordered alongside the *James and Mary* and all but a few of the *Henry of London*'s crew were transferred to mount cannon and helter-skelter clear the flagship's decks of diving tackle and other betraying impediments.

To Phips it proved vastly discouraging to note how sluggish were his crews' efforts; to a man they acted dog-tired, moved like somnambulists.

Gun ports which hadn't been open for weeks were prised up and readied. While the anchor was being heaved, powder, shot, and loading gear were fetched on deck. In less than an hour's time the flagship, under light canvas, spread to catch a mild breeze out of the south, was standing warily along the Vice Admiral's Channel.

Phips flung at First Officer Strong: "Break out the flags and show my pendant!"

While turning away to comply, Strong again couldn't resist a grin. Since the *James and Mary* was not a Royal vessel, the "Commodore" had no right to fly such a pendant. Still, Strong realized, the presence of such a streamer might serve to impress officers on that sizable vessel now surging over the horizon.

As best they might the flagship's crew set main courses, top gallants and royals in addition to topsails raised in the lagoon.

To his Master Gunner, Phips shouted: "Man the guns. Get ready to run out!"

This was but a futile gesture—not since before Porto Plata had he ordered gun drills of any description.

The unknown vessel proved to be a large brigantine pierced for what seemed to be about eighteen guns. Tensely, officers occupying the *James and Mary*'s quarterdeck studied the stranger through spyglasses. Although Union Jacks now were snapping from the frigate's three mastheads, the other ship obstinately refused to display colors of any description.

When less than a mile of ultramarine-blue and weed-splotched water separated the two, Phips ordered a gun fired to leeward as a signal for the other to identify himself.

The unknown had rakish lines and appeared a trifle heavier. Undoubtedly she was of European construction, but not along Spanish lines.

At a distance of about half-a-mile with the stranger still refusing to show colors Phips ordered all twenty-two guns run out, a maneuver only raggedly executed.

Next he bellowed through his speaking trumpet: "All hands get armed then climb the rigging, yell and shout fit to make yonder rascals believe we're fair crawling with fighting men!" God help us, was Phips's silent thought, if this stranger really means to engage.

The gap of sparkling water narrowed to within two hundred yards before the green-painted brigantine's Captain, after what seemed an interminable interval, finally ordered his helm put over which started veering her slightly to port. Only then did the English perceive that although this big vessel undoubtedly was heavily armed she was not a regular man-of-war. Her gun crews were lounging about their stations and none of the officers on her quarterdeck were wearing rich coats or uniforms of any description.

French? Dutch? Danish? No telling.

To Strong he snapped: "Order all hands to yell like hell and wave their weapons, then fire a shot across her bow. If she keeps on, give her the best broadside we can manage!"

To Phips it came as some consolation that, in all probability, low-lying Ambrosia Bank still remained below the horizon so her lookouts probably could not have sighted boats lying within a lagoon. But he couldn't altogether be sure.

Phips shouted: "Show colors, else I fire! Blow yer matches, boys!"

Eternities seemed to elapse before the green brigantine bore away downwind but not before Phips got a good look at her Captain, a thick-set bandy-legged fellow with a blond beard and wearing a rapier slung to a scarlet, gold-embroidered baldric. Clearly he saw the other sweep off his hat bow and heard his shout: "*À bientôt. N'en doubtez vous pas!*"

Chapter 42

THE KETCH, DOVE

THE BERMUDA KETCH, *Dove*, mounting six light 8-pound cannon and a pair of swivel guns, otherwise known as "murtherers," scudded smoothly back and forth over the diamantine, dark-blue seas off Cotton Key—a small outer island off the Turks Island group. Only a few cottonball white clouds afforded relief to the sky's brazen-blue.

Moog, the half-Mohawk whose bronzed and battered features were burnt to a dark mahogany hue, sat perched in the swaying crosstrees intently scanning the horizon—especially towards the south-southeast. Like everybody else aboard, the mixed-breed felt desperately anxious to find out whether the other Bermudian craft, Captain William Davis's shallop, *Experience*, would show at the rendezvous.

Although of but 37 tons and mounting only a pair of pitifully small 6-pound cannon plus one swivel gun, the shallop, nevertheless, carried a crew of seven and could sail as fast as the proverbial scared tomcat. Certainly two such vessels most likely would be able to drive all but powerful competitors away from Ambrosia Bank.

While the mast swung like an inverted pendulum, Moog fell to conjecturing on just what might be their final destination, Captain Adderly and John Dale having successfully kept that a close secret.

Captain William Davis, he figured, barring accidents, was bound to show up because that worthy had been confided only approximate information concerning the wreck's presumed position. Beyond doubt, Captain Adderly was continuing to track about Cotton Key in hopes that "Bloody" Bill Davis's shallop, although three days overdue, yet might put in an appearance.

Frowning, John Dale put away nautical dividers and parallel rulers, then rolled up a creased and salt-stained chart and passed it to Pegeen who was helping navigate. She was wearing fraying knee breeches and a blue cotton shirt so loose it served to reveal rather than conceal her full upstanding breasts. A sprinkling of not unattractive freckles still traversed her short nose, emphasizing the clear dark-blue hue of her eyes. She was wearing one of those wide-brimmed hats from Colombia so loose in weave the sun could beat through and faintly illumine smooth, nut-brown features.

Her wide, dark-red mouth still curved slightly upwards at its corners but beside it had appeared faint lines suggestive of cruelty.

Areas of her skin usually protected from the sun still shone as white and lustrous as that of the terror-stricken lass who'd pelted down the Sheepscot to Jeremesquam.

To a classically educated observer her figure was reminiscent of a well-proportioned Amazon such as ancient Greek sculptors loved to imagine and create; adding to the illusion there hung at her belt a heavy, ivory-handled dagger with which she never parted, day or night.

"Well, Jack, still figure the same as before?"

"Yep. Still reckon we ought to raise the Abroxes in around

two days' sailin' time. Next day we should sight the North Riff off Ambrosia Bank."

In the shade cast by the mainsail Captain Abram Adderly tested his jaw, hideously painful and swollen by an ulcerated tooth. Much more of this and he'd have Dale yank the damn' thing out with a pair of sailmaker's pliers. He hated the idea because this would leave him but a scant dozen choppers to chew with.

Aloud he growled: "God send them calculations prove sound. Still wonder if that feller Smith back in Port Royal spoke straight. Mayhap not; he were almighty drunk."

Dale came over, body swaying to the ketch's easy motion. "Reckon Smith must have spoke the truth."

"Why?"

"Account of that position he gave pretty near matches the latitude we noted on Salmon's map."

The ketch, brought into the wind lay wallowing comfortably so the crew promptly baited hooks. Fresh fish would afford a welcome change from boucan and salted pork.

Having spied a small green turtle asleep amid a patch of Sargasso weed, Pegeen went below briefly and reappeared wearing only an old nightrail, then, graceful as an otter, she dove and shot through the water. Moments later she towed the creature alongside.

Meanwhile Dale turned to Adderly. "How's yer bad fang?"

"Feels like a red-hot spike drove in my trap," groaned the black-bearded Bermudian.

"Shall I yank it?"

Adderly cast a glance at Pegeen, now deliberately wringing water out of waist-long red tresses. "What d'you think?"

Said she, grinning: "It's got to come out sometime, so I'd say the sooner's the better."

Adderly's puffy, red-rimmed eyes lingered on this young woman half-in half-out of her ragged nightshift. B'God, she was wearing that peculiar tight and mirthless half-smile she affected only when someone's wound was being cauterized or sewn up. Aye. He recalled first seeing it that time a swarm of black and brown "fishermen" suddenly had boarded the *Dove* off Puerto Rico. Pegeen had pistoled the leader, a huge Negro, through the belly just an instant before the *Dove*'s hurriedly manned starboard swivel gun roared and blasted the "fishermen" back over the side.

Neither Dale nor Adderly reckoned they'd ever forget how calmly the Second Mate had dropped her still-smoking weapon, then used her dagger to neatly slit the shrieking black man's throat.

Often Dale had found it nearly impossible to identify this impassive killer with the sometimes tender female he'd "married." Back in Bermuda, Pegeen on occasion, affecting frilly garments, would move gracefully about their house. The Lord alone knew where, when or how she'd come by so many gaudy furbelows and trinkets. Again, when the mood was on her, she'd spend hours dressing her hair, all the while lewdly cursing the clumsiness of a small Negro slave girl he'd given her. Once she'd got herself satisfactorily "doozied up"—as they'd say back home—Pegeen had insisted, even if they were eating by themselves, on dining off a gleaming mahogany table salvaged out of a wreck and by the light of fine French silver candlesticks fished from the same source.

Pegeen had been baffled about where eating utensils, plates, glasses and other tableware should be placed until, during a visit to Saint George's between trading voyages, she'd encountered Mrs. Aubrey—a distant and very poor relation of the Governor's who'd come out to the Somers Isles in hopes of improving the state of her lungs.

Mrs. Aubrey had coughed incessantly but had survived long enough to impart a deal of instructions concerning fashionable speech, genteel deportment and etiquette; all these the sturdy young woman from the Maine District took in with the readiness of sandy earth absorbing rain at the end of a long drought.

Among other things, poor Mrs. Aubrey had suggested certain books, pamphlets, and periodicals calculated to improve "Mrs. Dale's" mind and vocabulary. These Pegeen studied intently whenever the *Dove* put in for careening and overhauling against another voyage to the West Indies.

Thus far, such cruises had proved profitable and then some, thanks to her partners' bargaining ability and foresight about which goods would be in greatest demand.

Surreptitiously, bit by bit, Pegeen added cash, jewelry, and other valuables to a hoard cleverly concealed among the rocky heights of Somerset Island not far from that tall hill on which the natives were given to lighting false beacons in hopes of luring unwary seafarers to destruction.

John Dale, however, entertained few illusions about what his "wife" was up to.

One evening after she'd again practiced speaking, walking, and otherwise conducting herself like a lady of high society, she'd reduced her finery to a flimsy gauze shift and had joined him where he sat on their porch staring out over moonlit Great Sound.

"Jack, you thinking about buying yet another vessel?"

"Aye." He fanned away a mosquito. "How else can I become a power 'mongst the merchant of these Isles."

"You've no intent of ever returning to Boston?"

"Hell, no! Those penny-pinching, canting Puritans always did give me the pip. Besides, I like it here; know my way about and I've no idea what's goin' on in the Bay Colony nowadays. How about you?"

Absently, she wriggled bare toes in the moonlight. "There'd be nothing up there for the likes of me, either. I mean to become a real lady like I *know* that my Mother once was. I'm sure she was, even if it can't be proved."

A faint chuckle escaped him. "Well, now, such ambitions! Would you believe it if I say your ambition somehow don't oversurprise me. For a long while a blind man could have told how you're minded. Good luck to you. I'll help all I can."

He bent over to kiss her and was pleasantly astonished by the way eager, moist lips almost devoured his. Presently they'd revel in complicated transports of sensuality—transports shared more and more infrequently as time went by. Somehow, a tumble in bed, in the underbrush or wherever, now held no more significance than devouring a tasty meal or getting mildly drunk on fine wine.

Lively young fellows inhabiting the West End had soon become aware that when "the mood was on her," Pegeen might be willing to go for a "walk and a talk." Fortunately there were no results from such encounters—possibly because she was reported to be barren. Pegeen therefore received no offers of legal marriage. Eligible young men weren't about to get legally spliced since there could be no young ones to go seafaring, plant tobacco, build ships, or supply daughters capable of marrying to financial advantage.

A muffled groan from Abram Adderly abruptly ended Dale's reverie. Pegeen jumped up. "I'll fetch rum and laudanum. Jack, go fetch your pliers and we'll have that tooth out in two shakes of a lamb's tail." As if by accident she brushed the Captain's swollen jaw, thereby evoking anguished curses before disappearing below, wearing that peculiar smile of hers.

Once a single powerful yank dislodged the offending molar —amid a gush of evil-smelling pus and bone splinters—Abram Adderly felt a deal better, especially after sloshing out his mouth with fiery Demerara rum.

Just before dark the lookout bawled: "Deck there! Sa-ail to sta'board!"

From the crosstrees Dale called to Pegeen, clambering over the Captain's comatose figure: "Yonder comes the *Experience!*"

"You sure?"

"Aye. Recogize the yellow patch she wears in her tops'l."

Chapter 43

INTERLOPERS

RAIN SHEETING LIKE A WATERFALL from a wandering cloud bank reduced visibility until both Bermudian vessels arrived unobserved off the South Riff of Ambrosia Bank.

When the sun broke through with startling abruptness shouts arose from the ketch and then from the shallop half-a-mile astern.

Adderly scrambled up to join Dale in the crosstrees. Together they took in a vision neither would ever forget.

Within what looked like a great, nearly closed semicircle of white, seething rocks and shoals, two ships of European design lay at anchor: one was easily twice the size of her companion. Near the center of this wide lagoon could be seen something like a barge surrounded by many small boats.

If the "Commodore" of these European ships had been taken by surprise by the abrupt arrival of the two vessels, obviously not native coasters or sponge fishermen, his reaction was immediate.

The larger ship, a frigate by the look of her, quickly raised jibs, set topsails and got under way so swiftly she must have slipped her anchor cable and made for a buoyed channel undoubtedly marking the lagoon's entrance. She commenced to run out a few cannon. The frigate's consort remained where she lay. The officer commanding her by now must have noticed how puny and few were the guns mounted by both interlopers.

At a distance of half-a-mile the frigate showed a big Union Jack and fired a gun to leeward ordering ketch and sloop to veer off and come into the wind.

In a big hurry, Adderly and Davis ran up faded Union Jacks and came about until their craft lost headway and wallowed, sails slatting uselessly.

Francis Rogers—who'd happened to be aboard the *James and Mary*—noted at once the *Dove*'s peculiar design and rubbed his unshaven chin. "Seen such a craft somewhere before but I'm damned if I can recall whether 'twas in Antigua, Grenada, Barbados or maybe Port Royal? Hell no! 'Twas at Saint George's in the Bermudas. Look at that overlong bowsprit."

Phips, vastly relieved, snapped: "Good thing they're showing friendly colors and the weight of their broadsides can't amount to a pinch of 'coon shit. Signal 'em to send over boats."

The first head to show in the *James and Mary*'s gangway was the yellow one of John Dale. He paused, with Adderly and Davis a significant step in his rear. Unarmed, all acted apprehensive. Finally Dale began: "You signaled us aboard, Will. Hope we ain't altogether unwelcome."

Phips paused, bronzed features inscrutable. "Ye're not welcome, neither are you exactly unwelcome—provided you act sensible."

Rogers, Strong and Maddox exchanged glances. What the Hell was this? Surely Phips had intended to order off these piratical-looking rascals or order them sunk. Why not?

"Pity you didn't sign on along of me back in Bermuda, Jack.

You'd have made a heap more money than by trying on your own."

Dale grimaced. "Likely I should have but, all the same, I've done a heap of profitable tradin' since we last met. I own two vessels and am about set to buy some more."

Mr. Waddington advanced and whispered to Phips something which caused him to fix a grim stare on the weather-scoured and ragged group before him. "Any of you hold a license or warrant authorizing you to fish for treasure in these waters?"

"No," growled Davis, sweating harder than ever, "but who says freeborn Englishmen like us can't look around wherever we like in British waters?"

"Nobody," Francis Rogers rasped. "Look about all you please but send down a single diver and you'll be clapped in irons and tried for piracy."

The visitors looked glum while taking in the elaborate diving gear and dripping heaps of debris fetched aboard since the downpour had let up. Their expressions lit when they noticed how a large sow, accidentally split, released enough silver coins to form a bright puddle among seaweed yet clinging to the plunder.

Adderly gaped. "You've raised plenty like that?"

Phips nodded. "More than anyone can imagine, and there's as much, or more, still down there."

Dale noticed a couple of divers, resting supine under an old sail; they looked in wretched condition and one, a youngish white man, kept coughing up vivid, scarlet-streaked foam—the other diver, an Indian, was breathing so weakly he appeared to have collapsed for good and all.

The *Dove*'s First Mate drawled presently: "Say, Will, 'pears to me, like you been working yer men overhard."

"Why? I'm doing all right."

"Well, ye've taken on board so much weight this here vessel rides low in the water and I don't notice many o' your people fit to dance a jig."

Billy Davis and Abram Adderly concluded Phips's ship must

have been at sea a long while—too long, mayhap, for her standing rigging was badly in need of tarring, her halyards and stays showed frayed places, while long streamers of bright green weed were undulating along her waterline. She could sail only at a snail's pace, now—easy prey for corsairs or buccaneers.

Phips became aware that his visitors were taking in all this.

"Aye, we have been toiling hard," admitted John Strong, sucking a gashed knuckle, "but plenty more work lies ahead."

Another rain squall came roaring up, so Phips, accompanied by Mr. Waddington and Francis Rogers, led the Bermudians down to the "great cabbin."

When Abram Adderly queried, "D'you intend drivin' us off?" Phips shook his head and said thoughtfully: "No, whilst you and the rest of you have no legal right to fish here I don't aim to sink you or drive you off because—well, the season's shortening and the chance of pirates or privateers closing in grows every day. Besides, I need fresh hands, especially divers."

He turned to Dale whose butter-yellow head shone in the cabin's dim light looked his old friend squarely in the face. "All right, Jack, you've guessed right; I have raised a vast treasure, but, more, *much* more, waits to be salvaged." As if thinking aloud, he continued: "I'm fully aware my ships can't tarry here much longer—I'm low on water, growing short of supplies, my divers are sickening and all hands are slowing down.

"Then there's another consideration; a short time back a big French privateer showed on the horizon. I sailed out and bluffed him away but I ain't sure he didn't approach sufficient close to make out what was going on hereabouts. Whether she ran away only to collect enforcement, God only knows. I'd have stood in chase but my bottom's so foul I decided what with all the treasure I've aboard not to chance it.

"Such being my situation, I'll strike a bargain with you, Jack. Stay and help raise treasure, otherwise"—he stared ferociously —"I'll have to sink you both straightaway lest you carry news about the *Vice-Admiral* farther than it's already traveled."

William Davis spoke for almost the first time, "You don't leave us much choice, sir. What are yer terms?"

"Pass under my command, use yer vessels and divers just as I direct and"—he paused for effect—"I'll let you keep half of all you bring up, an you stay honest with me."

"*A half!*" Adderly burst out. "Ye can't be serious, Cap'n! Why—why that's a princely share!"

William Davis shook his balding head. "A damn' sight too princely. Minute we quit divin', this Yankee will go back on his word, grab everythin' and sink us."

Phips's huge fist clamped down on Davis's bull-like neck. He shook the powerfully built Bermudian as if he'd been a small child. "Blast your ugly eyes! I've *never* gone back on my given word."

Dale hurried to intervene. "Shut yer trap, Davis. I've known Will Phips nigh on thirty years and he's yet to hedge on a solemn agreement!"

Once Phips released his purple-faced victim Mr. Waddington said, "Now understand this clearly—*everything* brought up by either of your vessels *must* be discharged into the *Dove*; I'll send an accountant and an assayer aboard the ketch and Captain Phips's half-share must be delivered daily to the *James and Mary*. Is that understood?"

Incredulous, the visitors relaxed and, grinning like happy dogs, surfeited their thirst on tepid English beer. Meanwhile, under Phips's direction, Mr. Waddington drew up articles covering the agreement.

After negotiating the Vice-Admiral's Channel both Bermudians, obeying orders, anchored close by the *Betrag*, and at once sent down divers; Moog and Dale were among them.

Indicative of the exhaustion of Phips's crews they gave small attention to the Bermudians vessels' arrival. Only a few bothered even to wave half-heartedly.

Their attitude underwent a change once Pegeen's sinewy but unmistakably feminine figure was noticed moving about the *Dove*'s deck.

"B'God," gasped the Honorable Frederick, treading water

alongside the *Betrag*, "do I imagine things or ain't that a female aboard the ketch?"

When a few men gesticulated and yelled lewd invitations, Pegeen, unusually bewildered by this succession of events, deemed it only sensible to wave acknowledgment aware she'd been careless in not having donned a canvas vest which, when tightly laced, constricted her breasts to near invisibility.

The *Betrag*'s hoisting crane kept on raising strange new objects. To Pegeen's unbounded delight, Fast Otter who'd recognized her at first sight despite the passage of time, brought up a small, handsomely fashioned four-legged stool whitened by marine encrustations. One of its legs gave off golden gleams. Small wonder it had weighed so much.

Frederick Delacorte, on presenting the *Henry of London*'s daily tally in the "great cabbin," discovered the "Commodore" in an unusually affable mood, he having reached a decision of immense importance.

Expansively he indicated a flagon of taffia.

"Presume you noticed a woman on the Bermuda ketch?"

"Aye, sir. Seems well-built or maybe it's because I've not spied a female in so long."

"Ye won't credit this, Fred," said he to the assistant accountant, "but I've known that female nearly the whole of her life."

This the Honorable Frederick quickly estimated must have covered a period of around twenty-five years. All he said was, "How very interesting, sir, and how is she named?"

"Sit down and maybe I'll tell you something about Pegeen Hammond. Like I said, she comes from Hammond's Fort in the Maine District of Massachusetts Bay Colony. It lay a few miles up the Sheepscot from a shipyard I once owned on Monsweag Bay."

"You owned a shipyard there, sir?" The Honorable Frederick's question was suave, deferential. "What became of it, may I inquire?"

"Goddam redskins burned it back in '76. Pegeen was just a young girl when she made a great run to warn us about Blue-foot's raid. And ye're interested about that, ask her or Fast Otter or Jack Dale. He was my partner in the shipyard, and lost his wife and unborn child to them red hellions during the same attack."

The Honorable Frederick settled back, flexing bare brown toes before him. "I believe, sir, I have heard the—er—lady referred to as 'Mrs. Dale'? Is she indeed married?"

Phips set about loading a short-stemmed clay pipe. "Depends what you mean by 'marriaged.' In Bermuda she's counted as Jack Dale's common-law wife. She got wrecked there along of him, and, so they say, lost a baby."

"His, sir?"

"No. Pegeen was pledged to marry a local feller; guess they must have experimented some before the Abenakis struck. In any case, seems Pegeen miscarried once they'd reached the Bermudas but though she and Jack Dale have been living together quite a piece they ain't ever produced chick or child 'twixt 'em."

Why the "Commodore" should choose to unburden himself to such an extent was somewhat mystifying.

"Pegeen's shrewd and grown hard, I suspect—else she'd not be part-owner of yonder ketch." Using his pipe's stem the New Englander pointed through the stern windows at the *Dove* on which dim yellow-and-red lights were commencing to glow amid the brief tropical dusk.

"Wouldn't put it beyond her to have learned some Bermudian ways—the most of 'em I've met are tricky beyond belief and grasping as any merchant in Amsterdam. Remember the old jingle?"

"Sir?"

" 'In matters commercial the fault of the Dutch, is giving too little and asking too much.' "

"Yes, sir. I believe I understand."

"Hope so, for you're to live aboard the *Dove* as my tally master to make certain Adderly, Davis and company every evening send over my full share of their lift."

[323]

Beaming, the younger man jumped to his feet. "Sir, I'm truly honored and will do my best to serve your interests, sir."

"I hope so, but take care concerning 'Mrs. Dale.'"

"Certainly, sir, why not?"

"From what I've heard in London you've dallied only with lady 'friends'—and had few enemies."

The Honorable Frederick arose and bowed declaring earnestly: "Please rely on me, sir. Of late I've come to appreciate and value a reputation for honesty."

Returning on deck the Honorable Frederick gloated over this unexpected turn of fortune's wheel but sobered; where, aboard a craft as small as the *Dove*, could he hope to conceal his growing "private collection" of gems? There *must* exist some suitable place. Umm. Better delay till he found one and since daily he would be reporting aboard the flagship, he'd await an opportune moment to transfer his small but precious hoard over to the ketch.

Another pleasing prospect was the chance of again enjoying female society for, unlike certain of his cronies, he'd never fancied the company of lads, no matter how plump-bottomed and complaisant.

Chapter 44

COMBINED OPERATIONS

THE WATERS IN THE VICINITY of the *Nuestra Señora de la Concepción*, although roiled by another of those half-gales now blowing stronger and more frequently, were dotted by the heads of more swimmers than before.

Fast Otter was pleased that three of the newly arrived divers proved to be Bermudian Pequots—descendants of warriors reduced to slavery back in 1637 following Captain John Mason's decisive destruction of Narragansett Town near Stonington in Connecticut. John Dale and Moog brought the number of effective fresh divers to five who could penetrate the dark recesses in the *Vice-Admiral's* stern section.

Phips, concerned by the advancing season and the growing probability of attack, had concentrated all efforts on this part of the wreck. Silver, breath-taking quantities of it, still was being removed from the two forward strong rooms and wrenched free, bit-by-bit, from imprisoning layers of limestone and corals.

The "Commodore" ordered only trusty and especially qualified divers to work among the dangerously jumbled timbers of the "gold hold"—the sternmost strong room, where, for some reason, cuttlefish and octopuses, some of them quite sizable, liked to lurk, changing color so quickly they instantaneously could become all but invisible.

Selected to work the gold hold were Phips himself, the veteran diver Covell, Dale, Frederick Delacorte, and, of course, Fast Otter, Moog, and his handful of American Indians—the Caribs and Lucayans having given out completely.

Now and again sections of the stern laboriously had to be sawed and cleared of sand and corals; timbers must be levered and torn asunder to permit the raising of large strongboxes. Gold here was found in a wide variety of guises; bars, heavy chains capable of being chopped off link by link in lieu of coins, small casks of specie, more native idols and body ornaments, crucifixes, monstrances and church service utensils. Unworked rich red gold appeared in the form of bars, ingots, wedges, unstruck coin sheets and the like.

Phips, nonetheless, kept some of his swimmers at work on the *Vice-Admiral*'s submarine silver mine—silver at that time being far more valuable than it became later. There seemed no end to the heaps of dowboys, pigs, and sows crammed into the silver holds. Rubbing hot and claret-rimmed eyes, the twenty-first son could visualize the incredulous expressions of Kit Albemarle, Sir John Narbrough, and the rest of the shareholders when—and if—they beheld such amazing riches.

When the Honorable Frederick arrived alongside the ketch he hopefully looked about for the *Dove*'s Second Mate but "Mrs. Dale" wasn't to be seen.

Dale and Adderly accorded him only surly recognition; both knew Phips had sent this fancy Dan to spy and to keep tallies in order.

Adderly emitted a snorting laugh; instinctively, he mistrusted such a soft-spoken young man. "You notice that sail reported to the westward come daybreak?"

"No," admitted the Honorable Frederick.

Adderly growled: "I'm Captain, say 'sir' when you speak to me."

"Yes, sir!" Somehow, the young fellow in those two words managed to convey an infuriating contempt.

"Where shall I stow my gear?"

Dale snapped: "Come darkness, ye can sling a hammock to the main boom an ye know how."

One of the *Dove*'s boats pulled near gunwale—deep under her cargo of shapeless, gray-white salvage. A muscular young woman was steering. Hatless, Pegeen Hammond Dale was wearing a well-worn blue-and-white cotton jersey which signally failed to disguise her shape. Otherwise, this tawny-skinned creature, like other divers, wore only a scanty strip of cloth hitched up between her legs and secured to the belt supporting her dagger.

"Shake a leg, you lazy, sister-seducing bastards," called "Mrs. Dale." "Swing this trash aboard in a hurry, they've just come across a new mess of silver. Come along, Jack, we've got to get our share."

For the first time Pegeen and the assistant accountant exchanged sustained glances.

When, with sinuous ease, Pegeen swung up on deck Dale said, without glancing up from the irregular lump of coral he was chipping at with a short-handled cobbler's hammer, "Pegeen, this here feller is Fred Delacorte, an accountant the Commodore's sent to live on board and measure, weigh, and list our daily take and make sure Billy Phips gets his half."

"Welcome aboard." Pegeen smiled and deliberately surveyed this tall young fellow with long, yellow-brown hair and well-muscled shoulders.

For the life of her she couldn't decide why this newcomer seemed to stand apart from her associates. Perhaps this was attributable to his easy, confident bearing which narrowly escaped arrogance? Or was it a devilish-glint in his small, dark-blue and bloodshot eyes which seemed to sum her up in a single glance.

"Delighted, I am sure, Ma'am, to make your acquaintance." While sea birds shrieked and wheeled in the offing, the Honorable Frederick offered a curt bow and was intrigued to notice a sudden flush under her heavy tan.

He was sufficiently tactful to address himself to John Dale, busily freeing a cluster of fused silver coins from its limestone shell.

"May I say, sir, that I look forward not only to keeping the accounts but towards assisting with diving. May I?"

"Sure, why not? Time's runnin' out. Every hand helps."

"Thank you, sir. I'll set to work straightaway."

Pegeen hadn't heard such a rich, clearly enunciated voice very often; only a few times in Port Royal or in Saint George's when dignitaries were visiting. Umm. This striking young gentleman must already have been diving on the wreck if several half-healed coral cuts on his arms and thighs signified anything.

Dale came over. "This here's my wife, Second Mate and part owner. Come sundown, Fred, you can sling yer hammock and yer writin' gear in Abram's cabin. You'll have to work down there whenever the weather's bad or it gets too dark to figger by daylight."

The Honorable Frederick was experiencing pleasurable, well-concealed astonishment over "Mrs. Dale's" voice and general bearing, a surprise which continued to mount during the morning while she moved about and explained the methods employed aboard the ketch. He could have sworn that this strapping, bronze-haired colonial wench must at some time have enjoyed education in airs and graces which promptly disappeared when once she started rasping orders to her shipmates.

When Captain Abram Adderly and Dale departed to fish a new silver find Pegeen said: "Won't be much for you to do till the boats return. See you've been diving—want to try your hand?" She indicated a yellow-painted buoy bobbing about a quarter-mile distant. "They say a little mound of unexplored rubble lies over there."

"I'd be glad of the oportunity even though I'll get small interest in what's brought up by your craft whereas on the flagship I'd gain more."

When *Dove*'s gig shoved off with Pegeen steering and eyes squinted against hot sunlight, Fred and a pair of impassive Pequot Indians from Bermuda handled the oars.

Directly facing Pegeen sat the Honorable Frederick, stripped to the waist and like the rest wearing a shapeless, broad-brimmed hat. He now found ample opportunity to appraise the Second Mate's contours with an expert's eye.

From the set of her mouth he decided that here was one of those rare women who knew what she wanted out of life and fully intended to get it. On arriving at the yellow marker, the *Dove*'s Second Mate unconcernedly pulled off her striped, blue-and-white pantaloons. An ugly cotton loincloth was revealed above a delightful length of smooth, well-muscled thigh. Once she'd eased out of a loose shirt the points of her breasts were concealed only by a tightly knotted bandanna.

She grinned unexpectedly. "Take a good look. Expect it's been some time since you've viewed so jolly a pair of tits."

"Right. I seldom treated slatterns in Porto Plata to even half a glance." Smiling, he pushed a damp curl from his forehead and added softly: "'Twould appear there are more treasures around Ambrosia Bank than one has heard about."

Chapter 45

STERNCASTLE II

THREE MORE DAYS of furious effort by failing divers and weary hands went into raising only some fairly accessible articles: casks, cannon, sows, dowboys and pigs. Many promising pieces of plunder remained visible but unapproachable; they could only be secured through time-consuming battering, prising and chiseling, and time was running out along with water and food supplies.

Moreover, everybody sensed the weather, which had remained almost incredibly fair over all these weeks, was deteriorating. As if to emphasize the obvious a half-gale arose and blew for forty-eight hours so hard all diving had to be suspended.

During this gale Davis's *Experience* parted her anchor cable and, before sail could be made, the shallop was driven onto a seething boiler so hard her rudder carried away and her stern was so seriously smashed no choice remained but for her to seek some place where she could careen and make major repairs.

Once leaks in Davis's battered shallop had been stopped temporarily by nailing sheets of lead over thick wads of tarred oakum, Phips ordered the shallop to make for Port Royal—the only friendly shipyard within a reasonable distance. Sulphurously, Davis refused point-blank to depart, but was mollified when Phips assured him that, provided he left his divers behind, he might retain the *entire* sum of the shallop's last day of work in addition to one-half of total salvage raised by the *Experience*.

With the wind still screaming through the rigging and his ships heaving and straining at their anchors, Phips seized the opportunity to have all treasure on board stowed below in such a fashion as to trim the flagship and keep her on an even keel.

The Honorable Frederick, temporarily restricted to duty on the flagship to assist Mr. Waddington in the monumental task of tallying loot, found himself wearily studying the storm-tossed *Dove* and bebating what course he'd better adopt during the remaining time on Ambrosia Bank. True, his embezzled wealth now was hidden in the Bermuda vessel.

Aye. Although his purloined jewels remained few in number they were choice—very choice, as near as he could tell. Not for nothing had he so intently watched Mr. Waddington's methods of appraisal.

Although still far from an expert, the Marquis of Cranbury's second son felt confident his thefts must be worth hundreds if not thousands of pounds if—and this was a huge "if"—they could be kept secure and fetched out at the right moment.

How to effect this? Again and again he weighed a most critical decision. Should he return to England in the *James and Mary* or should he intrigue to remain aboard the *Dove?* To be sure he'd obtain better prices in London and in addition would receive a modest share in the flagship's profits.

However, it stood to reason Customs inspectors, in addition to Royal Treasury agents, would ransack the flagship from stem to stern and truck to keelson and thoroughly search every member of her crew and their effects in search of illicit items.

What would be the fate of the Honorable Frederick should he get caught? Beyond a doubt his life and dreams would terminate on Execution Dock. In Bermuda there'd be no such search if half of what was said proved true.

Aye, better take a chance and stick to the *Dove*, weak as she was; besides, Pegeen would be aboard.

At an officer's meeting in the "great cabbin," John Strong said wearily, "Why linger? We've already fetched up more than enough to satisfy the shareholders and make the lot of us rich for life."

Phips's deep voice filled the cabin. "I'm not gainsaying that. We could bring up a good bit more but the start of the hurricane season's at hand so why take a chance and risk losing all we've taken."

He fingered his jaw. "All the same, I figger with luck we can spend maybe a week longer here for all water and supplies are low and our bottoms so exceeding foul we wouldn't be able to make real speed on the need comes to run for it. Also, we mustn't forget that damn' big Frenchman we bluffed. Our presence hereabouts must have tipped him the wreck is nearby."

"Aye," Maddox said. "By now he'll have had time to recruit sufficient help to overwhelm us. Wouldn't it be folly to try matching broadsides when a lucky shot or two 'twixt wind and water could send us to the bottom and lose us everything?"

Phips turned to Rogers, practical, clear-thinking Rogers. "What's yer opinion?"

"Me? Well, I mind the old adage about a 'bird in hand.'"

"You?" He turned to Strong, sprawled with grimy fingers steepled beneath a long, sun-mottled nose.

"I'd say let all hands work like hell on the sterncastle for only so long as the glass stays high—it's falling, by the bye."

Another fear came to niggle at William Phips's peace of mind. What might have occurred when and if the *Experience* had arrived in Port Royal? He could picture easily tough old Davis taking aside a few rascally captains of his own stamp and cautiously speaking of a yellow-painted frigate lying in Ambrosia Bank's lagoon burdened by riches beyond imagination.

During the night of the 17th April, 1687, the twenty-first son remained up till the small hours watching Francis Rogers, Waddington, and Kelly sorting glittering piles of precious stones, tourmalines, opals, verdant emeralds and tawny topazes among others.

"Waddington, what d'you figure these trinkets will bring?"

Judiciously, the Treasury Accountant pursed thick, sun-cracked lips. "Not being an expert lapidary I can only guess—so I won't, but, certes, you have here more than enough to greatly pleasure His Majesty and satisfy the fondest hopes of your shareholders."

Once the stones had been swept into small leather bags and double-locked in a small flat, ironbound chest chained to ring bolts let into the side beneath his bunk, Phips, yawning prodigiously, rubbed burning eyes and announced: "Since the glass is dropping, tomorrow we'll make our final dives and depart next day. Come dawn send a message to the *Dove* and tell Adderly and Jack Dale to report aboard straightaway."

Rogers blinked like a sleepy hound. "What's on yer mind, Will?"

"Figure on leaving the *Dove* here a little longer—wouldn't do for Davis to come back and find the lagoon deserted so I'll allow the 'Mudians to rummage around two days more."

"What if they make a killing and clear out on their own?"

"They won't. They're too small and defenseless and Dale's word, at least, is good. Never fear, they'll rendezvous with us at Cotton Key come a few days' time. Besides, to keep an eye on Adderly, I've decided to transfer yer assistant, young Delacorte, to the *Dove* to make certain all loot recovered after we sail is honestly listed and delivered up for division on Cotton Key."

[333]

Chapter 46

ON THE DOVE

THE EVENING AFTER THE *James and Mary* and the *Henry of London* heaved anchor, set mildewed topsails and disappeared beyond the Vice-Admiral's Channel, a full moon arose. The color of a ripe mango to start with, it gradually paled until it drenched the sea and Ambrosia Bank with a silvery radiance so intense one could easily have read a printed page.

Also Moog decided that it was shedding sufficient light to work an area he'd become intimately familiar with. Once crew members had sunk into exhausted slumber about the deck, the half-Mohawk silently eased into the lagoon beneath the bowsprit.

Certainly, he departed unnoticed by Pegeen and the Honorable Frederick, who at present were seated close together on the poop enjoying the moonrise and wholly absorbed with each other.

No better opportunity, he decided, would ever present itself to retrieve a small canvas package concealed in the muzzle of one of the sunken galleon's stern chasers. Of course, complete darkness would prevail inside the hull, but Moog, swimming swiftly and silently in line with the *Dove*'s bow, felt entirely confident he knew the *Vice-Admiral*'s quarters well enough to work by sense of touch alone.

Once beside the sterncastle's buoy, the mixed-breed drew a series of deep breaths before making for that jagged opening in the stern through which he and many another had swum dozens of times. It all seemed ridiculously easy, for despite impenetrable darkness he readily identified key guide points. Easily as a hunting otter he avoided tangles of beams and jagged plank ends to enter quarters long ago occupied by Vice-Admiral Don Luis Villavincencio.

Almost immediately his groping hands located the barnacle-encrusted pommelion of the galleon's starboard stern chaser. Moog then worked forward along the tube until he could delve into the muzzle's bore until his fingers closed on a small, canvas-wrapped parcel. But then quite without warning, powerful arms encircled and gripped him crushingly hard and applied irresistible suction.

Although the half-Mohawk struggled frantically the octopus squeezed air from his lungs and did not let go until the naked brown body went limp and settled on the cabin's deck. The little parcel remained in Moog's death grip.

John Dale, yawning, arose. "I'm turnin' in. You two better do the same. Don't gab till all hours. Sure as shootin', weather's going to break mighty soon and we'll have to clear out of here in a big hurry."

He went below and presently joined in Abram Adderly's stertorous snoring.

Although bone-weary after the day's diving, Pegeen remained beside her companion on the settee on which she slept during fine weather.

Rolling onto his back the Honorable Frederick laced fingers behind his head and stared, unseeing, at the moon.

"Peg, what do you want of life? I don't mean to intrude on private thoughts, but you're such a mass of contradictions I'm truly fascinated."

Pegeen summoned her most polished accents.

"And what might you mean by 'contradictions,' sir?"

"For one thing you've got a rougher edge to your tongue than any female I've ever encountered—Billingsgate fishwives included; at times your cursing becomes inspirational. But when the day's work is done your speech assumes a quality which reminds me of voices I grew up among."

She smiled—momentarily ruffled her tangled hair then got to her feet, bare as usual. "I'm going below for a few moments. Mayhap after that I will attempt to explain myself as well as I'm able."

The Honorable Frederick nodded, relaxed upon the settee and turned his thoughts in a different direction.

Wasn't it something to have got the gems transferred to the ketch? He reckoned his little leather pouch would remain un-detected at the bottom of a small keg of caulking pitch he customarily employed to support the traveling desk on which he did his accounting.

John Dale he sensed would prove the key in this situation; all along he'd puzzled over Abram Adderly's First Mate. Bold, a consummate navigator, and often unscrupulous in avoiding certain Customs obligations, Dale remained a problem. Would loyalty to a boyhood friend prevail over oft-stated ambitions of becoming wealthy and assuming a dominant position in the affairs of the Bermuda Islands?

While the moon in the rigging wrought lacy black patterns of shadow across the encumbered deck, he again attempted to analyze his real sentiments concerning Pegeen.

Beyond doubt Dale and Pegeen were deeply attached to each other—had been for years.

What their connubial attitudes might be on land he'd no idea, but never since he'd boarded the *Dove* had either employed an endearing term or demonstrated an outward display of affection which seemed odd since they'd been living together for so long. Stranger still, both, on occasion, had admitted having had intimate relations with other partners.

Why should this bold colonial baggage hold for the Marquis of Cranbury's second son such deepening attraction? The conviction was burgeoning that, one way or another, he must have Pegeen. But what gambit should he employ?

Despite himself the Honorable Frederick's lids drooped over eyes burning from prolonged contact with salt water. To Hell with Pegeen! What could be keeping her below so long? Faugh! female capriciousness at a moment like this! He better get some rest. Tomorrow he'd have to rise, come first light, so as for once to beat Moog to the sterncastle. For some reason the mixed-blood always seemed to be diving alone, despite the danger.

A sound of light almost stealthy footfalls on the companionway roused him in time to take in an amazing sight. Pegeen appeared and was advancing with stately grace clad in an embroidered formal gown, rich but of long-outmoded design. Her hair effectively but simply dressed rippled over her shoulders.

In her ears and about her neck jewels sparkled faintly. She also was wearing a gem studded gold bracelet much too massive for his taste. So she, too, had been pilfering! To his utter astonishment this sturdy young woman spread skirts and offered a reasonably good formal curtsy.

Effectively as a theatre's footlights the radiant moonlight revealed fine, strong features but with an affected smile curving her wide mouth. "Good evening, sir, one trusts you enjoy good humor?" Her voice no more resembled that of the *Dove*'s Second Mate than the croaking of a crow resembles a linnet's liquid outpourings.

Surging to his feet, incongruous in ragged work garments, the Honorable Frederick returned the curtsy with an elaborate Court bow—left leg outthrust, right hand over midriff. Straightening, he offered an arm and conducted Pegeen to the wicker settee as ceremoniously as if that ugly thing had been a throne.

"How often do you masquerade as a lady?"

Haughtily, her chin went up and her voice hardened. "Sir, I do not 'masquerade.' No matter what you may think, I am of gentle birth—at least on my mother's side."

"And you are determined to regain your rank in society?"

"I am, sir," Pegeen admitted daintily smoothing skirts.

"But where in God's name have you acquired such moderately convincing airs and graces?"

Without hesitation she blurted out about having employed a distressed gentlewoman to teach her refinements.

"Well I'll be damned!" Consumed with admiration he added, "You truly are the most amazing creature."

She was struggling to control herself to keep on employing language suitable to the situation. She said archly, "Please, sir, I am a lady, not a 'creature.'"

He chuckled. "Your pardon, Ma'am. To employ such—er—gentlewomen must have been—er—costly."

"It was, but believe me or no, Mr. Delacorte, with Mr. Dale's backing I have become moderately wealthy and expect to become considerably richer ere long." Her voice soared. "Moreover I *will* attain a high place in society. Perhaps even gain a title."

He hesitated. "Ah. In view of what you've just confided, what about your—er—'husband'?"

"To realize my ambitions I would leave him as readily as he would part from me, an it stood to our advantage."

"I'll confess, Ma'am, I don't understand you. Am I mistook or haven't you two lived as man and wife over a long period?"

"Aye."

"And you're not in love?"

Mechanically, Pegeen again smoothed her skirt, looked him straight in the face and said carefully: "Things happened during a red Indian attack on our settlement which neither of us have been able to forget. Jack not only lost a beloved wife but also their unborn child whilst I lost Tom, the love of my life, whom I was pledged in marriage.

"Later on a baby which would have blessed our union was

[*338*]

born dead. Being shipwrecked in a foreign shore Jack and I clung to each other and agreed to dwell under common law—an accepted practice in Bermuda.

"I will not fatigue you, Mr. Delacorte, with a recital of all we have experienced together—pleasant and unpleasant." She drew a slow breath. "Jack admits to recently having become deeply attached to a rich widow in Bermuda. He intends to marry her upon our return."

She dabbed a curl from her cheek. "And now, sir, I believe I have talked sufficient. Is it not fair that you should tell me something concerning yourself?"

"True enough." The Honorable Frederick extended coral-scarred legs before him and in a low voice described his lineage and upbringing in a moldering castle dating from Norman times. He mentioned George, his elder brother, as frail, charming and utterly improvident. Then frankly avowed that his father, Lionel Delacorte, Marquis of Cranbury, always had been considered more than a bit irrational and had become increasingly so with the passage of time. For years Cranbury had deluded himself that, as the Duke of Albemarle's cousin, he was very influential at Court and enormously wealthy which misconceptions Lionel Delacorte all too successfully had implanted in his children—especially in the case of his second son.

"Of course," explained the Honorable Frederick, "I'd not the foggiest notion that the Pater only was able to maintain our once extensive holdings through, bit-by-bit, mortgaging or selling off the ancestral estate.

"I was sent up to Cambridge in style but roistered so much and studied so little I soon got sent down and took up residence in London where"—he smiled faintly—"I fell in with profligate rakehells who speedily assisted me in squandering the last of my funds through drinking, wild gaming, keeping women and dressing only in the latest *ton*—all that sort of thing.

"In short I became plunged so deep into debt the Pater simply couldn't bail me out. So, I—well, I had to run for it or face a debtor's prison for, at that very moment intelligence

[339]

was circulated that the Pater had been declared bankrupt; and was only able to occupy Cranbury Castle during his lifetime through the Duke of Albemarle's grace and favor.

"Have you ever been in debt?"

"No, sir, not moneywise, at least."

"Then you can have no idea how deeply fear and a sense of degradation can torment a debtor, especially when his obligations amount to near fourteen thousand pounds."

A gasp escaped Pegeen. "Did you say *fourteen thousand pounds*, sir?"

"Aye, give or take a few hundred quid." He shrugged. "Therefore you undoubtedly will perceive, Ma'am, why I dare not go back to England to claim the title when my brother George dies—as surely he must before long—he's far gone in consumption."

Pegeen, leaning forward, spoke in low, breathless tones.

"Then, when your older brother dies, you stand to inherit the title and will become a marquis."

"Aye. But 'tis an ancient and empty honor," said he harshly. "The new Marquis will be penniless since Cranbury Castle must be sold instanter the Pater departs to his questionable reward."

A breeze sprang up and set the rigging to humming gently. Sleepers about deck stirred, subconsciously enjoying the cooling air.

The Honorable Frederick resumed in bantering tones: "I could become the 4th Marquis if I dare show this sun-scorched beak in England. At the moment I cannot." Thinking of a certain keg of pitch, he might have qualified this remark, but didn't.

"But aren't you entitled to share in the treasure Captain Phips and the rest of us have raised?"

"Possibly, but such a sum wouldn't come close to getting me out of debt—when and *if* the Commodore"—a decisive note entered his voice—"manages to fetch the *James and Mary* back to England. Being rated as something less than a boatswain's mate I might receive all of a hundred pounds."

He sighed. Even by selling the embezzled stones to advantage he probably wouldn't realize near enough to settle those damnable debts.

Pegeen's voice impinged on his calculations. "In that case, sir, what might your next move be?"

For a moment he hesitated. "Since I presume I will return to duty on the flagship at Cotton Key I must return to England in her and risk shipping out again before the bailiffs learn I'm back."

Curiously, he regarded the sinewy but curvaceous figure by his side. "What would you do in my situation, Ma'am?"

This wasn't the moment to speak right out so Pegeen evaded; better learn a lot more concerning the Honorable Frederick— he might well prove no better than a well-bred if plausible blackleg.

She arose, employing her most polished accents. "Sir, you have evoked most sincere sympathy. An I arrive at some possible solution to your problems we will speak of them on another occasion."

His hands shot out and gripped Pegeen, but he only kissed her lightly on the cheek before releasing her. "I shall count the minutes till that happy occasion arises, Ma'am."

When Moog wasn't to be seen when breakfast was being devoured it didn't much surprise anyone; the mixed-breed was given to swimming over to the wreck before anyone else could get going. He would keep diving tirelessly till the midday break, then return to send up so much debris Adderly and Dale had promised him a bonus.

Despite his late retirement, the Honorable Frederick got into the first workboat to shove off as if abrim with energy. He was first over the side and, clutching a sinkstone, followed his shadow through pellucid depths until that jagged hole hewn out of the galleon's ornate stern carvings loomed before him.

This day, thank God, was bright enough to cast light into the Vice-Admiral's quarters sufficient to reveal Moog's contorted dark body lying, horribly crushed, between the two stern chasers; also it showed a small packet clutched in one of his skinny hands.

Controlling revulsion, the Honorable Frederick ignored the dead mixed-breed's reproachful black stare and, reasoning that not for nothing would Moog have clung to the parcel during his death throes, wrenched it free.

His breath near to giving out, he thrust his prize into the bottom of a net bag such as divers normally carried to contain small objects, then snatched a chunk or two of debris for covering and, lungs aching, returned to the surface and carelessly dumped the whole of his take onto the workboat's bottom where it soon should become indistinguishable since other swimmers were arriving alongside. He'd make another dive for effect, then plead acute pain in his side, remain in the boat and pretend to assist in stowing plunder.

Not until noon did he find opportunity to set aside Moog's little package for special examination; this was simple, such being his prerogative as assistant assayer. The prize he secreted under large pieces of debris littering the *Dove*'s deck where it remained until dark before vanishing temporarily into the sea-chest of the second son of the Marquis of Cranbury.

Examination set the Honorable Frederick's hopes to soaring. His own selection of stones had been good but this small little hoard of rough-cut and unpolished emeralds, rubies, topazes, and stones of unknown description generally were larger and, even to inexperienced eyes, more lustrous.

Even discovery of Moog's corpse failed to discourage frenetic efforts; new finds were made by men on the verge of total exhaustion. One fine piece was a bronze coffer filled with unusually thick gold necklaces one of which supported a curious golden fish so skillfully fashioned its body simulated the movements of a swimming fish.

A massive golden altar service was the last item of great worth to be brought aboard the ketch before a bank of livid, purple-black clouds charged over the southwestern horizon and an ominous, humid, curious-smelling calm robbed the atmosphere of vitality.

Chapter 47

COTTON KEY

WHY THAT TALL, green-painted ship had failed to reappear off Ambrosia Bank remained a happy mystery to the
twenty-first son. In any case, he felt unfeignedly thankful that,
at the moment, both the Company's vessels lay in a deep cove
ending in a gradually shelving sand beach ideal for vessels
needing to careen and at least partially rid their bottoms of
marine growths.

A thorough job, of course, would have entailed the landing
of all carriage guns which under these circumstances would be
the height of folly, especially because a nearly infallible sixth
sense warned Phips that news of his finding the *Vice-Admiral*
by now must have spread about the Caribbean with the speed
of a forest fire during a drought.

Therefore, Phips kept a full broadside battery on board
while bottoms were scraped after a fashion. From under an

awning rigged over his quarterdeck, William Phips surveyed the scene while listlessly fanning himself with a palm leaf.

While the belated arrival of the storm-battered *Dove* had brought relief, she also fetched worrisome intelligence; she'd glimpsed the tops of one large ship and of two smaller ones, all apparently making towards Turks Island.

"Looked like a sizable brigantine sailing in convoy with a pair of heavy sloops," Dale had told him.

"What color was the brigantine?"

"Dark green."

As soon as the weather-beaten ketch arrived alongside Adderly, Dale, and Pegeen were summoned on board and made much of. For some time Phips had been apprehensive she would ever appear, even with Jack Dale aboard.

The "Commodore" was as much pleased as he was astonished by the value of the ketch's cargo raised following his departure. Even more surprisingly, the tally presented to Mr. Waddington by the Honorable Frederick appeared accurate and complete when the take was counted after being transshipped to the *James and Mary*.

All the same, William Phips suspected not a few readily concealed items might not have found a place in other than on the assayer's scales, but he said nothing; God knew how many incalculable riches already lay beneath his feet.

Tomorrow, or maybe the next day, Mr. Waddington and his assistants would have reached a fair estimate of riches yielded by *Nuestra Señora de la Concepción*. God knew how it had hurt him to leave, unraised, a fortune which might even exceed what he already had on board.

Moodily Phips glanced over dancing silver-crested, ultramarine waves towards the *Henry*, doing patrol duty off the cove's entrance. Although her bottom had been cleansed of barnacles, weeds and strange marine growths he foresaw that the *Henry* would become lost to sight at some point during the long and perilous voyage home. With this in mind he ordered all treasure carried in the sloop transferred to his flagship.

What particularly worried him was Dale's report about that tall ship with consorts sailing in this general direction.

Again, who could tell whether Captain Davis, on reaching Port Royal, hadn't blabbed? The Bermudian, like everyone else on the expedition, must be fully aware of the fabulous treasure in the *James and Mary*.

"Bloody" Billy Davis would have had ample time to collect a force of buccaneers and pirates powerful enough to overpower the small sixth-rate under his command.

Worst of all came realization that he, the clever twenty-first son, hadn't used sufficient foresight and had given Davis a rendezvous at Cotton Key.

In relays Phips kept Fast Otter and other sharp-eyed lookouts scanning the horizon for the first flash of canvas. He must have time to get his ships under sail, man guns and run out of this dangerous pocket of a cove, unless that sail proved to be the *Experience*.

Above the creaking of whips lowering salvage equipment into the forehold and the ringing made by caulking irons at work on strakes, he heard a hail from the maindeck given in the Honorable Frederick's succinct accents.

"Permission to approach the quarterdeck, sir?"

"Come on up, young feller. What's on yer mind?"

The assistant accountant, eyes direct and steady said, "Why, sir, it's just that I have been doing a bit of serious figuring."

"About what?"

"Sir, I have been calculating on what my share in the treasure you've raised might amount to when it comes time to pay off. I figure my portion, while it would delight and enrich most officers and seamen, won't go far towards resolving of my—er—financial troubles."

"A pity!"

"Sir, have you any inkling of the extent of my indebtedness?"

Phips continued to fan himself before grunting: "I don't and I don't give a damn, but I've a notion it must be impressive."

[*345*]

The Honorable Frederick long since had discovered that if consideration was wanted from William Phips it was better to look him full in the face and speak right out.

"Sir, since I know I can't begin to clear myself, would you deem it the part of wisdom for me to return to England and face a debtor's prison?"

"You'd be a fool to. What d'you want of me?"

The Honorable Frederick drew a slow breath. "Your permission, sir, to remain in the *Dove* and proceed to Bermuda in her."

A snorting laugh escaped the "Commodore." "I presume Pegeen's presence has nothing to do with this request?"

Under deep, red-bronze tan the Honorable Frederick flushed darker still. "Sir, I will not attempt to deny that I have, er—conceived a profound affection for the lady."

"So I've noticed. But isn't she still sort of married to Jack Dale?"

"Not legally, as I am sure you know. In a long while, sir, they seem to have been more like business partners than man and wife."

"I take it Jack raises no objections?"

"No, sir. He's stated he intends to marry a rich widow in the Bermudas the moment he returns there. Pegeen does not object."

"Not surprising. She also entertains ambitions, perhaps too high for her own good."

"With her, sir, I might find a new place in life, especially if you would be so kind as to see that my share in the *James and Mary*'s treasure is deposited with my principal creditors." The Honorable Frederick hesitated. "Sir, were I to stay away from home I possibly might—er—come by sufficient moneys to discharge me from debt."

Phips hooked a forefinger, moodily scraped a beading of sweat from his forehead. "In other words, ye're begging me to release you from the Articles signed on coming aboard so's you can try your luck along of a shrewd baggage like Pegeen Hammond?" He took care to use the name he'd first known her by.

"Yes, sir. I would be most grateful."

"I promise nothing beyond I'll think on the matter. Seems you've thought things out pretty 'cute, but you'd better realize that, by transferring to the *Dove*, you stand a more than even chance of not only losing yer share in what the ketch has earned, but quite possibly your worthless life as well. Ain't pirates more likely to tackle a lonely little ketch than a heavy-armed frigate with a consort?"

The Honorable Frederick said gravely: "Sir, that possibility indeed has crossed my mind particularly since we've heard naught from Captain Davis."

Turning his big head Phips spat viciously over the rail. "You're no fool, Fred. I confess I am sore worried on that very score. So report on board at top speed ready to assist Mr. Waddington and young Kelly. I want our cargo checked and restowed for the home voyage."

It came about, therefore, that treasure packed any which way on Ambrosia Bank, was returned on deck unit by unit and, despite the sun's burning heat, separated into categories. Ugly, tarnished silver specie, bars and wedges were collected in one place, plate in another, golden church services, Indian idols and ornaments were stacked in a pile which captured and held all eyes as silver never could.

Even by the light of a dim and smoky lanthorn assayers toiled endlessly sustained only by the breath-taking value of what they were tallying.

Thousands of silver coins fused through action of salt water had to be reweighed. Individual coins which had been in contact with iron—pistoles, johns, Austrian thalers, doubloons, and "two-pillar" pieces-of-eight—were easier to assay and pack.

During a respite, Mr. Waddington commented that, back in the early 1600s, illegal trade with the West Indies must have flourished, so many foreign coins were present: English James I shillings, laurels, and crowns; Portuguese escudos; French écus and louis d'argent, Dutch and Hanseatic thalers—which, later on, came to be called "dollars."

[347]

Next day in the "great cabbin" precious stones, pearls, and elaborate jewelry of all classifications were resorted and tallied in a rough-and-ready way—although intrinsically of much greater value than gold, precious stones, emeralds excepted, failed to stir men's imagination as did any golden object.

What fascination, Phips often wondered, had gold held for humans since the dawn of history? He'd read sufficiently to understand that Egyptians, Assyrians, Babylonians, Persians, barbarians, Greeks and Romans alike—all mankind for that matter—had been mesmerized and maddened by the very sight of this ever-gleaming and completely odorless metal. How often had he himself spent hours feasting his eyes or sensuously stroking gold of any description?

Towards the end of the second day Phips was given by blear-eyed accountants what seemed an accurate estimate of the value of treasure lying in the *James and Mary*'s hold.

"Sir," Waddington told him, "I know full well we may be underestimating, but at the very least some thirty-seven thousand pounds worth—troy weight—in pieces-of-eight and twenty-eight thousand pounds' value in bars, cakes and ingots of silver are aboard."

The twenty-first son sighed: what a staggering, unbelievable sum. So, in the long run, his Star thus far hadn't misled him after all.

The accountant continued: "And then there are three hundred-odd pounds of assorted plate plus"—he raised tired, red-rimmed eyes—"near thirty pounds of pure gold, not counting the heathen gods and jewelries of near the same fineness."

Unexpectedly, Phips peered across the "great cabbin." He was fondling a delicate little female idol adorned with an inscrutable half-smile. Said he: "There's only one thing above all this which grieves me: Is there no way to prevent so beautiful a thing as this from being melted down in the Spanish manner? Such are too lovely to be reduced to ingots and bars."

"I fear not, sir, to people from the Mint gold is simply so much gold!"

Chapter 48

A DEAL

THE NIGHT was still luminous and fragrant. Abram Adderly drawled: "Smells like a real weather-breeder."

People lounging about the *Dove*'s tiny poop deck all looked worn out. Pegeen, especially, showed effects of never-ending and exhausting toil. Her wide sun-darkened face had thinned to refinement so much that her cheekbones had become more noticeable while her cotton blouse appeared to be nowhere near so well filled as she lounged in a canvas easy chair sturdy brown legs extended and apart.

John Dale's broad features also had become chiseled fine through fatigue. Only black-bearded Abram Adderly seemed unchanged.

Thoughtfully, the Honorable Frederick's gaze wandered from one weather-beaten countenance to the next. What were his companions thinking about? No telling.

Presently, Adderly yawned cavernously and disappeared below soon to be followed by the First Mate.

The young nobleman's expression softened when he crossed to sit beside Pegeen. How would she have looked some ten years earlier? Vaguely he wondered from whence she had derived such physical and mental courage sufficient to sustain her over nearly nine strenuous and often perilous years?

"You must know by now," she'd told him, almost defiantly, "if we ever should marry I probably never could give you an heir—unless—unless."

"Unless what?"

For once she acted flustered. "Since we got to Ambrosia Bank I've sometimes dived pretty deep."

"What of that?"

Pegeen stared at hands clenched on her lap. "Can't say for sure, Fred, but mayhap strong pressures have done something to my—my innards." She relapsed into natural speech. "Guess no man could understand this, but when I last was 'with the flowers' it felt considerable different than since I reached the Bermudas."

"You—you think it's possible that now you might conceive?"

"I'm not promising but I figure it just might come about." She shrugged. "So if you'd risk gambling on an heir—why 'tis up to you."

He had said slowly: "I *must* have an heir to succeed to the title, carry on the name and all that, but Hell, Peg, why not give it a try? I've always been a gambler."

"And generally a losing one from what I've heard."

"Granted. All the same, I have a feeling that this time I'm about to pick a winning horse—mare, I mean. Together, we might rise high, all-fired high somewhere in our colonies. Maybe I'll even buy a governorship. Who knows?"

"'Colonies'?"

"To be sure. In England with your and my histories we could get nowhere, title or no title."

"You're certain Jack Dale won't make trouble?"

"Hell, no. Even now, Jack's not poor. With the Widow Gilbert's wealth added to his share in this venture, he can and will establish a thriving trade with the West Indies—'specially since the Spaniards more and more are losing their grip down there."

She looked him full in the face. "What have you to offer me, aside from a title? Got any money?"

"Might have; maybe more than you would imagine."

Her laugh was soft, her smile enigmatic. "You've been diving a lot on the gold room, haven't you?"

"Aye. What of that?"

"Well, I've known plenty of divers, and there's never been one yet, myself included, who hasn't been holding something out."

Chapter 49

PURSUIT

ON THE AFTERNOON of May 22, 1687, William Phips
ordered all senior officers immediately to assemble on the flagship's quarterdeck. A rougher, more villainous-appearing con-
gregation of masters and mates would have been difficult to
imagine when in a big hurry they appeared in the flagship's
gangway. Even the least experienced seaman in the motley
little squadron had observed a gradual paling of the sky's brilliant blue, and the uneasy evolutions of seabirds as well as the
ever-increasing roaring of surf on clusters of reefs off the cove's
entrance.

Abram Adderly shuffled up to the "Commodore." "Hope
to Hell, sir, you're about to order us to hightail out o' here.
Look at that sky! 'Tis bound to start blowin' great guns before
long."

Phips reared back on his rattan armchair and its fabric pro-

tested his weight. He turned to Dale. "That's no vain pre-
diction, is it, Jack?"

"Yep. Sure smells like a hurricane's brewin'. Time's come to
clear out and seek weather room. 'Twould make small sense
risk sendin' our spoil back to the bottom."

Lieutenant Strong, who had been supervising the remounting
of broadside guns and distribution of loading tools, shot and
ammunition, clambered to the crowded quarterdeck.

"All set, sir," the lieutenant said. "I'll tell off gun crews and
start drilling—they've grown might rusty about serving cannon." He cast a glance at Captain Rogers. "See you, too, have
been readying your hardware."

"Good," Phips commented. "Somehow, I've the notion before long we'll be using every gun can be fired. Jack, you don't
throw much weight of shot, but get yer pop guns useful right
away." Now his big-jawed features turned to Captains Rogers
and Adderly. "You're wooded and watered up like I told you?"

Both replied that water casks had been topped off, that
they'd stowed a plentiful supply of fresh fruit and sea turtles.

"Good. We set sail tomorrow earliest moment the wind's
sufficient strong to give us steerageway. I'll order my canvas
kept short so's we can keep together.

"Now listen, all of you. To begin with we'll pass through
Mouchoir Passage, then shape a course for the Caicos Islands;
aim to stay in British waters long as possible.

"Should a storm or some other hazard separate us, this ship
and the *Henry* will rendezvous off Mariguana Island." He
glanced at Dale. "An trouble strikes you, being small and swift,
I grant you leave to make for the Bermudas. Pray God you get
your loot there, safe and sound."

From the lookout on the frigate's foretop sounded a long-
drawn hail: "Deck there! Sail ho-o!"

Phips snatched up his dented brass speaking trumpet. "Where
away?"

"Nor'west-by-west, sir! Seems heading this way!"

Everyone peered at the foretop, wearing strained expressions.
"How big is she?" Strong shouted.

[353]

"Still too far off to be sure, sir."

A griping sensation in Phips's bowels increased.

He spun about. "Get to yer ships and stations. Make ready to weigh and tow out of this trap the instant I signal."

While a rain squall during the critical next half hour obscured all sight of the unknown craft furious activity took place on all three ships. Soon the overcast broke to reveal a shallop, unmistakably "Bloody" Bill Davis's *Experience*, speeding towards Cotton Key, canvas straining.

A vast sense of relief briefly restored Phips's sense of confidence—a relief quickly dissipated when Davis sailed under the *James and Mary*'s counter bawling: "Get out of here quick! Sighted a heavy brigantine and two big sloops cruisin' this way. Can't be fifty miles off."

"Could they be British?" Phips shouted, heart hammering.

"No tellin'. They was too far off to make out their hulls."

"Thanks! Put about and wait offshore!" To Maddox, his signal officer, he roared: "Hoist the 'get-under-weigh' signal."

Great God! The tops of a big ship and two sloops might heave into sight before dark closed in on the gathering storm. What then would become of the Company's treasure?

There being scant wind small boats hurriedly were lowered and set to towing vessels out of the cove—a laborious task—but it came as a consoling possibility that those unidentified ships also might lie becalmed and so unable to close in before dark.

That night, for the first time in years, William Phips knelt beside his bunk, joined hands and prayed awkwardly but earnestly. If only Mary could be kneeling alongside to join in his supplications he'd have felt a sight more confident concerning the immediate future.

An unearthly windlessness prevailed all night. Just the same, huge, oily rollers continued to come racing up out of the southeast and started all four English ships to rolling so violently crews were forced to double-lash gun carriages, small boats and other deck gear which possibly might break loose.

When uneasy puffs of wind commenced to blow towards Mouchoir Bank, Phips raged and cursed because they were

[354]

coming out of the southwest just where Davis had sighted the three strangers.

"Damnation!" snarled the "Commodore." "They'll catch this wind before us and come roaring up." To John Strong he rasped: "Signal consorts to close in and clear for action soon's we get sufficient wind to fill our canvas and check this Goddam rolling."

Dawn broke tardily thanks to squadrons of livid clouds hurtling across a scaly, yellow-gray sky. The wind increased for a space then fell off again leaving the oddly assorted little squadron to wallow, all but helpless, among giant waves which, coming from different directions, creating dangerous cross-seas that sent crew members lurching about as on a drunken spree.

What Phips had been fearing all along occurred just as his ships were nearing the treacherous, reef-strewn entrance to Mouchoir Passage and a long succession of low-lying islets beyond them.

One after another the tops of three ships became visible astern; discouragingly soon, their hulls loomed, dark and ominous on the horizon.

From the fact that the strangers had reduced canvas to jibs, topsails, and an occasional staysail, they must be running before a slant of wind vastly stronger than that affording the English vessels only uncertain steerageway.

Guns were shotted and ports raised by men forced time and again to grab desperately for the nearest handhold.

"Look at the 'Mudians! Bastards are clearing out," stormed Strong. "Blast 'em for lily-livered cowards." To his considerable astonishment the grim-faced "Commodore" said, "I'd do the same in their stead; they can't throw sufficient metal to accomplish anything much. They're fast. With luck they may survive this tempest and win free."

The wind gradually increased until it commenced to whip stinging sheets of spray from mountainous wavetops. A curious haze materialized but not thick enough to obscure details of the foremost pursuer, a green-painted brigantine which Phips

[355]

judged to be armed with maybe twenty carriage guns. She was reeling hard to port and spewing great sheets of spray from beneath her bows.

Phips ordered a Union Jack hoisted. Immediately it flattened as if cut out of tin. He ordered both stern chasers manned, though with the sea rising so fast and the flagship's violent and unpredictable motions it seemed most unlikely that they could accomplish much.

One thing became certain. The *Henry of London*'s only chance of escape lay in veering westward in hopes that the pursuers, strung out according to sailing capacity, would keep after the flagship. Then a curious thing happened; the brigantine struck her foretopsail and bent on another showing a white skeleton painted on a scarlet panel.

"Pirates!" Maddox screamed over the whine of wind in the mizzen shrouds.

John Strong snarled: "Kind of him to let us know his intentions."

"'Intentions'?"

"If the background is red a pirate means he's willing to grant quarter—otherwise 'twould be black."

Soaked to the skin, Phips steadied himself against the taffrail. "Means he's sure we've got the main treasure on board so he don't aim to risk a fight and maybe sink us."

To the Gunner, Phips said, "When he comes within two cables' length try the stern chasers loaded with ball-and-chain shot—might score a lucky hit."

A chaser roared, its smoke whipped aside so instantly anxious officers on the *James and Mary*'s poop deck clearly saw a spout rise short by fifty yards and to port. The second shot, however, went unmarked—the seas having risen to an almost unbroken white lather.

Phips ordered canvas reduced or double-reefed lest a mast snap and put a bloody period to this adventure for, under no circumstance, did he intend to surrender: only fight to the last man.

He then struggled down to the "great cabbin" and personally trained the number one chaser. When the motion seemed right he jammed a slow match onto the touchhole. The piece lurched extra hard due to a violent dip and its recoil knocked him spinning to one side. Spouting profanities, the twenty-first son got back to his feet shouting: "Any luck?"

"Naw, sir," yelled the gun captain. "Ship pitched just as you fired—shot passed clear over the bloody rascal's tops—saw it clear."

By now the pirate had closed to a range of less than a quarter mile. So why the pursuer didn't open with his bow chasers remained a mystery.

Once number two chaser had been run out again, Phips waited to sense some sort of rhythm in his ship's motion but cross-seas rendered this all but impossible.

Sweating "like a whore in church" as Jack Dale would have put it, Phips blew on his match till it glowed like a demon's eye, poised it dangerously low over the priming till the ship dipped sharply then jammed down the match and got his brows singed by a dazzling perpendicular flash from the touchhole.

The cannon leaped suddenly like a spurred thoroughbred and blinding, rotten-smelling smoke swirled about the "great cabbin."

Someone screamed: "A hit! A hit! His top hamper's hit."

Phips peered past the tube in time to watch the pirate's straining foretopmast snap and its broken yard begin to flail about.

Whoever he might be, the enemy captain bore off to starboard, yawing and plunging but already he had sent men struggling into the rigging.

Phips risked much by ordering reefs shaken out and storm staysails set, even though the hurricane was increasing in fury and visibility had diminished to less than a cable's length. Even so, those on the flagship became aware that the pirate captain, disdaining to pause for repairs, had resumed chase at a speed which Phips judged roughly approximated that of the fleeing *James and Mary*, now pitching and rolling over mountainous and generally directionless gray-white seas.

Of consorts on both sides nothing could be seen once the haze thickened and the sky darkened into a sinister twilight.

Incredibly, the wind's already terrific velocity mounted. The *James and Mary* had assumed a 15° list to port when with a *crack!* audible over the tumult, the mizzen topgallant carried away. The flagship staggered and fell, groaning into the trough of the waves. Great, gray-green rollers started to sluice over the deck, carried away the gig and a pair of luckless deck hands, boiled among the guns and ripped away sections of bulwarks.

Ax in hand, William Phips, half-smothered by spindrift fought his way up the mizzen shrouds, directed a party hacking at tangling lines until the shattered mast and its burden of wreckage were freed to vanish amid screaming turmoil.

Possibly the eye of the storm had arrived in the vicinity. At any rate the wind dropped rapidly although the ocean continued to spout and roar as before. Visibility miraculously increased until it was seen that the crippled pirate, by pure chance, had been driven in the same direction. She was only some two miles astern and scudding past clusters of reefs and surfbordered keys. She seemed to be closing in with a relentless tenacity.

For all he felt confident his command could outshoot the pursuer, Phips had no mind to match broadsides unless forced to. Only a couple of lucky shots into his bilges could return *Nuestra Señora de la Concepción*'s riches to the bottom, together with all his vaulting ambitions.

Once the wind-filled darkness deepened, Phips, to Lieutenant Strong's incredulous dismay, ordered the stern lanthorn lit.

Strong knew better than to disregard this apparently daft command; the New Englander must have some valid reason for so inexplicable a move. Better than anyone else, the First Lieutenant knew Phips was familiar with this area through which his fleeing flagship was staggering through a maze of reefs, keys, and shoals among which, even in fair weather, one had to look sharp and then some. But amid such blinding rain squalls, increasing darkness and thundering combers which shook the frigate from stem to stern this resembled inevitable disaster.

In an iron grip, Phips clutched a lifeline long since rigged about his thickening middle and, shielding his eyes from successive stinging bursts of spray, found he still could discern outlines of his pursuers. By God, despite everything, that bloody pirate still was dogging him.

While entering a particularly narrow and tricky reach of the Passage he experienced an inexplicable sense of calm such as had steadied him in the face of many a critical situation.

After all, hadn't he negotiated this same channel several times on trading voyages which had rendered possible the construction, by Peter Sargeant, of that "faire three-story, brick mansion" on Green Lane?

The ominous, protesting creak of yards and the caterwauling of wind in the rigging eased during a brief let-up in the blast. By the last traces of daylight he was able to make out a pair of tall black and pointed reefs and a small island, topped by a conical hill barely visible beyond them.

He allowed the frigate to lurch and stagger onwards for a long five minutes before bellowing: "Put out light—ease all sheets! Ready both bow anchors. Quick! Quick for your lives!"

That great power lies in prayer, his intimate friend, the Reverend Mather, had preached more than once. Right now Phips felt more than willing to agree. Only the hand of God on the helm possibly could have guided the *James and Mary* in safety past spouting reefs once she had veered to starboard out of Mouchoir Passage and, amid rain-filled darkness, plunged into a narrow passage separating those sea-tormented twin rocks.

Little time was required for Strong and Maddox, half-suffocated at the end of their lifelines, to sense the "Commodore's" intent as he steered the *James and Mary* through that gap between the reefs and into a partial lee created by them. When the force of towering, unseen waves appeared to decrease somewhat, Phips at once ordered the bow anchors dropped and spares, such as the stream and sheet anchors, readied for instant use.

Everybody on board could feel anchors jar and grind along the bottom. Oh Christ, what if they refused to bite and hold? No one aboard ever would forget the awful roar of giant seas pounding the drifting and now quite helpless frigate.

Below, Mr. Waddington, no longer plump and roseate, clung to his bunk as never before. Oh, the pity of it! All this ingenuity, money, and energy was about to be thrown away. "Oh, Lord, into Thy hands I commend my spirit," he babbled when the ship struck and her entire fabric shuddered violently.

Mr. Waddington gulped now because that vast treasure once more was about to be strewn about the ocean's floor—this time never to be recovered.

Twice more Mr. Waddington felt the ship bump and twist, but not too savagely. Although no part of a seaman, the assayer nevertheless deduced that the frigate's rudder must be pounding upon a reef. From above sounded yelled commands distorted by wind. Mr. Waddington braced himself for the ultimate, rending crash. Yet there came no more violent shocks, only diminished grinding noises.

Only slowly did William Phips become aware that his Star still was shining. Incredibly, both anchors were holding so well that voracious reefs could only nibble at her rudder. Rubbing sea water from smarting, hollowed eyes, the twenty-first son peered into furious, lightless confusion but could see nothing at all. Betrag Eldritch? Could her incantations have guided him through one of three sleeves he knew to exist along the eastward reaches of Mouchoir Passage? Dully, he reckoned that, for the time being, the *James and Mary* was safe but only for so long as her anchors held and no hawser parted. Didn't it stand to reason the pirate, once the chase had extinguished her stern light, must have continued to struggle onward along the comparative safety of Mouchoir Passage?

Throughout the night of May 23, the *James and Mary* fought savagely to break loose. Should either anchor cable snap all the treasure below would not have bought even the faintest hope for survival.

Having done everything conceivable to restore a measure of

confidence and order, Phips sent all hands below but remained on the quarterdeck and once more addressed himself to that stern Puritan God who, for time out of mind, he'd been taught to fear.

The thundering of seas and groaning of the laboring vessel's timbers resounding in his ears and he gripped the taffrail, lifted streaming features, hair whipping, and shouted: "Hear this miserable sinner, hear me, Almighty God! Hear me and heed my vow an Thee carries this vessel safe to England, I swear I will devote my life unto the service of Jesus Christ, your Son, and ever will labor to aid them who truly believe in Him—especially those inhabiting Massachusetts Bay Colony, so help me."

Whether his prayer had been effective or not, William Phips never could determine, yet towards the end of an interminable spell of darkness rendered heart-shaking by the thundering of nearby reefs and the staccato snapping of tattered canvas, the wind began to abate and blinding rain squalls came less frequently.

Once dim and unsteady light commenced to penetrate low, scurrying storm clouds men struggled on deck. Soon it became apparent that while sections of the bulwarks had carried away, two of the flagship's three small boats somehow remained intact in their cradles.

Of the *Henry* and the Bermudian vessels there was no trace. Whether they had managed somehow to escape down Mouchoir Passage only time would reveal.

Lieutenant Strong, looking like a horse-faced scarecrow and bleeding from a gash across his forehead, viewed his superior with something like superstitious awe. "In God's name, sir, how dared you risk running into a place like this even by daylight?"

"Needs must when the Devil drives," Phips grunted. "Get axmen to work, there's one hell of a lot to be done if we're to win clear of this trap."

Chapter 50

GRAVESEND

OFF SHEERNESS THE *James and Mary* was bespoken by a speedy revenue cutter just before the sea-worn yellow frigate entered the Thames estuary with her Captain profoundly thankful that intermittent fogs had veiled the final stretch of his voyage from corsairs and the like.

Thanks to the cutter's quick report, the Company of Gentlemen Adventurers learned that the flagship had reached London on a morning in late summer, 1687, and now was lying at Gravesend. The Duke of Albemarle and the Royal Mint Master were the first to be informed.

At once, Kit Monck jubilantly invited the Company's principal shareholders to assemble posthaste at Newcastle House but, long before they arrived, word flew from borough to borough that that redoubtable New Englander, Captain William Phips, had returned from Hispaniola with holds abrim with gold, silver, and jewels. Wildly excited mobs collected and started for the Thames chanting: "To the river! To the river!"

Although Albemarle and friends ordered coachmen not to spare their horses, officers representing the Admiralty and the Customs Service already were in Gravesend and had posted a cordon of guards about the wharf to which lay the seaworn yellow frigate.

Hard on their heels appeared Commissioners from the Royal Treasury determined to thwart the least attempt at embezzlement and to make certain His Royal Majesty would receive every farthing due him. A cheering and wildly excited human tide surged along beside glittering coaches until the guards' curses and fixed bayonets restrained them.

Dignity forgotten, the Duke, crusty old Sir John Narbrough, Lords Sunderland and Oxford, and other shareholders ran over the wharf's splintery surface towards that spot where Phips, together with his principal officers, stood waiting, hats in hands and grinning hugely.

Albemarle wasn't above shedding a few tears while hugging Phips, then shouted: "Let my health be drunk by every man and boy of this ship's company!"—an order immediately obeyed not once but many times.

In Newcastle House all but a few of the Company's shareholders assembled next day, jubilant and not a few roaring drunk. Following still fresh rounds of toasts, Phips remarked: "I say, Kit, I don't see Sir Richard Haddock. Hope he ain't ill."

Someone burbled: "Oh, Dick's sick all right, but only because, two months back, he sold his shares for a paltry ninety pounds! Doubt if the poor fellow will ever recover."

After awhile Albemarle managed to guide the New Englander into a small library where he said, "'Tis fortunate you've returned at this time."

"Why so?"

"His Majesty daily grows more unpopular."

"Why?"

"Because of ever-increasing taxes, of his stubborn friendliness towards the King of France and his tolerance of the Roman Church in general." With a wry smile, the Duke added: "An Jamie's share in the treasure proves sufficient great he may be able to settle pressing obligations to the so-called 'Sun King' and regain a measure of public approval at home."

He frowned annoyance when young Lord Oxford burst in, red-faced, his wig's long black curls asway and his coat of embroidered silk splashed with liquor.

He lifted a brandy glass. "Here's to you, Captain Phips! If rumors flying about town prove even half true you are a made man—ten thousand times a made man! So are we all! Thank God you've come home safe!" Draping an arm about the twenty-first son, he adopted an absurdly secretive manner. "Take it you'd no trouble with pirates? No threat of mutiny among your crew?"

"No, my Lord. All along, the men knew I'd promised to pay them their cut out of my own share if need arose."

To the host's obvious displeasure, others came crowding into the library behind Sunderland, flushed and unsteady.

"Come on, Phips, give us some inkling of the worth of these riches you've raised home."

Phips said boastfully: "They must be worth well over three hundred thousand pounds, sterling, in coinage alone and that's not counting the value of bronze and brass cannons and culverins, gold, and silver plate, Indian ornaments, idols and the like."

"Three hundred thousand in specie alone!" burst out Albemarle. "God's teeth!"

"Aye, my Lord. God's teeth."

"What about jewelry and precious stones? What sort did you raise?" Narbrough cut in sharply.

"An assortment of topazes, amethysts, emeralds, sapphires, and pearls." Hugely enjoying this supreme moment, he announced loudly: "Friends, for your delectation I've fetched along a few of the finest gems."

Spirits soaring as never before, the twenty-first son from his coattails produced a pair of leather wallets, crossed to a table desk and with a flourish scattered their contents across it. Breathless gasps, exultant screeches, and resounding shouts made the stuffy little library reverberate.

"God in His High Heaven!" Lord Oxford burst out, goggling, "you have won us all a fortune!"

Several days were required for the Mint Master, assayers and other Treasury Officials to tally precisely and check the weight of all bullion against the impeccably accurate report of Mr. Waddington, Mr. Charles Kelly, and the Honorable Frederick Delacorte.

On a warm summer's afternoon the Mint Master completed the last in his findings for the King's Warrant Book. Lips pursed, he passed it to Mr. Waddington saying, "Pray read this certification and sign it, if you approve."

King's Warrant Book XII

pp 343–8

Royal Warrant to Clerk of the Signet for a seal to remise and release to Christopher, Duke of Albemarle, his Executors, lands etc. and all the partners adventurers and undertakers who engaged with him in recovery of treasure on the north side of Hispaniola, et supra.

All manner of further reckoning (by reason of the King's Admiralty droit to a moiety, et supra.) Touching valuables there recovered by Captain William Phips and the other persons employed by the said Duke and his partner's and brought home to London about June last in the *James and Mary*.

But this is to apply only to valuables so brought home as above and is not to apply to any other such carried to Bermudas or any other place whatsoever; all by reason that the said Duke and partners did equip said *James and Mary*, and Captain William Phips did there get up a great quantity of silver and a considerable parcel of gold, which was brought home as above (besides certain other quantities which were carried away in other vessels to Bermudas (or elsewhere).

The Mint officials did weigh the said valuables on the *James and Mary* and find them to be 37,538 lb. Troy of pieces of eight (of which the King's tenth is 3,753 lb 9oz 12dwt. Troy) and 27,556 lb 4oz bars and cakes of silver (whereof the King's tenth is 2,755 lb 7oz 12dwt. Troy) and 347lb of plate (whereof the King's tenth is 34 lb 8oz 8dwt Troy) and 25 lb 7oz 19dwt of gold (whereof the King's tenth was 2 lb 6oz 15dwt 21 grains Troy) The silver which concerned the seamen is 3,770 lb 3oz (whereof the King's tenth is 3,07 lb 8oz 14dwt Troy) all which have been received by the said Mint Officers.

After Mr. Waddington had surveyed the certification with great care he announced: "I will attest this, provided a notation is made that no estimate of the worth of jewelry, artifacts, and precious stones is here included."

Further calculations indicated His Majesty's share alone would amount to something worth well over twenty thousand pounds sterling: that the portion of the Duke of Albemarle, as owner of the largest number of shares, was likely to realize near fifty thousand pounds, while the rest of the shareholders would receive around eight to ten thousand pounds for every one hundred pounds sterling invested in the Company.

On the other hand the twenty-first son's share, it was calculated, would amount to a scant sixteen thousand pounds—largely due to unquestioned probity in the matter of accounting and generosity towards his officers and men.

Declared the Duke at a sumptuous banquet later that week: "It ain't fair, Will, that you, who brought all this about, despite all hazards, shouldn't be more handsomely rewarded. You must accept some jewelry. Certainly your good wife back in Boston would relish some?"

Slowly, the New Englander shook his big, dark-wigged head. "'Tis generous of you, Kit, but Puritans abiding in the Massachusetts Bay Colony ain't given to adorning themselves in any way. Were my Mary to flaunt rich finery she'd expose herself and me to dangerous gossip which might cost us dear."

Burst out Lord Oxford: "But surely, man, your wife, whom you've left deserted so long in our interest, should be rewarded? Hah! I have it! I've noticed a heavy golden goblet with its rim studded with little emeralds which might solve the problem of demonstrating the Company's gratitude for her loyalty towards you."

Phips's features, already flushed a deep, wine-red, turned a deeper hue. "That's truly a handsome notion, my Lord, yet I can't accept, lacking knowledge of the goblet's true worth."

Albemarle ceased fingering jewels, raised a glittering hand. "In that case you must know the said goblet is valued at around a thousand pounds—a sum which we trust won't stick in your Puritanical craw. Even a pack of blue noses couldn't construe it a sinful act for the two of you to toast from it us and those brave fellows who accompanied you on the expedition."

Phips ended by nodding. In all fairness wasn't Mary deserving of more than trivial recognition for long patience and unswerving trust?

Towards the banquet's conclusion, Lord Falkland, somewhat soberer than his fellow shareholders, called for attention. "Captain Phips, will you, in your own words and at whatever length you choose, give us an account of your adventures off Hispaniola?"

The New Englander, mellowed with good food and copious wines, became boastful as of yore and rendered a fulsome but accurate rendering of his chance meeting with Ottavio Gallucio, the diving operations, the chase by the green brigantine, and his anxiety during a potential mutiny on the homeward voyage. Shamelessly, he enlarged on the appearance of the green brigantine and his bluff to send the Frenchman away, on his own courage and astuteness in evading the pirate's pursuit along Mouchoir Passage.

Thinking ahead, Phips concluded by reciting his reasons for breaking off operations at the moment he had, even if it meant leaving plentiful plunder behind. "A great fortune remains in

[367]

the *Vice-Admiral* but her location's now known, so we'll have to move fast—very fast."

Avidly, the shareholders listened and loudly silenced anyone attempting to interrupt until the New Englander sat down, heavily, to swill a tall glass of cognac.

"By God," roared Albemarle, "an you ever give up the sea, Will, you can make your fortune as a teller of tales. When this story spreads you'll have half of London fighting for passage on any ship bound for the West Indies!"

Brandy and champagne was offered until Phips's head swam pleasantly and he sensed himself floating luxuriously on a soft pink-and-golden cloud. Only now was he commencing to perceive the importance of his triumph. With a share amounting to at least sixteen thousand pounds, a gold goblet, some jewels and his Star to lead him on, what lofty goals could he not achieve? How pleased Granny Eldritch would be were she still in the land of the living.

The Duke's bejeweled hand decanted a small measure of champagne into Phips's glass as he said thickly but steadily: "This, my lad, must suffice for tonight. May I suggest you retire early?"

Something in his manner brought Phips up sharp, sobered him a little. "What's your meaning, Kit? Ain't this by rights my night to howl?"

Albemarle, swaying a trifle, bent and breathed vinously into Phips's ear. "Summons arrived this evening from Windsor Castle where His Majesty will deign to receive us tomorrow."

"But, but why?"

"No doubt Jamie wishes a firsthand account of your doings."

As if to cap this transcendent moment, a messenger arrived bearing news of the arrival at Greenwich of the *Henry of London*, badly weather-scarred but with ship and crew intact.

Next day, June 28, the Duke of Albemarle's ornate coach's tires crackled over gravel paving the long and stately driveway, through the Home Park and the Forest up to Windsor Castle and there pulled up to discharge a pair of passengers. The taller was wearing an elaborate white wig of the newest and most fashionable design to which his deeply bronzed skin offered an effective contrast.

William Phips's scarlet long-skirted silk coat sparkled with a plethora of gold lace while a waistcoat of sky-blue satin glittered with arabesques executed in the same precious metal. The New Englander's big hands, marred by ugly calluses and reddish scars, were almost concealed by deep cuffs of delicate Belgian lace. At his side swung a magnificent gold-hilted and emerald-studded dress sword he had personally raised from *Nuestra Señora de la Concepción*'s gold room.

Invisible under a shirt of the finest lawn dangled that same Cairngorm broach, recently altered into a pendant, which Betrag Eldritch had bestowed, half-a-lifetime ago it seemed, aboard the *High Hopes*.

Even more resplendent was the appearance of His Grace of Albemarle wearing a multitude of high and distinguished decorations and orders and clad in a coat of peacock-blue satin, canary-yellow breeches of the same material and bright green hose.

Little delay attended the appearance of the King's black-clad Chief Chamberlain, gold-topped staff of office and all. Gravely, he informed the callers they might enter at once.

After mounting a flight of wide steps the Chamberlain ushered the visitors into a small private antechamber and bade them to make themselves comfortable for a space, adding: "Pleased you are so punctual; His Majesty may keep you waiting but he dislikes subjects to be lacking in promptness."

Once they had settled themselves, Phips inquired in Court-inflected tones: "Why is this audience granted to me—a mere colonial commoner?"

"The King, above everything, is a sea-loving man. *Vide* how much he has done to restore his Navy to fitness. I venture he is curious concerning the methods you employed while raising the treasure, jubilant though he may be over your honesty and the amazing size of his share, he very urgently needs more money."

To both men's astonishment the Chamberlain reappeared almost immediately and announced His Majesty's readiness to receive them. He led off along what appeared to be an interminable route through the upper ward to the Presence Room in the Chapel of Saint George. Here, James II, King of England, Scotland, Ireland, Wales, and France occupied an elaborately carved and gilded armchair set upon a low, crimson-carpeted dais.

Announced the Chamberlain: "Your Majesty, his Grace the Duke of Albemarle and"—in less pompous tones—"Captain William Phips."

The King's posture was stiff and in no way resembled the easy grace affected by his late brother, Charles II.

"Your Majesty," commenced the Duke bowing deeply, "I have the honor to present your most loyal subject, Captain William Phips, whose valor, seamanship and integrity have brought great honor and wealth to England."

The gleaming parquetry floor commenced to heave like the deck of a vessel fleeing a storm when a page boy ran up to place a red velvet cushion before James II's chair.

On signal an impassive Officer of the Royal Bodyguard slipped his sword from its sheath, but paused before the King, who at the moment was extending a pale and slender hand.

"Kneel, you flaming fool!" hissed Albemarle.

Although the twenty-first son's head was whirling, he knew enough through previous experience to obey and brush hard lips across the Royal knuckles.

The impact of a blade on one and then the other of his shoulders was featherlight, but its touch, to the twenty-first son, felt as crushing as the blow of a hard-swung cudgel. At the same instant he fancied he could hear Betrag Eldritch rejoicing and see Mary Phips fighting down unseemly pride.

As from a vast distance, he heard the words, clearly spoken: "Arise, Sir William Phips."

Epilogue

THE CAREER of William Phips subsequent to his ennoble-
ment proved to be almost as checkered and stormy as that span
of his life preceding his raising of the *Nuestra Señora de la
Concepción*'s treasure. Once Sir William Phips was knighted
he became the toast of London, was followed by swarms of
admirers and nearly overwhelmed with a dazzling variety of
honors bestowed from all directions. As an example, the Company of Gentlemen Adventurers ordered a handsome gold
medal struck in his honor and presented it suspended from a
heavy chain of that same precious metal.

Similar silver medals and chains were bestowed on every
member of the *James and Mary*'s company. The medal, dated
1687, showed the King and Queen in profile on the obverse,
with the *James and Mary* riding at anchor and attended by
small diving vessels on its reverse.

For a long while Sir William continued to be inundated by

invitations and offers of patronage from the great and the near-great. Such flattery, however, failed to turn the massive head of that hardy individual who, as the twenty-first son of the same parents, first had seen the light of day in a log cabin on Jeremesquam Point on the Sheepscot River.

William Phips thus became the first American-born English subject ever to be knighted by his King, an honor which had been too-hardly earned to lend the new nobleman more than passing illusions of grandeur.

Once Sir William Phips had located the wreck of the *Vice-Admiral*, as British mariners termed it, on Ambrosia Bank— later, it was, and still is, named "The Silver Bank" because the bulk of treasure raised there was largely composed of that metal—news of the find and its location spread with gale-speed about the West Indies, to Bermuda and the length of the American seaboard, especially since it was reported that William Phips had failed to completely despoil the galleon's considerable wealth.

The King, the Duke of Albemarle, Sir John Narbrough, and Sir William Phips, therefore, were in a great hurry to fit out a second expedition to complete the ransacking. The Duke of Albemarle, although in ill health, was especially eager since he was nearing bankruptcy. Also, he had recently pleaded successfully with the King to appoint him Royal Governor of Jamaica.

King James II, being agreeable for Phips's swift return to Ambrosia Bank, assigned the *Assistance*, a well-armed Royal frigate, to lead this second expedition. A new stock company was formed and soon a squadron of four stout vessels was assembled to return to the wreck under the acknowledged leadership of Sir William Phips—although old Sir John Narbrough had been designated to serve as titular Commander-in-Chief in H.B.M.S. *Foresight*.

On this occasion Sir William commanded a vessel bearing surely the strangest name ever to appear on the Royal Navy List: *Good Luck and a Boy*! Commanding another ship, the *Princess*, was Captain Francis Rogers, steadfast veteran of both previous attempts to raise the *Vice-Admiral's* treasure.

The expedition sailed in August 1687 and on the 7th of December reached Samana Bay there to receive most unwelcome intelligence, for by this time some twenty-seven sail—mostly small craft from Bermuda and other British colonies—had been sighted anchored near the wreck of the *Nuestra Señora de la Concepción!*

When the expedition reached Ambrosia Bank the wreck proved to have been so thoroughly gutted that only a few little vessels were lingering there in the hopes of discovering overlooked trifles. Lacking legal permits to operate these promptly fled when Phips arrived at the lagoon.

Not much time was required for the King's expedition to ascertain that the *Vice-Admiral* indeed had been most thoroughly plundered.

Sir William and the rest of the expedition's leaders naturally experienced bitter disappointment. Characteristically, the twenty-first son was first to point out: "When the cream is taken, 'tis useless to skim the milk." Thereupon he ordered the *Good Luck and a Boy* on a course for Boston intending to exercise his responsibilities as Provost-Marshal-General and High Sheriff of the Dominion of New England—a recent appointment covering all the New England colonies.

While Sir William Phips sailed northward he envisaged certain critically important social reforms and planned increased security from the French for his native land. On arrival in Boston, however, he became aware of the jealous enmity of the Royal Governor, arrogant, narrow-minded, and unbending Sir Edmund Andros. However, he was overjoyed to reoccupy his "Faire brick house on Green Lane" where Lady Mary, his able and faithful spouse, eagerly awaited him with pride and open arms.

Before long the new knight discovered he could accomplish next to nothing against the entrenched influences of Sir Edmund Andros and that dour Puritan theocracy which for so long had dominated not only Boston but most of New England. Never one to fight against patently hopeless odds, Sir William, at the end of only six weeks, sailed for London to protest the

Governor's tyranny and to plead for a new Charter calculated to rectify flagrant abuses of the colonists' civil rights as free-born Englishmen.

Alas, on December 10, 1688, James II found it advisable, as a secret Catholic, to flee London hurriedly and take refuge in France thereby evoking a turmoil which forever ended the Stuart dynasty's rule.

Thus passed from the scene the second of the kings whom the suspected witch, Betrag Eldritch, had predicted young William Phips would "stand before" some day.

The next monarch before whom the twenty-first son was destined to appear would be Prince William of Orange of Holland, summoned to the throne by Parliament by right of his marriage to Mary, Protestant daughter of James II.

During upheavals and intrigues preceding the reign of William III and his Queen, Mary, there was little Sir William could do save to rally old friends, mend political fences and gradually, but with consummate skill, to insinuate himself into the new rulers' good graces.

Abandoning all thoughts of further treasure-hunting, Phips now dedicated himself in fulfillment of his oath towards planning the correction of deplorable political conditions in New England. To compound Sir William's difficulties came the sad news that his great good friend and most powerful sponsor, the Duke of Albemarle and Royal Governor of Jamaica, had died in November 1688. But at almost the same time he received a measure of consolation in the fact that, in December, the General Court of Boston finally had become sufficiently exasperated to depose Sir Edmund Andros and in his stead had appointed elderly but able Simon Bradstreet as provisional Governor.

Once Sir Edmund Andros was out of the way, Phips, in May of 1689, abruptly returned to Boston, organized and headed an expedition which captured Port Royal in Nova Scotia, a strategically important base from which French and Indian attacks for a long while had been launched against the New England frontier. With Port Royal taken, the whole of

Acadia passed under British rule and Sir William Phips on his return to Boston was widely acclaimed and became the hero of the hour.

Sufficiently shrewd to capitalize on this outburst of popularity, he promptly made sail for England where, in October of 1691, King William and Queen Mary issued a Royal Governor's commission to "Our trusted and well-beloved Sir William Phips, knight, to be our Captain-General and Governor-in-Chief in and over said Provinces of Massachussetts in New England, and to rule over the Massachusetts Bay and Plymouth colonies, Nova Scotia and Acadia, to restore peace." Equally important, he carried with him a new Charter for the Massachusetts Bay Colony which at Phips's urging, among other reforms included far-reaching curbs on witch-hunting.

On the whole, the man from Jeremesquam proved a successful Governor. Among other accomplishments, he ordered a powerful stone fort constructed at Pemaquid near his birthplace to forestall further French and Indian depredations.

However, an attack on Quebec launched too late in the season proved a costly failure and afforded his enemies opportunity to decry his administrative reforms which included relaxation of qualifications for the right to vote for representation in the General Court.

Once a fairly durable peace had been established with the Indians the Royal Governor at once sailed for England to defend his actions against powerful enemies at Court. Scarcely had he arrived in London than he fell ill of "a grievous fever" —probably some form of influenza—and on the 18th of February, 1694, died at the age of forty-four.

Pegeen Hammond and the Honorable Frederick Delacorte, together with Captain Abram Adderly and John Dale, managed to survive the hurricane in Mouchoir Passage and returned to the Bermudas in the *Dove*—as also did Captain William Davis in his *Experience*.

Among ancient Bermudian records appears a notation that treasure "officially" fetched back in the *Dove* amounted to no less than £15,000: also, that the *Experience* brought home loot worth around £12,000.

On returning to Bermuda, the Honorable Frederick learned of the almost simultaneous deaths of his father, Lionel the 3rd Marquis of Cranbury, and that of his elder brother, George who, being childless, ensured that the title would pass to him, but with a seriously encumbered estate.

At this point the 4th Marquis of Cranbury and his stalwart wife made calculations and arrived at a conclusion that the future appeared bright since The Honorable Frederick's "official" shares in treasure raised by the *James and Mary* and proceeds of the *Dove*'s voyage to Ambrosia Bank amounted to just over £8,000 while Pegeen's interests came to almost the same sum.

In addition the new Marquis realized some £6,000 on his "private loot" while Lady Pegeen's illegal profits eventually fetched around £3,000 which gave the young couple a total of some £25,000 with which to shape their future.

This sum—very considerable for those days—not only enabled the Honorable Frederick to pay off those long-standing debts at home but also left a surplus of £9,000 once debt-ridden Cranbury Castle and the remaining estate lands had been sold. Frederick retained the gatehouse and sufficient adjoining acres to keep alive the property's identity.

The newly wedded Marquis and his bride found further cause to rejoice in that Lady Pegeen—as if to make up for lost time—embarrassingly soon gave birth to twins, a boy and a girl and later to another girl.

Friends of Sir William Phips, the late Duke of Albemarle, and others of the Company of Gentlemen Adventurers saw to it that the new Marquis of Cranbury should receive appointment to be Royal Governor of the Bahamas.*

He and his Marchioness built a handsome mansion near New Providence and lived in a style which Pegeen, even in her wildest dreams, never had hoped to enjoy.

Ably, with great dignity and grace the Marchioness of Cran-

* This appointment is difficult to substantiate.

bury assisted her husband in the discharge of many responsibilities, official and social, and with firm kindness reared their
lusty offspring who, after being sent to England for education,
served their country—and themselves—with distinction for
many generations.

Captain John Dale with his £9,000 share in the *Dove's*
earnings also was content to give up treasure hunting and to
settle down in Somerset in the Bermudas close to that spot
where, long ago, he had been cast away.

Added to his personal fortune, the dowry of his wife,
Anne Gilbert, a well-to-do widow from Mangrove Bay, en-
nabled him to build or buy a fleet of stout merchant vessels
with which he conducted a thriving business in Turks Island
salt and to engage in general trade with the West Indies. In due
course Dale and his wife begat a lusty brood some of whose
descendants still inhabit the beautiful Somers Isles.